Praise for
The Undetectables

"Unputdownable. Grim and caring, twisted and witty, *The Undetectables* is gripping and charming in equal measure. You won't want to leave Wrackton, while also being really glad you don't live there."

Deirdre Sullivan, author of *Savage Her Reply*

"A compulsively readable race against the clock to stop a supernatural killer – downright delightful and unapologetically queer."

Polygon.com

"If you aren't already deep into spooky season then here is the perfect book to get you in the mood."

Irish Examiner

"A fun and breezy urban fantasy novel that has an interesting take on using magical forensics."

SFBook Reviews

"If you're looking for a mystery that makes you think, mixed with a healthy dose of supernatural, diverse representation and some of the best dialogue I've seen in a long time then [...] *The Undetectables* is the book for you."

Geeking By

"An urban fantasy that feels light but has a lot of heart, with a fantabulous cast and oddly adorable glowing beetles, *The Undetectables* is my new favourite friendship-fantasy. I strongly advi

Eve

T0182476

An UNDETECTABLES Mystery

The UNDEAD COMPLEX

COURTNEY SMYTH

TITAN BOOKS

The Undead Complex
Print edition ISBN: 9781803364803
E-book edition ISBN: 9781803364810

Published by Titan Books
A division of Titan Publishing Group Ltd
144 Southwark Street, London SE1 0UP
www.titanbooks.com

First edition: September 2024
10 9 8 7 6 5 4 3 2 1

A CIP catalogue record for this title is available from
the British Library.

Printed and bound by CPI (UK) Ltd, Croydon, CR0 4YY.

For Jacq
A gold-star friend

ONE

104 years ago, give or take a day

In all ways but the one that matters most, Heather Larkin was dead. Once again, she is not who the story is about, but it is important to know this.

Heather was dead to the extended Larkin family, who had never forgiven her for engineering her inheritance of Oakpass Manor and the annexed film studio, usurping them in the process. It was not, she believed, her fault that her forged path did not allow for anything less than a charmed existence, and so she became estranged.

She was dead inside, though she pretended she was not. This was easily achieved with a bright smile, some hair pins and an air of cold exclusivity that encouraged others – Apparent and Occult alike – to follow her every move, wanting to touch the light she emitted, but being too afraid to get close at the same time. Not that Heather dealt with those undeserving of closeness. All her relationships were built on a healthy foundation of give and take – where others gave, and she graciously accepted, leaving them open-mouthed like baby birds awaiting a worm. Even that image of desperate social hunger would have Heather recoil in disgust, despite it coming from her very own mind.

And presently, Heather Larkin was dead to the world. The potion – for want of a better description – her doting husband Howard had slipped into her night-time sherry had taken hold. Her breathing was shallow though, crucially, still there, for that was the only way in which Heather was not dead.

So far.

Her husband, as mentioned, was doting – though this was seldom reciprocated – and his reasons for using a potion-by-any-other-name were both acceptable, for she had a headache, and also unfortunate, for Heather had expected to receive a guest that night in the second-best parlour of Oakpass Manor. An interviewee, to be precise; one who had hopes of joining Heather's Society.

The Society itself was a gift Heather had the pleasure of bestowing on the best of Occult and Apparent society, all for the low, low price of marrying her least ugly and most biddable (third) cousin, capable of taking the title of Lord. The house – for she called it a 'house', both to appear somewhat demure and because 'manor' implied staffing that Heather was loath to admit she did not have – was as grand as the beliefs she had about the world she inhabited. It was Heather's world, for the most part, and she held the respect of the most important folk from Wrackton, Oughteron and beyond in her pale, delicate little hands.

Of course, her being dead to the world and dead in all those other ways meant her husband was left unsupervised. So when a knock sounded on the great doors of Oakpass Manor, Howard Larkin began to panic.

'Early, early… Biscuits, Missy, do you have them?'

The maid he was speaking to, who was not and had not ever been named Missy, obliged nonetheless by pointing at the spread of sandwiches and tea on the great table beyond them. The interviewing chairs were waiting, and Howard's favourite fountain pen rested on the side table with sheafs of paper that he presumed were the contracts. He had never liked this parlour, and gladly went to meet his guest.

The guest was a woman he'd recognise anywhere, not least because he had a framed film poster in his study sporting a carefully illustrated likeness of her.

'Hello. Erm. Hello,' Howard tried, unsure – even after all this time – how to start a Society interview.

'I'm Delfina Sackville,' Delfina Sackville said.

'I know,' Howard said, at the same time as she added, 'For now.'

She winked, and Howard smiled at her, unsure what to make of this woman. She had single-handedly launched the family-run Larkin Studios into renown. She was Apparent, he was quite sure; being Apparent himself, he had to look hard to find the signs of Occulture that came easily to other, vastly more magical members of the Society. As she was dressed in mourning colours, he chose to assume she was intimating an impending re-marriage. If he had learned anything from Lady Larkin, it was not to ask questions about private matters.

Not surface-level ones, anyway.

'A pleasure. So what brings you to— Candles. Hold on, where's that… Missy? Can you— Never mind, I have it here. Ceremonial candle, we need it to… rationalise the space, I expect,' he said, not entirely sure both of the wording his wife usually used, or of its intended meaning.

'Frankincense,' Delfina said, crossing her legs. Howard did not know what to make of that, either, and looked away.

'Quite,' Howard said vaguely. 'I am to ask you some questions, before I let you into the Appoccult Society. Rather, before we carefully assess you for suitability to join,' he said, flustered. 'I trust you are familiar with our admittance requirement?'

Delfina nodded once. 'A trinket, yes? Something of intrigue to you and your contemporaries.'

'And in the case of our Apparent members, they must maintain a lifelong connection to Occulture. That connection is at your discretion, but we in the Appoccult Society—'

'An ingenious name. Your invention?' Delfina continued without allowing him to respond. 'Lord Larkin, forgive my forwardness, but I had hoped to meet with Lady Larkin tonight, as I have…' She paused demurely. 'An unusual offer to make.'

At this, Howard began to perspire – both because 'unusual offers' were very much his wife's domain, and because the last time he had admitted an individual to the Appoccult Society without her present, it had ended in tears.

Mostly his.

'Well. Lady Larkin is currently… indisposed. You could come back?'

Delfina rose to her feet, smoothing her skirts. 'I'm afraid, Lord Larkin, that this is a one-time-only offer.'

This panicked Howard even more, because he had no idea how Heather would respond to this unusual creature before him, or how she would want him to. The last time he had acted rashly, Heather had been forced – under mighty duress – to excommunicate a demon from the Appoccult Society. This demon had created undesirable ripples at meetings; despite his repeated promises of connections and information, the information had seemed increasingly implausible. All had tired of his insistence he knew better than everyone around him, including the vampire Society members. The demon had been on the Ghoul Council, and losing him was a blow the Society – and Howard – had fought to absorb.

Howard was sure that this was an opportunity Heather would freeze him out for losing, and it was slipping through his fingers with every slow step Delfina took towards the parlour door.

He urged Delfina to sit and asked her to explain the offer. Her dark eyes lit up as she reached into her pocket and slid a black stone across the table between them.

'Not sure of the provenance, but I can promise you it is Occult,' Delfina said, as Howard held it up. He recognised it instantly as a planchette, but this one felt old, and heavy.

'It feels haunted,' Howard said, at the precise second Delfina said, 'It's haunted, if that helps.'

He stared at it, rolling the object around in his hands. The Society would assess it, even in the absence of a Ghoul Council member – the tears he had shed over that fiasco really had been proportionate – and decide Delfina's merits. He was just about to make this clear to his guest when she held up her hand.

'One-time offer, Lord Larkin. The trinket for me – for it is haunted, I can assure you. The second gift is more unusual, but I think you'll like it.'

She leaned forward. Her lipstick was very red, he noticed, her teeth very white. She had a way of commanding attention, the way she did on film, that even Howard couldn't miss. She spoke at length, and when she finished, leaned back and waited.

'Just to be clear. You'd like the Society to accept… a dollhouse?'

'A perfect replica,' she said.

'Made by, you say, your "dear friend"?'

'The dearest.' That smile again, that Howard couldn't interpret. He supposed women did have their close girlhood friends.

'And you'd like me to give this bespoke object…'

'To your youngest child, yes. Or the child most receptive to ownership of such an object. You have, how many children was it again?'

'Three,' Howard said absently.

'Splendid.'

'So I give one of my girls the dollhouse, and then…?'

Delfina stood again, but with curiosity rather than an *I'm leaving* finality as she had before. She pressed one hand covered in rings to the terracotta wallpaper.

'Lord Larkin, would you say you know the history of Oakpass?'

'I would say so,' he said, but it was a lie.

'More history than your own family's. Hundreds of years back. No matter,' she said, seeing his face as he battled with the urge to not lie and the desire to appear competent. 'My dear friend makes dollhouses as gifts. She's talented beyond measure. Her accuracy, her attention to detail, just…' She exhaled. 'Sublime. This would be the finest replica of Oakpass Manor one could ever hope to acquire.'

'And would your friend need measurements, and that?' Howard gestured vaguely.

'We have another friend who has… shall we say, *intimate* knowledge of Oakpass Manor, so my dear friend would never have to set foot inside.'

'And who is this other friend? A Society member?' If Howard had been prone to stabs of fear over anything other than what pleased his wife, he'd have felt one at the fleeting thought that this could be a Larkin cousin trying to worm their way back into Heather's good books.

As it was, he felt no apprehension whatsoever.

'Never mind who. That doesn't matter. The dollhouse would be, in itself, a kind of magic.'

'And this is… No, sorry. You've lost me,' Howard said.

'This would ensure my friend's entry to the Society. I told you it was unusual. This way, she does not break your Society rules about objects, but she does not put the work in for no gain. This will be *her* trinket, so to speak.'

'And it's Occult?'

'Magical. The sort of magic that appreciates in value. Beyond your wildest dreams.'

It was an offer Howard couldn't refuse.

It was an offer Heather would have.

The dollhouse was a promise kept. Delfina's dear friend – though we all know what she means by that, really – was admitted to the Society. The three Larkin children played with their gift, and Heather forgave Howard in time. The Appoccult Society continued to meet.

The five Larkins, attached as they were to Oakpass, vanished without a trace four years later.

All they took with them was the dollhouse.

TWO

NOW – Seven days to the Spring Equinox ball

Diana Cheung-Merriweather was many things – a private investigator, a skilled prop-maker, an excellent friend, and, perhaps first and foremost, a brilliant liar.

She had been lying about many things in the five months since their last major case, mostly by omission.

'Thank you *so* much for contacting the Undetectables,' Diana said into her phone, her face pressed in despair to the table it rested on, but her voice bright and cheery. 'As always, we endeavour to help you detect the undetectable. In this instance, it was a very detectable, but very, very unfortunate case of old age.'

'My husband was in the prime of his life,' the phone, or rather the elderly witch at the other end of it, squawked indignantly.

'I am truly sorry for your loss, Mrs...' Diana paused, lifting her eyes to Mallory, who slid the case file towards her. Diana slapped her hand down on the file. 'Blackburn. Truly sorry. I have no doubt that at a hundred and two, your husband Phil—'

'Paul!'

'Bit of static on the line. As I said, your husband Paul was indeed in the prime of his life. We've concluded our investigation now, and have liaised with Wrackton's Medical Examiner. You will receive a finalised report email in a few minutes.'

Just as soon as Cornelia finished writing it.

'Put the Medical Examiner on,' Mrs Blackburn said sharply. 'I want to hear it from her. I need to know you're telling the truth. My husband was *poisoned*.'

Diana glanced at Mallory again, who held her hand out for the phone.

'I am going to pass you to our agency director now, who spoke to Dr Ray, and can reassure you as to her, and our, findings.' Diana gestured at the phone with what she hoped was an air of renouncement and walked away, leaving Mallory saying in soothing tones, 'Yes, I'm the agency director. I can confirm all the details of the case with you by phone, but there will be an email soon with everything in writing, if you'd rather wait for that?'

An email, and the outstanding balance for the rest of their bill.

Diana left the basement where the Undetectables operated, sliding past the benches of Theodore and Mallory's lab, and climbed the steep stairs to the kitchen. She flicked a hand in the direction of the counter and warm brown bread started to slice itself. She muttered under her breath and the kettle boiled as she rummaged around for her favourite mug. It was much too early for arguing with folk. She hoped breakfast would make things better.

'What's that then, the tenth or eleventh case?' Cornelia said, startling her.

'Hex*ana*, can you announce yourself when you enter rooms?' Diana pressed a hand to her heart, annoyed at herself for not hearing Cornelia's approach more than anything.

'I'm sorry, I didn't realise I needed permission to walk around my own house.' Cornelia grinned. She reached over and grabbed the freshly sliced bread and waved over a jar of jam, which bumped against the table.

'Oops, careful now.' She looked tired, her short hair in disarray and her ubiquitous undulating jumper consuming more of her person than usual. Diana figured that she herself didn't look much better.

'To answer your question, it's the eleventh.'

Eleven cases that hadn't required private investigators in the first place. Eleven cases that had been ostensibly baffling, but easily solvable.

'So we've had stolen jewellery—'

'Found down the back of a couch with a simple finding spell, though I maintain he was gaslighting his husband about it,' Diana said, biting into her bread.

'—a missing person—'

'You would think that someone upping and moving across the country would be enough of a suggestion that a person was not so much *missing*, as they did not want to be contacted by our client.'

'As I said at the time, *I agree with you*, but that's how the case was presented to us. Then there was… what was next?'

'That was our eighth murder-that-wasn't-murder case, if that helps,' Mallory said, climbing the stairs. She grabbed the other slice of bread Diana had prepared for herself and joined them at the table.

Diana scowled at Mallory as Cornelia handed her a knife.

'Is there tea?' Mallory asked, smiling at Cornelia – one of the small smiles that Diana often caught passing between them, but very kindly did not point out. 'I calmed Mrs Blackburn down for now, but she'll likely call back in a few days demanding we reopen the investigation when she's had time to stew over our findings.' Mallory pulled her long dark hair out of its ponytail, rubbing her hand over her scalp. 'Hexana, I didn't realise how difficult it would be to liaise with grieving people if there *wasn't* a murder. With murder, we can at least do something about it – seek justice, find someone to hold responsible. But with regular old death it's… *I'm sorry for your loss, please don't forget to pay us.*' She grimaced.

'You handled that one very well, I thought,' Diana said, smiling fondly at her friend. '*Director* of the Undetectables.'

It gave Diana a thrill to say it, albeit mostly to see how delighted Mallory initially looked every single time, before doubt kicked in. It had been an easy majority-rules vote.

'I've had five months of case practice,' Mallory said. 'And we agreed I'd call myself the director! Didn't we?'

'Diana is being mean,' Cornelia said, giving Diana a playful shove. 'But nonetheless, we both reserve the right to tease you about your title if and when it feels socially relevant.'

Mallory visibly relaxed.

'And we won't do it too much,' Diana said, feeling like she was saying it more for Cornelia's benefit than her own. While she and Cornelia had the sort of friendship where they could rip into each other whenever the mood struck them and it be a sign of love, Diana knew that Mallory looked for meaning in interactions that Cornelia hardly ever intended. Every day was just a day, and Cornelia just contained multitudes.

'That's only ten cases altogether,' Cornelia said. 'We're missing—'

'Ghost,' Theodore said, appearing in the kitchen, bringing with him an enveloping warmth that Diana was thankful for on such a chilly spring morning. Mallory shifted happily in her seat, her mouth full of brown bread as Theodore brought his hand down on her hair, static sparking visibly from the contact.

Theodore Wyatt was their resident ghost who had lived and died and become semi-corporeal in the Broadwicks' basement where the Undetectables headquartered, all while wearing a pair of cat ears. There had been a brief period where Diana was sure they'd lost him forever, when he became a victim in their last big murder case. He had returned – as a ghost, and still wearing the cat ears – thanks to Mallory, but Diana got the sense she wasn't alone in feeling relieved whenever Theodore came into the room. As though being able to see him would stop anything bad from ever happening to him again.

'Are you announcing your presence, or answering my question?' Cornelia asked, sliding their phones into the little iron bags they'd installed on the edge of the table. Theodore's presence had the tendency to ruin electrical items, and it happened whether he wanted it to or not, unless there was some kind of iron-based buffer to stop him.

He paused. 'Both.' He drew himself up to his full height, which was taller than Diana and approximately the same height as Cornelia, but several inches shorter than Mallory. 'I am once again registering my full chagrin with this fact, though – I am unhappy there was a ghost case at all to begin with.'

Diana sighed. 'We know, Theo.'

Unhappy didn't quite cover it.

'I will always be unhappy with ghost cases,' he said. 'It is in my nature to be marginally unhappy with everything, and ghost cases fall under the umbrella of *everything*.'

Theodore did not do emotions by halves.

'We have to take on anything and everything at the moment, ghost cases or not. We aren't getting enough work to not do it, so we just have to take what we can get,' Diana said, a buzzing sound in her ear making her jaw clamp with annoyance that she fought to disguise. This was one of her lies-by-omission: since the Mayoral Offices explosion, her hearing had not returned to normal, and her days were frequently interrupted by a high-pitched ringing that made it hard to focus on what was going on around her. Theodore, unfortunately, seemed to be a major trigger, though it was unclear if that was his static charge, or the fact he could get very loud.

'And it wasn't really a ghost case,' Mallory said. 'Just someone concerned that their cousin *didn't* become a Samhain ghost.'

'It's hard for the ordinary folk to understand us,' Theodore said, brushing at the whiskers on his face, his hand passing through the blurry outline of the permanent tears on his cheeks that had appeared after his unlikely return. 'They will never know the song of my people. Of which I am the only one in this town. So, song of my person.'

Mallory's mouth folded into a line, and Diana looked away. This was a lie; they had not only encountered a second Samhain ghost in the Mayoral Offices, but that ghost had known Theodore. Theodore was the only one in the room who didn't know that they knew and as far as Diana could tell, Mallory intended to keep it that way until she figured out why.

'We had to prove a lack of evidence on that case, and they almost refused to pay, which is fast becoming the song of *our* people,' Diana said, pressing a hand to her ear in hopes that would stop the buzzing coming from within.

'Ah, like taking a photo of nothing. Which is incidentally what would happen if you were to photograph me. Nothing,' Theodore said.

'It's not like we're going to run out of money,' Cornelia said around a mouthful of bread, as though someone had just mentioned the agency money woes.

Diana shot her a look that she hoped conveyed all fifteen intentions behind it. Although they both came from wealthy backgrounds – wealthier than Mallory, who wasn't doing too badly either, mostly thanks to their hometown's insistence on a universal basic income – Cornelia's family had a wealth bordering on monstrous that frightened Diana to think about too much. Diana was set to inherit a lot of money when she was twenty-five, but had been raised to want to make her own name and her own fortune. It did not surprise her one bit that Cornelia didn't quite understand how she and Mallory felt about earning – Mallory for reasons of achievement, and Diana for moral values.

'I do feel guilty taking money from people who just want answers, though. It feels…' Diana searched for the right word.

'Bad,' Mallory supplied.

'That's what I was going to say!' The buzzing got higher pitched, and Diana snapped her mouth shut.

'We could take those as pro bono cases?' Cornelia suggested. 'I can cover the agency fee.'

'We are not doing that,' Diana said. 'A benevolent idea, but we are not letting you pay to keep our business running.'

'I can't see that being a long-term answer, either,' Mallory said. 'We need something sustainable, before anyone starts planning an exit from the agency.' She laughed, but Diana could detect barely concealed panic behind the joke.

Diana wished she could say Mallory was catastrophising.

'Nobody's leaving. Nobody would *have* to leave if you'd let me keep us afloat. We could do a proper business plan with charts and shit,' Cornelia said. 'Or whatever folk do when they have to care about budgets. We'll find something proper to get our teeth into soon, this will keep us going.'

'Or you could shut the hell up,' Diana said, sharper than intended. Cornelia making long-term promises Diana could not necessarily keep was not helpful, even if Cornelia didn't know it.

Cornelia scowled, then scowled deeper at the sound of the agency phone buzzing against the wooden leg of the table.

'Heads that's Blackburn again, tails it's Ingram asking us to follow his wife to the gym and I told him already I am NOT DOING THAT,' she said emphatically. The buzzing stopped.

'How did your meeting go?' Mallory asked Theodore in the resulting silence, who fixed her with his full attention.

'The meeting! Ahh, meetings. When groups of folk come together to make resolutions, yes.'

'Was this the Unified Magical Liaison meeting?' Cornelia asked around a bite of bread. 'They're awful pricks, aren't they?'

'You made that so clear when we did the tribunal with them after the Whistler case,' Diana said. 'I believe you actually said "you are all awful pricks" at one point.'

'And?'

Diana did not dignify that with an answer.

'Yes, my wonderfully observant friend,' Theodore said. 'To both observations. This was *the* meeting with the Occulture overlords about the Mayoral Offices that the Ghoul Council rescheduled a mere eight times over the past few months, which of course is no big deal for me, a Samhain ghost who cannot use a phone or receive electronic mail. No big deal at all, to sit in a room alone in the dark waiting for a meeting that will never start, as though I have an eternity stretching out in front of me.'

'What did they say?' Mallory prompted.

'Well. As you know. The Mayoral Offices have been in a state of disrepair since you— since the— since... five months ago.'

As nobody liked saying Jacob's name in front of Theodore – or, indeed, particularly enjoyed discussing what Jacob had done to them and several people they'd loved – 'five months ago' had become their shorthand for all the consequences of the Whistler case, including Theodore's temporary demise. The Whistler had killed several of their friends in an effort to become a fourth member of the Ternion, Occulture's main goddesses, and the Undetectables had narrowly escaped. They'd defeated him by blowing up the Mayoral Offices – or so Diana was told, as she'd been unconscious for most of it. The Offices had been out of commission ever since, meaning Theodore had been waiting to restart his job.

'Nod if you're with me, Mallory,' Theodore said seriously. 'Great. Okay, well, the repairs are still going very slowly, and after much discussion they've decided they're ready to deal with the spectral disturbances once and for all.'

'That's your job, right?' Diana said. She had never been willing to admit to Theodore that she didn't quite know what he did for an unliving, apart from despairing over paperwork and bureaucratic rules that made the paperwork difficult. 'Did they give you a start date?'

'Yes! Well. The Ghoul Council, along with the UML, have decided that they're going to treat the spectral activity like it is something that can be smoothed over. Like a brick wall, for instance. That's the plan. They're going to brick off the back offices with iron-lined bricks and hope for the best. They have suggested a timeframe of somewhere between one and eight business weeks, though the count might've started last week, so that could be a skewed timeline. All nice and vague. But fear not, the good news is I can join the agency full time! PI Wyatt has a nice ring to it,' Theodore finished cheerfully.

'Sorry,' Diana said. 'They *fired* you?'

'It would appear so, yes,' Theodore said. 'I was dismissed.'

Diana tensed for the dramatic explosion. A quick glance around the table told her the others were also waiting; this surely fell under the umbrella of something Theodore could be at least marginally unhappy about.

'Theodore, I'm so sorry,' Cornelia said. 'I could call my parents, see if they can convince whoever in the Ghoul Council decided this that it is a very shit idea?'

Theodore waved a dismissive hand. 'Let's not bother the Broadwicks with things that may or may not be relevant to them, just because they're in the Ghoul Council.'

'They should've been there for this. You live – sorry, *reside* – in their house!' Cornelia said.

'It's okay if you're upset,' Mallory said gently.

'Why on earth would I be upset?'

He looked genuinely baffled. Diana felt a chill run down her spine as it became clear the explosion wasn't coming. He was completely and utterly calm.

'It's just that, previously,' Cornelia started. 'And I'm sure Diana and Mallory can back me up here. But previously, you *have* stated that your *raison de la mort* was your job in the Mayoral Offices. You know, given that you're tethered to this plane because you had unfinished business. The unfinished business being' – Cornelia made some grasping motions with her hands – 'whatever it is you usually do in the Mayoral Offices.'

'Whatever it is I usually *did*. Grammar tenses are very important.'

'Remember Cornelia pointed out your *raison de la mort* was because someone had murdered you and that you additionally cannot substitute common French philosophies with words that relate more to your state of being, and you got very upset and did some shouting and sprayed static around the place and we calmed you down with a big hug?' Diana tried.

'My memory is fine, Diana. Now, if you'll excuse me, I better – oh! Habit. I better go tidy up my paperwork, I expect. You know, the bane of my life is paperwork. Every day, paperwork. Paper, paper, paper… That's a great word to say. Say it with me, Mallory. PAPER.'

The paper choir was interrupted by Diana's phone dinging once, then twice.

She flinched, thinking it was a message she was waiting on that she did not want to open in front of the others, before realising what it actually meant.

'Was that your phone?' Mallory said, peering into Diana's table pocket.

'Was that your phone with *sound* on?' Cornelia asked, eyeing her suspiciously.

'Oh, maybe,' Diana said airily. 'You must've knocked a button putting it in the pouch.' She left her hands where they were, focusing on stopping her fingers from twitching towards it. She wasn't hiding anything; 'hiding' implied she spent an inordinate amount of time working to conceal something. Things were simply stuffed into miniature compartments in her brain where nobody could get at them.

'Well on that note,' Theodore said. He paused, like he was waiting for the right words to come to him, then passed through the basement door, leaving the Undetectables staring at each other.

'Well,' Diana said.

'Well,' Mallory said.

'That was fucking weird, wasn't it?' Cornelia said. 'I did witness that correctly? He's been fired and he… didn't react. At all.'

'I'm worried,' Mallory said. 'Not just about Theo – I'm beyond concerned about that. But the Offices.'

Diana knew what she was going to say. The Undetectables'

very first case had been Theodore's murder, and it remained unsolved. Meeting Katherine the Samhain ghost and learning she had met Theodore *before* he'd died had been the first semblance of a lead. If the Offices were going to be bricked over, they'd lose their chance to get back in to talk to her.

'I'm going to reopen Theodore's case, as a matter of urgency,' Mallory said decisively. 'I can work on it alone; you two can keep our current cases afloat and keep an eye out for anything new and interesting. If that's okay? I can't lose this lead.'

There was something else under the surface, something Diana felt Mallory had been dancing around ever since Theodore had come back. She just didn't know what it was yet.

'Of course it's okay,' Cornelia said. 'You're the director, it's your call.'

'This is urgent, now. Who knows if they'll actually brick it up within the next few weeks?'

'Of all the things they could choose to be expeditious about, it *would* be this, if only for the sole reason that it's a bad idea,' Diana said. 'It's not exactly solving the spectral problem, is it, locking up a load of hideous giant insects?'

'*Beautiful* hideous giant insects,' Cornelia corrected. 'But yeah, feels like something they'd do. I can see if Mother will halt it, but that might involve her asking *questions*, and I'm quite sick of *questions* after being interrogated by the UML all those times over the Whistler.'

'Then that's decided. I'm going to take a nap first.' Mallory stretched her shoulders, wincing as she touched the skin of her upper arms. 'But then I'll get started right away.' She headed for her room.

'I'll go see who that was calling and write the email to bloody whatshername. Hexana love the poor dear, I am very sorry for her and have no idea what she's going through, et cetera, but...' Cornelia waved a hand.

'Yes, Cornelia, I find it's all very emotionally convincing when you say things like "et cetera", et cetera.' Diana playfully flicked Cornelia's hand. Cornelia shot her a glare as she stuffed another slice of bread into her mouth and bounded down the basement stairs.

It was only then that Diana allowed herself to reach for her phone. The compartments in her mind had opened and all the baggage she had stuffed in there was rapidly unsealing like it had been vacuum-packed. The message may not have been what she was waiting for, but it was another thing to wrap beneath layers of brilliant lies.

There was only one person who had the ability to make her phone make a noise.

Only one person that could make Diana's heart feel as though it was beating out of her chest.

She looked down at the screen, heart palpitating so loud she could hear it in her ears as her eyes skipped over the texts, once, twice, trying to take it in, trying to understand what it meant.

Taylor
hey angel baby (sorry, let me have this one)

got a live one for you (and by that i mean dead)

PERIMORTEM I

Taylor Rose O'Gorman was perfectly aware of the moment she died.

It had come as a bit of a shock, all told. The body does strange things while dying; it can be like falling asleep, or it can be a battle of wills. A soul straddling the two options. Taylor's death was of the die-screaming variety.

Or it would've been.

She was making noise, her larynx straining beneath her skin, tendons pulled taut with the effort, but no sound would come out. She'd been feeling funny right before it happened, come to think of it, though Taylor couldn't actually *think*. She just knew she was dead, and if not now, imminently.

A backlit figure moved beyond the scope of her vision. Coming into frame, their appearance disorganised and unrecognisable, her eyes no longer making sense of the images they were witnessing, and Taylor was screaming, oh how she was *screaming*, but there was no audio track to prove it.

The figure didn't seem to notice. They approached her – maybe had been beside her the whole time – and she felt a weightlessness, her body lifted up, up and out of frame until she wasn't sure where she was anymore, until she was carefully lowered onto something soft and pink and brocade. *Chaise longue* floated into her head and left as quickly.

She turned her head – no, moved her eyes, the only part of her still capable of moving; the figure turned her head, settling her limbs into an unnatural position. Her fingers fell to the floor, draped in a pool of something wet and warm and pungent and then her hands were lifted again and placed over her chest. She thought she could feel something: eyelet lace. It reminded her of someone, faces floating in and out of close-shot memories that refused to cement into anything she could make sense of.

The figure came closer again, placed their hands over hers, then raised one, closed Taylor's eyelids, shut out the last of the light in her fade-out final scene.

A warm trickle of something flooded over her hands, but it was dark, dark, nothingness.

THREE

Mallory Hawthorne was many things – director of the PI agency she and her friends had co-founded, an excellent friend (when she wasn't getting in her own way), a resourceful inventor and, first and foremost, a scientist.

When she had cast the spell to bring Theodore back from the undead after the Whistler had killed him five months prior, hope had been dwindling away to an accepting ache of loss, until the moment he appeared in the basement of Broadwick Mansion and enveloped her in a hug.

She had so many questions about what it had been like for him when he was gone – if he knew he had been properly dead, if there'd been a confrontation between him and Jacob, if it had hurt or if he'd been aware when Jacob had put his soul into the death blade – and how he felt now that he was back. The only sign anything had changed was the permanent addition of twin tracks of tears on his cheeks. He refused to speak on any of it.

'I'm back now,' he'd said. 'Isn't that the true meaning of Yule, and so forth?'

Once she had gotten past the tears, relief, and the realisation that he wasn't going to share anything with her, she selected a fresh notebook, her favourite pen, and began to take notes. Extensive, copious, scientific notes on everything and anything Theodore did, said, or seemed to be thinking about doing and saying.

Theodore flickered twice today, once at 13:21 and once at 20:33, but on both occasions he said it was a 'ghost sneeze'.

Theodore shouted at a pigeon through the basement window at 14:14.

Theodore in good mood today.

Theodore is not quite right.

She hadn't told him she was doing this, both because she was mildly embarrassed at her scrutiny, and because she didn't want him to ask why; she wasn't sure herself. Perhaps it was the idea that he had not been totally honest with her before his second death. Theodore was not supposed to communicate with other ghosts, and yet he had – with a ghost who had known him longer than Mallory herself.

While Mallory was many things, she tried not to be a liar, so she had not lied about taking a nap, craving the darkness of her bedroom, the comfort of her bed. But when she crawled between the sheets, her legs grateful for the relief, her body readily sinking into the mattress, her knee struck the hard edge of a book. She nudged it away, wrapping herself carefully in the duvet and closing her eyes, willing sleep to overtake her.

But the book called to her. Not literally, as it was not a magical book, but emotionally. Mallory felt the urge to start now, the UML's vague one to eight business weeks looming over her head like the threat to her investigation it was.

In the dark, she mentally turned a page in her Theodore Field Study/Cold Case notebook, to a scribbled drawing of a witchlight and a small Polaroid of the shelf in Cornelia's basement – she had been going through a photography phase at the time, though Diana did most of the image recording these days – where they'd found the witchlight extinguished near Theodore's body that night. The Whistler had known the trick of witchlight travel; it stood to reason other witches did too, even though the Unified Magical Liaison had been shocked to learn of it when the Undetectables attended the case tribunal. It felt most likely to Mallory that a witch had snuck after Theodore in the dark while the lights were off, then teleported somewhere else in Broadwick Mansion, and nobody was any the wiser. She'd compiled lists of witches who had been in attendance at the Samhain ball, comparing statements the Undetectables had taken all those years ago, when they were still children and were not taken seriously.

But perhaps Katherine had some answers for her.

She opened her eyes and took in the quiet darkness for a few more moments, willing her arms and legs to relax. Then she eased herself towards the lamp, propping pillows behind her so she was half-reclining, pulled her knees up, and rested the book on top of a soft bee-shaped plushie her friend Felix had given her. She took up her notebook, holding the pen loosely as her joints protested the movement.

Katherine herself presented an interesting issue, both because she was trapped in the destroyed Mayoral Offices, and because officially, Theodore was the only Samhain ghost in Wrackton. Trying to find out who she was had led Mallory on an unorthodox ghost hunt. Even with Theodore back, Mallory had not been able to get a straight – or indeed gay – answer out of him as to how he knew Katherine on any of the three occasions she'd asked, though the answers he did give could be arranged in order of least to most interesting.

'In a way we're all Katherines, aren't we? At some point in our lives we've all been a Katherine. Perhaps some more literally than others,' Theodore had said the second time she'd asked.

The first time she'd asked, he had said, 'Katherine? No, sorry, I don't know any ghost called Katherine, especially not one who spells her name with a K.' And then scrunched up his face, because Mallory had not specified the Katherine she was inquiring about was a ghost.

The third time she'd asked, Theodore said, 'Mallory, I care so very deeply about you. And because I care so very deeply about you, it pains me to say – stay out of this.'

Although he hadn't quite said the last part so much as screamed it, then carried on as though he'd said nothing, leaving Mallory staring at him in horror as he hummed to himself, busy analysing something in the lab.

Thinking of it, and writing it into her notebook, made Mallory's stomach drop, though it had been weeks since that had happened. It was not very *Theodore* of him. Sure, he'd always had a flair for the dramatic, and sure he was always a little mercurial, but this was not what Mallory would happily describe as 'normal behaviour'.

Nor was his underreaction to being fired.

'Who are you, Katherine?' she whispered.

She had subscribed to a genealogy database to try to get a handle on past generations in Wrackton, but without Katherine's surname, her ghost hunt had stalled. She had the sense Katherine was much older than Theodore, that she had died a very long time ago, but with only the knowledge that Katherine had had a sister, Mallory was chasing the ghost of a ghost.

Her next port of call was speaking to the new Night Mayor, Dr Priyanka Ray, who also happened to be Wrackton's Medical Examiner. These were hats she wore both with pride and with exasperation, mostly as it increased her dealings with the public tenfold. Dr Ray had granted Mallory access to the written census books, which weren't many, given the oft-relevant explosion of the Mayoral Offices, taking with it a lot of irreplaceable records.

Somehow, even with the tribunals and the UML scrutinising their involvement, the Undetectables had avoided taking any direct blame for that.

What Mallory had now was the oldest record book that had been recovered, dating back to the early 1800s. It didn't feel old enough, but she was hoping for some kind of lead. Katherine had to be findable. Mallory had noticed that generations of witches, demons and vampires in Wrackton had used a regular naming scheme, skipping a generation or two, keeping the spirit of someone alive by using their name again and again. It was honouring their personhood, in a way, and giving someone guidance on who to be. *Your great-aunt Bunice was a wonderful woman, she'd be proud you were called Bunice today*, they'd say, to the poor unfortunate soul who was named Bunice in this day and age.

So far, Mallory had narrowed down the possibilities – *if* Katherine had originally lived within Wrackton's walls – to around two to three hundred families, based on the occurrences of Katherines. It was going to take forever, but if she had to go to them one by one, she would.

She could not let Theodore down again. She could not lose the lead. And though hunches were more Diana's territory, Mallory could not help the knot in her stomach that told her that Katherine was the key to finding answers. If she solved the mystery of who she was, she'd solve Theodore's murder once and for all.

There was something there, just beyond her reach.

Answers that had been waiting for six years.

All she needed to do was get to them.

FOUR

Diana stared at the name at the top of the screen, her fingers shaking.

'Oh get a grip,' she told herself. 'Stop that. You are strong, you are confident, you are beloved, you are in control of your emotions, and you do not *shake* when—'

> **Taylor**
> you should turn off read receipts if you're not going to reply, i know you're there
>
> please call me, it's really important

'Fuckingggg...' Diana heaved in a breath, and forced her shoulders to relax. She was not panicking. She famously did not panic, even when the situation maybe called for it. Her ear rang in the quiet of the kitchen, but not so badly that she couldn't handle talking.

Diana
what's a call worth to you?

She watched the message change to *read* and waited, pushing an email she had also been waiting for off the screen as it pinged in in real time:

Re: Prop dept Larkin Studios, Undead Co...

One pressing issue at a time.

It had been a long time since she'd heard from Taylor.

Five months.

Five months, two weeks and three days, to be exact.

As much as she could, Diana trusted her friends with every single part of her. But just as Cornelia contained her multitudes and Mallory contained a lifetime's worth of built-in shame, Diana contained many omissions.

Such as Vancouver. And Taylor. And what she left behind. Or rather, the *possibility* she left behind. The potential version of Diana she'd discarded like an old jumper to hop on a plane and return home to the familiar, the comfortable – or so she thought, before everything went to shit.

For Diana, opportunities either worked out, or they came back to her in a different form if she made the wrong choice the first time. For the most part, Diana could not fail. She'd been raised with the belief she was naturally lucky, and Diana had never seen any evidence to the contrary.

Taylor
i wouldn't be asking if it wasn't dead serious

video call in three

unless you really don't want to see me

Diana pressed the call button herself, twirling on the spot so she could find a part of the Broadwicks' kitchen that served as a good background. She rested the phone on the island and leaned forward, adjusting her hair and swiping a finger under her lip to be sure her lipgloss hadn't smudged.

She ignored the way her heart beat strangely into her arms when Taylor answered, her face filling the screen. Her green hair fell messily around her pale, freckled face, her deep blue eyes wide and dancing.

'How's it going?' Taylor said.

'Hi.' Diana cursed herself for not saying something snappier.

'So biting,' Taylor said playfully. 'I'll get on with it in a second, but seriously – how's it going?'

'You know how I am, otherwise you wouldn't have called.'

Enough time had passed that Taylor could be sure Diana wouldn't burst into tears at the sight of her.

'That's true. I mean, it's rude of you to suggest an Apparent has some sort of all-knowing powers when you, an actual witch, could probably have divined I was going to call, like. But it's still true.'

Taylor smiled, her lips pink and soft-looking, and Diana fought the urge to look away.

She wasn't even there *in person*. Get a grip, Diana.

'Did you know you still talk to yourself out loud when you're flustered? It's cute.'

'Taylor, why…'

Why had she called? Why had Diana left her? Why was this happening?

'All right, for the love of… whatever it is you believe in. Here's the story, chicken: I'm working on a pilot of a show called *Undead Complex*. We're on location up at Oakpass Manor, which I believe is—'

'Did you say *Undead Complex*?' Diana shrieked. 'Why didn't you say something?'

'Ah yeah. Five months of radio silence, and I'd just send you a little message to say I got a job on a low-budget pilot.'

Diana knew she was being unreasonable, given the circumstances, but she felt a flash of anger, her thumb finding the email she'd dismissed earlier.

Hi Diana,

Thanks for sending your CV, you're exactly what we're looking for. We'd love to have you on our team…

It was a secret she'd been determined to keep from Mallory until she was forced otherwise. Diana had always been a fan of keeping her options open, and she missed working on a set. She hadn't necessarily intended to go looking for jobs; she'd seen the posting, had sent an email before she'd really thought about it, then realised she really, *really* wanted the job. It would take her away from the Undetectables for a while, but cases were slow, and Diana was bored, and she figured she'd find a way to make Mallory understand it wasn't a permanent departure. More of a weeks-long detour, mostly so she didn't lose her skills. She didn't expect the show would get picked up.

'Larkin Studios, right?' Diana said instead.

'They're having a little revival moment, yeah. They're filming on location in Oakpass Manor itself, which apparently features really heavily in the comics the show is based on. Place is in shite, but that's beside the point. Just listen to me for a second, would you?'

'I am listening, you're not saying anything!' Diana tried not to think too hard about how weird it would've been to turn up for her first day and find Taylor there, practically in her back garden after all this time. Oakpass Manor was barely twenty minutes from where Diana was standing.

'Aha.' It was a humourless laugh. 'Wait and I'll tell you though, cause this is an absolute shit show. You're not going to believe any of this.'

'You have thirty seconds,' Diana said firmly. 'Not to tell me about the shit show, about why you're calling.'

'I'm working away in the prop department, which surprisingly has the highest concentration of staff, but it's a very visual concept so I guess that tracks. I'm doing a great job, if I do say so myself. My talents amaze me. Ceaselessly, you might say. And I wake up one morning, and I'm dead.'

'What?'

Up to this point, Diana had admittedly thought this was all some kind of ruse to get her attention.

'I'm dead. They've found my body in one of the sound stages. I died. I'm lying across one of the sofas on set like fuckin' Ophelia at the lake, all dead and shit, except the lake was my own blood. But I – obviously – wasn't dead, cause I was able to look at photos of it.'

'How did this happen?'

'I was off sick – some kind of twenty-four-hour bug yoke, and had taken the day off. Under duress, and with twelve servings of guilt from the showrunner. But I was gone for a day. Naturally, everyone else assumed I had wandered back on set and died, and they shut down production. For a day, mind. I'm but a lowly crew member, and the police had the scene cleared within hours. I hadn't signed in, which nobody seemed to think was weird. When I showed up confused about all the aforementioned police, they looked at me like I was a ghost.'

For one split second, Diana wondered if Taylor *could* be a ghost, before remembering that technology and ghosts did not mix.

'Taylor, when was this?' Diana was having trouble understanding what was going on, but she knew what the growing feeling in her stomach was: excitement. Possibility. Opportunity. *A case.*

'This morning,' Taylor said lightly. 'I'm feeling much better, thanks.'

Diana blinked. 'So they found…'

'My body on set this morning. Me, dead. But I'm not dead. They're quite sure it's me, the propmaster made a formal identification. They called my ma. They called my *ma*, Diana, first thing in the morning, and told her I was *dead*. By the time I woke up and seen all the messages and missed calls, she'd gone from wailing to starting absolute war that I'd gone and got myself murdered, when didn't I know that was "the one and only way to break her heart".'

Diana had heard much about Mrs O'Gorman, but Taylor seemed to adore her, even given her absolute dramatics, justified and otherwise.

'So naturally I frightened the shite out of her by calling and asking what the fuck was going on. My brother, you remember Tommo, is still alive and hasn't become the second O'Gorman sibling to trans their gender, so it wasn't him they found. And I dunno how else they found a freckly sea-green-haired Irish youngwan the spitting image of me to replace me at such short notice, but… that body has my face and name, but it isn't me. Just cause Taylor Rose kinda rhymes with Jane Doe if you squint a bit, doesn't mean anything.'

Diana sensed that for all Taylor's casualness, there was genuine fear underlying everything she'd said.

'What do you want me to do?'

'I don't want *you* to do anything.'

'Then why—' Diana started, anger flaring.

'I want you to get your pals up here. The Undetectables. And I want you to find out who's targeting me, if that's what's happening, and if not, find out why someone's leaving bodies that look like me around the place.'

'Oh. You're hiring us?' Diana cycled through a range of questions that started with "How do you know about us?" and ended with "Could this have been an email?"

'You're the only private investigators I know who specialise in magical happenings, so who else was I going to call? And by "only" I mean "the only ones that came up when I tried searching about an hour ago, and discovered what you've been up to for the last five months, and knew there was no one else I could call".'

'I'm sure you could've thought of someone or other.' Diana looked away for a moment, trying to gain her composure in a way that looked effortless. 'I need to discuss it with my team first, make sure it's something we want to take on. Can you get up here? Are you still sick, or…?'

'I can come to you, text me the address. I'm fine.'

'I'll brief the team, but you'll need to sell it to them yourself. We're very in demand, we can't go taking on cases… willy-nilly.'

Taylor's eyes danced. 'Grand so. Wouldn't want you to make any rash decisions now, would we?'

And there it was.

'Leaving Vancouver wasn't a rash decision, it was—'

'Life-altering, course-correcting, accidental chaos. I know. I was there when you told me you were leaving.' Taylor looked down at her smart watch, notifications flooding in. 'Shit, I've to go, the police want to talk to me. I'll come by later.'

'Will you be okay?' Diana wasn't entirely sure what she was asking; would she be okay with the police?

'I managed the last five months without you, and managed my entire life before you. I think I'll be grand.' She winked, and ended the call.

Shit.

The first potentially real murder in months, and Diana was going to have to swallow her pride over it.

'It's a what?' Cornelia said. She was holding envelopes in one hand and something in her other that looked like a piece of textured black paper until it flapped, revealing a pink underbelly and legs, and Diana realised it was some sort of terrible moth.

'A doozy,' Diana said for the second time, recoiling from the moth as she rummaged through the snack cupboard in the

Undetectables' research room, which had doubled as Theodore's remote office during his employment.

She was beginning to question if she'd used the word correctly, when Cornelia said, 'Oh yes. Short for whoopsadoozy.'

Diana said a phrase in Cantonese that she knew Cornelia didn't understand, but would grasp the sentiment of regardless.

'Hold on a second, before I forget.' Cornelia handed her a heavyweight cream envelope. Diana tapped her fingers to break the seal at the back, monogrammed with *GQ*. She scanned the card inside.

'Invitation to a Spring Equinox ball, from Grey Quinn,' she said, skipping over the details. 'For me and two guests.'

She was secretly pleased one of the most connected demons in all of Occulture had remembered her – he had extended an offer to meet for drinks during the Whistler case, when Diana had pretended to be a socialite, but she hadn't expected he'd follow up.

'We could go, try to drum up business like old times?' Mallory suggested.

'We could,' Diana said. 'Or you could both *listen to me*.'

Cornelia and Mallory looked up, Mallory's hands poised over her case notes.

'Sorry. I've been trying to tell you, I think we *have* a case,' Diana said. 'I was waiting for Cornelia to finish that email to Mrs Blackburn.'

'That's been an entire hour, almost,' Mallory protested, which Diana was all too aware of, but she did not want to snap at Mallory for no reason.

During that time, Diana had run through no fewer than

twenty ways of delivering the information about the murder that best concealed Taylor's identity, and what she meant to her.

Had meant. Didn't anymore.

Fuck.

She gave them a brief run-down. 'So like I said, a doozy.'

'That's easy for you to say twice,' Mallory said, closing her file. Diana bit back a smile; Mallory was on board already. 'You heard the first-hand account. Who is Taylor?'

'She's an old friend, someone I worked with in Vancouver.'

This much, at least, was true.

'How did she know what you do?' Cornelia interrupted.

She was surveying the state of their research room with dismay; this was another thing they'd let get away from them. She muttered spells and waved her hands around as objects piled themselves into corners, the moth flapping indignantly. It gave the illusion of both more chaos and that it was somewhat organised.

'Sometimes Apparents know things,' Diana said.

Mallory waited for Diana to continue, the cogs clearly turning in her head, her eyes shining in the way they did when something had her full attention. Diana grinned.

'She searched magical murders, and found us. We've paid for advertising. And she recognised my name, found the articles from the Whistler case, gave me a call, Bob's your uncle.'

'I've never had an Uncle Bob,' Theodore said from the doorway. Diana hid her involuntary flinch of surprise; she hadn't heard him approaching. 'It's strange, really. I had uncles of course, six of them, but they're all dead now – properly dead, not undeadly dead – and not a single Robert among them.'

'*Six* uncles dead? I don't think you've told us that story,' Diana said, ignoring Cornelia's vehement headshake.

'A sombre tale for another time.' Theodore didn't seem to notice Cornelia's instant relief.

'Did you say the show was called *Undead Complex*?' Cornelia prompted, the terrible moth now climbing up her arm. 'That name rings a bell.'

'Felix,' Mallory said suddenly. 'That's the comic series they love, isn't it?'

Cornelia snapped her fingers. 'That must be it, they've been trying to get me to read it for years.'

'What in the name of Blair is an undead complex?' Theodore asked. 'If I didn't know any better I'd say *I* was an undead complex, which could be my own version of Cornelia's containing multitudes, just… deader.'

'It's… I don't know,' Cornelia said distractedly. 'I've never actually read more than a couple of pages.'

'Zombies,' Diana said, her mind full of the illustrations she'd pored over while waiting to hear back from the job. 'It's a fantasy zombie necromancy… horror-y comic series that Larkin Studios are adapting into a TV show – or trying to; they're filming a pilot episode. I think it's loosely inspired by Occulture.'

'Where did this all happen?' Mallory asked. 'The murder, I mean. Assuming we take this case on, if it's far, I can always stay—'

'Oakpass Manor, and Larkin Studios beside it. It's about twenty minutes' drive from here. Thirty in traffic. Maybe thirty-five if it's really bad.'

Chronic pain from fibromyalgia meant travel was difficult for Mallory; the relief on her face was palpable.

'Oakpass Manor? The big castle-looking thing?' Cornelia said.

'It never ceases to amaze me how you know so much about so much, and so little about literally anything outside your own carefully crafted bubble,' Diana said.

Cornelia scowled at her, and Diana was grateful for the opportunity to deflect. Cornelia's ability to match her verbal sparring made them both utterly armoured against ever having to meaningfully discuss their feelings with each other except in extreme circumstances. It made them brilliant friends and terrible friends all at once. They needed Mallory to keep them functioning.

'What's Oakpass?' Theodore asked. 'Or rather, what's the significance? I daresay I should know, but whatever is outside of Wrackton I cannot go to, and apart from that one-time to two-ish-month stretch where I ghost-sobbed into a stack of *National Geographic* every night, I have stopped being interested in what's outside of my own little bubble. Which is probably wrong. Is it wrong? Can I, a ghost, have specific concepts of right and wrong?' He paused, rubbing a hand over his chin.

'I don't know a huge amount, but I'm quite sure Oakpass Manor has vague ties to Wrackton,' Mallory said. 'It was a vampire-owned castle a long time ago – or rumoured to be, anyway – and then was inhabited by Apparent families. The last family to own and live in it were the Larkins in the early 1900s, and then it was privately sold, though the original furnishings were retained. They do tours and stuff out there sometimes. Or they used to, when we were kids. There was a tea shop and gardens and it was all staged like the family were going to come home at any moment.'

'Original furnishings? What happened to the Larkins?' Theodore asked, seizing upon the strangest thread in everything Mallory had just said.

'That's a good point,' Diana said. 'I have no idea. We visited it when we were really young, as a school thing.'

'This is also ringing a bell,' Cornelia said, squinting.

'I think Cornelia and I wandered off somewhere because I don't remember the rest of the talk. Or any of it, come to think of it. There was the bit about the dollhouse; that whole exhibition room was nice even though the dollhouse itself wasn't there. Even then I was partial to miniatures of things.'

'So it's a museum?'

'No, not really,' Diana said.

'So it's... a what, then?' Theodore frowned. 'This is twenty questions on architecture, and I am running out of valid guesses.'

'I don't know what you'd call it. A private exhibit, maybe? I don't think it's that important,' Cornelia said. 'Especially as now it's a zombie film set.' She made a low, guttural noise, raising her arms and gnashing her teeth.

'Eww,' Diana said, at the same time as Mallory said, 'Please stop that, I'll have nightmares.'

'Did this Taylor send you any more information?' Cornelia dropped her stance and patted Mallory lightly on the arm.

'She'll be over once she's done answering police questions, and you can ask her anything you need then.'

Cornelia put the moth down on the desk in front of her. 'She doesn't happen to know a good nightshade supplier, does she?'

'Must you?' Diana wrinkled her nose as the moth flapped and wiggled its feathery antennae. Diana had never hated a bug more in her life, and she'd had to disembowel a giant mantis five months ago.

'*Acherontia gravis* deserves more respect than this. Don't you, Travis?' Cornelia ran her finger over Travis's back, because of course she had named something so scary and imposing something as ridiculous as Travis.

'I regret Mallory getting the idea into her head that you needed a terrifying insect that would only feed on poisonous plants. Why couldn't you get a nicer bug that likes lavender?'

'Grave moths hate lavender; it destroys the potency of their preferred nightshades. They are incredible, and so is Mallory for finding me one.'

Mallory blushed and stared down at the desk in front of her.

'Unfortunately I need a nightshade supplier because it turns out one of the new rules is that I can't purchase a large amount or it "looks suspicious". Speaking of, we got another letter from the UML telling us we cannot take on cases until they've officially closed off the Whistler case,' Cornelia said.

'What do you mean *another* letter?' Mallory and Diana said in unison.

'Shit,' Cornelia said. 'I was sure I'd told you. They've sent two now, but they didn't suggest a penalty if we didn't comply, so I just… forgot.'

'You forgot,' Diana said acidly. 'Just… *forgot*, that the Occulture regulatory body had sent us – a PI agency whose entire operation relies on the existence and acceptance of cases – cease and desist letters. Twice.'

'Diana,' Mallory said warningly. Diana took a deep breath.

'I'm sorry,' Cornelia said. 'Sincerely. As sincerely as I can muster.'

This was not, in fact, very sincere at all.

'Anyway,' she continued without waiting for acknowledgement, 'we got another letter from the UML asking for another hearing to talk about what happened with the Whistler. They haven't recovered his ring, or his body, so we've still got more interviews to do. They did find his tongue, which is great, but they seem to be having trouble finding the rest of the man that should be attached to it.'

'How can they not have found either?' Mallory asked. 'We told them everything we knew.'

Diana pulled out her phone, studiously ignoring that last point. Theodore had conspicuously moved from the doorway at the mention of the Whistler, and Diana took advantage of the deflection.

'We can talk about that later,' she said. 'She's on her way.'

If seeing her on video was bad, Taylor standing in the research room was worse.

Living, breathing Taylor had her green hair pulled back in a ponytail and tied with a pink bandana, and living, breathing Diana had to focus to remain living and breathing in the same space instead of the much more desirable opposite of running away, or perhaps dying a convenient death.

'Everyone, this is Taylor. Taylor, this is Cornelia and Mallory.'

Mallory shook her hand and offered her tea. Within minutes Taylor had wrapped her arms gently around Mallory.

'I think I love her,' she said, pressing her head against Mallory's, who was oddly receptive to the whole exchange.

'That's Theodore,' Diana said as Cornelia poured tea, pointing to where Theodore was intently working on something in the lab. 'He's a bit busy at the moment.'

Taylor quickly filled the others in on what she'd already told Diana, talking to Mallory and Cornelia like they were old friends.

'So we've got the case of the mistaken identity,' Mallory said when she finished.

'Snappy,' Cornelia said.

'Shut it,' Diana said. 'Any questions? Mallory?'

'What do you do on *Undead Complex*?'

'I work in the prop department. It's a bit of an unusual set-up, this one – the show is based on the comics, have you heard of them? They're pretty popular. Most of us are double jobbing in other roles, but the prop department always has extra bodies. No pun intended. It's fairly low-budget, so we're operating on skeleton staff. Also no pun there.'

'And what is your relationship like with everyone you work with? Any issues?'

Taylor shook her head. 'It's stressful, I won't lie. There's too few of us to get everything done on the schedule they want us to, but apart from the showrunner, everyone is really nice and friendly. Like if you're ready to have a full breakdown, someone is around to get you a coffee and to slap a bit of cop-on into you. It's all banter and joking most of the time. They're a really sound crew; even the few actors they have around are nice. It's just...' she hesitated. 'It's hard not to feel targeted, you know?'

'What's the showrunner like?'

'Orson – Orson Webb. To put it kindly, he's a bit of a wreck-the-head. He's grand, like, but… I don't know. We've barely interacted, and I wouldn't point fingers at him. Not readily, anyway.'

Diana saw Mallory write that down.

'To go back to this morning,' Mallory said smoothly. 'What happened again?'

She was clearly trying to check how watertight Taylor's story was, and Diana couldn't complain.

'I was due back in after a day off – it was a day and a half, really. I had a vomiting bug.'

'What time did you arrive?'

'I had an eight a.m. call time, so I showed up just before that, still feeling like a boiled shite, and everyone there was looking at me like they'd seen a ghost.'

Theodore looked up at that. 'I know that one,' he said wearily.

Taylor grinned at him. 'Eventually Xander – he's one of the actors – showed me photographs.'

'Do you have them?' Cornelia held her hand out.

Taylor passed over her phone and Cornelia sent them all to the printer, which responded with uncharacteristic speed. Diana hung them up on the murder board so everyone could see, her fingers trembling as she took in the images.

Taylor in a white nightgown draped over a long couch, her hair trailing in blood, her hands pressing down on her own chest which had a massive hole in the centre of it, visible through the unbuttoned top of the dress. Her arms, her hands, her clothes, the chair and the floor were all stained dark.

'Hexana, is that all blood?' Cornelia pointed at the floor.

Taylor nodded, her expression unreadable.

'We need to go have a chat,' Diana said after a moment. 'Theodore will entertain you while we're gone.'

'Oh yes, that's fine. I'll stay here and rot like a forgotten cabbage while you go have a secret meeting without me. Hello, Taylor. Welcome to the Rot House.'

Taylor, appearing utterly unshaken by this, stuck out her hand. After staring at it for a moment, Theodore pulled her into a hug, and the rest of the Undetectables left them standing there in a cloud of static.

'What do we think?' Diana closed the door to the basement behind her, the three of them standing in the kitchen.

'She seems nice,' Cornelia said. 'Weird how you've never mentioned her before. Though she does explain why you came back from Vancouver with the word "gobshite" suddenly added to your lexicon.'

'Of the *case*,' Diana said impatiently, ignoring the barb. 'Pro bono, of course.'

Cornelia broke into a smile, but didn't say anything, which was somehow worse than her gloating.

'It certainly seems weird enough for us to take on,' Mallory said thoughtfully.

Cornelia looked less certain. Diana noticed the flicker of something Cornelia almost never displayed – hesitation.

'What is it?'

'The last time someone brought us a murder case, we made a lot of mistakes. I don't want us to make a lot of mistakes this time.'

'I'm going into this with eyes wide open, trust me,' Mallory said. 'And for the sake of professionalism, because you know Taylor, I think that our official case communications with her should go through either me or Cornelia. If that's okay?' she added uncertainly.

'You're the director.' Diana flashed her a smile. 'Are we in?'

'I'm in,' Mallory said. 'Cornelia?'

'I'm in. But, assuming we are going to try to check out the scene for ourselves, I think we should leave one of us here to hold down the fort, keep our other cases ticking over.'

'That'll probably be me,' Mallory said. 'And that's fine, I have stuff to be getting on with. Someone should see if Sully could get us access, even if the scene has been reopened. I can do all that sort of thing.'

Detective Inspector Alyssa O'Sullivan was something of an ally to the Undetectables, though they largely tried to operate outside of the sphere of the police.

'Well, actually,' Diana said. In running versions of how to present the case, she'd solved a problem of her own making. 'The show is hiring prop makers, so I could get in pretty easily. And not only that…'

'Why do I feel like I'm going to hate this?' Mallory said nervously.

'I was pretty sure you were going to say yes,' Diana said.

'Oh here we go,' Cornelia said, but the eyeroll seemed good-natured, so Diana didn't hex her for interrupting.

'I was proactive! We don't need to say anything to anyone, because in addition to needing a prop maker, they're down a featured extra for a key scene tomorrow. They're not going to think too hard about qualifications or past experience.'

It seemed dreadfully disorganised, but that was the sort of chaos Diana had come to expect from this line of work.

'The featured extra needs to be approximately five foot ten and comfortable with appliances,' Diana continued.

Mallory nodded, the nod turning slower as she realised what Diana was implying.

'I do love a good toaster,' Mallory said hesitantly.

'Do you have any allergies?' Diana asked, moving to open the basement door. 'Or any qualms about wearing a latex mask for a few hours?'

She was already visualising what they'd need, thinking about what materials she had jammed into her kit upstairs. Moulding masks wasn't *entirely* her forte, but she'd told the propmaster that she could help out even further, and she was not a witch who liked to go back on her word.

'Taylor, could you come up here? We're taking your case, and my moulding skills are a little rusty.'

FIVE

Six days to the Spring Equinox ball

It is often the stuff of disappointment to return to a place once visited in childhood. Perhaps it's the combination of a smaller vantage point – though Diana's vantage had not changed much – and the act of simply *experiencing* for the first time. As though the blank young mind presses the stamp of memory upon its surface, creating an impression that erodes over the years, leaving a lasting sense of grandeur that never was and only serves to disappoint when the reality is later revisited.

That didn't happen when Diana followed the curve of the road past Oakpass Manor on the way to Larkin Studios, as the two present members of the Undetectables audibly gasped at the glimpse of the estate visible through the gates.

If a building could be tall, dark and handsome, Oakpass Manor was it. Grey stone walls and sweeping turrets, balustrade balconies in jet-black stone and ivy creeping up the sides that loomed over well-tended lawns and tree-lined walkways, green lights along the paths giving the manor an air of something otherworldly, set so far in from the road. For all the opulence readily available in Wrackton, Oakpass Manor demanded to be seen as special.

The same could not be said when the road continued to curve past the Manor grounds and, minutes later, they caught their first glimpse of Larkin Studios. Even with the presence of trailers and scaffolding, signs of life, Larkin Studios did not look good. A weather-beaten, hand-painted sign declared they were in the right place, the temporary grey metal security hut the newest building alongside run-down concrete structures that did not look to be in use.

Even still, Diana felt a bubble of excitement. This wasn't just revisiting the subject of a distant childhood memory.

This was like coming home.

Diana pulled up to the gates. She had done some late-night liaising with the first Assistant Director – who seemed to be quadrupling as a PA, a runner, and a general hiring manager – and a courier had brought them access passes that morning.

'Hi,' Diana said cheerily to the gate guard, rolling down her window. 'Where can I park?'

He blinked at her. He was a demon, his uniform crisp. Diana couldn't read his name tag.

'Haven't seen you before. Either of you.' He had an easy way of speaking, but something about his voice made Diana's scalp tingle, demanding to be heard.

'We're new,' Diana said, her tone still light and just as controlled. 'Do you want these?' She waved the access cards at him.

He gave both cards a careful once-over, in no hurry. Mallory inhaled sharply beside Diana, evidently feeling the same strange tension, but Diana tapped her hand casually off the side of her car and waited for him to hand them back.

'Mmm,' the guard said noncommittally. 'Crew car park is around the side, follow the cones.'

Diana winked at him as he opened the gates and they wound around an outer path, getting a sense of the vastness of the studio lot. Oakpass Manor couldn't be seen over the horizon of stages and workshops, suggesting they were at least a mile away, if not more. Circling faded sound stages and offices she was sure were not in use, she could see trappings of materials and cars, from this century at least, though the whole lot felt uncannily empty. Taylor had not been exaggerating when she said they were operating on a skeleton crew; even for a pilot, it felt thin on the ground.

Excitement fizzed in her stomach again.

'I used our real names because fuck having to remember to be someone else. I am going to try talking to everyone who works in props and design. You, Mallory, are—'

'In desperate need of a wee,' Mallory said. 'Do we know how long I'll have to sit for?'

'I've been assured it's all face and upper-body makeup. If the artist likes the mask Taylor and I made, great, if not, they'll figure something out. There might be a bit of makeup on your hands, but you'll be wearing the uniform they've prepared and that's going to cover most of you. I got Felix to loan us their knee-high platform boots because they're the brand they suggested, and there's a pair of socks to stuff the toes with, but you'll be lying down for the whole scene, so don't worry about them being too big. Just don't worry.'

'The more you say "don't worry"…' Mallory started fretfully. They had kept her awake to work on the mask, trying to take a mould as quickly as they could, and she looked tired. Diana felt bad, even though she herself had barely had three hours' sleep. She was running on pure adrenaline. For the first time in a long time, Diana had woken up to silence, the buzzing in her ear quiet, her heart soothed by the smell of liquid latex burned into her nose from the night before.

'You sit there, you ask some questions, you lie down and pretend to be dead until they tell you to sit up, that seems to be the gist of it. I promise it'll be okay. Head down, ears up.'

'Okay.' Mallory flashed her a smile. Her phone buzzed with a call and she put it on speaker.

'Nice of you to join us,' Diana said, checking her lipstick in the rearview mirror.

'Theodore was right, this is the Rot House,' Cornelia said sleepily, her voice crackling through the phone. 'This is not a real time of day. Are you in?'

'In the car park, about to begin our mission,' Diana said. 'It's six o'clock, Cornelia, and you are being ridiculous.'

'Great. I'll have sixteen coffees and maybe be repeatedly hounded by one of our existing clients. I was thinking how I wouldn't mind if they kept coming back for more, if only they were offering something interesting.'

'Like money?'

'Yeah,' Cornelia said vaguely. 'I guess.'

'While I have you both here,' Mallory said. 'As agency director, I made an executive decision this morning and let Sully know we are working a new case.'

'What! Why?' Cornelia demanded.

'I think Cornelia hates it.' Diana hated it a little bit too. Voluntarily working with the police when it was not to their personal gain was not something she particularly condoned.

'I knew neither of you would be pleased, but I decided it was necessary in case we need her or Dr Ray to call in a favour for us and get Tay– *the* body brought to Wrackton instead of a mortuary in Oughteron, where we have no connections or semi-legal ways of pulling strings. She has already filed a request with Oughteron and the UML to transfer the body to Wrackton, on account of it being a magical murder – assuming, of course, that we can confirm it's magical.'

'Who in the name of Elisabella would let us do that?'

Mallory shrugged, then seemed to remember Cornelia couldn't actually see her. 'They readily handed over the last one, it's just a question of what the UML wants this time. They're petrified of a repeat of the Whistler. The tribunal showed us that. Besides, she won't mention our potential involvement in the case until she's asked about it, so we might not have to worry about the cease and desist situation until after we've solved it.'

'I think you made the right call,' Diana said, running it through in her head. It was why Mallory was director and not her or Cornelia; neither of them would've thought of a time-saving exercise. 'It's two against one, Cornelia.'

'Fine. It sounds disgustingly sensible, but seeing as it was Mallory's idea, fine. And anyway, she's already done it.'

'Plus, it's Taylor's body, technically. I daresay she gets a say in who cuts it open,' Mallory said.

'If that's everything, I will get on with my day of drudgery.'

Even to Diana, it sounded like Cornelia was laying it on a bit thick. Diana had offered to get her a role as a PA or something Cornelia could've play-acted at for a day, but she had all but shouted Diana's suggestions down.

'You got the most important job and you know it,' Diana said.

A golf cart pulled up beside them, and Diana took that as her cue to exit the car. She handed Mallory a bag containing Felix's boots, a box she'd carefully packed the mask into, and her forensics kit that thoughtfully included several drinks to keep her energy up.

'New people,' a pale, skinny witch boy said. He had a tablet in one hand, balancing a phone against the steering wheel.

'Diana, props. Mallory, extra.'

'Right. Fred,' he said, pointing to himself with the phone. Diana caught a flash of a vinyl melting-smiley-face sticker on the back of it. 'First AD. Assistant Director, you know.'

'I've worked on sets before,' Diana said politely.

'You got past the dragon okay?'

'What?'

Fred shook his head. 'Nathan, our security. He gives folk a hard time, don't worry about it. Are you ready, Diana props and Mallory extra?'

Mallory tucked the box closer to her chest, and nodded.

Fred dropped Mallory off at the MUA trailer on a backlot ten minutes from the carpark – after a quick pitstop to the toilets, at Mallory's behest – then neatly manoeuvred the cart past the sound stages, towards what would be Diana's home for the day: the props workshop.

'This feels like a lot of grunt work for the first AD,' Diana commented after a few minutes, trying to memorise the layout of the studio as it whipped past them.

Fred made a soft noise in his throat. 'I'm glad I don't actually have to *run* anywhere, it's a good ten-minute walk to the Manor from the studio. Here we are,' he said, slowing to a stop. 'I'm sure I'll see you around.' He tipped a finger against his forehead, and drove away.

'New girl,' a voice said. 'Welcome. I'm Rachel, the propmaster.'

Diana turned to see a tall pale woman with burnished red hair, her lipstick drawn perfectly to accentuate her cupid's bow. She spoke without moving her eyes, forcing Diana's attention to her mouth, making Diana feel particularly uselessly gay.

'Diana,' Diana said, pointing to herself. *Get a grip.* 'We talked over email.'

Rachel broke into a seamless smile. She was pretty the way film stars were pretty – ethereal and impossible – even in unfavourable lighting, a pale denim jumpsuit tied around her hips, her t-shirt showing off toned arms. 'Come meet the rest of the team.'

The workshop was cramped, despite the distinct lack of living folk inside.

'The team' amounted to a mousy-seeming faerie girl with heavy-lidded eyes who did not look at Diana once, intently pouring rubber into one of the moulds in front of her. 'This is Alannah,' Rachel said. 'When she gets really into her work, she ignores everyone around her, so don't take it personally.'

She smiled again, and Diana forced herself to look away from her mouth. 'We've got another girl too, but she's off sick at the moment. Though whether she'll come back is a question for another day.'

Taylor had agreed to stay home for another day to give Diana and Mallory space to investigate, citing shock, which was very much the essence of the truth.

'She will,' Alannah said without looking up.

'Lovely,' Diana said vaguely. 'What are we working on?'

'We're finishing props for the background of a scene – we've got the green screen props and the retractables covered, so this is just moulding rubber weapons for some of the melee shots,' Rachel said. 'They're based on authentic medieval weaponry that's been hanging up in Oakpass Manor, so we have to be careful not to damage anything, but Himself wanted everything authentic so we're following our orders. We're about a day behind, because of...' She broke off. 'You said you'd worked in props before?'

'I have. I pivoted into set dressing for a while, but I'm keen to get back into the practical side of things.' Diana wondered who Himself was, assuming it wasn't Fred. Perhaps the showrunner Taylor had mentioned.

'Are you good?'

'I'm not bad,' Diana said, meaning she was excellent.

'I'm getting a sense you're being modest,' Alannah said, surfacing from her work. 'I think you look kind of familiar?'

Not recognising her, Diana named the shows she'd worked on before, which felt like a lifetime before she'd come back to Wrackton. Before her life as she knew it had changed forever.

But maybe she'd started down that path a long time ago without realising it.

'Oh, so you must know Taylor, then?'

Diana made a split-second decision. 'Taylor Rose?'

Alannah nodded, but said nothing else, and Diana saw her first chance to ask questions slipping away from her. 'Where do you want me?' she asked Rachel.

'We've got you right where we want you,' she said, that smile creasing her mouth again.

It was past lunch time when Diana was confident she could ask about the body. She had noticed the energy in the department was subdued, a little distracted. She heard voices outside as Rachel wandered in and out, and Diana cast a listening spell, furious she was too far away to really enhance her hearing, and annoyed at herself when the buzzing in her head got too loud to hear what was being said. A few times Alannah caught her listening intently and frowned at her.

'Ringing in my ears,' Diana muttered, then clamped her lips shut. She hadn't told Mallory or Cornelia about it; she wasn't talking about it here. All she'd gotten from the conversations happening outside was confirmation that there had been no major news outlet reports and they were 'lucky on that front', and someone mentioning Taylor was coming back tomorrow.

Fred walked in looking for the acting script supervisor, who, after some panicked back and forth between Rachel and Alannah, transpired to actually be Fred himself. Diana seized her chance.

'I hear there was something strange going on here yesterday, who wants to fill me in?' She said it lightly and eagerly, hoping she sounded exactly how someone who wanted to fit in with her new peers would sound in response to on-set gossip without knowing the details.

'I'm surprised it hasn't hit the papers,' Rachel said.

Fred shook his head in agreement. 'Orson will be trying to keep this quiet, but I doubt it'll last long. There were journalists sniffing around earlier this morning, asking if there was an *Undead Complex* curse. I made short work of them, but they'll be back.'

Rachel set aside a mould cast and rubbed at her forehead delicately, taking the papers from Fred. 'I don't want to alarm you, Diana, or risk scaring you off on your first day, but a body was found on set yesterday.'

'My goddess,' Diana said, her eyes widening. 'What happened?'

'We thought it was a prank at first, someone messing around.'

'But it wasn't pretend,' Fred said.

'The body… the body looked like Taylor's. That's why she's not here today. She's still alive, but… Make of that what you will.'

'Goddess, that's horrible,' Diana said. 'I'm sorry. And so horrible for you, to think a colleague was dead!'

'It was awful. I tear up thinking about it,' Fred said. Diana scanned Rachel and Alannah's faces; Alannah appeared to have not heard, while Rachel nodded solemnly.

'Who was… I mean, is it insensitive to ask who… who found her?'

'One of our actors,' Rachel said. 'I heard him shout and came running.'

'Xander?' Fred said uncertainly.

'Xander,' Rachel confirmed. 'Alannah was there too, and so was Sandi – she's our lead, playing the necromancer. Sandi said she was fine to keep filming, so the rest of us needed to be okay too. Gosh, we're so lucky you turned up today, we're already doing such a massive production with very few hands.'

Diana held in her questions, unwilling to press. Waiting for someone to fill the silence was always more beneficial.

'I thought I was the one that screamed,' Alannah said suddenly. 'Fred was in the bathroom and came running. Sandi came in last with her phone, and Xander strolled in afterwards.'

'I was having a little wazz,' Fred said. 'But I heard someone scream from the set, and I went running. I don't remember seeing the two of you at all. Not till later, anyway.'

They all frowned at each other and Diana tried not to explode from the need to ask more questions; two people having conflicting stories was one thing, but three entirely different stories meant she needed to talk to the rest of those present. No matter what the real story was, there were plenty of people in the vicinity, and that meant anyone could've done it.

'Poor Taylor,' Diana said, hoping she looked as wide-eyed as she was trying to. 'Who'd want to do a thing like that to her? It must've scared her so badly.'

'You'd be surprised what people want,' Alannah said darkly.

'Oh but nobody here would want to harm anyone, surely?' Rachel said, her brows furrowed. 'I thought, despite the difficulties, we were getting on great. Her work is excellent, she gets on with everyone.'

'And yet someone staged a murder using a replica of my ex-girlfriend,' Alannah said, wiping her arm over her eyes. She wasn't crying, but there was something in her face Diana couldn't read, her mind chewing over *ex-girlfriend* like a hex.

That was why Diana was familiar to Alannah: she and Taylor had been talking about her.

Rachel nodded, her eyes still full of concern. 'Right, yes. It's strange. You're all safe in here though.'

'Does anyone have an idea who the body really is, then? If Taylor's okay,' Diana said.

Fred looked at her quizzically. 'It's obviously not real? It *looked* real, but Taylor's alive and well – well, I don't know that she's well. But she's alive, and that's what matters.'

'Would *you* be well if that happened to you?' Alannah snapped.

'Okay, Alannah, I'm sorry for not using the right words.' But he said it with a salty tone.

'Sorry,' Alannah said. 'It wasn't exactly a fun start to the day, and we've had a hell of a week, and I thought… I don't know what I thought. But I'm sorry.'

Diana needed to get Alannah alone to talk to her.

'Has anyone brought Xander some chocolate or anything? That helps me when I've had a shock,' she said, knowing it was pushing things a bit.

'Xander is fine,' Rachel laughed. 'Water off a duck's back. I've worked with him on a couple of projects before, he's seen all sorts. Though not anything like this. Anyway, let's stop talking about it. It's depressing, and we can't afford to lose more time. I'm going to put our afternoon tunes on.' She pressed play on a speaker in the corner and Apparent chart music filled the space. Diana's ear chose that moment to ring, the noise of it mingling unpleasantly with the sounds of her equipment, the music and people talking in low voices.

'I'm going to step outside for a minute,' she said to Rachel, pressing a hand to her face. 'Two minutes, tops.'

Rachel said something, but Diana couldn't hear it. She gestured for Diana to go on and she hurried out, not looking at anyone until she found an exit. She hadn't realised until she was out in the cool spring air just how warm it had been inside. She pulled a water bottle from her bag and took long, careful sips.

'You okay, darlin'?' a melodic voice said to her, and she jumped, realising the ringing had dulled to a buzzing whine. She came face to face with a man she recognised in that vague sort of celebrity sense, his brown skin glowing in a way regular Apparent folk's couldn't. He looked as though it was not the first time he'd asked if she was okay.

'Yes, sorry. Overheated in there a bit,' Diana said, smiling. 'How are you?'

'If I had a hundred quid for every time I was asked that in the last twenty-four hours, I'd have… a lot of money,' he said, rubbing a hand through his magnificent, perfectly manicured beard. On closer inspection, Diana could see it was dyed.

Diana cocked her head, making sure puzzlement was evident on her features.

'They haven't been talking about it?'

'About…?'

'Never mind.'

'The body, is it? I've heard a bit about it,' Diana said, brow furrowing. Then she widened her eyes. 'You were the one who—'

'Yeah,' the man – who Diana was now certain was Xander Crane – said. He fumbled in his pocket and pulled out a cigarette, finding a dry spot to sit down. 'Look, let's not worry too much about it, all right?'

'Sorry. I bet people are pushing you for all the gory details,' Diana said. 'I imagine it's a relief to know there are still folk out here who haven't a clue what really happened.'

'To be honest, nobody really does. Lots of people came running, but… I don't even know what I saw, to be honest. I thought it was that girl. People were screaming "Taylor!" and I was so sure I was looking at her. And the way she had her hands over the hole in her chest, like she'd… but it's impossible, of course. She's still alive. We don't know who that is.'

'Did you know Taylor? I mean, do you know her?'

'Crew's small, it's hard to not get to know everyone,' he said. 'She's a sweet girl.'

Fred's golf cart crunched to a stop several feet away, and he shouted something that Diana couldn't hear.

'No,' Xander shouted back.

'—laugh a minute here,' he shouted, and drove away.

Xander took a long drag on his cigarette and Diana looked at him questioningly.

'He said the director of photography hasn't been seen in thirty-six hours, was wondering if I'd heard from him.'

'Is he a friend of yours?'

'Donny Baker's a friend of everyone, as long as they carry a lighter in their pocket and don't piss him off.'

'Did he know Taylor? I mean, if he's missing and someone that looked like her turned up…' Diana let the implication land.

'Nah, I don't think so. They're double and triple jobbing here, but I can't imagine him getting his hands on makeup and it looking like it did.' He shook his head, exhaling a cloud of smoke. Diana shuffled back a couple of steps. 'Decent at his job, but I can see him cutting his losses and running – every time I've seen him he's threatened to quit, so it wouldn't surprise me in the slightest if he had. They're using magic on the cameras, apparently, and he keeps saying he could quit and they'd never manage to replace him. I've never seen a DP not having any assistants – even on a skeleton crew – and Orson is doing his head in. Have you met our showrunner? Woeful bastard, but that's always the way. Another reason to call this place cursed.'

'Cursed?'

'Ah, usual shit, you know. Horror show in a crumbling old shithouse with a studio that shut down when its owners went missing… I'm surprised they're not making a show about that instead of this zombie bollocks. What's worse is every prick here seems to have some sort of attachment to the place. I'll tell you what, I'd absolutely murder a pint right now.' He ran his hands through his hair. 'You're dead good to talk to.'

'I try,' Diana said. 'It must've been something though, walking in on that?'

He paused, and she worried he was going to bolt. 'It was… weird… to walk in and see that poor girl dead, but she's not, is she? It wasn't real. Just some shit someone decided would be fun. Joke gone wrong, I don't know. Between you and me…' He took a drag from his cigarette, squinting at Diana. 'Nah. Never mind.'

'You can tell me. I'm dead good to talk to because I'm dead good at listening.'

'I'm regretting taking this job on,' he said, rubbing his face. 'I wasn't going to, my gut told me no... It'll be fine, we're in it now.' His face was grim-set. He stubbed his cigarette out on the ground, standing to go. 'You just take care of yourself, you hear me? Or I'll have something to say about it.'

SIX

Mallory was not having what one would call 'the best of times', though it also was not the worst, should she come to think of it. She was in pain from sitting for Diana and Taylor's moulding process, stiffness radiating along her shoulders. She'd timidly asked where the bathrooms were and Fred had stopped at a bathroom attached to Stage One. It was cleaner than she'd expected, but she'd been hit with a blast of artificial-smelling apple air freshener and it made her feel nauseated on top of everything else. It had been a considerable effort to coax herself out of Fred's golf cart and into the makeup trailer, the apple scent clinging to her.

'She'll be right along to look after you,' Fred said, taking off again and leaving Mallory with a box and a bag and a sense that she was ill equipped for whatever she was about to step into.

She knocked on the trailer door – certain it was the right one, because it had a sign that said MUA/SFX in bold black letters taped to it – and when no one answered, she stepped inside. The trailer door banged closed behind her.

She was alone.

The trailer was cramped and smelled of fake wood and fresh carpet, a lingering scent of liquid latex and something vaguely antiseptic. Mirrors with character sketches from the comics and hand-scribbled costume notes stuck to them were set over two long benches covered in bottles and brushes and tubs. Directly to Mallory's right were shelves holding silicone and latex zombie masks on model heads, as well as some other monsters she couldn't begin to identify. Diana had assured her the makeup she'd be wearing wouldn't be particularly complicated, but that her mouth would be partially covered, and she tried to ignore the swoop of terror she felt at potentially not being able to breathe properly.

Mallory was staring aghast at a tub of something called scab blood, wondering what in the name of Elisabella she'd gotten herself into, when the door banged open and a wholly familiar blonde woman walked in. She looked at Mallory. Mallory looked at her, her hand clenched tightly around the tub. The woman edged around Mallory, eyes locked on hers, until she had folded herself into a seat down from the one Mallory had chosen. She settled back into the chair. She had not blinked in a long time. Mallory's eyes started to water.

'Hi,' the woman mouthed.

'Hi,' Mallory mouthed back.

'I'll just sit here,' she said at normal volume. 'This is my chair. I'd prefer it if you didn't sit in my chair.'

'Of course,' Mallory said, completely baffled by this entire exchange. 'That's no problem at all.'

The woman spread a newspaper out on the table in front of

her, one that screamed a headline about a body discovered under a bridge in the Lake District. She folded it in half, placing her hands on top of it.

'It works best for me, because she likes things to be done from the left. Like a server at a restaurant,' she said, except she pronounced it '*REE*staurant', with the emphasis on the wrong part of the word, which jarred with Mallory's assumption that this woman was American. 'I'm Sandi,' the woman henceforth known as Sandi continued. 'Clementine. You probably knew that.'

'Mallory, I'm an extra.' She held out a hand. Sandi placed hers in it, as though waiting for Mallory to kiss it. Unsure of what to do, she shook it a little, and Sandi beamed.

'I think you're playing the fallen soldier today, if I'm not mistaken,' Sandi pointed at the masks behind her. 'She didn't say, but I know things. It's kind of magic, you know.'

Mallory did sort of know, but she wasn't entirely sure Sandi did. It had just clicked into place for her who she was: Sandi Clementine, twelve-time prestigious TV award nominee and all-time favourite among queer Apparents, best known for playing quirky, quotable characters. What the general public – including Mallory – had not known about Sandi was that she liked to talk, endlessly, and she filled the next twenty minutes telling Mallory in great detail where 'she' liked things to be placed – name and occupation unclear, unless Sandi was talking about herself in third person – what 'her' preferences were, why she was the best MUA she'd ever worked with. She pronounced MUA like *moo-a*, which also amused Mallory.

'Thank you,' Mallory said when Sandi paused. 'That was

very... informative. It's my first time on a set, I'm really interested in how everything works.'

She wished so much for Diana's ability to find openings for the questions she needed answering. There was a reason Mallory preferred the seclusion of back-office forensics.

'She's late, she's not normally late,' Sandi said. 'Sad.'

'Sad,' Mallory agreed, scrambling for how to rescue this. Diana had suggested she'd mostly be working with other extras, giving her a chance to snoop around and ask questions of the makeup artist, who would have access to the key actors. She had not, despite her usual brilliance, foreseen a situation where Mallory would have to be charming, and Mallory tried to channel her friend as best she could.

'So,' Mallory said, hoping Sandi would not immediately realise she had an ulterior motive. 'Do you have a big part in the show?'

'Oh, yes. I'm playing a necromancer,' she said, pronouncing it '*neecROMancer*'. 'A big one. Not, like, tall, you know, just big in importance. Her name is Ruthless Monroe. I love that. I storm the castle, I do magic. You know there are people out there who do magic every day? Occult,' she said, pronouncing it like the beginning of *Occam*. 'My grandmom was English and she spent a lot of time around magical people.'

'Oh,' Mallory said, teetering on the edge of something. Sandi could either see her as helpful, or she'd run scared. Mallory had not met many folk who did not take kindly to Occulture; though she and her friends had survived the slings and arrows of an Apparent secondary school, they had largely been ignored, both for their unbreakable friendship bubble and because they refused to engage in the sort of chaos classmates wanted them to. Cornelia was her own chaos, of course, but not in a way that would've benefited those who wanted to be entertained.

'I'm actually a witch,' Mallory said quietly. 'I don't do magic much though.'

'You *are?*' Sandi gasped, pressing a hand to her chest. Mallory was not sure if her entire persona was acting, or if Sandi was just like that. She was used to Theodore's dramatics and largely understood he was partially joking but mostly not, but she could not read this situation at all. 'That's so wonderful. You know I was really excited to film here; my great-grandmom used to live in Oakpass Manor. Apparently she really liked magic. Occultical, I think you said.'

This had Mallory's attention, ignoring the fact she had not managed to say anything about Occulture, wrong or otherwise.

'Really? When was that?'

'A lady never reveals her age, or the age of her great-grandmom. Although I was never great at numbers...'

'Me neither, don't worry. What was her name?'

Sandi flashed her a beaming smile. 'I kind of hoped to do some family tree work while I was here. Spend a bit of time learning about magic, the Occultical, snoop around Oakpass a little. We should totally hang out, dollface.' She brushed Mallory's sleeve with the back of her hand, not giving her a chance to respond, or ask again for a name. 'It made sense for me, given my family history, to play the part of a magician. No, necromancer, I'm a necromancer. Or a wizard? You know, I've asked Hollis a bunch of times to really explain to me this world we're in, but he never will. He's the creative director. I think he writes comic books or something? Hey, hold on a second.' Sandi reached into her bag and rummaged around until she pulled out a call sheet. Mallory took the opportunity to take a deep breath, incredibly overwhelmed. 'Oh no, this is yesterday's. Hold this, please.' She thrust it at Mallory, who cast a cursory glance at it. A list of names, times when Sandi was supposed to be on set. Things that might be useful to them. While Sandi was occupied, Mallory casually slipped it into her own bag.

'Here we go.' Sandi smoothed a sheaf of script pages covered in green and yellow sticky flags in front of her, notes scrawled on every single inch of the paper so the print was barely legible. 'So here, when it says the necromancer "casts a spell", what sort of arm movements should I be doing? Like…' She wobbled her hands around in front of her. 'I want this to be authentic, you know. Really raising people from the dead.'

Mallory briefly explained how magic worked in her world. How it simply *was*, how you thought something and made it happen, but that it followed rules in the same way everyone followed gravity – they weren't rules she was particularly cognisant of, but rules that she was forced to live by.

'Well if it's just energy, honey, why don't you do magic?'

'Because I don't have any, a lot of the time.'

'Right, right. Right, right, right. Okay.' Sandi nodded emphatically. There was silence for a moment, then, 'I actually had another question about this necromancer, if you've got a second—'

To Mallory's relief, the trailer door opened.

'Sandi.' A short, pale-skinned, flame-haired demon walked in. 'Sorry I'm late, babe, having a mare.' She brought with her a waft of perfume that tickled Mallory's nose, mixed with something earthy, mingling unpleasantly with the air-freshener scent clinging to her clothes.

'*Jenna!*' Sandi threw her hands in the air. 'You're here! I have a new friend, her name is…'

'Mallory. I'm the emergency featured extra. I hope I'm in the right place?' Mallory looked at her nervously.

'You're exactly where you need to be. I'm Jenna White, the head MUA here, although it's not like there is anyone else around to do it. I was promised an assistant that never materialised.' She rolled her eyes. 'Do you have much experience?'

Mallory shook her head. 'It's my first time on a TV set.'

'So you've done film before, right?'

'Yeah,' she lied lyingly. 'Though I haven't spent much time having makeup applied, I know I'm… comfortable.'

Jenna waved a hand, which Mallory noted was encased in a compression glove. Jenna saw her looking. 'I have a condition,' she said.

'I have gloves just like them.'

Jenna smiled. 'We'll get you sorted first, Mallory, and get you both off to set.'

It took over an hour to wait for the pieces of Diana's mask to dry – those that Jenna wholly approved of – and to get Mallory into her costume – consisting of a black button-front jumpsuit, several looping weapon belts, and a helmet that helped hide her hair. Then Mallory, Sandi and Jenna were bundled back into Fred's golf cart and taken to a small set that proudly declared itself to be Stage Three, directly across from Stage One and notably nowhere near Stage Two. She wondered how anyone found anything in Larkin Studios.

Mallory did not know what she was expecting when she walked in, but it wasn't a series of cameras pointing at a dimly lit, narrow cellar with a big bundle of clothes in the centre of it, and nobody else around. An empty set that could've been one of Diana's dioramas made life-size.

As Mallory approached, she saw the bundle of clothes was not a bundle of clothes at all, but piled life-size mannequins made to look like rotting corpses.

'Oh,' Mallory said.

'This is the bit where the zombies take over the castle,' Jenna said, as Fred led her to the stage.

'Showrunner should be here in a minute,' Fred said, checking his tablet. 'You got here early, which is great.'

'Puts us only about thirty hours behind,' Jenna said, and they both laughed tiredly. She pulled out a chair next to a small white table and set up a few tools on it that Mallory assumed were for touch-ups.

'Where… where's the crew?' Mallory asked.

'We're trying some magic,' Fred said. 'Larkin Studios was known for creating movie magic, and part of the revival attempt is to mix old and new methods. State-of-the-art cameras set to run and record with minimal interference. It helps that our DP is a witch too. And especially helps given that he hasn't bothered to show up to work today.'

Mallory did not know much about how a TV set should be run, but this sounded like a nightmare way of doing anything.

'Are you worried that he's not around?'

'Nah. I think he's made good on his threat to quit. Good riddance, honestly. He's left the cameras set up, which is all that matters until we get another DP in place. Wild, isn't it?' Fred said, flashing a grin at her. 'Fun, though. Nobody's ever done anything like it.'

Sandi was busy mouthing lines to herself as she paced in front of the craft services table – Mallory assumed that was also Fred's doing – a robe tucked over her shoulders.

'Action!' a voice called, and nobody but Mallory jumped. 'My little joke,' the owner of the voice explained as he got closer, swinging an oddly shaped cane with every step. He was a troll, his skin a pale blue-grey, his face handsome enough. He wore a brimmed hat pulled low over his eyes, casting shadows over the sockets.

'Are we ready?' he said, barely glancing at Mallory. 'Time is money, Fredrich. Hollis will have my hat.' He was close enough now that she could see the cane was not a cane at all, but some sort of short, barbed spear. Nobody else seemed remotely alarmed by it, which suggested this was a regularly occurring barbed spear.

'Got it, Orson, just a sec,' Fred said. Orson took the spear between his hands, turning it pensively as Fred sprang into action, directing Mallory to her mark.

'Basically we get a wide shot of the full pile of bodies, then get a close shot of your eyes snapping open. We'll try a few where you sit up towards the camera. It's going to move towards you on the dolly,' he said. 'And I want you to try looking into it, then a few a shots where we look past it.'

Mallory nodded. 'Can I also ask what the scene... is?'

Fred paused. He pulled the script from under his arm and scanned it. 'It's supposed to be the moment where the first zombies appear. "Immortalis", I think it's called, something to do with Occulture. I've never heard of it, so it's probably bullshit—'

'Fip fip,' Orson interrupted, finally looking at her. She had the sense her face was being recorded in his memory.

'I... what?'

'Fip fip, short for "fix it in post". It means hurry up, we don't have all day, we can fix mistakes and misunderstandings later. Saves time,' Fred said, a small smirk on his lips. 'Ready? Quiet on set!'

Mallory did the scene twenty or thirty times, her pain levels rising even as she baked alive inside her costume under the stage lights. She broke for touch-ups, Orson and Fred deep in conversation on the other side of the set.

'What's Orson like to work with?' Mallory whispered to Jenna.

'He keeps things running,' Jenna said quietly, taking Mallory's chin gently and forcing her to stay still. 'Moreso than Hollis, who... is also here.'

'What are we talking about?' Sandi whispered. 'Also, Mallory, can you help me with one more thing? I tried asking Hollis earlier and he dismissed me, like I don't know what I'm talking about or something. It's very strange.'

'Of course I can. What's he like?' Mallory asked as soon as Jenna released her chin, glad she could still somewhat speak behind her mask. 'Hollis.'

'Oh he's a very, very busy man,' Sandi said. 'I shouldn't be badmouthing him. He keeps an eye on Xander and me, but via text. Though he doesn't reply very often. And he doesn't tend to appear until there's actual filming happening – filming with dialogue, though.' She said it like *dee-alog*. 'He's usually hiding in the Manor thinking. He's a little… weird, you know? He acts ways that make other folk look at him and wonder what he's doing.'

Mallory fought back a smile. 'I know the type. Listen, were you here yesterday? I don't like to gossip…'

'I *love* to gossip,' Sandi said. 'Is this about the murder?'

Mallory nodded, casting a glance at Jenna, who didn't seem to have heard her.

'Well, I was the second one to arrive, Jenna and I ran over. So horrible, I really thought it was acting, you know. Nobody should die like that. First they said "Taylor", and I thought, "oh no, Taylor's dead?!" and I was *so* upset. But then I realised they were not talking about my personal tailor, but a girl who worked in the prop department here. So sad. Even though Tailor Taylor Dufresne would've been much sadder and more personally concerning. Taylor's been my tailor since I was a little girl. I just wish everyone had been clear about *which* Taylor they meant.'

Mallory was quite sure that '*Du-frezz-ney*' was not how anyone's surname was pronounced.

'Did you know Taylor? The prop maker.'

'I've only been here a couple of days – they don't need me to build, they need me to create, you see. So I missed out on making a friend, which is so sad.'

'Sad,' Mallory agreed.

'All I know is that she's dead, they shut down production for the day so I go take a bath and read my lines for today, you know, that's my job, so I keep working even in the face of tragedy,' she said seriously. 'And hope we wake up in a better world. And then you show up, and it's great again.'

'I can't imagine anyone wanting to kill a person from the prop department randomly,' Mallory said carefully. 'It seems so strange.'

'There's a lot of strange things going on here. This place? I wish I could ask my great-grandmom questions about it, but she's been gone a long time. This place is haunted. It feels so haunted.' She pressed a cold hand to Mallory's, who blinked back in surprise. 'Doesn't it give you chills?'

'What are you two talking about?' Jenna asked, as though surfacing from a daydream.

'Murder,' Sandi said. 'Murder is the word... er.'

Mallory wished more than anything she could bring Theodore here to meet Sandi. They'd get on like a house on fire.

'Oh, no. I was late to the whole thing. So awful at the time, though apparently she's fine now? The prop girl?' Jenna's face creased with worry.

'She's not dead? Oh what a miracle! Was it a necromancer?' Sandi asked, a look of genuine-seeming fear on her face.

'Do you know her?' Mallory asked.

Jenna shook her head. 'Not well. Small crew, we got to know each other quickly, but Taylor keeps to herself. Rachel runs a tight ship. That's the propmaster, but she sometimes steps into a more senior role when things call for it,' she added for Mallory's benefit. 'She's helped out on some of the appliances though, it's great to have someone multi-skilled around to help out on something this big, but our interactions were limited. I was naturally horrified when I did hear about it – even when you don't know each other well, it's human to be shaken by that kind of news, you know?'

Mallory nodded. 'What do you think happened with the body, then? A case of mistaken identity? It's so scary to think about. You hear of cursed sets...' Mallory wished Diana could see her steer the conversation. She half-wondered if the mask covering her face was making it easier to function, somehow.

Jenna's face dropped, just enough that Mallory noticed. 'I'd say it was something of a mistake.' She paused with a brush over a pot of loose powder. 'I was setting up when the alarm was raised, though I didn't even hear there was anything going on. All of it happened in Stage Two, and that's a five-minute cart ride away from our trailer, or at least a fifteen-minute walk back to the car park. I was working on Sandi at the time, and didn't hear anything until it was all over and they were taking the body out.'

'So you never saw the scene?'

'No, the two of us were in here the whole time.' Jenna shook her head. 'They took the body away, but it wasn't Taylor's, cause she's fine. I guess it wasn't really a body? I don't know. It *looked* real. But then that would mean...'

Mallory waited to see if she'd add anything else; it contradicted what Sandi had told her.

'There's something really weird about this place. The manor itself, too. There's all these rooms we can't go into. The owner granted us special permission to film in the drawing room, but he wasn't keen on letting us.'

'I always thought the manor was nationally owned,' Mallory said.

'So did I! But it was purchased years ago from the last family that lived in it. The current owner is some guy who owns hotels. Quinn-something. Apparently there's plans to make it a hotel within the next few years. I assume big money was dropped to get him to hold off on that while we filmed. That, and Hollis is an old friend. Speculation, of course, I don't know who this guy is.'

Mallory knew precisely who she was talking about.

'And what kind of permissions did you have to get? Sorry, I'm so new to the world of TV, it seems amazing to me that everyone comes together to make something and have it look so seamless.'

'Ha,' Jenna said, rather than laughing, which suggested that whatever was to come next was not going to be funny. 'I have yet to work somewhere where things *do* feel seamless. I don't know the ins and outs, I never do. I pick up things here and there, but that's all it ever is. I know Hollis is a very convincing man, that's for sure.'

'What's he like to work with? Brilliant, I bet.'

Jenna nodded. 'He sure is.'

She didn't elaborate, instead catching Orson's eye as he walked by. She dropped the brush she was using to add more scab blood to Mallory's nose and hurried over to talk to him, turning so Mallory couldn't see their lips move. Fred, who had been peering at the cameras, called Mallory back to lie once again on the bodies of her fallen comrades, staring up at a stage light until she felt it burn into her retinas. She was not sure what she'd gathered, but a clear picture was starting to form in her mind: something strange was happening here.

SEVEN

By the end of the day, Diana was dying to go home. Her muscle memory led her to cast and mould props, her hands guiding her into remembering exactly what she loved to do and how good she was at it. Her mind strayed more than once to how Mallory was doing, and if she'd found anything out, either about the body, or why someone would want them to think Taylor was dead.

She wondered if there had been anything to find.

During a five-minute break everyone else used to smoke, Diana had checked in with Sully, but there had been no reply, which either meant she was transferring the body, or hadn't gotten around to making the requests. Both were fine; they'd get to see the body one way or another. The DP going AWOL in the same timeframe as 'Taylor's' murder was interesting as well; Diana was eager for the agency to look into him.

She looked to Alannah, who was deep in her task, moulding bone-shaped candles. Diana had no idea if she'd have the guts to keep coming back if she couldn't tell Mallory the truth about what she wanted; if this was her last chance to speak to Alannah, her last time on set of *Undead Complex*, she didn't want to waste it.

'You've been quiet,' Diana said to Alannah. 'I was thinking about what you said earlier, about Taylor being your ex and then the... the whole thing. Are... are you okay?' She kept her tone soft and delicate, as though she was trying to be very thoughtful and not at all nosy.

Alannah seemed almost bored by the question. 'Yeah. I mostly work on horror shows, blood and guts and shit doesn't really bother me. Everyone's secretly freaking out about it, but I swear it looked like a prop. I think it probably was a prop,' she said.

Diana blinked at her, thinking about the photographs she'd seen, how much she'd had to convince her own mind that it wasn't really Taylor. And yet Alannah was faerie; she could not lie.

Alannah sighed. 'Did you not hear about the last show Jenna worked on?'

When Diana was not forthcoming, both because she hadn't heard and because she had no idea who Jenna was supposed to be, Alannah flicked her tongue over her lips before continuing in that same bored voice. 'Lots of freaky things kept happening on set, but it was mostly the actors playing pranks and the pranks seeming weird in isolation. You know, ghostly writing on the walls, things floating in mid-air, that kind of thing, but there were a bunch of Occult folk – including witches – working on that set. I bought none of it. When we were in pre-production here and fan forums got wind the pilot was happening, there were a bunch of people saying we should keep an eye out for hauntings because she was working on the show – I mean she's a makeup artist, how important could she be, really, and why did they keep letting her do interviews? It was bullshit then, and this is bullshit now. I didn't get too close, but it looked like dodgy SFX makeup and a shitty wig to me, and if it wasn't a wig...' She looked to the side. 'I'm just saying, Taylor not being around right now is suspicious as fuck, but I'm not allowed to say that.'

'Who said you can't?'

Alannah side-eyed Diana. 'I don't want to be accused of creating "workplace animosity", I roll with the punches. They said she's "sick" now, and she'll turn up tomorrow, but based on how everyone's acting, I don't think we'll ever see her again. I mean, look around.' She swept a hand behind her. 'There's no one here. Apparently some investor poured money into reopening Larkin Studios just to make the pilot, and yet they can only muster a skeleton crew. Doesn't make sense, unless there's something seriously dodgy going on behind the scenes. As far as I'm concerned, there wasn't a real body. And everyone else will know when one doesn't turn up at a mortuary, and there isn't a funeral. If it looks like a duck, and walks like a duck...'

'Then quack quack,' Diana finished.

'Are you done now with your fifty questions, or can you find someone else to bother?'

'Oh don't mind me, I love chatting and learning things,' Diana said, hoping Alannah could hear how badly she wanted to hex her.

Alannah shot her a look and put her headphones back on, signalling the end of the conversation. Diana picked absently at the smears of latex stuck to her wrists and forearms, trying to process this. Alannah was faerie, which meant that she couldn't lie, but she had been so defensive of Taylor earlier in the day; now she seemed convinced she was part of a hoax.

'You mentioned miniatures in your application, didn't you?' Rachel asked, startling Diana. For at least twenty minutes Rachel had been staring at a series of prop drawings tacked to the wall, occupying the only space that various panels from the comics didn't – intended as 'aesthetic setting' guides – and Diana hadn't heard her approach.

'It's more hobby than professional. And I meant miniatures in the diorama-dollhouse sense, rather than miniatures for set,' Diana said. She regularly wished everything had its own word; it would make communicating that bit more efficient.

'That's exactly what I was hoping you'd say.'

'What I want to show you is up here. It's a bit specialist, so if you're not up to it, you won't be fired or anything,' Rachel said with a laugh, leading Diana and Alannah on a short walk back to the road Fred had driven her and Mallory down some hours before. Stage One and Stage Three were in full darkness and for one heart-stopping moment Diana thought they were going to Stage Two, where Taylor's body had been found. Alas, Rachel steered them into the smaller building in front of Stage Two, equally run-down as the prop warehouse, peeling red paint on the roll-up shutters. Just as the cool night air was beginning to settle into Diana's shoulders, she saw Mallory pass on the golf cart from the direction of the MUA backlot, her face scrubbed clean. She waved and Fred slowed. Mallory cast a confused glance over the entire prop department that was now waiting for Rachel to rummage through her bag for a key.

'Here's my ride home, can we bring her?' Diana asked Rachel sweetly.

She eyed Mallory for a second, then nodded. Diana sagged in relief as Mallory fell into step behind her. She seemed stiff and sore, but she looked okay.

Rachel unlocked the door, leading them into a cluttered workshop in even more disarray than the one they'd left. There was a scent of something heavy and synthetic in the air, like fake apples, and Diana's ear, which had not been bothering her since her run-in with Xander, chose that moment to ring loudly.

'So this is a bit special, I'm very excited about it,' Rachel said, sounding like she was underwater. She turned so her body was hiding something behind her. 'Have you heard of the Larkin family?'

Diana cut a glance to Mallory, who nodded. 'Yeah, they owned the studio and the manor, right?'

'And they disappeared some time ago. Historical records suggested there was once a scale model of Oakpass Manor, but it left the same time they did. It was the only thing they took. You should've seen Hollis's face when we showed him,' Rachel said, or at least Diana thought she did, stepping aside.

Diana was looking at a house.

A dollhouse, though it was not just any dollhouse: it was a perfectly scaled, impossibly detailed, miniature replica of Oakpass Manor.

Her jaw dropped taking it in, no longer trying to listen around the screaming in her own head. Drawn closer as though it was magnetic, Diana moved to it, her eyes skating over the tiny ivy that climbed determinedly up the window frames, some browned as though it was in active decay. The walls were covered in tiny, painstakingly applied slivers of what Diana knew, instinctively, was the same dark rock that made up the real Oakpass.

Rachel touched the side and the front wall sprang open, revealing scaled grandeur perfectly preserved from a century ago. Thick, plush velvet hangings in reds and greys and blacks, a marbled entrance hall with five pillars stretching up to an ornate roof, spear-like weapons hung on the walls over the doorway to the rest of the house. A ballroom with polished wood floors, a perfectly rendered kitchen. A library crammed with mini leather-bound books, lavish bedrooms with four-poster beds. She took in the acid-green wallpaper in the hallways above the tiny oak-panelled staircase. Picture frames and paintings hung carefully from string and the tiniest nails, the way they would've been in the real Oakpass. A tiny figure was draped across a fainting couch in a formal study, others in the bedrooms and drawing room, one in the enclosed courtyard beyond – a clever trick where Diana could peer through the entrance hall to the courtyard for a doll's-eye view. She could've spent hours taking in the painstaking detail, her eyes discovering something new and fascinating every second she looked. It was like something Francine Leon might've made.

'Oh my goddess,' Diana breathed. 'What is… where did…'

'Isn't it incredible? Alannah found it,' Rachel said.

Diana turned to her. 'You *found* this?'

Alannah shrugged. 'They wanted some sort of in-house dollhouse to display, so I went rummaging around on resale sites. Apparently this is *the* dollhouse.'

'How?' Mallory asked, giving Diana a second to squeeze her eyes shut and will the ringing to dull. It was annoying at the best of times, but now it was actively hindering her fascination.

'Ugh,' Alannah said. 'Historical collectors have apparently been trying to find it and it's been a mystery, but this old woman in Bath had it this whole time. Her daughter sold it online and they had no idea what it was that they'd sold and everyone clapped,' Alannah said.

'There was a huge fanfare when it happened. I was brought in about a week later, and I've never seen anything like it,' Rachel said.

Diana was speechless, a rare occurrence for her.

'Are you okay?' Rachel asked.

Something dropped on the other side of the workshop, like a metal tool striking a metal bar, and the sound reverberated in Diana's head, growing and ringing louder than before, making her miss the next bit of what Rachel said.

'—models, her name was Francie,' Rachel said. 'And she made these dollhouses that helped solve crime.'

'The love of Diana's life,' Mallory said, smiling.

'Francine,' Diana said, catching on. 'Francine Leon. I love her, she's… she's amazing.'

'Oh! You've heard of her? Normally people haven't heard of her.'

'Diana does not count as people,' Mallory said. 'In this particular instance, anyway.'

Alannah snorted, and Diana wished she would go back to not speaking to her.

'What do you need me to do?' Diana reached out a hand towards the dollhouse.

Rachel said something and Diana shook her head a little to clear it. She pushed Diana's hand gently.

'We're handling it with gloves, these are all the original fixtures and furniture. There are bits missing, we think – based on old photographs of the Manor. We want someone who can make tiny props for the close-up shots.' Her mouth turned down for a split second before the smile returned. 'I was going to ask if you'd be okay with staying back, but seeing as you've got a ride home, and you do this kind of work already, what do you say to moulding some pieces for us for tomorrow? I can give you anything you need. It would be such a big favour, and you're under no obligation to say yes, but...'

'I'm up for it,' Diana said, hoping she'd understood properly.

'You're a lifesaver. Hollis wants a lot of atmospheric shots of the location, but we're to do it as "creatively" as possible. AKA the budget isn't there for the VFX. There is a reason the prop department is the most populated – aesthetics are everything. Some of us *should* be in special effects and costumes, but we're doing our best here. Alannah and I came up with using the miniatures for the rooms they're not shooting in. Took a bit of time we didn't have to convince him, even with Orson putting the pressure on, but here we are.' Rachel rolled her eyes. She described what Diana would need to do, and Diana had never been so grateful to see

Mallory taking notes as she was in that moment, nodding and smiling but only able to hear bits of what was being said.

'Thanks, Rachel,' Diana said at what she thought was a suitable interval. 'I'd love to do this work.'

'Great. I'll sort—'

'Well, well. It's always nice to see the crew taking a moment to stop and smell the roses,' a voice said. For a moment, Diana was sure this was Hollis Hadley, but then he stuck a hand out to her, the other resting on some sort of spear, or a particularly scary poker. Not even Mallory looked surprised to see him with it.

'Orson Webb, showrunner.' He was a troll, she realised, his pale skin tinted blue, like his veins were leaking colour into the rest of him. 'We've met,' he said to Mallory, who did not seem like she knew what to do with that information.

Rachel introduced Diana.

'Ah, our new prop maker. Hollis will be pleased. Don't be alarmed if he comes to talk to you; our creative director takes his job title a little *too* seriously.'

'I'm happy to talk about any aspect of my work to both or either of you at your earliest convenience,' Diana said, flashing Orson a brilliant smile, but he had already lost interest.

'Busy, Rachel?'

'Just a second – Diana, materials are over on that bench, Alannah will help you box them up.'

Diana nodded, her eyes catching on something. The tiny figure draped over the pink fainting couch in the otherwise austere study had its arms pressed to its chest, and the back of Diana's neck tingled.

'Does that remind anyone of anything?' She pointed.

'What?' Alannah asked.

'I should think it would remind you of Oakpass,' Orson said, squinting at her.

'No, it's just…' Diana trailed off, realising she couldn't say it looked like 'Taylor's' murder scene, because she wasn't supposed to have seen it.

'We haven't touched it,' Alannah said. 'To the best of my knowledge, this is exactly as it came.'

Mallory bit her lip and Diana took it as a sign of agreement: the positioning of the figure was odd. Diana took some photos as Alannah grabbed a sturdy box and a hand cart and waited impatiently for Diana to figure out what she needed. While she had a lot of moulding materials at home, the paints were the most important part, for the sake of continuity.

'We'd better be going. See you all tomorrow, thanks for today.' Rachel checked her watch and ushered everyone back out, Orson following at a short distance, their voices lowered and out of earshot.

Diana and Mallory stood outside the warehouse, Stage Two behind them, the number stark black on greying white background. Diana made a show of rummaging in her bag as Mallory carefully shook out her arms and legs. Rachel and Orson walked back in the direction of the workshop.

Alannah had put her headphones back on and was already walking towards the car park; there was no sign of Fred and his cart. Diana darted to the door of Stage Two and had magically opened the door in the time it took Mallory to pull out a lock pick set.

'Hurry as fast as you possibly can,' Diana said sweetly, darting inside. She pulled out her camera, swallowing down her urge to stand and goggle at what she was seeing.

Without a body, the crime scene was just a dried rusty stain all over the floorboards and chaise longue in the middle of the room. The stain could've been made with fake blood, but there was an energy hanging over it that Diana knew was not right. She pulled out her phone and started filming, taking photos as Mallory snapped on a pair of gloves and pulled her kit out of her bag, dropping swabs into evidence bags as fast as she could.

'Do we think that blood's real?' Diana asked quietly. She'd witnessed a lot of death recently, but nothing that felt so violent.

'Can't you smell it?' Mallory rummaged in her kit and produced a tube Diana hadn't seen before. 'Cornelia found presumptive blood tests for me a while back.' She swabbed the blood and dropped the swab into the tube, capped it and squeezed it, timing it with her watch. Diana's gaze darted back to the door as the seconds dragged by.

'Blue,' she said. 'That's blood.' She slipped the test back into her kit. 'There's some grass here, which could've been tracked in by anyone, or could've been brought in by the killer – there's no grass that I could see in the entirety of Larkin Studios, but plenty back up at Oakpass Manor. There are drag marks here, see on the edge of the pooling, but no cast-off or spatter like you'd expect if someone was attacked here. A nightmare to analyse. I'm not ruling out this being a secondary location though, even with the volume of blood present.'

'Killed elsewhere in Larkin Studios, brought here?'

Mallory hummed in agreement, her face thoughtful.

'Take some grass samples, I'm sure there's some sort of test you and Theodore can do.'

'What, like fingerprint it?' Mallory said exasperatedly, before clamping her mouth shut. 'I'm so sorry, that was uncalled for.'

Diana laughed. It was endlessly amusing when Mallory got short with her. 'Do you have what you need? I don't want to get caught in here.'

'I wish we'd brought a beetle,' Mallory said fretfully, pulling her gloves off and following Diana out. Diana made sure to lock the stage behind her and they took a slow walk in the direction of the car park, the cartwheels the only noise on the lot.

'Are you okay?' she asked, as Mallory lowered herself into the passenger seat.

'Fine,' Mallory said shortly, meaning she was not fine at all. 'Nobody seemed to dislike or have an issue with Taylor, and I found out nothing that suggests she was targeted directly. You?'

'Nothing here either.' Diana started the car, waiting for Mallory to settle herself. 'Lots of odd little things going on, though – the main thing that jumped out is that lots of the crew seem to think it was a hoax, that it's a fake body, but it looked real to me in the photos.'

'If we assume it *is* a real body, figuring out who was there at the time of the murder will help, assuming "Taylor" died not long before she was found. We had to sign in to get in, so presumably so did the killer. If there is a killer... although the test I did proves the blood is real, so *someone* was likely murdered here. We'll know more if Sully manages to get the body sent to Wrackton.'

'I also learned the DP hasn't been seen since before the body was found on set – either he's dead too, or…' Diana said, ignoring the squeeze in her stomach at the idea of dead Taylor.

'Or he's a person of interest.' Mallory nodded. 'Fred said he'd likely quit – the exact words he used were "good riddance".'

'Funny, Xander said that Orson had made things immensely difficult for Baker and he'd threatened to quit every day as a result, something about not enough crew.' Diana drummed her fingers on the steering wheel, thoughtful. 'Good start, anyway.'

'I don't…' Mallory broke off, yawning. 'Hexana, sorry. I don't know about you, but I feel like there's a case here, even though nobody else seems to. Something with lots of layers to unravel. I can feel it.'

Her eyes were shining, and Diana tried not to latch onto it. It would not be fair to encourage her for her own selfish reasons, but there was a flutter of hope in her chest. One that said that if she played her cards right, she could have her case and eat it.

'I wonder what Orson wanted to talk to Rachel about,' she said.

Mallory looked at her askance. 'Rachel asked Orson to talk to her, I thought?'

Diana frowned, replaying the memory in her head. She was sure she'd heard Orson ask Rachel to speak; there was an urgency to it.

'She walked up to him and asked if he was busy,' Mallory said, frowning. 'Semantics, I guess.'

'Semantics,' Diana agreed.

'Sandi said something interesting I'll look into – possible link between her and Oakpass.' She yawned again. 'I'll fill you in properly later, I need a nap.' She settled back in the seat, stretching her shoulders, clearly in deep discomfort.

'I hope Cornelia has something for us,' Diana said, waiting at the gate for the demon security guard to open it. He did so while barely looking at them, which made Diana's scalp prickle for some reason, but then her tyres hit the road and she could feel some of the tiredness leaving her body.

Mallory was right. There was something here.

EIGHT

Mallory disappeared off to bed as soon as they got in. Diana knew she should've followed suit, but she was wired, a frenetic energy buzzing through her despite the long day on set.

A phrase she'd got out of the habit of thinking.

She made a coffee and grabbed a snack before heading to set up the research room. A low-level hum continued ringing in the back of her head. She could almost ignore it when she was alone, but there were times when she'd look around to find the electrical socket making the noise, and then remember it was inside her head, inside her ears, which may never ever go back to the way they were before the Whistler case.

Theodore was standing in the middle of the lab when Diana turned the witchlights on with a wave of her hand, looking a little lost. He twitched slightly, like he was trying to decide on something, or like something was pulling him away from where he wanted to be.

'Theodore?' Diana pulled her long dark hair up into a bun on the top of her head. 'Are you okay?'

The twitching stopped and he turned.

'Interrupting me is exactly the sort of thing that would rustle my jodhpurs,' Theodore said, a huge, over-produced smile on his face. 'Or it would, if I rustled, or had any sort of affinity for horses in life.'

'You looked like you were a little stuck.'

'Horses and ghosts do not mix, you know. There should be a mnemonic for that, keep the people aware. Avast, a ghost! Horses leave them alone the most! Or something,' he continued, pulling his cardigan around him as though she hadn't spoken.

Diana smiled a little, mentally noting that she needed to tell Mallory about it later.

Theodore drifted back into the lab and Diana got to work pinning the fresh crime scene photos up and scrawling down all the information she'd gathered so they could have a proper meeting. She had just pulled out her kit and gotten to work on making a scaled diorama of the studios so they could start plotting crew movements, when Cornelia bounded down the basement stairs.

'Theo, could you stand on the iron plate for a second while I pass?'

She gestured at the laptop clutched under her arm.

'Theodore move, Theodore go, Theodore, Theodore, Theodore, no,' he sang miserably, schlepping to the plate. Cornelia blew him a kiss as she darted into the research room, grabbing Diana's arm and steering her onto the sofa.

'So glad you're back, it's been *so boring* without you. No offence, Theodore,' she said. He had already drifted off the plate.

'Hexana forbid any ghost get ballyhooed around here,' he said, flouncing to his bench.

'I got ahold of Sully, finally,' Cornelia said, ignoring him. 'She and Dr Ray have had to go through the UML to apply for jurisdiction on this case, which could take a lot longer than anyone wants it to. They already knew about it, because someone in the Oughteron mortuary called Dr Ray and asked for advice on magical autopsies, and they found out about it, which is...'

'Pretty bad,' Diana said. 'Pretty bad indeed. So it's a real body, then?'

'Hexana forbid anyone be subject to the same circular bureaucratic trials of red tape and nonsense that your friend Theodore is,' Theodore said loudly.

'Also pretty bad,' Diana called back, which seemed to satisfy him.

'Yes, real body. Dr Ray doesn't want anything to do with this either, but after the Whistler hearing, the UML are adamant that magical cases are an Occulture problem and so by default are the responsibility of the nearest local Occult community – but the UML still need to approve any and all interference if it happens in an Apparent jurisdiction, which is why she's willing to help, essentially. This is going to be much more difficult than the Whistler case – the UML are determined to not let anything happen on their watch again. Particularly if we're involved, which so far has escaped their notice.'

'Technically it was the last Night Mayor – may he rest in pieces – who caused the trouble because he refused to let them watch in the first place,' Diana said. 'So thanks, Vincent Van Doren, for that little posthumous gift.'

'They said, among other things, that they need next-of-kin clearance to perform the autopsy,' Cornelia said. 'Which is impossible, because Taylor's not dead, so...'

Diana felt her face brighten as an idea occurred to her.

'So? We've got next-of-kin clearance. We've got the permission of the person whose body it ostensibly is, because they're alive to give it.'

She pulled out her phone and called Taylor.

'Seeing you *and* hearing from you in twenty-four hours? Did you miss me that mu—'

'You're on speaker, I've got Cornelia here,' Diana said, cutting her off. 'We need you to do something.'

'Anything,' Taylor said, and a shiver went up Diana's spine.

She told her where to go and what to do.

'I've sent Sully a text,' Cornelia said afterwards, 'so they'll be expecting her.'

'We got samples from the scene,' Diana said. 'I don't think Mallory will mind us starting without her if it's to confirm something.'

Something, meaning *anything* about this case.

She moved back to the lab and pulled out the sample bag. She was about to ask Theodore to help, but he lifted his chin, huffily pretending he couldn't see them. Cornelia jammed her fingers into her jeans pocket and pulled out a beetle box containing a *Sonata lutumae*, and introduced it to the sample.

Diana hated the beastly things, but had to admit they were useful; in the presence of magic, for reasons she vowed to never ask Cornelia about again as the explanation was both convoluted and boring, *Sonata lutumae*, or sound beetles, changed from orange to luminous green and made an annoying noise.

Except, this time, there was no noise and no colour change, though the beetle did flicker green once before settling back down to its usual burnt orange-yellow.

'What does that mean?' Diana demanded.

'I...' Cornelia bit her lip. 'I don't know. It could be magic, but possibly not? I've only ever seen them react properly, or not at all. Not this in-between thing.'

She tried it again with another, and the result was the same, as was a third and fourth attempt, producing little boxes of beetles from various pockets and the tops of her boots like a clown with never-ending scarves, until she reached down the front of her sports bra and Diana begged her to stop.

'You're just jealous you can't fit dioramas down the front of your top,' Cornelia grumbled.

'Do you want my opinion?' Theodore asked archly from his corner.

'Of course, come here please,' Diana said.

Theodore bent his head until his whiskers were almost touching the beetles.

'I think...' he said slowly.

'Yes?'

'I think,' he said again. 'These beetles are tired. But as that is only one plausible limitation of your study – of which there are many, largely because Mallory is not here – we have to accept that this is not necessarily magic in its most conventional sense.'

He looked pleased with himself. Diana scratched at her forehead, unable to stop herself cracking a smile, despite the problem at hand. It was not the best start to evidence-collecting.

'In that case, we'd better hope Mallory can get something out of the Magic Magical Machine, and hope that what Taylor's about to try doing works in our favour.'

It did, in fact, work in their favour, and within hours. Before nine that evening, Diana and a still-quite-mangled Mallory were at Dr Ray's mortuary, outside Room Two, waiting to see the results of an autopsy. Cornelia had stayed behind to get Mallory's crime scene samples ready to test in the Magic Magical Machine – a machine that was magical by name but not by nature, in that it was a mass spectrometer Mallory and Theodore had cleverly adapted for the Undetectables' magical needs – as per Mallory's precise, neatly hand-written instructions, so Theodore could get started on analysis. They all agreed the motives for killing 'Taylor' weren't clear, the opportunity wasn't clear, and the weapon used to do so wasn't clear, though Diana hoped they'd know more about that after the autopsy.

A prospect she was not looking forward to nearly as much as Mallory was.

'Come in, then,' Dr Ray said, and they walked into a room occupied by Dr Ray, a body, and someone Diana wanted to see even less than the corpse: Izna, who was both Dr Ray's assistant and one of Diana's exes who had tried to be not an ex anymore a few months ago. Diana had originally thought of it as a standard-quality breakup – some tears, but still reasonably amicable, and she hadn't felt bad about it at all – but the second breakup had considerably soured things between them. There were accusations that Diana had 'used her for information' and was 'clearly thinking about someone else the whole time'. Diana, however, was quite sure Izna was with someone else now and wore this belief like armour, even as Izna forcefully opened drawers in an effort to not have to look directly at her.

'Mallory, welcome back. Ah, Diana,' Dr Ray, the sometimes-pathologist and always-Night Mayor of Wrackton said, noticing Izna's body language. 'One of the best things about working with the dead is that they don't talk, which means all manner of conversations are had within these walls.'

Diana translated that to mean her name had been said in here a lot, and not in favourable terms.

'I'll be on my best behaviour, I promise,' Diana said. 'It could be much worse: I could be Cornelia.'

Dr Ray snorted, and Diana chose to take it as a compliment.

Her eyes strayed down to Taylor laid out on the slab, and her heart jolted into her mouth. It wasn't really Taylor, she reminded herself. The smell of formaldehyde burned in her nose, and her head felt like it was being squeezed into a tube.

Perhaps she was panicking, though she wasn't sure.

Mallory reached over and squeezed her hand, either sensing that it was hard for Diana, or simply feeling the weirdness herself.

'Did we find anything out?' She gestured at Taylor. *Not Taylor, not Taylor.* She'd seen too many bodies, folk she cared about, folk she knew, to be able to afford panic now. 'We've been to the scene—'

'Cornelia did lay out the facts of the case as she knows them when we spoke on the phone, but I must insist that there is no case, that you have not been to the scene, and you know nothing other than what's occurring in front of us, because the UML don't know anything about what you've been doing and therefore neither do I. Are we clear?'

Dr Ray's face was set, serious, and Diana nodded. 'Of course.'

'So what I can tell you, from the autopsy and the official information I've gleaned from Oughteron police, is that the fingerprints match Taylor's, and she was ID'd by her colleagues. She died of a stab wound, it seems, but it also appears that there was respiratory failure that I can't ascribe any particular cause to.'

'Interesting. A knife?' Mallory asked.

'Interestingly, no. Whatever the weapon was, sharp force trauma caused extensive damage to the chest. The heart was effectively macerated, for want of a better word. I'm thinking something sharp and barbed, like a lance, maybe some sort of spear. Dreadfully medieval, whatever it was.'

Diana and Mallory exchanged glances and Diana knew what she was thinking: the object Orson had been carrying around.

'There was no weapon officially recovered from the scene, so I can't be certain. The angle of entry suggests she was stabbed by someone shorter than her, but that's a fallible observation and would be dependent on elevation of the area the murder occurred in, shoes the subject was wearing, and so forth. No defensive wounds, so whoever got her, she didn't see them coming. There's some lividity here contrary to the body's discovered positioning.' Dr Ray lifted Taylor's body and rotated it so they could see her back, where a dark bruise spread across her mottled skin. Tears pricked Diana's eyes and she fought them back down. *Not Taylor. Not Taylor.*

'And you know what that means,' Dr Ray continued.

Diana did not know what that meant, and Mallory leaned over to whisper, 'It suggests the body was moved; it's a precursor stage to rigor mortis. Basically, it's confirming the set we saw is a secondary location.'

If Mallory was not already a witch, Diana would consider this interpretation to be a type of witchcraft.

'Yes, we do know what that means,' Diana said instead. 'Do we have an approximate time of death?'

'Lividity sets in around the thirty-minute mark, but can take up to four hours, sometimes longer. Rigor had set as far as her legs, and it took time before I got hold of the body, which suggests it's more along that thirty-minute to two-hour window. As she was found at approximately eight a.m., I'm tentatively – *tentatively* – suggesting TOD to be between six and seven thirty a.m.'

This was a big window – maybe too big to account for, especially if the killer got into the studio grounds undetected. Diana bit her lip.

'What about her hands?' Mallory said suddenly. 'Was she wearing any jewellery, or were there any cuts around her fingers?'

'No,' Dr Ray said shortly. 'Hands were covered in blood, but it was from the chest wound. No injuries to the fingernails.'

Mallory sagged a little. 'I was wondering, after the Whistler… the UML never did find the ring he used to change his appearance.'

Diana swallowed and looked away. The omissions she'd made in the last five-and-a-bit months were numerous, and she wasn't getting into this now.

'No evidence of that that I can determine,' Dr Ray said.

'Can we take a sample?' Mallory said, thankfully changing the subject. 'From the body, directly.'

'As long as I don't see you do it, you may break whatever rules your little hearts desire.' She pulled off her gloves. 'I will be back in precisely ninety seconds. Izna, could you go get a restock of the small gloves?'

As soon as Dr Ray and Izna left, Mallory pulled a beetle out of her bag.

'Cornelia let you take that?'

'She was trying to get me to bring more creatures in, for testing.' Mallory shuddered. 'I asked for one beetle, and here it is.' She let it walk on the body.

The same thing that had happened earlier that night happened again – a shudder, a flicker of green, and then a return to orange-yellow.

Mallory scooped the beetle into its box just as Dr Ray walked back in.

'Now, Mallory, I am aware you and Theodore have access to a GC-mass spec and could potentially run a toxicology analysis, seeing as there isn't the facility for it here. Any longer.'

Another victim of the exploding Mayoral Offices.

'But I am also aware that Theodore cannot operate the machinery himself due to his…'

'Ghostliness,' Diana said.

'Yes. And you are not trained in toxicology, so I will have to send off to an external lab to obtain these results. It is going to take time, thanks to our Mr Whistler, to even get the UML to pursue this as a magical murder, even though they permitted the autopsy and will make this Wrackton's failure if we don't solve it, the circular nature of which is not lost on me. The fact of the autopsy was sheer luck and quick thinking on your part, Diana, don't let me congratulate you again. It may be that we have no way to investigate this. Larkin Studios is in Oughteron, and Oughteron are keen to distance themselves from any further Occult murders.' She clasped her hands, latex squeaking. 'With Alyssa— Sully,' she corrected, as if Diana and Mallory didn't know Sully's first name or that she and Dr Ray lived together, 'now the DI in Wrackton, the Oughteron police have made it impossible to investigate anything regardless of if it's required of us. It's all very boring. But crucially, it's going to take a while before we can get a lab to agree to take on the work. I feel I must make it clear that that is *not* an invitation for Cornelia to grease an axle with money. I cannot be accused of political corruption to that degree. Give me an indication you heard me.'

Mallory and Diana both nodded vigorously.

'Toxicologists are not paid well enough to be worth contending with the UML's new rules, so we'll be lucky if we get anyone on board.' Dr Ray pressed a hand to her forehead. 'I'm ageing rapidly. That is a cue for you to tell me I'm not ageing rapidly and then I will tell you to stop putting so much emphasis on beauty standards, only for you to stutter out an apology, realise you've outstayed your welcome, and leave.' She smiled, and handed Mallory a file. 'This is a copy of the report, which you have because you stole it from me when my back was turned. Have fun.'

She opened the door and Diana and Mallory left, Mallory leading the way out.

'Was that okay for you?'

'It was a rip-roaring laugh a minute. Fun for all the family.'

'*Diana.*'

'I know it's not actually Taylor's body – I don't know what's going on, really. But it was weird,' she said, as truthfully as she could. She could tell Mallory anything, but not this. Not what seeing Taylor had actually felt like in the moment.

Heart-wrenching, gut-punching. A searing tale of loss.

Mallory carefully picked her way down the steps, seemingly accepting Diana's answer. The mortuary was far enough away from the Mayoral Offices that the interior hadn't been damaged in the explosions. Though the stairs had been repaired, the front-facing pillars were wounded, like the world as they knew it was crumbling down around them.

'I don't know what Taylor was to you, or even is to you now,' Mallory said. 'But you can tell me anything. If you don't want me to repeat anything you say to anyone else, I won't. All you have to do is say it, and I'll listen. That's all.'

'She was just a friend,' Diana said, hating herself for outright lying to Mallory. Mallory, who wore all her feelings on her face like a pair of flamboyant trousers. Mallory, who was trying so hard to be a good friend to Diana, trying to make space for her.

'If you say she was a friend, I believe you,' Mallory said, then went quiet.

Diana was wondering if Mallory still hadn't gotten used to the idea that she was not going to be replaced by someone less chronically ill when she saw what had caught Mallory's attention.

Theodore, moving swiftly towards the ruined Mayoral Offices. His face was calm, his cardigan was billowing, and he moved with purpose, static springing up all around him as he got closer to the site.

Mallory frowned. Diana went to lift her hand to wave, but Mallory forced her to lower it.

'Watch him,' she whispered.

So they did. They watched as he stood at the destroyed doorway of the Offices. Watched as Theodore flickered once, twice and pulled away from the entrance. Watched as he turned back the way he came, his features creased. Watched as he flickered again, pivoting on the spot like he was making a decision. He approached the doors of the Mayoral Offices a second time, closed his eyes, and disappeared.

'What the fuck was that?' Diana asked, gripping Mallory's wrist too tightly.

Mallory shook her head. 'I don't know, but he's been doing that ever since he came back.'

NINE

There were a lot of things Mallory had not been able to voice to her friends in the last five months. They had grown closer than ever, but there were nights when Mallory remembered what Diana said to her as they were about to face down the Whistler. Specifically about what she should say out loud, and who she should say it to, though in classic Diana form, she had not expressed it in so many words. These were the nights where tendrils of insomnia had her in their unforgiving grip, her hips and lower back aching, and no sleeping position was comfortable. She'd go from worrying about Theodore, to thinking about what Diana said, and why she'd said it.

There was no timeline when it was appropriate to discuss feelings one might've had for one of their best friends, particularly when said friend had just lost a would-be ex-boyfriend, so Mallory had been waiting. She'd originally thought six months would be appropriate, but now that six months was approaching rapidly, she'd amended it to twelve to be certain. In those sleepless nights where she'd have given anything to lessen the blanket of exhaustion, the lids over her eyes scratching even while they were closed, she had thought through all possible negative outcomes: her friend not processing grief properly, her becoming a rebound, and, perhaps worst of all, risking their friendship forever.

And so Mallory, seeing Diana as she looked at Taylor's body, knowing intimately, horrifically, what grief looked like on her best friend's face, knew what she was feeling, even if Diana did not want to admit it. And Mallory was not keen to throw stones from her precarious position inside a glass house, lest she shatter walls and be forced to tell someone in so many words that she, Mallory Hawthorne, was in love with Cornelia Broadwick. Always had been, in one way or another, always would be, in as many forms as were humanly, magically, eternally possible.

She had been about to gently push Diana on Taylor, push her usually incautious friend into talking about what, exactly, was making her cautious about this particular girl, when she'd spotted Theodore making his approach on the Mayoral Offices.

A part of her hoped that he would behave normally, and that she'd been worried for no reason.

A part of her knew it would go into her notebook.

'I have a confession to make,' Mallory said. 'I think I brought him back wrong.'

A final part of her hoped Diana somehow hadn't noticed, but her friend closed her eyes for the briefest of seconds.

'I only started wondering about him a couple of days ago,' Diana said finally. 'He's… weird at the moment. Mostly he's himself – completely, utterly, insufferably so – and sometimes he's… not.'

Mallory felt guilt seep down into her stomach. A familiar, unwanted friend.

'This is all my fault. It's also why I thought it was important I looked into Katherine – not just because she's a lead on his murder, but because I'm afraid if we *don't* solve his murder soon, we're going to lose our chance before… I don't even know what I'm afraid of. He's just not right.'

It was as desperate a confession as the one she'd planned to make to Cornelia, but saying it aloud didn't make her feel any better.

'I don't think this is your fault. It wouldn't make any sense,' Diana said breezily. 'The spell worked and Theodore came back, or it didn't work and he didn't. But he came back. A little… waterier around the face than before, maybe. And occasionally a bit odder, but why would it start five months in, instead of immediately?'

Mallory could tell Diana was being facetious – she was too observant a witch to have missed the emergence of the Theodore notebook five months ago, even if she hadn't read any of it, and much too clever to have not put two and two together.

'What if my magic wasn't strong enough? The spell required a sacrifice of the heart, but what if it wasn't big enough? I assumed it should be meaningful, but maybe I was meant to cut out my true love's heart, or—' She stopped short, but Diana had the sense to not needle her. 'I don't know. I do know, based on my observations, and the thing he did in front of us… he's not right. He was *fired*: why is he going back in there?'

Diana sighed. 'He did something odd last night, after you went to bed,' she admitted. 'It was like how he was there at the doorway, but he was in the middle of the lab... glitching, almost, staring at nothing. When I spoke to him, he sounded a bit forced, maybe? But by the time Cornelia came down, he was a regular amount of dramatic, as though nothing had happened. He's always been a bit mercurial, though, so maybe we're overthinking it.'

'But don't you see? One minute he's quipping and flouncing around, the next he seems likely to blow at any moment, then inappropriately calm the next. He's been coming here, even though he's not meant to – nobody is – but he's especially not meant to anymore. And he won't tell me *anything*,' Mallory said, frustration flaring through her.

She hadn't meant to have this conversation here, even though she clearly needed to say it to someone, and Diana was clearly going to let her, if only to distract from the secrets they both did not want to share.

Mutually assured indestruction.

'Anything?'

'*Anything.* I've asked him so many times about Katherine – who she is, what he promised to help her with, why she knew him pre-cat ears. Every time, he shuts me down. Either he deflects, tells me to stay out of it, or pretends he doesn't know what I'm talking about.'

'Maybe we need to sit him down and make him talk,' Diana said.

'But what if that's too much for him? There's something ticking under the surface, and it's something I think I'm afraid of.' It felt awful to say that she was afraid of Theodore in any context. Her sweet, kind, eccentric friend whom she'd spent the past almost-six-and-a-half years convincing he was good and worthy.

'What's the worst that could happen, really? It's Theodore.'

'First of all, Diana, *please* don't say things like "what's the worst that could happen", that nearly guarantees the worst possible outcome!' Mallory squeaked, even as Diana grinned at her, clearly trying to break the tension. 'I am very worried about him accidentally, or on purpose, breaking Ghoul Council rules, particularly in light of him being fired. The Broadwicks being out of Wrackton and the Offices being' – Mallory gestured at the ruined building – 'like that, mean he's got very little to protect himself with, particularly as he technically passed on during the Whistler case, so what rights does he really have? He's been in a ghost light before, I can't risk that happening to him again. We don't even know where he went,' Mallory said, biting her lip. 'When he died a second time. I don't know where I called him back from. This could break him.'

'Could do. He could also fold under the pressure.' Diana pointed at her. 'I think the Undetectables are long overdue for a full-scale interrogation of a suspect; we could do with the practice.'

'I need something concrete, though, before that happens. Something that'll make him talk himself around in circles until he tells us what we need to know. Goddess, Diana, if he *knew* I was afraid of him, or that we were thinking any of this...' She rubbed a hand over her forehead, her eyes burning. 'I'm telling you, this is all linked to his murder. His first one.'

'Okay fine, no interrogation until you're ready,' Diana conceded, pulling out her phone. 'Let's not stay standing here, unless you want to get caught. Walk or taxi?'

'Taxi. But we'll get it from around the corner.'

Safely away from where Theodore might see them, Mallory leaned against the grey stone of a building, her hands in her pockets as they waited for a taxi to show up.

'I have an idea,' Diana said suddenly, 'of who you could ask to help you with Katherine.'

'Who?'

'The trolls. They never forget a face. You could start with Observer Johnson. He's surely got some musty old records in the Observatory, and it was usually trolls who kept them – maybe some records will note someone who died in Wrackton under mysterious circumstances, even if she's not named. Or maybe he'll know her family based on a description? I don't think she looked that old, so perhaps he's even met her – though I was running past and had hit her in the face with some salt before I'd got a proper look, so what do I know?'

Mallory's mouth creased into a smile. 'That's actually a really good idea.'

'Actually!' Diana said, mock-offended.

'You know what I mean!'

'Yes, I do. I know you meant "Diana, you're a motherfucking genius and I bow at the altar of your wit".' Diana patted her hand, an expression on her face Mallory couldn't read. 'Are you sure you don't want to go in there and see what Theodore's doing?'

Mallory shook her head. 'I tried before; it's warded until the repairs are complete. Or until they find Jacob's body and close off the Whistler investigation, whichever comes first. I don't know why the wards don't apply to Theodore, but I've been trying to figure it out, because of the wider implications.'

'That whatever is being contained in there isn't actually being contained,' Diana finished.

'Exactly.'

'Cool, that's one for the nightmares,' Diana said, as the taxi pulled up. 'Directorially speaking, you call the shots – but time *is* of the essence in both our active murder cases. You should keep focusing on Theodore where you can.'

'Directorially speaking, that's actually another good idea.'

They walked into the research room to find Cornelia waiting with a pot of tea and a terrifying smile on her face that Mallory hoped meant something good and case-related, and not that a bug had learned a new trick.

'Are you ready for this?' Cornelia bounced on her chair, narrowly avoiding knocking the beginnings of Diana's Larkin Studios diorama off the coffee table with her knees. Diana had also spent a lot of the time Mallory was asleep crafting miniature weapons for the dollhouse as requested, and a photo of the doll on the fainting couch had appeared on their murder board. Diana's work for the pilot episode made Mallory very nervous for reasons she couldn't articulate. She was sure Diana missed working on a set, but part of her worried that, now she'd been back for a day, she'd realise she didn't need the Undetectables anymore.

'Theodore wasn't here when I got back to show him what I'd found, so I've been waiting here grinning to myself, waiting for you.'

'It's good for workers to take breaks,' Diana said.

'Of course it is, how else are we meant to keep going? Anyway, shut up, look at this.'

Cornelia held up a massive piece of paper that had been folded several times. The paper was yellowed, black spidery ink stark against it, even with its considerable age.

'You know what this is, right? Right?' Cornelia asked, her voice muffled behind the page.

'Blueprints and a map,' Mallory said, smiling at Cornelia's enthusiasm.

'*So* useful at this point in our investigation,' Diana said.

Cornelia lowered the paper so Diana could see her scowl. 'It's exciting and you know it. It's got the full floor plans of Oakpass Manor *and* Larkin Studios, and I got this for you, so you could make a diorama.'

'Oh,' Diana said, brightening. '*So* useful at this point in our investigation, good work!'

'This is the last time I do anything nice for you,' Cornelia grumbled. 'I got Felix to drive me to the Oughteron Historical Museum for that. Apparently the castle really has ties to Occulture – someone suggested vampires, but they did not seem certain or to have any further detail, which was useless to me – so it was in their Occult section.'

'Is this the *original* map of the grounds? And how did you get the full blueprint and not a copy?' Mallory asked, knowing the answer could not be good. 'Or do we want to know?'

'Nope!'

Mallory peered at the hand-drawn images, the drawing scale confirming, to her best estimation, that Jenna had been telling the truth that the MUA trailer was situated almost a mile from

Stage Two. Oakpass Manor was about a mile away from the studios, a path leading over the river and disappearing off the edge of the page.

'Okay, so. Here's the case, if Mallory doesn't mind me chairing the meeting,' Diana said, shooting her a glance for confirmation. Mallory felt a jolt of surprise at being asked, though tried her best to hide it.

'The floor is yours,' she said.

'The case is that of the death of Taylor Rose O'Gorman, twenty-two, Irish. Her body was found two days ago at Larkin Studios on the set of a show called *Undead Complex*, on a set situated in—' Diana consulted the pages Cornelia had brought, or bought, Mallory was not sure. 'Goddess, who wrote these? The handwriting is worse than yours, Cornelia. Situated in Stage Two on the east side of Larkin Studios, where production on the pilot of *Undead Complex* is still ongoing.'

'Great, good start,' Mallory encouraged.

'The body was moved and the scene cleared before we had a chance to look at it, but Mallory and I were able to access Stage Two and take photographs, collect samples, and confirm blood at the scene. We also viewed the body at autopsy, where it was confirmed that the victim was killed by stabbing, but there was also signs of respiratory failure, which Mallory assures me is possibly relevant.'

'No more knives, please.' Cornelia covered her face. 'I have had enough with bloody knives.'

'Dr Ray confirmed that the weapon was not a knife, bloody or otherwise, though she believes it was something sharp.'

'The word "macerated" was used,' Mallory added. 'So it's something horrible, but she mentioned something barbed or spear-like, and while we were there—'

'Orson Webb, the showrunner, was walking around with some sort of spear thing in his hands. That could very well be the murder weapon,' Diana finished. Mallory was glad to know they'd been on the same page about that.

'Would he walk around with it in the open like that?' Cornelia mused.

'Unclear at this stage in the proceedings,' Diana said. 'Dr Ray confirmed that fingerprints were a match for real Taylor's, and has sent off for a toxicology report because we aren't licensed to do accurate ones here.'

'I'm still technically unqualified, though in September I'm hoping to start a distance course so we don't run into this kind of barrier again,' Mallory said, trying not to smile at the looks of delight that passed over Cornelia's and Diana's faces. 'And Theodore is Theodore, so we've a conundrum there. As Diana said, we retrieved samples from the scene—'

'And we've run tests on some of those!' Cornelia interrupted, producing beetle boxes.

'Great. So I'll do a preliminary test for fibres and magic traces with the Machine, see if we can get anything that way while waiting for the tox reports. Back to you, Diana,' Mallory said, ducking her head to hide her smile. It didn't help her that she sometimes wanted to take Cornelia by the hands and tell her she was adorable over and over until the word lost all meaning.

'Thank you, news correspondent. Okay, now our findings from visiting the set: I spoke to the first AD-slash-multi-job-person, and the entire prop department – which has three, now four members. I also met that actor, Xander Crane, briefly. He was allegedly first on the scene – but accounts of who else was present are scattered and contradictory.'

Cornelia set the blueprints down and got up to write names on the murder board as Diana called them out. 'What do you mean contradictory?'

'Some of the crew think Xander was the first to come running,' Diana said, 'but Alannah thinks she was the first one there. Fred says he was in the bathroom and came running when he heard a scream. So nobody seems certain who came running, and in what order. When I talked to Xander, he implied people kept asking him how he was – suggesting he saw something others didn't.'

'Very strange,' Mallory said, though it reminded her of earlier, when Diana had insisted Orson had asked to speak to Rachel. She was sure it was the other way around, though the memory was fuzzy. It was possible she was wrong.

'But very us,' Cornelia said. 'We can deal with strange.'

'I can focus on trying to untangle who actually went where and we can run scenarios when your diorama is finished,' Mallory said, anxious to make it clear she wasn't wholly focusing on Theodore; she'd promised to work on it solo only until a bigger case came along.

'Good plan! Possible witnesses, then, are Xander Crane, Rachel Lyons – she's the propmaster. Fred Hill, the first AD-slash-whatever, Alannah Roache – she's faerie and says she has nothing to do with it, so definitely a witness – and they said Sandi Clementine was there—'

'—I *love* Sandi Clementine,' Cornelia said.

'Cool, she could be a murderer, but still cool,' Diana said.

Mallory, sensing an impending hex war, stepped in. 'On Sandi – Jenna White, the head MUA, which translates to being the entire makeup and costumes department, said she wasn't there until after the alarm was raised and that Sandi was with her. Sandi said that she was second on the scene and that Jenna was with her.'

'And Rachel told me that Sandi, Alannah and Fred were there, but didn't mention Jenna,' Diana said.

'Okay, either Sandi wasn't there and neither was Jenna, Sandi *was* there and Jenna got there later and everyone's somehow confused... or someone's lying,' Mallory said. 'Sandi also said that her great-grandmother lived in Oakpass, which is a possible connection.'

Cornelia scrawled these onto the board, circling *SANDI* and writing *POTENTIALLY DANGEROUS*, which made Mallory laugh.

'While I was with Xander, Fred came by and said that the DP, Donny Baker, hadn't been seen for thirty-six hours, which is before fake-Taylor turned up dead. Mallory and I established that while Xander said that Baker had been threatening to quit for ages because Orson's management of the filming side of things wasn't great, Fred told her—'

'That they were glad to see the back of him, essentially,' Mallory said. 'We should definitely try speak to him, as the timing is a little coincidental.'

'I'll get right on that,' Cornelia said, jotting his name down. 'I'll see if there's a missing person report filed. Did nobody seem suspicious of the timing?'

'No, they're all under immense pressure. Hence why I've been given the job of dressing the dollhouse in my own time,' Diana said. 'This is my immense pressure.'

Mallory looked thoughtful. 'It's still strange that nobody had suggested a link between Taylor's body and Baker's sudden departure. Did Alannah have anything interesting to say? Since she's faerie, her account makes the most sense to start with.'

'She not only isn't involved, she thinks it was a prank and that Taylor was in on it. She said something similar happened on the last set Jenna White worked on – not murder, but orchestrated events – and that it's all a PR stunt because production is such a shitshow.'

Cornelia was already typing it into her laptop.

'Yup, haunting rumours on a horror set that was having funding problems,' Cornelia said. 'Happened a couple of years ago and it was a confirmed hoax. Did Alannah see the scene?'

'She said she heard Fred shouting and ran, though he says he heard her scream and followed her voice. She said it looked like a shitty wig, and like the wound was special effects work, and that it was meant to unsettle everyone.'

'That doesn't make sense,' Mallory said firmly. 'Faeries might not be able to lie, but surely a high-stress situation could make her *believe* she'd seen something fake? She wouldn't be lying if she was convinced by what she thought she'd seen. But we've seen a real body, there was real blood, there was a real autopsy.'

'If it's easier to believe there's a conspiracy to generate news about a soon-to-be popular TV show instead of the idea that someone killed your colleague, I know which one I'd prefer,' Diana said.

'If only murder wasn't your job,' Cornelia said.

'I agree with Mallory,' Diana continued, ignoring her. 'I don't think Dr Ray could be fooled by a wig and a jar of scab blood.'

Nor, to that point, could Mallory.

'And say it was a hoax,' Diana continued. 'There's nothing to say it's not a hoax gone wrong. I have reason to believe Alannah and Taylor were in a relationship at some point, so there are some questions to be asked – is anyone else interested in Alannah? Could someone be trying to scare Taylor away?'

'Could Baker have a romantic interest in either of them?'

'It would be very, very boring if that was the motive, but it wouldn't explain how he'd managed to change the face of whoever he'd murdered to convince everyone Taylor's dead. Worth looking into while you're tracking him down,' Diana said.

'Good to consider everyone, trust no one,' Cornelia said.

Mallory felt that right to her core. They had made so many mistakes already in the concise history of the Undetectables; she did not want to make a mistake again.

'And that means we're considering Taylor herself,' Mallory said quietly. Diana's face crumpled a smidgeon.

'Yeah. That seems fair. That—' she stopped, like she'd been about to say something else, but Cornelia filled the silence.

'It's hard when it's someone you care about. I was very displeased when you were investigating Beckett, even when the rational part of me knew it was necessary. The irrational part was annoyed you'd question my judgement, because he was my boyfriend and I wanted you to like him.'

That was, to say the least, an understatement.

'Beckett was easier to suspect than Taylor,' Diana said. 'But we've all learned from that incident.'

'It was easier when he turned up dead, I guess,' Cornelia said, the casualness of the statement not matching the expression on her face.

'This is different though, because Taylor's turned up alive *and* dead—'

Diana was interrupted by a gentle knock on the door that was still enough to startle them. They exchanged glances that confirmed none of them were expecting a visitor at this hour.

Mallory was closest, and she stood carefully to open the door, a very forced smile plastered onto her face. She did not have the energy to deal with whoever was on the other side, especially not if it was a surprise client.

But it was not a client, nor anyone she could've expected. Her heart dropped at the sight of the familiar face that greeted her.

His hands stuffed in his pockets, leather jacket over a t-shirt advertising a band Mallory had never heard of, black hair falling artfully onto his forehead, piercing gaze levelled at her.

'Hi,' Beckett said. 'Hope I'm not interrupting.'

TEN

Diana was on her feet instantly, her hands reaching for Cornelia, who had lurched forward, as if holding onto her friend could take back the last few seconds.

Mallory had staggered back from the door in shock, which Diana could barely process – Mallory, who had befriended Theodore first, who stepped into everything she was afraid of with curiosity, was backing away from the door like she had seen a ghost and was afraid.

'Sorry, is this a bad time?' Beckett said again.

Beckett. The tall, pretty – if you liked that sort of thing, which Diana didn't – vampire boy Cornelia had briefly dated and Diana had briefly hated. The boy who had died five months ago, who had been burned up in a ceremony the night he passed and then interred in the Vampire Cemetery, was somehow standing in front of them.

Diana felt a chill pass over her.

'Kingston,' Cornelia said, and he wrapped his arms around her, burying his face in her shoulder.

Loud sobs wracked his body.

Diana and Mallory exchanged glances. This made no sense, and Diana hated it. Mallory skirted around the sobbing mesh of bodies in the middle of their research room and sat next to Diana, her arms folded around herself, her eyes haunted. Diana was feeling a combination of rage and revulsion and, for a moment, fury on Mallory's behalf, irrational and gleaming, a sense of wanting justice for her friend while knowing that, whatever this was, it was Cornelia's prerogative.

All of these thoughts happened in the space of seconds, before Beckett – not Beckett, someone she was calling *Kingston* – pulled away.

'Man, I'm sorry for dropping in like this, it wasn't cool of me,' he said, wiping his eyes.

Diana stared at him, trying to take in the ways he wasn't Beckett. A snake tattoo that started from his hand and wound up into the sleeve of his leather jacket, tattoos on his knuckles she couldn't read. Black nail polish. His face the same, but as he spoke, Diana saw a flash of what looked like a metallic tooth. His mannerisms were not dissimilar to Beckett's, but his voice was softer, lacking a tense demand for attention.

She was reasonably certain he was a different person, and this made her angrier still.

'Sorry, I bet this is a little confusing. A little pre-warning might've helped, but too late now. Mallory, Diana, this is Kingston,' Cornelia said, wiping her eyes. She'd been crying too. 'He's Beckett's cousin.'

'The illustrious, studious cousin who told him he should drink your blood that time?' Diana demanded.

'What?' Kingston's face furrowed. 'No. No, I didn't tell him that. He did *what*?'

'Why are you here?' Diana asked. 'I know that's pretty rude to ask, but you…' She searched for an ending to the sentence, not entirely sure what her issue was. 'You frightened Mallory, and made me confused about our case-solving skills.'

'I… I didn't know Beckett was gone until about a week ago. We were camping on Mount Hallow since before last Samhain and I planned to stay for another week or so, but…' He brushed a hand over his head. Same ridiculous hair Beckett had, just longer and a little more unruly.

'That was five months ago,' Diana said, but Kingston didn't seem to hear her.

'Sit down, I'll make you some tea,' Cornelia said.

Diana flicked a hand out so the kettle would be nearly boiled by the time Cornelia got up the stairs.

It was just Diana, Mallory, and a guy who looked like a dead guy.

A guy who looked like a dead guy Diana hated.

'I'm really sorry, this must be so weird for all of you. I found out he was gone, and I didn't realise how much time had passed.' His eyes were wider than a startled cat's and he looked between them with an expression Diana couldn't read. Muted fear, perhaps.

'You spent five months camping?' Mallory asked. 'And didn't die? What did you do for food?'

'That's… yeah. I was fine, don't worry.'

Diana did not think either she or Mallory could be classified as having ever been worried.

He scratched his face, and Diana could finally read what was written on his right hand – the letters *KING*. She could only assume the other hand said *STON*.

There were many reasons she didn't have anything to do with men, most of them gay, but she particularly wished she didn't have to have anything to do with the sad strays Cornelia kept bringing home.

Cornelia came back with a peace offering of a fresh tray of tea and some cakes she'd gotten from goddess knew where. Diana begrudgingly helped her pass out cups, her eyes never leaving Kingston.

'Introduce yourself properly,' she suggested.

'Okay. Hi, I'm Kingston, I'm Beckett's cousin,' he said. 'I found out he died a week ago, as I said, and I missed it all. I missed him dying, I missed the funeral, I missed the grieving period. I apparently missed him fucking drinking fucking blood, the fucking fuckhead.'

Diana could feel herself warming to him, against her better judgement.

'And… did you…' Mallory seemed to be searching for a diplomatic way to ask her question, as was her habit.

'Why do you look identical to him?' Diana cut in.

'What?'

'Your face, your clothes, your body, your *hair.*'

'Diana,' Mallory said reproachfully.

'These are all valid questions,' Kingston said, raising his hands. His palms had been tattooed with what looked like ruler markings. He closed his fists and Diana could see his knuckles on his left hand did not, in fact, read *STON*, and the vague embers of warmth she felt towards him died a timely death.

KING SHIT.

Shit King, more like. Diana fought the urge to snort.

'Sorry, Cornelia, I'm really sorry for barging in here, I should know better than to have done that, it was just when I texted you and... I didn't meant to upset you, or to— whoa,' Kingston said, his eyes lighting on the murder board behind them. He squinted for a moment longer than Diana thought was necessary. 'Is that a dead body?'

'Hexana,' Diana said, pressing her face into her hands. They didn't have time for this.

'This is what we do. We're the Undetectables, private investigators.'

'Helping you detect the undetectable,' Mallory said quietly.

'And we solve murders, among other things,' Cornelia continued. 'Our most notable to date being the case of the Whistler.'

'So you solved Beckett's death,' Kingston said.

'Yep.' Diana did not think Shit King deserved to hear all of this. There was a dull sense of alarm tingling in her stomach, a gut feeling she didn't want to ignore. She knew what Mallory would say – two didn't make a pattern – but two people had shown up looking like two other dead people, and that felt weird enough to Diana that she did not want to be having a conversation with this particular vampire.

'And he was... he was murdered, then,' Kingston said. 'Officially. Nobody at home wanted to fill me in properly, which I suppose is understandable.'

'Yep,' Diana said again, forcing Mallory and Cornelia to remain silent. Cornelia looked like she wanted to lop Diana's head off and press it onto a stake on the external stairs, and Diana did not care one bit.

'And you just… do that, here. You get evidence together and you solve stuff.'

'Yep.'

'And you don't answer questions with any other words.'

'None of those were questions,' Diana said pointedly. 'Look, I'm sorry, if you wanted to chat with Cornelia, do you think you could wait a few minutes in the kitchen or something? We're trying to finish something here.'

'Yeah, go wait in the kitchen. Take the cakes with you, I can make you some proper food in a bit. Guess what we've got?' Cornelia nudged him playfully.

He looked at her blankly. Somehow, he seemed even more gormless than Beckett had been. Not a single gorm to be found.

'Eggs,' Cornelia said, a glint in her eye. 'Lots and lots of eggs.'

'No, thank you,' he said weakly.

'Sure you don't want an omelette? Fried? Poached?'

'I can make myself some toast, or something, if you show me the way.'

Cornelia led him to the stairs.

'What the fuck, Cornelia?' Diana hissed as soon as she came back. She had seen Mallory try to compose herself again. They did not have time for any of this, whatever *this* was.

'He's grieving,' Cornelia said. 'He's not thinking properly, it's okay.'

'Were you not going to mention it?'

'Mention what?'

Diana gestured towards the stairs. 'Shit King himself!'

'Should I have?' Her brow furrowed, looking to Mallory, who made a noncommittal head movement. 'I didn't think it was significant, except when he arrived here. Also, don't call him Shit King.'

'Did you know what he looked like?' Diana demanded. 'Also, he has it literally branded on his own hands. If he didn't want to be called that he should've been cleverer about what he was permanently adorning his body with.'

'Yeah, I'd seen photos of him and Beckett ages ago, back in uni,' Cornelia said, completely ignoring Diana's excellent point, which Diana took to mean she'd won. 'He had some photos of the two of them on his wall. I don't see why this matters?'

'Cornelia,' Mallory said finally, having finished cooking up whatever diplomacy she wanted to serve. 'It's a strange coincidence that Kingston, with his face just like Beckett's, appears two days after we get wind of a murder where the victim looked identical to someone who's alive. Don't you think?'

Diana could see the words *I don't follow* live and die on Cornelia's lips. She did follow. She absolutely did follow, and Diana would hex the truth out of her if need be.

'When you put it like that,' Cornelia said. 'Okay look. I texted Kingston back in the Whistler case like you asked, to get Beckett's alibi. The message didn't go through, and I thought nothing of it, especially when the investigation moved on. I completely forgot about it – until it delivered, and he texted me. I forgot to reply, but he texted again a few days later, having just heard the news from the rest of his family.'

'When was this?'

'It was… it was two days ago,' Cornelia said, scratching her forehead. 'Yeah, actually, Mal. It is suspicious timing, when you think about it.'

Mallory nodded. Diana did not react, focusing on keeping her features smooth and reasonably non-judgemental.

It was taking all of her patience and most of her energy.

'Do we think that's a valid line of inquiry?' Mallory asked.

Cornelia considered in her usual way, bouncing from foot to foot with her eyes closed.

'I think I believe him, and, Diana, you're going to wait to hear why, but – he's not trying to look exactly like Beckett. That's his face, and he had it first. This case, now, with Taylor, the killer is trying to make us think Taylor is dead, for some reason. This is different. I think he really was camping for months on end. From what Beck told me about him, he sort of does his own thing. It's weird, and I know it's weird, but I think for now, we should consider it unrelated weird.'

Diana looked to Mallory, who had not moved at all while Cornelia was talking. She nodded tiredly. 'Unrelated weird unless otherwise indicated.'

'Okay. Moving on from our poorly timed interruption, then,' Diana said, hoping this would pivot her and Cornelia away from a fight. 'Mallory, can you fire up the Magic Magical Machine, please? We need to see if our autopsy samples have anything worth thinking about.'

The Magic Magical Machine worked in mysterious ways, and Diana preferred to keep it that way no matter how much Theodore and Mallory tried to get her interested in it. As far as Diana was concerned, a sample went in, then a terrifying feat of science – and potentially lasers – turned magic samples into a chart with wavy lines, and colour-specific smoke that Mallory could collect and look at in a vial. And this was either good or bad, depending on what they were looking for.

'Here we go,' Mallory said after the first set of tests, then frowned. 'Oh.'

'What is it?'

She held up an empty vial. 'The chromatographic— the smoke sample,' she corrected herself, clearly remembering she was talking to Diana. Having to repeatedly explain what was in the vial would do that to a witch. 'It dissipated.'

'Is no smoke sample even an option?'

'An Apparent magic sample would be white smoke and they're not magical – so no, colourless isn't really an option.'

She tried again, the results the same. She took the spectrum charts into the research room and laid them out so everyone could see, comparing them to the results from the crime scene samples.

'I don't know what I'm looking at,' Mallory said finally. 'Part of what worked for us before was that I had a hypothesis first, and the hypothesis happened to fit. Which is the basis of the scientific method, of course. I don't know what this is.'

'Shall we try the Sprinter, too?' Cornelia suggested. This was, to Diana's understanding, a database Mallory and Theodore had built of all the spells they could reasonably know – and then some – that they could use to later try find a match to any magic they came across in their cases. It worked similarly to a fingerprint database, but even Diana knew there was no point in trying. They hadn't seen whatever this magic was before.

Mallory stood, her lips pursed. 'I don't think there's any point, but I'm very keen to learn from our mistakes last time. No stone unturned.'

She was back within a few minutes, shaking her head. 'Not a spell, no match found at all. I don't... I don't think this is magical.'

'What does that mean?' Cornelia asked.

'That this is a regular murder,' Diana said. 'A regular murder that might have an Occult explanation, but possibly doesn't. Maybe Alannah was onto something, that it was some kind of stunt.'

'A real person was killed, though!' Mallory said. 'The body Dr Ray has is real. And there's a person missing from set, who is either also dead or is a very clear suspect. So it's been taken really far for a stunt.'

'One of Taylor's questions was to find out if someone was targeting her, right?' Cornelia asked. 'And the second was to find out why someone would leave a body that looked like her. What if it's the latter, but it's actually nothing to do with her?'

Diana held her arms out. 'I am open to all possible explanations at this stage. I want to look into Baker, Xander, Sandi, Jenna, Fred, Rachel. Everyone we can get our hands on.'

'Oh wait!' Mallory said suddenly. 'I pulled a Diana and stole something.'

'I am not loving that "pull a Diana" means stealing,' Diana said, but inside she was beaming. It meant everything to her when her friends were able to recognise her talents. Mostly because it meant she didn't have to do it out loud herself.

'I got this,' Mallory said, ignoring her. 'It's Sandi Clementine's call sheet, but it has the full cast and crew who were meant to be there on it, and it's from the day of the murder.'

Diana stood up and kissed Mallory's forehead. 'You are a star.'

She looked at it, recognising some of the names as folk they already had on their board.

'Baker was meant to be there,' Diana said, pointing. 'And it only says SECURITY, so we'll need to figure out if that's the same guard who was there when we were on set. I can use this to work the diorama properly, see where people should've been situated at the time of Taylor's murder. Maybe we can get camera footage somehow? I didn't notice many cameras around, now I think about it.'

Cornelia jotted that down as an action to take. 'Did you get anything on time of death?'

'Dr Ray has tentatively, and she put emphasis on tentatively, suggested a two-hour window. She's allowing for delays and improper handling of the body,' Mallory said. She explained in slightly more detail, pulling out 'algor mortis' along with 'rigor mortis', and Diana was glad not to have to know any of these things. She did dioramas and connections, and she did them both exceptionally well.

'So is that everything? A possible time frame, no magic source, inconclusive accounts from eyewitnesses. A body that's not the body of the person it's supposed to be,' Cornelia said, ticking the items off on her fingers. 'Diana was right, this is a whatsit. A doozy.'

'Short for whoopsadoozy, I hear,' Diana said. 'What now?'

'Now, I think Cornelia should look into Baker and try to make contact,' Mallory said. 'That's the first port of call. We also need to crack the timeline somehow. I'd like us to see what we can dig up on funding, in case this is about investors and the show itself.'

'You said Orson was the showrunner?' Cornelia asked, unusually thoughtful.

'Yeah. He's...' Mallory searched for the word.

'Oily,' Diana said.

'It would make sense to look into Orson and Hollis, then, in case it is financially motivated.'

'We should try to figure out a way to get close to Orson to find out more about him. All of them, really; Hollis especially is going to be difficult to get ahold of. He wasn't around when we were on set,' Diana mused. She hoped it wasn't deeply transparent that she was situating herself to keep returning to set; or that if it was, that it seemed to be entirely case-motivated.

'That's something Sandi said – that he's a strange man who's difficult to pin down,' Mallory said, looking at Cornelia's nonsensical note about Sandi on the whiteboard and smiling to herself. 'Jenna White was talking about Hollis and said he's, quote, a "convincing man". Oh wait! She told me who owns Oakpass these days! It was bought and sold privately over the years as we thought, but recently – as in, very recently – it was bought by someone we know very well.'

'Who? Who? Don't make me wait, just tell me,' Cornelia said. 'Especially as I looked extensively while you were off gallivanting and didn't find this information.'

Mallory smiled then, very brightly, and Diana wished she could bottle her friend's confidence to give back to her later.

'She said it was going to be turned into a hotel.' Mallory flipped through a stack of letters until her hand rested on the invitation Diana had tossed there. 'Equinox party hosted by Grey Quinn... at *Oakpass Manor*,' she said, holding it up.

Diana couldn't even be annoyed at herself for missing it, because Mallory was so pleased with herself for figuring it out.

'I realise that doesn't answer who owns Larkin Studios currently, but...' Mallory took out her phone and searched for something, scrolling until she found what she was looking for. 'On both Oakpass Manor's website and the old website for Larkin Studios, copyright attributions for this year are to the Quinn Indigo Group.'

'Beautiful. Ten out of ten stars.' Cornelia blew her a kiss. Mallory turned a very interesting shade of pink.

'Um. Anyway,' Mallory said, ducking her head. 'Jenna said they needed special permissions to film at Oakpass Manor, but that Hollis was an old friend of Quinn's. Even if the nature of their relationship is speculation, if Quinn's involved it would mean he's at least met Hollis before, and maybe Orson, and maybe he could tell us something we don't already know. Plus I think it would be good to know more about Oakpass Manor itself, seeing as we've no idea what's going on and we need to examine every single avenue we find. We should talk to Quinn.'

'Oakpass Manor itself is an interesting angle,' Diana said. 'There's mystery surrounding it already, what with the Larkins disappearing. Why not make things more mysterious? There has to be something tying all this together.' Diana looked at her photos of the dollhouse again. She stared at the doll on the fainting couch, willing her brain to make the connection. 'Xander said that everyone on set has some story about Oakpass, that there's all sorts of mystery surrounding it. But how does that result in a murder?'

'And why would a murderer pretend to kill someone who's provably alive? And, crucially, what does it mean that it wasn't actually Taylor? Like, who is that body, if it's not her?' Cornelia rubbed a hand through her hair.

'And fourthly, why does it look magical but all evidence points to it not being?' Diana said, not expecting an answer. There wasn't one yet.

'I don't know, but Quinn feels like a good starting point,' Mallory said. 'It's going to be the wolf who cried demon someday – Quinn will do something awful and we'll have spent so much time fluttering around him trying to establish his involvement in a murder, we'll never make it stick.'

'Maybe that's a risk we need to take,' Cornelia said. 'We need to know. If he does have a personal relationship with Hollis Hadley, maybe we can pin down the difficult man that way. Make it happen, Diana. The Undetectables versus Quinn: the rematch.'

'I'm on it,' Diana said. 'Would you like to accompany me?'

'I need to go talk to Observer Johnson,' Mallory said. Cornelia looked at her quizzically. 'Theo. I'll fill you in later, but this is a matter of urgency.'

Cornelia nodded, biting her lip.

'So you two go to Quinn tomorrow, and I'll take Johnson?' Mallory finished. 'Then we can report back on findings.'

'I'll get on to Sully about Donny Baker.' Cornelia rubbed her arms self-consciously, looking up the stairs. 'But before we do anything, I need to go talk to…' She jerked her head upward.

'Whatever,' Diana said, not bothering to hide her annoyance.

Cornelia had never been like this when they were teenagers – Diana might've done the lion's share of the dating and drama growing up, but she had half-expected her friends would've learned from how annoying she was and not repeat her mistakes. 'Why not interrupt our murder investigation by introducing another vampire boy to us at the exact same point in the process as the last big murder case we had. What could possibly go wrong?'

'Thanks for being so understanding,' Cornelia said, reaching over to flick Diana's arm. Diana whispered a hex and Cornelia jumped, clutching her side. 'That is NOT fair,' she said, and stomped up the stairs.

'I'll have to bring the dollhouse pieces in,' Diana said to Mallory, checking the time. 'And work tomorrow's shift, if we want to keep eyes on our suspects.'

'Of course,' Mallory said. 'It's a pity you didn't have time to replicate the house, but you got some really good photos.'

She smiled, and Diana felt the tiniest pang of guilt, but she pushed it down. They'd solve the case soon, and it would make no sense to quit if they had nothing else on their plates. Mallory would understand.

Diana pulled out her phone, taking a deep breath. She had two main skills; it was time to use one of them to its fullest extent.

ELEVEN

Five days to the Spring Equinox ball

Armed with pages of notes, a heart full of questions, and a tiny sliver of hope, Mallory caught a taxi to the Observatory and stood in the fading watery sunlight, trying to work up the courage to go in.

She had not particularly wanted to talk to Observer Johnson, either alone or at all, but she needed answers about Katherine, and this was the best chance of getting them.

'Not you again,' Observer Johnson said, pushing open the glass door. His face was furrowed deeper than the last time she'd seen him, the blue-grey of his skin less troll-like and more reflective of poor sleep. Mallory could relate.

'Hi,' Mallory said quickly. 'I actually have come for your expertise.'

'I'm pretty sure that was the line you used last time. What delights do you have in store for me today?' He led her inside, and Mallory could not help but notice he was being slightly nicer this time.

'Take a seat. Tea?' he offered, sitting down as though he had no intention of bringing her any.

'Please,' Mallory said, settling beneath a statue of Morrigan and Hecate holding hands. The mothers of the Ternion rarely got a look-in in Occulture, as the Ternion were the upholders of Occulture post-Vampire Wars, but there was still something comforting about the old goddesses.

He sighed audibly, but rose to make her a cup, bringing her sugar packets and a spoon, before sitting down very deliberately.

'What brings you in today?'

'I suppose I feel a bit guilty,' Mallory said, then frowned. She hadn't meant to say that. Thoughts of Larkin Studios, Oakpass Manor and 'Taylor' mingled with questions about Katherine and Theodore and his murder, repeating over and over until she felt like there was no room for anything in her head.

'I see. Guilt can be quite consuming. Do you know the source of this guilt?'

'I think I've hurt someone. Not intentionally. I helped them as best I could, but I'm not sure I did the right thing in the first place. They haven't really been the same since. It's someone I care about so deeply, and I thought I was doing the right thing, but it's possible I was being really selfish in insisting on doing it in the first place.'

Observer Johnson nodded. He seemed much more at ease without Cornelia around. Mallory took a shallow breath through her nose and smelled cinnamon. She felt safe and cocooned, the teacup in her hands pleasantly warm.

'So it is guilt over the outcome not being what you expected? Or guilt that your helping was not an act of complete altruism?'

'Both, I think.'

He sat back. 'Guilt, or shame?'

Mallory looked at him blankly.

'Well?'

She hesitated. 'Both, I guess? Seeing as they're the same thing.'

'Could be. Could be both. Of course, it *could* be both, but only if you understand shame as it really is, as it really functions – which is an internalised sense of what the world wants from you. Perhaps your actions have harmed this person – but have they said so? Have you asked? Did you help because you had no other option?'

Mallory shifted in her seat, uncomfortable. His words were landing with a particular sort of clarity she usually only let Theodore have.

'I guess they haven't really said anything, even when I've asked. And I guess I'm worried because I still need to help them – with something I promised to help with a while ago,' Mallory said carefully.

'Then I think you need to trust your gut. Something led you to try to help, and your intentions were good. If your friend was bothered by this, they would say something. And I think you need to give yourself a break.'

She blinked at him.

'You're thinking now, how do I know this applies to you?' He pointed up at the ceiling, painted in little black stars. Mallory let her gaze follow. 'The Ternion bring me knowledge sometimes, and I dispense it as best as I can. Perhaps you'd like a biscuit?' He stood and left the room, leaving Mallory a moment to gather her thoughts. She decided the best thing to do would be to examine those thoughts later in the safety of her room, like a pelican storing food in its gullet.

'Now,' he said, returning with a plate of biscuits. He had made himself tea too this time, and seemed at ease. 'What really brings you here?'

Mallory laid out her questions about Katherine. She did not tell him she had met her, or that she was a Samhain ghost, or anything other than the barest of facts she had, but she did say what she wanted – namely, to know who she was.

'I see,' Observer Johnson said after she described what she'd been trying to find in the records. She had to wonder if he did; if he knew, somehow, what she was really asking. 'And did you happen to get a physical description of this young woman? How she might've looked at any point in her life?'

'Close to… close to her death, she had short-cropped hair. She would've worn a long dress coat. And she had a sister, who was either missing or still alive at the time, and Katherine was looking for her.'

A strange expression flickered across Observer Johnson's face. 'Do you happen to know if she has been buried anywhere?'

'That's what's not clear. Her grave wasn't found.'

'Mallory,' he said. 'I'm going to ask you to be honest with me, because I can't help you if you aren't. Whatever you tell me in this room will stay here. Have you met Katherine?'

Mallory nodded.

'Have you met her recently?'

Mallory nodded again.

'And she was…'

'Dead.'

'Samhain ghost?'

'Appears to be.'

'Hmm.' Observer Johnson scratched his beard. 'And where? No, wait, don't tell me. The Mayoral Offices.'

Mallory nodded a third time, feeling like her head was too heavy for her neck. 'Deep. Deep inside the Offices.' She relayed the encounter as honestly as she could, leaving out Theodore's involvement. If she got in trouble for not reporting a Samhain ghost, so be it, but she refused to get Theodore in trouble too. At least until she understood what was going on with him.

'Hexana,' Observer Johnson swore. 'Okay. Here's what we're going to do. I'll go through the anointment records here and see what I can find.'

'But—'

'I didn't say that was all, did I?' he said impatiently. Mallory had evidently worn out his goodwill for the day. 'I'll call you if I find anything out. Give me a little bit of time. Failing that, you'll just have to go back to the Offices to ask her directly for more information.'

Mallory brightened.

'There's no guarantee I'll find her, but if she's Occult it's the most likely place. Did you get a spelling on Katherine?'

'She didn't exactly tell me what it was, but I knew – instinctively, I guess? – that it was with a K.' And not because Theodore had specifically, albeit accidentally, told her.

'Interesting. And she gave no indication she was Occult, you didn't see anything?'

Mallory shook her head. 'She's a ghost, so it's hard to know if she was a troll. Could've been a witch, or a demon – possible she was a demon, she was trying very hard to persuade me.'

'Good, good, that narrows it down slightly.'

'Could've been a vampire, as well,' Mallory said after a minute. 'It was really hard to tell.'

'There's nothing to say she wasn't Apparent, was there?'

'No, but I didn't get the sense she was.'

Mallory tried to replay her memory of their interaction, but everything had moved so fast.

'Did she mention speaking to anyone else?'

'No,' Mallory said, hoping he didn't notice how quickly she said it. 'It was just me.'

'Well. I can do my best, sort through the records as we have them and see if I can narrow anything down for you. How old would you say she was?'

'I initially mistook her for my friend Cornelia, so she could be young? But it really depends on when she was alive. And genetics. And my ability to notice those sorts of details. Also, it was dark. And I was a bit stressed.'

Observer Johnson gave her a tight-lipped smile and surreptitiously glanced at his watch.

'Is there anything else?'

Mallory thought for a second, a question forming. She wasn't entirely sure how this was going to help them, but she wanted to know nonetheless.

'Has there ever been an instance you can recall of seeing someone whose face you remember, but it turned out to not be them?'

'What do you mean?'

'Say you met someone, and they looked like the person they said they were, and acted like them, but were not them. Would you know?'

'A sort of doppelgänger situation, is it?'

'Hypothetically, yes.'

He shot her a sharp glance. 'The last time you asked me a hypothetical question, a terrible thing happened.'

Mallory did not have the energy to point out that that wasn't entirely her fault.

'Hypothetically, yes. Such as in the case of twins, often they are identical but not so identical I cannot tell them apart, even if I don't know their names.'

'And you would *always* know?'

'Yes. I never forget a face. No troll does. That means noticing differences, even if you're not looking for them specifically.'

It confirmed what Mallory had half-wondered about Orson Webb: as a troll, he might've known if Taylor's body wasn't hers. And if he knew that…

'Do you know a man named Orson Webb?'

At Observer Johnson's blank expression, she described him briefly.

'Not ringing any bells. Is that everything?' He stood to dismiss her.

'I need to find Katherine sooner rather than later,' Mallory said. 'So if you've any suggestions of anywhere else I might find records…'

'If waiting is truly an agony, the only thing I can suggest is going and checking every single headstone in the witch cemetery, or the demon mausoleums. I have a map, somewhere; they're all in the lower end of Wrackton. Just a moment.' He left again, with distinctly less energy than before, and returned with a badly photocopied map of Wrackton, small plots hastily marked with a biro. The sites were, at least, reasonably close together.

'Thank you. You've been immensely helpful.' Mallory left an envelope on the table. 'For your troubles.'

'I have troubles of the sort you couldn't even begin to imagine, or indeed cover. But thank you. Between this and my impending dinner, I expect some of the work of papering things over will have been completed.'

Mallory excused herself, unable to think of a decent response to that. She hovered at the great glass doors of the Observatory waiting for a taxi, feeling she'd made some space in her brain to think about Taylor's murder case. She wasn't used to juggling priorities, a tug of guilt in her stomach making her wish she could focus wholly on Theodore and Katherine.

On her phone, she searched for Sandi Clementine, hoping it would help point her in the direction of her alleged Oakpass Manor connection. It transpired Sandi Clementine's real name was Sandra Miller-Davis-Anderson-Harris-Clark, and the good people who compiled alarming amounts of information about public figures did not know if any of those were maternal or paternal surnames. She climbed into the taxi, almost melting into the heated seats. Her body was still exhausted from yesterday and she slumped against the window, the realisation setting in: all of this was going to be unimaginably harder than she'd anticipated.

TWELVE

'I hate this.' Cornelia pulled at her silk shirt, which she'd only put on after Diana had adjusted the fabric so that it was loose and baggy the way Cornelia liked it, but still neat enough that the more sartorially minded would believe she'd intentionally put an outfit together. And given who they were going to meet, she was sure he'd notice.

'It's Valentino, you can't hate it. My mother can hate it, after The Incident. But you can't,' Diana said firmly, shutting the taxi door behind her.

'It doesn't look like me *at all*.'

'That's the idea. It says "I'm not a private investigator, I'm just a little guy",' Diana said, tugging gently at the tails of Cornelia's shirt so they sat flat against the leather trousers she'd also bullied her into. 'You should be thrilled.'

Diana shivered as they walked the cobbled Oughteron side street past a row of restaurants and bars, already freezing in her own dress. There was no turning back now. She'd taken a call from Quinn while working an otherwise silent shift alone at Larkin Studios, everyone scrambling to get pieces together for the next day's shoot, headphones on and not much conversation flowing, no opportunities for investigation, even though she'd asked Taylor to stay away for one more day, to see if her absence sparked any commentary. The best she'd been able to do was get a photo of Donny Baker from his Larkin Studios staff ID, which he'd left behind him.

Then she'd slammed home, showered, and forced Cornelia into a respectable outfit. She smoothed her ponytail, glamoured pink by Felix, who had been unsubtle in expressing their offence at not being invited. They'd also suggested wearing a pair of glasses, so Diana put those on too, hoping the tinted frames would be enough of a disguise that simultaneously wouldn't raise too much suspicion from Quinn.

'A tremendous disguise,' Theodore had commented as they were leaving. 'Genius, really, to add an accessory designed to confuse and befuddle. Never thought of before in any form of media, ever! A fashion imposition, if you will. But you know what they say: nobody expects the Fashion Imposition.'

He had sulked because they didn't laugh enough, and because he also wasn't invited. Even still, there was a third individual in their party whom Diana was trying to ignore.

'I'm thrilled,' Kingston said, twirling a little as he fell into step beside Diana. 'I've never worn a skirt before.'

Diana was not thrilled by the fact Kingston was coming with them, or by the fact that Cornelia had pointed out that bringing him as part of her entourage would make more sense than if it was just the two of them. She did not like being wrong.

'But if we're committing to the bit, yes you have. You wear

skirts all the time. You are a skirt machine. You are fashion, baby, fashion, baby,' Diana instructed. 'He thinks I am an heiress – and apparently doesn't read local news, so has no idea we're a PI agency. So for the bit, I ooze wealth and opulence, and you are a social climber who wants to be around me as much as you possibly can.'

'So I'm a beskirted hanger-on.' Kingston nodded. 'Sounds legit.' His pupils were so much bigger than the night before, his eyes more black than blue. There was a sense he wasn't quite *present* that Diana couldn't put her finger on, though she did not want to spend too much time thinking about Shit King in principle.

'Diana, you *are* an heiress,' Cornelia interrupted.

'Not until I'm twenty-five,' Diana said, glaring at a passing Apparent who was gawking at the three of them. She hated having this conversation. The money itself was not as embarrassing as admitting that just because she came from it and was working towards it that it didn't mean she shouldn't be making something of herself in the meantime. Cornelia – who Diana did not dispute wanted to make something of herself also; her friend was too talented not to – both wanted to spend as much of the Broadwicks' wealth as possible in an effort to redistribute it in whatever manner she saw fit, and could not fathom a world where she did not have money at her disposal. Diana's time outside the bubble of Occulture had taught her that life did not work like this for most Apparents; the ones that had money thought they were entitled to it and actively pushed others down, preventing them from making it. In Wrackton, folk were generally some kind of wealthy and it was shared. Cornelia's family was on another level.

'So practically tomorrow, seeing as you're nearly twenty-one,' Cornelia said. 'Do not hex me, I'll go home. And I won't throw you a party half as good as mine was.'

'To sell this tonight, we need to understand our roles. We are emulating an Apparent friendship trope,' Diana said, ignoring the barb. 'It's the trope of person who wants wealth' – she pointed to Kingston – 'person who has wealth and is sort of terrible about it' – she pointed to Cornelia – 'and person who has wealth who everyone wants to be.' She pointed at herself, brushing her hair off her shoulder. 'Who is also sort of terrible about it, but equally clueless about her actual worth and value, and has a wide-eyed approach to the world outside her orbit, very fascinated by things that glitter, because she thinks she should be part of them. We stick to our roles, nothing goes south.'

'I would like to argue that maybe that is not a friendship at all,' Kingston said. 'On account of the fact that that sounds horrible.'

'It does sound horrible,' Diana agreed, hating herself for agreeing with anything Shit King had to say. 'Fix your jacket.'

She stopped walking, turning abruptly, and led her entourage back up the street, frowning.

'I always have to walk by it at least three times before I find it,' Diana said, before Cornelia could say anything.

'Is it a glamour?' Kingston asked politely.

'No, it's hard to find. Here!' Diana said, grabbing the hand rail and lowering herself down a steep staircase to a basement bar, teetering dangerously on her heels. She stopped before opening the door.

'How's my resting face?'

'Bitchy,' Cornelia said.

'And bitchin',' Kingston said.

'I do not appreciate your input.' Diana cleared her throat. 'Right, everyone follow my lead.'

They were led around the corner into an intimate – meaning small – space with sofa booths.

'I wish Mallory was here,' Diana whispered, but Cornelia was deep in a conversation with Kingston, who couldn't stop staring at the warm white bulbs hanging from the vaulted ceiling, and didn't hear her. A frisson of annoyance bubbled through Diana and she felt her face set. At least her air of irritation would be authentic.

Grey Quinn, Wrackton's most notorious hotelier and Theodore's only enemy, was waiting for them. His arm rested across the back of the booth, his tie slightly undone, a half-empty wine bottle and two glasses in front of him. His expression was the same as ever: mildly amused with a side of boredom. He lifted an ornate silver pocket watch from his waistcoat and clicked it open with an exaggerated flourish, his intention clear, albeit obnoxious.

'Grey, darling,' Diana said, swooping to kiss the air either side of his face. 'Sorry we're late. I brought some dear friends, I hope you don't mind. You know how it is.'

'Not at all, not at all.' He kissed her cheek, raising a hand to summon a waiter. The waiter approached with trepidation, eyeing him like they were afraid one wrong move and their job would be over. It was probably true – Grey Quinn owned most of the hospitality venues in Wrackton, Oughteron and beyond.

Diana ordered the second-most expensive bottle on the menu, earning a look of approval from Quinn, and she relaxed into her role, knowing she'd struck the balance between vapid display of wealth and taking advantage of Quinn's hospitality.

'Is he here?' Diana whispered loudly.

'He's here.' Quinn brushed at his suit jacket. 'But he's here to have fun, so try not to upset him.'

'I wouldn't dream of it.'

Kingston stared around the room like he'd never been in a bar before, his eyes wide and unfocused. It occurred to Diana that he was high, and had been last night, too, though she hadn't seen him take anything. She side-eyed Cornelia, but Cornelia was busy folding a cocktail napkin over and over into a shape that Diana thought might be a beetle. The bar was quiet enough, but the background noise was distracting.

'He's a fascinating man,' Quinn continued. 'Apparent, of course, but we can't all be perfect.' He said the last part loud enough that a figure moving towards them chuckled, and Diana sat up straighter, the last piece of her hastily assembled plan falling into place.

Hollis Hadley was not the striking man she was expecting. He had a friendly, open face, but a shuffling gait that suggested he'd be happier hidden from everything and everyone until the end of time. He paused beside a waiter, slipping something into their pocket, and circled the table until he was sitting next to Quinn.

'Diana, this is Hollis Hadley,' Quinn said.

This was the riskiest part of the whole plan, and Diana hoped her glamoured hair and glorified-sunglasses-indoors disguise would be enough to prevent Hollis from remembering her on set if she came across him again. Given his general avoidance of the crew, she hoped it wouldn't be a problem.

'Hello.' He reached a clammy, limp hand across to her.

'Pleasure,' she said, making sure the word suggested she was both delighted to make his acquaintance and trying to be very cool about it.

'I was hoping I could introduce the two of you soon,' Quinn said. 'Diana's been interested in expanding her empire.'

Diana hesitated. They *had* talked about hotels the first time they met; she'd got him to agree to introduce her to Hollis because she'd expressed being somewhat of a fan of the comics. 'I'm a big fan of your work,' she said silkily.

'And my dear Hollis is making some sort of television show. Not exactly my idea of cinema, you understand, but I do recognise the interest to the masses.'

What a dick.

There wasn't so much as a flicker of a reaction from Hollis, who was studiously following Cornelia's folding technique. She was still buried deep in the process. Kingston lunged across the table several long and uncomfortable moments too late to shake his hand.

'Hi,' he said, almost too loudly. 'They call me Kingston.'

'Now that that's sorted.' Quinn turned his attention to Diana, but the drinks arrived, giving her a moment to steel herself.

'Are you filming close by? I won't lie, I heard you were in town and asked Grey to introduce us. It's always nice to have mutual friends.' Diana took the tiniest sip of her drink. She licked her lips, but could not honestly taste the difference between this and anything else she'd snuck a drink of at parties growing up until she was old enough to walk around with a glass of her own. Either her parents and their friends had expensive taste, or the second-most expensive bottle of whatever the bar had on offer was shit.

'We've recently reopened Larkin Studios,' Hollis began. 'They had some success in the last century, then closed down for a time. I've always wanted to create there, ever since I was a boy, and the opportunity finally presented itself.'

'You've never really been a boy, Hollis. You've been an old man since you were eleven years old. Boarding school,' he said to Diana's raised eyebrow, which did nothing but confirm they really were old friends, as rumoured.

'I'm surprised you haven't jumped on the opportunity to gloat, given that I handed you one a moment ago.'

'Do shut up.' Quinn smiled, lazily running a finger up the side of his glass. 'Larkin Studios is mine,' he clarified. 'I'm sure you've heard of Oakpass Manor?'

'That's the—' Diana started, but she was interrupted by her entourage throwing her carefully constructed script away.

'Oakpass! That's the place with the cool plants,' Kingston said, enthusiasm making him elbow the table.

Diana tried to kick him, catching the table leg instead.

'Cool plants?' Quinn asked, his gaze sharpening.

'So there's a river at the back, right? Crossing onto Larkin Studios, with a big oak tree in the middle?' He waved his hands slowly, painting a dexterous image only he could see. 'I got in to catch tadpoles once and got swept down the banks to this little island thing. That was before I realised rivers can have currents. I find time can distort memories so you feel as though they're happening to you in your current form. But yeah. First time I saw bog asphodel and henbane not in a photo. The nightshades, man. Rare individually in this region, but together? All part of the same little ecosystem? That was magic. Fuck any other kind of magic, that place is magic,' Kingston said, slapping the table.

This time, Diana was pleased to see Cornelia actually making eye contact when she looked over at her, and the look on her face said she hadn't known Kingston knew anything about Oakpass Manor at all.

'And when was this?' Quinn asked. There was a tone in his voice, something that made Diana's skull prickle.

'Nine, ten. Eleven, perhaps. Certainly no more than twelve. Years. Could've been minutes also, but I think that's how old I was. Although—'

'So before my time.' Quinn relaxed. 'We're planning protective measures going forward. The flora in that area – and, I daresay, the fauna – is endangered. I was hoping any tours that had been accessible to... children' – his mouth curled down like he'd thought of something disgusting, which Diana supposed the touring public often could be – 'or wandering adults, were not putting those plants, or the tree, at risk.'

Diana had not come here to talk about plants, but she was not opposed to ending her evening with hexing Kingston into the nearest sun.

Hollis sat forward. 'You saw it, as a child. The magic of the place. The whole river. The whole Manor. The plants, the trees, the grass, the lighting. I visited many times in my youth, imagined all the ways I'd craft a scene there, then I wrote it into this series, hoping one day I'd make it work. And when Grey contacted me, told me he'd purchased it… that's a high I've been chasing ever since. It takes my breath away every time I see the manor.' He kissed his own fingers. 'Bellissima.'

'You're Italian?' Kingston asked, his eyes following Hollis's hand a split-second too late.

'No. I'm not Occult either, but it doesn't stop me respecting' – he nodded upwards, to where Occulture assumed the Ternion were – 'in conversation.'

'I love Italian food. Italian *ice cream*. Diana, can we get some ice cream?'

'Shut up,' Diana whispered, the kick landing this time. She smiled brightly at Hollis.

'That sounds like a dream come true,' Diana said breathily. 'And I bet you've got so many amazing actors working with you to bring your vision to life. I heard Sandi Clementine is involved, she's amazing.'

'Who told you that?' Hollis asked, his tone sharp. Any concrete details about the filming of *Undead Complex* were limited, relegated to rumours without substance. Videos Diana had found about the show were removed within hours of uploading.

'I saw some article, or maybe a post somewhere.' Diana waved a hand. 'Rumours spread fast when there aren't meant to be rumours at all. Don't worry, I won't tell anyone anything. What's Sandi like?'

'If there's one thing I learned early on, it's that if anything was worth reading about, I'd know it before it was printed.'

So there really was a strong possibility he had no idea Diana and Cornelia were private investigators. Had perhaps never heard of the Undetectables.

'If it's celebrity shoulder-rubbing you're after, there's far better, less time-consuming ways to achieve that,' Quinn continued dryly. 'Like coming to the unofficial wrap party, that I believe you were invited to, and have not RSVP'd.'

'Oh, no,' Diana said, turning her head, pretending to be embarrassed, like he'd caught her out. She hoped he saw a raw, poorly disguised desire to social climb. 'That's the Equinox party, right? When is that?'

'On Equinox,' Quinn said. 'Saturday.'

'I'll be there. I haven't had my assistant reply yet.'

'Your assistant has been very busy writing emails,' Cornelia said, not looking up from her napkin.

'Perfect,' Quinn said, ignoring her. 'Now ask him what you really came here to ask.'

There was a heart-stopping moment when Diana wondered if he knew what they were doing, but he looked away, his gaze alighting on Kingston, who was counting the ceiling tiles.

'Okay look,' Diana said, leaning towards Hollis. 'I love the idea of your vision becoming something bigger, you know? This is totally off the record, but what kind of financial investments do projects like these take?' She softened into a loud whisper, 'It's so hard to know if what they're telling you is the best thing to do with your money really is the best thing, or if it's a scandal in the making. Trust is so important. I mean, that's why they call it a trust fund, isn't it?'

'My love, I fear you had some horror stories to tell.' Grey quirked an eyebrow at her and she fought the urge to smile. She loved being underestimated, when it suited her.

'You can't even begin to imagine,' Diana said, a flash of

disembowelled giant mantis appearing behind her eyes. Not the sort of horror stories he meant.

'We're taking risks,' Hollis said. 'Big ones, by resurrecting the studio—'

'Fitting,' Quinn said.

'And trying to keep things under wraps is proving difficult.'

'Why is it so secret?' Diana asked.

A pause hung in the air.

'For the fans,' Hollis said, and Diana knew he was lying. 'I'd rather only the relevant parties see the pilot, see what it could be with the right backing. But it's a risk I'm willing to take. Grey has been an enormous help, with Oakpass Manor. We're setting up a scene to film there soon and there's so many art pieces, so much richness to the history of the place. Other studios, bigger studios… they didn't get the vision. My vision. How important Oakpass is. How much of the story came straight from my nightmares, and how Oakpass is the best representation of that. Filming in Norway or Vancouver or wherever else they suggested… that wasn't going to cut it. We're making a taste of what it could be if done right.'

'And here I thought you were trying to butter me up so I'd agree to cut corners,' Quinn said archly. Hollis laughed and Diana followed suit, her thoughts scrambling to catch up: that he and Quinn weren't just old friends, Quinn was actively involved in the making of *Undead Complex*. Maybe they weren't wrong in looking at him with suspicion again.

'The only thing more expensive than money is time. So many forms, so much permission, so much red tape. Getting a crew together who'd agree to work on something this intense has been difficult, but we're making it work, letting the right people be... ostensibly... in charge.' He paused, and Diana had to wonder at the choice of words. There was no doubt he meant Orson; it had to be about funding. It explained, better than anything, the terrifying lack of crew.

'I'll be sad to see it become a hotel, but Grey will treat her right.'

'The studios will stay as they are, and the hotel will mean the Manor remains standing. Let's be real, some of what you're calling art and history is worthless,' Quinn said. 'There are some priceless fixtures, some artefacts that aren't priceless at all. But generally speaking, you can't own a piece of the Larkin fortune and not wonder what on earth made it so coveted by folk like me.'

'Who's the Larkins?' Cornelia asked, the rudeness and grammatical inaccuracy of it seeming deliberate, like she'd just woken up from a nap.

'You Broadwicks certainly vary in quality, don't you?' Quinn said. 'The Larkins were to Apparents what Broadwicks were to Occult, I suppose. Although the Larkins were much more involved with the Occult than the Broadwicks likely are with Apparents. Who knows, who cares.' He poured himself another drink. Diana wondered how many he'd had before she arrived, and how many it would be before he stopped making sense.

'Apple cult,' Kingston mumbled. Diana was sure she had misheard him, and he didn't elaborate.

'The Larkin family owned Oakpass Manor for generations,' Hollis said. 'I was privileged enough to learn that Oakpass Manor was once a vampire stronghold, at some point during the Vampire Wars. Much of it is private information, you understand. Shared among vampires' – he nodded to Kingston – 'and previously, a Society.'

Cornelia raised her face, something flickering across it. Diana wished she could reach right into her head and find out what it was, in case it was useful.

'And the Larkins passed it down through the family, until 1924.'

'What happened in 1924?'

Hollis shrugged. 'I have no idea. Nobody seems to know. They vanished, and left all their belongings.'

'Are they, like, dead?'

'Well they probably are, like, dead now. Unless they were vampires,' Quinn said.

'Vampires,' Kingston repeated.

Quinn stared at him for a moment, waiting for him to continue.

'Vampires. Oaks... oakspass. Stronghold. Makes... makes sense. Apples. I'm tired, Diana,' he said, his head dropping towards the table at an alarming speed.

'Take a nap, then,' Diana said through gritted teeth. 'He's had a little too much to drink,' she said apologetically. 'He's normally...'

'We all have one like him. And I suppose if we don't, we *are* him,' Quinn said.

'I work with one just like him,' Hollis said. 'But what can you do with a showrunner who thinks he's actually running the show?'

He exchanged a glance with Quinn.

'Trouble in paradise?' Quinn asked.

Hollis leaned in and whispered in his ear. Even with a carefully aimed listening spell, Diana couldn't make out what he was saying.

'Would this have something to do with the two who cornered me earlier?' Quinn asked, loud enough for Diana to hear. He dipped his head.

'—Tate I've heard of, but Whitlock?' Quinn said, then whispered something unintelligible. Hollis patted Quinn on the shoulder, and Diana filed the names away, just in case. No stone unturned.

She waited until they were multiple bottles in, though she had been trying to pace herself, before asking what she wanted to ask.

'Did I hear something bad happened on set of your show?' She leaned towards Hollis. 'It felt like a different sort of rumour.'

Grey Quinn smiled, all his teeth showing. 'I don't think you want to ask about that.'

She felt the tug of persuasion; demon magic trying to force her to change the subject.

'I heard someone went missing,' she continued.

'And how would you have heard about that?' Quinn asked.

Diana felt a flutter of nerves, but held up her phone. 'People like to talk.'

'And what are people saying?'

'That someone went missing.'

'I suppose they could be saying worse things,' he mused. 'And he is an argumentative little prick…'

The last bit was an aside, but Diana took it as confirmation that there *was* someone missing; Donny Baker had not resurfaced.

'Who is?'

'Someone I will be glad to get out of my hair,' Hollis said. 'But no matter.'

'What worse things do you mean? Did something really bad happen?' she asked, opening her mouth in surprise. 'Did someone… die?'

'Yes,' Hollis said, before Quinn could say anything else. 'Someone died. But it's all right, these things happen. They're tragic and terrible, but making a TV show is a physical job. Above all else, the show must go on.'

'Who? Goddess, was it one of the actors?' She pressed a hand to her mouth. 'Was it Sandi?'

'She was a crew member, nothing to worry about.' Quinn waved a hand.

'No need to be so harsh, Grey,' Hollis said. 'She was a valuable member of our team. Anyway, it's all over now, nothing to fret about.'

'Whoa,' Cornelia said. 'A whole crew member died and you're able to not fret about it?'

'Not so loud,' Quinn hissed. 'Can't have this making front page news. Anyway, I think it's clear neither of us are in a right mindset to talk shop.' Quinn reached over to top up Diana's glass. She had drunk more than she intended. 'So what do you say we stop, have another drink, and see where the party takes us?'

Diana felt pressure on her mind again and made a decision. She touched her glass to his, letting him change the subject.

Try as she did, she didn't get a single useful word out of him after that.

THIRTEEN

Four days to the Spring Equinox ball

It was with a heavy heart and a heavier, pounding-er head, that Diana wrenched herself into the land of the awake.

'About time,' Mallory said from the end of the bed, smiling at her. Or at least Diana thought she was smiling at her; her eyes were gummed shut with sleep. She tried to remember if she'd taken her makeup off before she'd crawled into bed. A quick glance at her merely eyeliner-smudged pillowcase told her yes, albeit unsuccessfully.

'What time's it?'

'Eight. Breakfast is on the way. Here's some coffee.'

'You are a goddess.' Diana held out her hands and Mallory shuffled forward stiffly. Slowly waking up, Diana could see Mallory looked as though she hadn't slept much at all, and she felt a pang of concern she swallowed down with the first sip of her coffee. Mallory would tell her if she wasn't okay. She always did.

'Cornelia?' she asked, unable to form a coherent sentence.

'I found Kingston passed out in the hall outside the bathroom.

Cornelia was curled in a ball in the corner of her bed with about six blankets piled on her.'

'She did keep saying she was cold last night.' A hazy memory of them piling into a taxi at some ungoddessly hour surfaced, along with a wave of nausea.

'Luckily I'm here to warm her up,' a voice said, and Theodore appeared in the room. 'Just call me a toaster, because I'm—'

'Reactive with water, prone to starting fires and… something else witty here,' Cornelia said, crawling into the room. She had one of the aforementioned blankets wrapped around her.

'You look like a pupa.' Diana ran a hand through her hair and noticed it was no longer pink; Felix's glamour had worn off.

'Is that coffee?'

'I can make—' Mallory started, but Cornelia waved a hand and a cup appeared in it as she heaved herself onto the end of Diana's bed, curling into as small a ball as she could.

'Got it myself. Are we doing a meeting? Hexana, it's so nice and warm in here.'

'That's thanks to me,' Theodore said loudly. 'Me, Theodore.'

Mallory glanced at him, a calculating worry that even an extremely hungover Diana could see plainly on her face.

'You'll keep the coffee warm too.' Cornelia shivered. 'Get on the bed, Mallory.'

Mallory sat gingerly beside her. She looked vaguely panicked when Cornelia shoved her head onto her lap, her coffee cup held aloft, but still found it in her heart to carefully stroke the hair above Cornelia's ear. Diana wished it was socially acceptable to smush people's faces together like dolls.

'You go first,' Diana said. 'I need to collect my thoughts.'

At least the thoughts that weren't doll-shaped and meddling.

Mallory looked at Theodore and shook her head slightly, an almost-warning behind the action. 'I can go later, I didn't find anything important yesterday. I spent most of the day trying to untangle the timeline and establish whereabouts, but I haven't cracked it yet.'

'Mallory. How many times? Everything you say, everything you do, is of the utmost importance,' Theodore said, wiggling his shoulders so that static sprayed around him.

'She was born to stroke my poor hungover head,' Cornelia said sleepily.

'And to be a gentle alarm clock,' Diana added.

'She was also born to carefully step over a sleeping vampire in the hallway,' Theodore said. 'Which is much nicer than I would've been. Trampled heads for all!'

'I woke up at one point to get more blankets and realised he'd left the room; I assumed he'd slipped out.' Cornelia yawned and Diana shot her a quizzical look, one she hoped conveyed a combination of 'not again with the bad taste in men' and 'not in front of Mallory' that only Cornelia could interpret, but Cornelia didn't seem to notice Diana's valiant attempts at unspoken communication.

Mallory cleared her throat. 'What happened with Quinn?'

Diana took a deep sip. Mallory was additionally born to make coffee. 'He brought Hollis Hadley along as planned. Quinn has bought Oakpass Manor and is behind the resurrection of Larkin Studios, and it sounds like he's more involved than just providing premises. He and Hollis have known each other years.

They were both cagey when I brought up hearing rumours about goings-on on set – I got the sense they've both poured personal funds into *Undead Complex*, and they're trying to avoid any negative press – I surmised there are investors they're trying to avoid looking into how poorly run the whole thing is.'

'There appears to be little cooperation between them and Orson Webb; they were very dismissive of him in passing. Something about him thinking he's the actual showrunner, perhaps implying it was supposed to be an ornamental title rather than literal,' Cornelia added.

'That tracks as the opposite of how the crew talk about Orson, but it could be that Hollis and Orson are both difficult in their own unique ways.'

'It's a pity we didn't get more time at Larkin Studios, or to really look around Oakpass – going undercover would've been easier if there had been more folk on set to blend in around.'

Diana did not typically 'do' feeling things while hungover, but this sentence spiked a sense of something she'd felt so rarely in her life, she could count the instances on one hand.

Panic.

Albeit low-level panic, because even while in the misery of a hangover, she was not beholden to something as fleeting as an emotion.

'What did either or both of them say about the body?' Mallory asked.

'This was interesting,' Cornelia said, her eyes still closed. Mallory had not stopped petting her hair, as though she was afraid of breaking some kind of spell, and Diana fought the incredible urge to draw attention to it. 'They both refused to discuss it properly. Hollis said, quote, it was "nothing to fret about". Quinn said he didn't want it to be front page news.'

'He tried to stop me asking,' Diana said, remembering the tug of persuasion she'd felt, how easy it would've been to simply declare she wanted to do shots and run off to the bar. 'Demon magic, just a little nudge to steer me away. He didn't try again after I resisted, I assume because he knew I'd notice if he pushed any harder.'

'Or he was so fucked up he couldn't be any more persuasive than he was being,' Cornelia said. 'Given that he nearly had a coronary when Kingston brought up being at Oakpass before, even if it was rambling about plants.'

'What did he say?' Mallory asked. Her fingers hesitated on Cornelia's head, and Diana saw one of Cornelia's eyes open a crack.

'He named a bunch of them. Nightshades, I think he said, and henbane.'

'That's what the episode of *Undead Complex* Mallory's going to be in is called,' Theodore said absently. '"Henbane". I read it on the call sheet.'

'So he's been to Oakpass, then?' Mallory said slowly.

'I wish I could go to Oakpass. It sounds a little fancy, doesn't it? Where are you off to, oh to Oakpass!' Theodore said.

'Yeah he has, years ago,' Cornelia said. 'He said something about a vampire stronghold, actually. Hollis, I mean. Kingston wasn't making a lot of sense. But it made me think of something Beckett told me once, about… keepers? Something to do with chess?' Cornelia wrinkled her nose. 'It's gone, sorry. But it reminded me of him telling me about it, so there must be some truth to it.'

Mallory bit her lip. Diana could practically see the diplomacy cooking in her brain, or would've if she wasn't intent on drawing out the last of the coffee. She would never be able to move normally again. She would never feel okay again. There was a dull ringing in her ear, brassy and uncomfortable.

'I just want to say again,' Mallory started, 'that I don't want to make the mistakes we did last time. We overlooked Jacob as the Whistler because we liked him and we completely ignored how he was always there, always conveniently popping up places. We can't make that mistake this time.'

'You're quite right, Mallory. No one is to pull the wool over our eyes this time! Though I wouldn't say that the wool was over my eyes, so to speak. I always knew there was something off about him. Nobody is that nice,' Theodore said.

Diana shot him a look, but refrained from pointing out that if Theodore hadn't been infatuated with Jacob, there would've been no wool for him to pull over anyone's eyes in the first place. She was not in the business of shattering Theodore's heart. No matter how tempting it was.

'Quite right,' Mallory said, smiling at him. 'Any leads on Donny Baker?'

'Hollis and Quinn confirmed that he's still missing,' Diana said.

'There seems to be little love lost between Hollis and Baker,' Cornelia added.

'They were dismissive, to say the least,' Diana continued. 'He's apparently argumentative, and Hollis was, quote, "glad to get him out of his hair". Which sort of matches what everyone else said about him.'

'But there are no specific leads,' Cornelia said. 'There's no missing person report, according to Sully, though he lives alone. I got contact info and tried to call before I came in here, but his phone's switched off.'

'Xander said he's nice as long as you have a lighter and don't piss him off, Hollis seemed to dislike him quite a bit, and Orson suggested he was argumentative, but nobody seems worried,' Diana said. 'I can keep asking folk today, see if we can get anywhere, but the main thing is how unconcerned everyone is. He could be a killer, or he could be another victim, and until we find him we've no way of knowing.'

Mallory took a deep breath. 'Okay. That doesn't leave us with very much. Hollis Hadley downplaying a murder on his set – could be suspicious, but could also be someone trying to not get their show shut down, particularly when Taylor bounced back in. Quinn trying to persuade you away from asking questions – could be suspicious, could also be that he is investing a lot in this show and doesn't want to lose. Donny Baker missing when there's a murder on set – could be suspicious, but could be that he really did cut his losses and walk away from a very stressful workplace where he was neither well liked or appreciated. The body having Taylor's face and her reaching out to Diana specifically could be suspicious, but there's some reason she was chosen. Then of course Kingston turning up with the same face as Beckett – which I'm aware he probably always had, but the timing, coupled with his seemingly specific knowledge of Oakpass Manor, could be suspicious, but equally could be a coincidence.'

'And you know what they say about coincidences – they only happen twice. A third time makes it serial, and then we have a problem. Of course, if a coincidence only happens once, I think that makes it an anomalous outlier that shouldn't be counted,' Theodore said sagely.

Mallory cracked another smile at him. 'As long as we avoid serial, I'm okay with coincidences.'

'Any word on the toxicology report?' Diana tried to keep her voice level, though she sounded to herself as though she was underwater.

Mallory shook her head. 'It could be weeks before we hear anything back from that. Theodore and I have been trying to narrow down what the beetles were picking up – or not, as the case may be. At the moment we're trying to establish any kind of fact, something concrete we can use to firmly find the killer, and we're going to have to make do with what we can. It seems between the UML and the Ghoul Council trying to stop us doing anything, we are going to have next to no help from Sully or Dr Ray, as Sully can't look into anything without UML approval, even if Oughteron were to specifically want Wrackton police – or us – involved.'

'Which they surely do, if they let Dr Ray have the victim's body and asked her advice,' Cornelia said.

'You'd think that—' Mallory started.

'—And you'd be grossly wrong,' Theodore said. 'Ask me how I know this. Ask me how years of dealing with the two-punch combination of the UML and the Ghoul Council has left me jaded, but well-informed.'

'Basically, if Oughteron's mayor or their police force make a direct request, Wrackton can seek approval from the UML. But even if the Wrackton police were to link every single case

Oughteron had had in the last ten years to this case, it would be seen as falling outside of their remit and they'd need to apply for permission for each individual piece.'

'Plus I imagine Oughteron would tell them, and by extension us, to fuck off for telling them how to do their jobs,' Cornelia said.

'Yes, basically.'

It meant the official channels were limited, and put Diana in a strangely advantageous position, should she play her cards right.

'I suppose I could continue being a prop maker for the next while? I think tonight I'm scheduled to be in the manor itself, which would give me a chance to explore the grounds,' Diana said, carefully modulating her tone so her eagerness wasn't audible. 'Plus it'll keep our lines of enquiry open, keep folk talking.'

'That sounds like a good idea,' Mallory said decisively. 'Maybe this case requires more observation, to fully understand what we're up against.'

Diana wanted to stuff Mallory inside a teddy bear's skin and squeeze her tightly. Even in the face of Mallory not at all sounding like she thought they really had a solvable case, she wanted to cover all her bases.

'Thank you, Director Hawthorne.'

Mallory grinned. 'Oh!' she said, jolting Cornelia on her lap. She placed a careful hand on Cornelia's cheek, as if to apologise. 'I did tell Dr Ray about the object Orson was carrying, and she sent over example photos of what the murder weapon might be. There're no guarantees until we can either get the object ourselves, or someone can properly test a range of instruments, but she thinks it's something called a…' Mallory squinted, like she was trying to remember.

'Pike!' Cornelia said. 'It's what they use to take down the zombies in *Undead Complex*. I did some research, by which I mean I asked Felix to give me a run-down on things they thought were interesting to know about the comics. But that's how they stop other necromancers reusing the zombie parts, they destroy them with a short pike.'

'There were some on the wall in the entrance hall of the Oakpass Manor dollhouse. I bet there're murder-sized counterparts in the real Manor,' Diana said.

'How on earth does that work?' Theodore said. 'Although you said the show takes place near a river, so I suppose it's not completely unfeasible.' He swung an imaginary object around the room in a static spray, holding it as though it was going to leap from his hands at any moment. 'I can't imagine how this would have killed someone quite to the extent as befell our young Taylor doppelgänger but… well, it's inventive. Maybe they've got teeth I've forgotten about. Do they have teeth, Mallory? Why are you laughing?'

Mallory, to her credit, was the only one of the three of them not *crying* with laughter. Diana had to put down her coffee cup to press the heel of her hand to her face in an effort to compose herself, and the sight of Cornelia shaking with the corner of her blanket pulled over her head made a small howl escape her.

'She meant a pike like a spear,' Mallory said, her voice strangled with effort. 'Not the fish.'

'Not the fish. Right.' Theodore dropped his hands and pulled his cardigan around him, his face twitching. 'Well, that would've made for a more inventive story. Killers these days, they're not very clever with weapons, are they?'

'I'm gonna gut you with a fish,' Cornelia whispered, and to Diana's delight, Mallory broke.

Theodore huffed into the corner, offering a sarcastic 'HA!' every few seconds that only served to set them off again. It felt good to laugh. It reminded Diana that they hadn't had much reason to laugh together for a while.

'So… so maybe,' Mallory said, recovering. 'Sorry, Theodore, I'll show you photos later so you can see what kind of thing she means. Besides, your confusion is warranted: technically it can only be a proper pike if it's over five feet long.'

'Otherwise it's just a sparkling poker,' Cornelia added. Diana shot her a look.

'The semantics of medieval weaponry do not interest me, particularly not while I'm this hungover,' Diana said shortly. 'As far as I'm concerned, it's a pike.'

'Maybe look into that while you're undercover, Diana,' Mallory continued, ignoring them both. 'It's possibly the murder weapon, so if you can somehow swab it, or even liberate it from Orson, great.'

Diana nodded.

'It begs the question of why someone would use something so strange to kill with,' Mallory continued. 'It could be something else, though; finding the exact murder weapon is actually quite difficult if it wasn't left at the scene. It's worse than no body no crime sometimes, as it's harder to prove how a murder was carried out. Though this pike would have to have been incredibly sharp and a specific shape – she thinks it was barbed, which is…'

'Horrifying.'

'But not magical,' Mallory said. 'Which means we are no closer to answers than we were before.'

'I'm switching to nights tonight for the next shoot, which gives us the day to do some work. Really get moving on things,' Diana said, then flopped back against the headboard. 'But maybe in a few hours. I think I need to sleep, and I definitely need to shower before I can PI again.'

'Is that a good idea?' Cornelia asked sleepily.

'Is what a good idea?'

'You, spending time on set with Taylor, when we don't know how involved she is or why she was the potential target. It seems like you're old friends,' Cornelia said. It was so diplomatic, so Mallory-like, that Diana blinked twice at the lack of a tone to *friends*. It was possible she'd gotten so good at hiding how she felt that Cornelia didn't know.

Or that Cornelia just hadn't noticed.

'It'll be fine. It gives us a chance to observe, to really follow what she's doing and who she's speaking to, in case we're wrong and it is about Taylor specifically. Cover all the bases.'

The others nodded, and Diana felt something uncurl in her chest. Going back was the right thing to do for the case. It was only mildly selfish.

'I have emails to write,' Cornelia said, shifting so her arm was draped over Mallory's lap. 'What's the polite way to say "I've told you several times we don't do stalking and stop asking me, you creep"?'

'Try "as per my last email",' Diana said. 'Keep swearing to a minimum.'

'I have things to do too, if anyone cares,' Theodore said.

'I always care,' Mallory said, and Diana wondered if he could hear the note of sadness. He patted her on the head and left.

'Ugh,' Cornelia rolled and sat up, her hair sticking up at all angles. 'Maybe I'll take a nap too, see if Kingston wants to take one of the spare rooms.'

Diana shot her a look.

'Hold on, what happened to "we'll be better this time"?' Mallory asked. 'We can't waste a whole day. And this is coming from me!'

Diana let her head loll against the headboard. 'We're not at our best, currently.'

Mallory closed her eyes.

'Fine, you two sit around. I have some things to be getting on with, with my… other case, and I've thought of a potential lead we've been ignoring.' She whispered the last part, casting a glance at the wall Theodore had walked through.

'What're you going to do?' Cornelia asked sleepily.

'See a boy about a troll.'

FOURTEEN

Approaching ten p.m., Diana was having no regrets about returning to Larkin Studios, elbow-deep in a task while the rest of the prop department darted around gathering the last pieces needed for a night shoot in Oakpass Manor. Her hangover was finally wearing off and she'd left Broadwick Mansion just as Mallory emerged into the lab after a nap, having clarified the 'boy' in question was their friend Langdon Ericsson, whose uncles ran the faerie and troll underworld. If anyone would know Orson Webb, it would be them. It was a beautiful approach in its simplicity, and Diana kicked herself for not being the one to think of it. She'd left Cornelia curled around her laptop all but crying about the agency inbox.

She adjusted her position, cross-legged on the floor beside the Oakpass Manor dollhouse. She had taken many photos and a walk-through video, but couldn't stop looking at the details. It was meticulously constructed, no expenses spared: wall hangings and upholstery made from real silk, real wood panelling, burnished silver candelabras standing on oak tabletops, rooms separated by carved and stained doors that Diana was certain matched the real thing. She had been tasked with making it look like the real set, so that close-ups could be used for transition scenes, and was cutting pieces of acetate and replicating the flooring and one of the walls so bloodied zombie parts could be splattered without damage. She'd completed countless little knives and mini body parts in between wishing for an early death, and they were waiting in a box beside her. Diana was starting to think the potential success of *Undead Complex* was riding entirely on the abilities of the various departments to make up for a lack of substance with incredible style.

'How are you getting on?' Rachel asked.

Diana made a muffled noise she hoped sounded positive, a small medieval axe clamped between her lips, her palms full of tiny weapons she was deftly stacking into a trunk. Taylor looked up from where she was painting an assortment of fake food that would be used to dress one of the set tables – the perfect assortment of high fantasy bread, cheese, apples and various roasted meats and fruits that made Diana want to fill a tankard and run a sword through her enemies.

'I'll run this over to Oakpass myself as soon as you're done. Fred's left us a cart, he'll meet us over there.'

'I can come with you,' Diana said quickly, slotting the tiny axe into a holder on one of the walls. 'It's heavy, and we've made it heavier with the additions. These were the last bits, it's good to go now.'

'I'll come too,' Alannah said. 'Better than sitting here in the warehouse by myself, it gives me the creeps.'

'I'll just go and shite, then, shall I?' Taylor said wryly.

'I assumed you were going with them,' Alannah said, shrugging.

The initial shock of seeing Taylor back at work had worn off among the crew, who were glad to have an extra pair of hands. It was as though the murder hadn't happened at all.

'We'll all go,' Rachel said. Diana helped her carry the dollhouse to the cart, climbing in the back and resting it on her lap. It wasn't a comfortable fit, but it wouldn't be for long. 'There's a little bridge across the river, it'll save us going all the way around. Oops,' she said, the cart lurching.

They stayed quiet on the trip over, the golf cart whirring beneath them, and Diana held her breath as they went over the river, afraid something was going to fall out of the dollhouse as they passed the gnarled, bare oak tree silhouetted against the sky, a small fenced plot of plants beneath it. She relaxed as Oakpass Manor neared, majestic even from behind as it towered above them. Green floodlights lit the walls from below, casting the rear courtyard in a ghostly glow that made her shiver.

Alannah took the other side of the dollhouse as Diana disembarked.

'I've been reading about the house,' she said. 'The dollhouse, I mean.'

'Find anything interesting?'

'Depends on how you feel about dollhouses.'

'I hear Diana loves them,' Rachel said.

'Okay, well,' Alannah said, her tone bored, 'there were rumours after the Larkins disappeared in the dead of night that the dollhouse contained treasure – belonging to Lady Larkin, maybe, or something that would ruin them, though most rumours agree it's actual treasure.'

'How does anyone know it was the dead of night?' Taylor asked. 'Could they not have wandered off at three in the afternoon and it took a while for anyone to notice?'

'I… don't know,' Alannah said, and Diana knew it to be true, faerie or not. 'It's just what I read.'

'It's possible staff showed up for work and they were missing,' Diana said. 'Maybe that's where the dead-of-night bit comes from.'

'What kind of treasure could really be in a dollhouse, anyway?' Alannah asked.

'Money. Really small money,' Taylor suggested.

'World's tiniest emerald earrings,' Rachel said, hurrying ahead to make sure they could walk onto the set. Diana looked down at the dollhouse, not meeting anyone's eye.

There was plenty you could hide in a dollhouse, and even more you could hide in a diorama. And Diana had done just that.

She was saved from having to comment by a shout, and she looked up to see Xander, standing in the fold of one of the turrets, pull abruptly away from someone, moving with the others towards the sound.

'—you are IMPOSSIBLE. Why would you hire me if you didn't want me to run your damn show?' a voice continued, coming closer. Orson Webb and Hollis Hadley burst out of Oakpass, their faces eerily lit.

Diana took a step back. She'd hoped to avoid running into Hollis until he'd had enough time to forget all about the girl with pink hair and sunglasses Quinn had brought to drinks, but he didn't even glance in her direction, much less recognise her.

'Orson, I made it patently clear when—'

'Oh PATENTLY clear, is it? Make this patently clear: I QUIT!' Orson roared, stalking across the lawn.

'You can't!'

'Watch me! I'll be in Barbados within hours and you'll be here trying to rescue this sinking ship. And the only person who sank it, Hollis, is YOU!' he shouted.

For a moment it looked like he was going to take the cart they'd abandoned, but he kept going, disappearing over the bridge into the darkness.

Hollis pinched the bridge of his nose, eyes closed. Diana didn't know what to do, her fingers straining to hold the dollhouse up, worried Alannah was going to let go of the other side. Xander had drifted back inside. Rachel beckoned the others forward and Diana was glad to be close to setting the dollhouse down.

'Fred?' Hollis called as Diana passed. Fred stepped out of the shadows where Xander had been moments ago. 'Obviously this is not good for the project, not good for us. Continue as we were. I will have to immediately begin hiring for a new showrunner, perhaps someone with directorial qualities, and there'll be fires to put out with investors. We'll likely need a new producer on board, assuage any concerns.' His gaze softened. 'Nothing worth doing well is easy, I believe the saying goes. Fred, Rachel, I'm trusting the two of you to keep the schedule.'

'Hollis, Orson said I—' Rachel started.

'You have to. You two are the most senior here.'

They were also, perhaps, the only two crew members he knew the names of.

'We're going to need to regroup, though,' Fred said seriously. 'We need him. Can we push?'

'Push, don't push, make sure it gets done on time. No one is to bother me for the next forty-eight hours. I'm trusting you. I am putting my full trust in you. Fip fip?' he said, a hint of mockery in his tone.

'Fip fip,' Rachel and Fred said in unison, though there was a look on Rachel's face that said this wasn't a responsibility she wanted. Fred darted back into the manor ahead of them, and Rachel guided them across the threshold, her eyes glued to the clipboard in her hands as she flicked through the pages, the sudden tension palpable. A slight breeze misted through the entrance hall, taking with it a vague scent of apples that made Diana's ear buzz as she and Alannah set the dollhouse down carefully next to the pillars. Diana looked around quickly, the grand effect of the hall dampened by all the equipment and set pieces stacked and scattered haphazardly around them. It was as though someone had blown up the miniatures she'd been working on or allowed her to step inside the dollhouse itself, all the tiny details made life-size. She turned once, under the guise of checking she hadn't dropped anything, noticing two empty sets of hooks over the doorway to the main hall – where the pikes had been in the dollhouse.

Taylor met Diana's eye then, her face mirroring what Diana suspected her own did.

'Well,' Diana said, at a loss for anything else. 'I suppose things can only get less exciting from here.'

PERIMORTEM II

The body was awake but already dead, even if they didn't know it yet.

They were on a bed. They knew that much; *whose* bed was another question. Something soft under their head. Furs. A roil of terror raced up their spine, but movement was beyond them.

A figure panned into focus, mid-action, hands tearing and ripping, tearing and ripping like they had been. The body remembered that from before. The back of a head jerking into action, surprised, then the body was not in control anymore.

A face swam into close view and the body's heart should've leapt, but the body could not feel a heart. The figure was touching them, but they couldn't see how, or why. Their frame of reference shook, backlit by tiny, hot lights that cut the scene with an ambient glow.

The body could taste apples and smell ammonia, a sharp scent that made their eyes water. Their vision swam as the figure moved their limbs, arranging them like a four-legged spider on the bed.

The body *knew* them. Knew their face, knew what they were looking at, but couldn't name it. The words wouldn't leave their tongue.

They tried to move an arm, a leg, uncurl from the staged pose, but nothing happened. The figure dipped their head, seeming to grow smaller with the movement, and worked with something cold and damp, running over their skin until the body could imagine they were sleeping. This was a nightmare.

It was a nightmare they'd had before.

Something rattled. The figure pulled a bottle out, emptied it into their palm and the body tried, tried so hard to see it as it was. A tearing sound. Pieces tucked away in pockets.

The body's vision darkened.

Their eyelids were opened. A final scene in front of them, the bottle placed beside their head for a rough-cut close-up.

A torn label and a stark warning: DO NOT EXCEED THE STATED DOSE.

FIFTEEN

Three days to the Spring Equinox ball

Diana was not often wrong. She'd thought she'd have days or even weeks to further investigate – and enjoy being on set again, in Taylor's company – but not twenty-four hours. She also hadn't anticipated another murder, which both put a dampener on her outlook, and made her worry she'd missed an obvious sign somewhere along the way.

But, alas, the killer had struck again.

'What's happening?' Diana rolled down her window at the security booth the next morning – under Fred and Rachel's ad hoc showrunning, she'd agreed to an early shift to help the crew catch up after last night, violating all kinds of workers' rights in the process. As she'd passed Oakpass Manor, it had been crawling with police cars and an ambulance, the entire crew standing outside the front entrance.

'Security issue,' a demon security guard she'd never seen before said. He might as well have said, *It's a secret.* 'Pull in out of the way.'

She squinted at his name badge, thinking about what Theodore had said about coincidences – or rather the essence of what he'd said, because the whole thing had been reasonably unintelligible. One demon security guard was unusual, but two was certainly something of a coincidence. His name was Lyle Whitlock, and the name rang a very faint bell, though she couldn't think why.

Taylor hurried over as soon as Diana rounded the back of Oakpass Manor, having walked the long way across the backlots of the studio.

'What's happening?' Diana said, accepting a hug and trying not to enjoy it.

'Someone else has been found dead.'

'Who? What's happening? What did you see?'

'Would you stop for a second? I didn't see anything. They were resetting the shoot after last night, then everyone was told to assemble over there, and an ambulance and police cars showed up. That's all I know.' Taylor's hand brushed Diana's and she subtly pulled away.

Alannah, Fred and Xander had clumped together on the grass verge behind a crime scene cordon. Diana took off towards them, when she heard a voice behind her.

'He's DEAD,' Sandi wailed, stumbling towards her. 'Orson is *dead* and it's all my *fault.*' She sobbed into her hands, teetering until Diana and Taylor both caught her.

Orson Webb was the victim this time. A chill ran through her, one of both excitement and horror. Diana patted Sandi on the arm while Taylor murmured comforting things. Diana could not help but notice that there were no actual tears falling from Sandi's eyes.

'What happened? Oh my goddess, you poor thing,' Diana said, fighting the urge to roll her eyes.

Sandi lifted her head mournfully. 'I killed him.'

Diana froze, not daring to take this as a real admission of guilt. 'What do you mean, you killed him?'

'He… He… heeeeeeee…' the last part came out as a whine. Even without tears and snot – a magical feat, even by Diana's standards – Sandi seemed genuinely distressed.

'It's okay. Oh,' Diana said as Sandi hit the ground with a bump. 'Let's come down to your level. What do you mean?'

'It's okay, chicken, you're grand, I promise,' Taylor said soothingly. She cast a worried glance at Diana. 'Tell us what happened, it's okay.'

'He is in recovery. He's in recovery and I knew this, but when he said, "Sandi please, dollface" – I love it when he calls me dollface, it's so endearing – "do you have any aspirin?" I was like, "Yes, of course, baby" – I call everyone baby – "of course, here's some aspirin," and I … I gave him the whole bottle,' she wailed. 'Just handed it over, like some evil temptation. Like some sort of demon succubus fresh from the depths of hell! Like a true *necromancer!*'

Diana was not quite the scientist Mallory or even Cornelia was, but she knew that this didn't sound quite right.

'So you gave him the aspirin bottle, and then what?'

'He snorted it, or did *something* with it, and he's *dead* now. They said he overdosed. And it's all my fault!'

Diana stood up abruptly, letting Sandi's arm fall to the ground.

'Ow,' she mumbled, before dissolving into tearless sobs again.

Diana wasn't paying attention. She cast around for someone she knew, finding Xander standing uncertainly at the part of the set they'd tried to cordon off, Lyle beside him.

'Xander, do you know what's going on?' Diana said, turning the lines of her mouth into a pout. 'I'm so worried.'

'I think… I think old Orson's had a bit of a turn,' he said. Up close, Diana could see how drawn he looked, his mouth clamped around his vape like it was oxygen.

'Who found him?'

'I think it was Sandi,' he said, but he didn't look certain. 'Or maybe Alannah?'

'No, it wasn't me,' Alannah said. 'Must've been Fred or Sandi, I remember being called over here.'

Diana frowned; more contradictions.

'I feel bad about yesterday,' Xander continued.

'What about yesterday?'

Xander shook his head. 'I was… he… I feel terrible. He had a row with Hollis,' he said, and Diana realised he hadn't seen her yesterday, didn't know she'd seen him in a shadowy corner with Fred. 'Big blazing one, shouting that he was the glue holding this show together, Hollis would be nothing without him. I have a video of it,' Xander said. 'I was sent it.'

Lyle looked at him curiously. 'It's only a video, it's not like—'

'I posted it online,' he said in a rush. 'Stupid of me, but he…' He trailed off, and Diana didn't know if he meant Orson or Hollis. 'It's done,' Xander said. 'I've taken it down. I took it down not long after I posted it, but the damage is done.'

Diana patted him on the arm. 'I'm sure he'd understand.'

'Yeah. Yeah,' Xander said, pulling himself upright.

'First day on the job and this is what happens, eh?' Lyle said, getting a laugh from Xander that Diana did not think he'd earned. She wished she could remember why his name rang a bell.

'Hey, you don't have Rachel's number, do you?' Diana asked, a thought seizing her.

'I think so.' Xander fumbled in his pocket, handing over his phone, unlocked. 'Rachel's our propmaster, though she's co-acting showrunner at the moment,' he said to Lyle, who nodded thoughtfully. 'You'll get the hang of them all, there aren't many of us. If we can even keep going after this.'

'There's nothing one can't do if they put their mind to it,' Lyle said, rolling up his sleeves, revealing a lion tattoo that took up most of his right forearm. Diana felt it was the definition of *a choice*. 'That has always been the way of Occulture, and it should apply here too.'

Lyle and Xander chatted quietly, though Diana was barely listening, finding the video in Xander's deleted folder, sending it to Cornelia and Mallory and deleting the evidence. She pulled up Rachel's number and sent it to herself.

'Oh look, here she is now,' Xander said as Rachel hurried over, unusually dishevelled. She breezed past Lyle to put her hand on Xander's shoulder.

'I slept in, I can't believe I slept in. What's happening? Diana?'

'We think Orson might be dead,' Diana said, not bothering to sugar-coat it.

Rachel's eyes widened. 'Fucking hell,' she said, then clapped a hand over her mouth. 'I mean… wow. Where's… what's… I need Fred. FRED!' she shouted, and he came running to her. They spoke in hushed tones, and Diana turned away as her phone buzzed.

> *Cornelia*
> Really was as bad as you said
>
> Filmed from the left of the manor, did you see anyone there?

It occurred to Diana that Xander could've filmed it himself, but she wondered if someone else had – Fred had been where Xander was standing. She'd seen him pull away from him, like they'd been embracing.

> *Diana*
> Xander or Fred. Orson might be dead also
>
> *Mallory*
> DIANA way to bury the lede!
>
> *Diana*
> Check socials, he left here last night and said he was quitting, there was a video of the fight going around too

'Diana, have you seen Alannah or Taylor?' Rachel asked.
'I saw Alannah earlier, Taylor…' She pointed to the Taylor-and-Sandi-shaped heap on the ground. 'Sandi is very upset.'

'Get her out of here,' Rachel said. There was a note of authority in her voice. 'Take her back to Larkin Studios. Just get her calmed, the pair of you.'

She turned to speak to Lyle, her voice low and anxious, though Diana couldn't hear what they were saying.

Cornelia
Found his socials – he made a post four hours
ago saying he's in Barbados and, quote, 'fuck all
of y'all'

Mallory
Which is exactly what he said he'd do in that video.
Is this a second body with a living counterpart?

Diana took a deep breath.

Diana
I think we need to get that body out of there before
the Apparent police come in

they're saying overdose but we don't know for sure

and frankly it could be a rumour

Mallory
Cornelia is on to Sully as I type, she's getting hold
of Dr Ray

'Let's go for a walk,' Diana said, and Taylor pulled Sandi to standing, looking grateful. There was no sign of the body being removed, but police were walking in and out, which Diana found worrying from a scene-contamination point of view. Mallory's habit of sticking to the rules was rubbing off on her.

They supported a still-wailing Sandi between them and quick-marched her back to Larkin Studios, Diana deeply reluctant to move away from the scene. They made it as far as the first building, where she insisted on stopping next to an overflowing skip surrounded by boxes.

'I'm calming myself,' she explained unnecessarily, taking deep, gasping breaths. 'Acting technique.'

Diana and Taylor exchanged glances. It was all Diana could do not to burst out laughing at this whole thing; had someone told her that her next job on set would involve standing in a semi-abandoned film studio with a hyperventilating Sandi Clementine between her and the girl she'd been in love with since the moment she'd first set eyes on her, she'd probably have hexed them into oblivion, then laughed at them too.

'Could you calm yourself somewhere with chairs? I'm absolutely banjaxed, it's been a long week,' Taylor said, rubbing her lower back.

Diana was about to try coaxing them back towards Oakpass – she didn't want to leave the scene – when Sandi inhaled as though she was about to scream. Seemingly unprompted, her face cleared and she approached the skip. Diana stared at her as she pressed on some of the boxes before using them as leverage to clamber *inside* the skip, humming to herself under her breath.

'Is this also part of the technique?' Diana asked.

'No, this is where the good stuff is.' Sandi held up a rubber arm. 'This was one of my children, you know.'

'What?' Taylor craned her neck into the skip.

'My children. Necromantically. Quick, girls. Look with me. Find the things you want. Ah,' she said, lifting a rotting rubber leg. '*This* is coming home with me.'

'I fucking *made* that, why's it in a bleedin' skip?' Taylor exclaimed, outraged.

'There was an unfortunate incident where Xander Crane's character was hit in the face by Ruthless Monroe, and the leg tore. I tried to explain I was fully in character and Ruthless *would* hit him in the face, but he didn't quite get it. So sad. Just like…' Her eyes welled, but she blinked them away. 'Just like Orson dying, so sad. But these are the props I love most, the ones with stories. Someone comes to your house and compliments you on your zombie leg, you say thank you *so* much, let's talk about *you* some more. But someone comes to your house and you have a zombie leg *story*, that's showbusiness, dollface. Open boxes. Live a little.' She sniffled. 'We owe it to Orson to live.'

An exceedingly pissed-off Taylor opened some of the boxes, and Diana joined her after a beat, her hands landing on a box half buried under the others. Taylor helped her pull it free and they opened it together.

'Are you for *real*?' Taylor exclaimed, at the same time as Diana swore in disbelief.

'What's…' Sandi's brow furrowed, and she clambered out of the skip with difficulty, her zombie leg clutched under her real arm, as Diana and Taylor carefully lifted out their find: the dollhouse

Diana had spent forever furnishing, that they'd delivered to Oakpass Manor mere hours before.

'Hexana' was all Diana was able to muster before a scream of anguish tore from Sandi's throat. Diana was quick to stop Sandi's reaching hand touching the evidence, for this was undoubtedly a crime scene.

'There's been a ROBBERY!' Sandi shouted, more distraught than ever.

It had been ransacked. Tiny furniture pieces upturned, doors ripped off hinges, papers and tiny cups and tiny ornaments scattered on the floor. Some of the walls had been opened up, gilded cardboard torn to reveal their inner layers.

This wasn't mindless destruction: someone had been searching for something.

Diana remembered what Alannah had said about treasure, and her stomach twisted.

'Hexana,' Diana said again. It was like looking down on one of her dioramas but worse, somehow. Perhaps because this was never intended to show something awful.

And then she stopped. The figure in the study on the fainting couch was still there, but it had a friend: in the drawing room they'd repurposed as Xander's character's bedroom in the real Oakpass Manor, lying on the floor with a very, very small open pill box beside it, was a doll. The room around it was destroyed, but the position of the body, the scattered tiny pills beside it, was unmistakably implying an overdose.

There were three more figures among the wreckage: one in the dining-room entrance below the main staircase, draped as though it had fallen. The tiny pikes had been ripped off the entrance hall wall, leaving one miniature hook in place. Diana could only see one of them, lying in the middle of the cracked floor between the pillars, singularly identifiable in a sea of illogical violence. She knelt so she could see right through to the enclosed courtyard where there were two more figures, among the uprooted bushes and shattered glass that seemed to come from a dome covering what Diana assumed was a well, sprawled opposite each other with their feet touching.

There were tiny daggers, daggers Diana had made with her own hands, protruding from their chests.

And they were all posed to look just like the comic frames on the mood boards all over Larkin Studios.

'Oh, for the love of fuck,' Taylor gasped, leaning over the dollhouse. 'This is awful.'

'I'm going to fix it,' Diana said, taking photos as quickly as she could. 'I have to, I can't leave it like this.'

Taylor blinked at the figure on the fainting couch, but she didn't comment on it.

Diana wasn't sure she would if it was her, either.

Taylor had called Rachel before Diana had a chance to think about what to do next.

'She said load it on a handcart and bring it over, she can't leave Oakpass until the police are done.'

'Where do we find one of those?' Diana turned in a circle.

Sandi lifted her zombie leg and pointed into the skip. 'The first rule of necromancy is that all you seek will be made available to you. There's a folded handcart there, beneath my children.'

'Shit,' Rachel said, her fingers pressed to her face in horror as soon as she saw the house. Taylor kept Sandi calm, or calm-ish, while Diana presented their findings. She'd had Taylor distract Sandi long enough to examine the cart for anything that might've been useful for Mallory, in case the culprit had used it, but it was clean. The crowd had grown in the time they were gone; Lyle had given up trying to control the situation and was letting the Oughteron police do their job badly instead.

'I could cry,' Rachel continued. 'Who would do this? Where did you say you found it?'

'In a skip near the studios. I was hoping you could tell *me* who might be capable of ruining a piece of history,' Diana said, softening her tone so she sounded the maximum amount of bewildered. It wasn't far off how she actually felt.

Rachel shook her head, glancing back at the gathered crowd. 'I've no idea. I don't know what to do now.'

'It's okay,' Diana said with confidence she didn't quite feel in the moment. 'I can fix it. It won't be quick, but I can fix it. It's the least I can do, for Orson.'

'Thank you. I can bring it to you later. I don't know if the police want it, or… but text me your address? Production will have to shut down.' Rachel rubbed her face. 'Hollis picked the wrong time to be on sabbatical.'

Diana's eyes narrowed in confusion. She was certain Hollis had said he was speaking to investors.

Diana sensed Taylor approaching before she reached her side. Sandi was still hunched on the ground, her arms wrapped tightly around her zombie leg.

'I'll help, this will take hours on your own. For the love of Blair or whatever her name is, who'd do this?' she said, with such ferocity Diana actually smiled.

'Thank you, Diana,' Rachel said. 'You're a lifesaver.'

'Wha—' was all Cornelia managed when Diana arrived back at the research room with an armload of emergency dollhouse-repair items.

Mallory was seated with a list of their case notes in front of her, a big piece of paper divided up into headings of ORSON, TAYLOR, STATEMENTS, INCONSISTENCIES scrawled with notes she'd been compiling over the last few days. The look of despair on her face suggested she hadn't made much headway.

Diana filled them in briefly on Orson's death and the dollhouse, showing them pictures nobody would admit to taking, but they all had on their phones. A blurry photo of Orson on a bed in the drawing room of Oakpass Manor, curled and rigid. His skin was more grey than blue, his eyes open and empty, the scene lit by an orange glow from behind; candles, perhaps, though Diana couldn't see. The aspirin bottle was there, as Sandi had said.

'Grim,' Cornelia said. 'Who took them?'

'I can't establish that. It sounds like Sandi was first on the scene this time, but it could've been Fred; they were all confused when I asked. Alannah says the only thing she's certain of is being asked to assemble with the others. They all have the photos – metadata doesn't tell me anything useful.'

'Grimmer,' Cornelia said.

'Rachel's going to bring the dollhouse by later.' Diana printed off the least-blurry images and stuck them to the board. 'Here's the state it's in.'

'It looks like it was properly ransacked,' Mallory said.

'It was. Someone tore it apart looking for something, then tried to hide the evidence by dumping it next to a skip. Had Sandi not wanted to go foraging, I'm not sure we'd have found it – Oughteron police were clearing out the scene and taking evidence, it could've been days before we figured out the dollhouse was missing.' Diana pointed inside it, trying not to entertain that thought too hard. 'And that's not all: what does this doll remind you of?'

'Orson,' Mallory said.

'And here, and these two.'

'Fuck,' Cornelia said. 'This is serial, isn't it?'

'It's about to be. The killer is using the dollhouse in a *very* annoyingly clichéd way – this is a warning, I think.'

'Then why also ransack it?'

'They must think there's something in here. Alannah said there's a story about Lady Larkin's lost treasure, maybe the killer wants… whatever it is. I'm going to put it back together, and I'm going to try find out what they were after. Taylor's coming to help, she just wanted to go change.'

'And that's useful because…?' Cornelia asked.

'It's a big job,' Diana said. 'Anyway, the question is this: which came first, ransacking or using the dollhouse to indicate future murders? Either the killer was pissed off and destroyed the dollhouse then wanted to stage, or the killer was staging and lost patience. Or another secret third thing.'

'That's not actually that helpful, but I'll allow it,' Cornelia said. 'I'll see if I can get Sully or Dr Ray about getting Orson's body for autopsy. We need to know for sure if that's him, or someone wearing his face – though I'm inclined to believe his socials.' She pulled out her phone.

Mallory examined the photos of Orson and the staged dollhouse murders. 'This suggests the pike wasn't a necessary component in the first murder,' Mallory said, pointing. 'The killer didn't bother putting blood in the dollhouse, also didn't leave a weapon in the doll's body, yet did with the two out in the courtyard. Maybe it's a weapon of opportunity? Or else the various methods mean something—'

The doorbell rang in the main house and Diana scrambled to the basement stairs, shutting the door firmly even as Cornelia crashed in behind her, trying to straighten up the kitchen as Diana walked as slowly as she possibly could to answer the door, only turning the handle when she heard the clear sounds of the basement door slamming again, Mallory and Cornelia's muffled voices fading.

Rachel and Jenna stood in the doorway, the dollhouse between them, a box under Rachel's arm. Jenna seemed to be struggling, Rachel bearing most of the weight. Diana ushered them in, the dollhouse worse-looking in the warm light of the kitchen. Fragments of wall fell as they set it on the table. Diana peered into the box that Rachel set down, little figures and furniture pieces carefully wrapped and stacked on top of each other.

'Oh, you took all the pieces out,' Diana said. She had assumed it would come to her as it had been found.

'Safer to transport it that way,' Jenna said. 'My solution had been to pack it full of bubble wrap, Rachel's was better.'

'I can't imagine how difficult this is going to be,' Rachel said, a look of disgust on her face that Diana could relate to. She hated seeing anyone's work destroyed the way the dollhouse had been, much less the work of someone with significantly more analogue tools than she had, and potentially much less magic, if any.

'It won't take me long, a few days at most.'

'I'd love to bottle your confidence,' Jenna said. Diana laughed, though she wasn't sure she meant to.

'What do you think whoever did this was after?'

'Job loss,' Jenna said. Rachel smiled at her, her lips perfectly painted and her hair smoother than it was that morning.

'Whatever they were after, I hope it was worth it. Lady Larkin's fortune would want to be worth something.'

'What do you mean?' Diana said sharply.

'What Alannah said yesterday, about Lady Larkin's fortune hidden in the dollhouse. A map, or jewellery. You were there, you had some guesses,' Rachel said.

'I heard that, she was telling me about it,' Jenna said.

Diana smiled uncertainly. This was happening a lot, this sense that there were conversations happening differently to how she was remembering them.

'We'll get out of your hair now,' Jenna added. She rested a hand on Rachel's shoulder. 'Come on, let's get you back.'

Diana seized her chance at the door. 'Does anyone know what's been going on? Two people turning up dead on set is so scary.'

'I would love to know too,' Jenna said.

'Well Orson had a lot of troubles, you know,' Rachel said. 'I shouldn't discuss him like this, it's not fair to his memory.' She drummed burgundy nails on the door frame.

'It's all very sad,' Jenna said. 'Both of them, but Orson especially. Big coincidence, I say, that there were two. Tragic. But Orson…'

'I've never seen it happen before, but I know it does. Lots of pressure in this industry. Pressure that never really goes away, to be something greater than you were yesterday. If you don't act on it, someone comes in and steals your spot, steals what was meant to be yours, and they'll never apologise for it. Ruthless. Just awful.'

Neither Rachel nor Jenna seemed to realise Orson Webb was still, apparently, alive and well.

'It seems to me like he's in a better place,' Diana said, subtly opening Orson's account on her phone where he was replying to the tens of comments his latest post was getting with *NO COMMENT*.

Rachel raised an eyebrow.

'Not an online sort of person?'

'What do you mean?'

She let a beat pass; they clearly hadn't seen.

'Lots of nice tributes pouring in,' Diana said, pocketing her phone. 'Anyway, did Orson say anything about that? Someone stealing something from him?'

'I didn't know him personally, but you know how rumours go,' Jenna said, stopping when Rachel silenced her with a look.

'Diana, I'm a professional. *We* are professionals. I can't discuss this,' Rachel said. 'I'm sorry, it's not right. He's… we weren't friends, but there's a certain level of discretion I try to employ. I'd like to think if you shared something with me, that you'd know I'd keep it safe.'

Jenna had been rummaging in her pockets, and pulled on a pair of gloves just like the ones Mallory often wore. She flexed her fingers, keeping her head down.

'Of course, it was just curiosity. Always the way when someone... dies, isn't it? Wanting to know what's happened.'

Rachel nodded, looking relieved. 'It's human, really. Thanks again, Diana.'

Diana opened the door to the basement to reveal Mallory and Cornelia standing right behind it.

'What did Sully say?'

Mallory walked into the kitchen, casting a wary glance at Cornelia, who groaned.

'They're having immense difficulty with the UML and the Ghoul Council has put their oar in, Hexana knows why. Dr Ray has seemingly managed to convince them that letting Apparents trample all over a potentially magical crime scene would be detrimental, and that there is something decidedly Occult happening here that impacts Occulture esteem. They seem to think pushing the Apparents will make us – Wrackton, but also Occulture as a whole – look bad, and weren't considering the possibility that we'd look just as bad if we didn't try in the first place.'

'Fair point. Mallory,' Diana said, raising an eyebrow at her. 'What are you doing?'

Mallory paused over the dollhouse with her hand halfway inside a latex glove. 'Securing the scene?'

Diana considered her for a minute. 'Well continue, detective. It is a crime scene after all.'

'I want to see if we can get anything that might indicate what's going on here – DNA, prints, fibres. Then perhaps you should take photographs?'

'This enthusiasm might be spurred on by the fact I ordered a borescope so we could all look at the tiny details up close,' Cornelia said dryly. 'Sully said once Dr Ray has the body, we can attend the autopsy this time.'

'There's still no word on the toxicology report,' Mallory said. 'Needing an outside lab to do our work is slowing us down.'

'And now you know why I decided pursuing a career with the Apparent police would've been a disaster – everything is so bloody slow.' Cornelia scowled.

Diana waited while Mallory got to grips with the borescope and swabbed and tested around the dollhouse, using small precise movements and the tiniest pair of tweezers she'd ever seen – which was saying something, given that Diana often worked with miniatures.

'There's some fibres here, a couple of hairs, but I think this is a cat hair. And honestly, given how old this is, that could be from a century-old cat. It'll give me something to catalogue, anyway, while we wait for the autopsy.'

Diana wanted to ask her if she was resting, if she was pushing herself too hard, but her ear was whining away and she was having trouble focusing.

'Look at this,' Mallory said suddenly. 'In the room with tiny Taylor, over the torn wallpaper. And here again, under the floor in the drawing room where Orson was found.' She used the tweezers to point out vertical lines carved deep into the walls with crossbars on the top and bottom, like a capital *I*. 'It seems at odds with the care that went into the rest of the Manor. I don't think these were added after the ransacking. They're too specific. I can see four so far, all the same length. Another here at the bottom of the main staircase, and one in what looks to be the youngest Larkin's bedroom upstairs... Could be some sort of symbol, or sigil?' She moved the borescope through the entrance to the courtyard, where the two figures with knives in their chests lay. She carefully picked glass away from the shattered dome. 'Look. The dome was covering this pattern. It's some sort of knot, I guess, over a circle... with half the circle filled in? It looks like it was drawn on with pen and ink. Cornelia, could you—'

Cornelia had anticipated the question and had the blueprints ready. 'There's no designation in the courtyard for what the dome is meant to be. I assume it's a well or something?'

'That's what I thought, too,' Diana said. 'So four lines, and a knot.'

'Five,' Mallory said, angling the borescope back. 'There's one more line on the courtyard door. Think this is the killer's signature?'

'Sounds about right,' Diana said.

'Go back to the knot for a second. I'm sick of symbols,' Cornelia said, but leaned in close to Diana to peer at it, the frames of her glasses touching Diana's cheek. Diana held her in a hug for a moment as Cornelia scribbled down an approximation of the symbol, which looked like a complex tangle of rope, but one Diana felt she'd seen before somewhere.

Mallory removed the borescope but stopped in the entrance hall. 'Interesting.' She shone a light in, where they could all see a hair-thin circle cut into the tile beneath the pillars.

'Odd,' Diana said. 'It feels vaguely Occult, but not in any way I can concretely name. The lines and the circle look like they were always there. Was this a thing that was done with Occult dollhouses, or can we conclude it's something special about this particular dollhouse?'

Cornelia heaved a deep sigh. 'I thought I was done with dusty Occult books, but alas.' She moved to the haphazard stack in the corner that was almost taller than her. 'We might think of getting bookcases at some point. Dibs not building them, though.'

'So I can go work on this with Taylor, then?'

Mallory pulled off her gloves and nodded. 'Make sure you ask more questions. Find out as much as you can.'

Diana and Taylor spent hours working, propped up by dinner Diana threw together with leftover rice from the fridge, and several rounds of coffee. Sitting either side of the dollhouse gave Diana enough distance to keep herself together, even as her stomach flipped at the proximity to Taylor.

'That's funny,' Diana said after a while, looking into the miniaturised version of the drawing room where Orson's body had been found. 'The entrance hall is completely backwards. Those doors lead out to the wrong rooms on either side.' She pulled up a picture of Cornelia's blueprint. 'The rest of the house is right, it's just this bit.'

'You and I have vastly differing ideas of what constitutes "funny",' Taylor said, holding a tiny picture frame. They were carefully removing every loose piece and using Mallory's tiny tweezers to pry up the remaining floorboards, laying them out so Diana could see which pieces needed to be replaced, and which could be repaired with epoxy.

Diana waved a hand to turn the house and Taylor squeaked. 'Sorry, I forget you can't do this.'

'I know. I remember, from Vancouver.'

Diana met Taylor's gaze, and lowered her eyes until she was peering at her through her eyelashes. She had not realised how intimate repairing a miniature could be until the only thing between her and Taylor was a table and a sense of propriety. And also Diana's morals, whatever they were supposed to be.

'That feels like a really long time ago,' Diana said softly. 'Now that I'm back home, magic is much more accessible to me in a way it isn't anywhere else. I don't have to consider the optics. I just do it.'

A text appeared on Taylor's phone screen, and Diana saw the name before Taylor could push it away.

'Alannah. She mentioned you were together before, how's that going?' Diana asked casually, pressing a floorboard into place.

'Fuckin' faeries really do have to tell the truth, don't they? We weren't what I'd call together, and we aren't now either. We weren't compatible as anything other than friends. That's my truth.'

Diana didn't know what to say to that, so gave Taylor a knowing smile that she hoped would make Taylor roll her eyes.

It did.

'She's busy playing Nancy Drew out there. Obsessed with Orson dying,' Taylor said. 'She's rethinking her assumption the first death was a prank – she thought I was part of it, can you believe it?'

Diana, in fact, could.

'She's gotten a list of who was signed in on set at the time of both bodies being discovered, and also checked for security clearance.'

Diana frowned a little. She didn't need another amateur detective muscling in on their case. 'What's she got?' she asked, curiosity getting the better of her. It was information she wanted too.

'She's asking what it's worth to me.'

'Tell her you'll take her on a date.'

Taylor raised an eyebrow.

'What? It works for me ninety-nine percent of the time.'

'Now I'm beginning to understand the latent success of your agency.'

'Shut up.'

'I've told her I'll owe her a favour if she tells me.' She snorted. 'And she clearly had this paragraph typed out already.'

She forwarded the message to Diana.

SET ONE: 'TAYLOR'

Rachel

Orson

Donny

Alannah
Fred
Sandi
Jenna
Xander
Hollis
Tate

SET TWO: ORSON

Jenna
Lyle
Fred
Sandi
Alannah
Taylor
Xander

'Who's Tate?' Diana said, examining the list. The name reminded her of something she couldn't quite remember.

'Nathan, the security guard,' Taylor explained. 'Alannah never calls him by his first name.'

'Ah.' She scanned the list again for names that appeared twice, thinking about Sandi and Jenna's inconsistent alibi and noticing other names that repeated.

'Xander,' Diana said. 'What's his story?'

'Nice fella, seems good craic to be around. I don't really know anything about him, bar what people say.'

'And what have they said?'

'Okay, Sherlock, relax would you,' Taylor said, laughing. 'I don't know. There's always some sort of shite going around. We're running on fumes and idle gossip, cause it's either that or rip each other's throats out. I heard someone say he'd had a thing with Jenna before, on another show or a film or something. But that was yonks ago.'

'And has there been anything else about him, about the current crew?'

'What are you getting at, Diana?'

'I thought I saw something last night. Xander and Fred.'

'*Fred?*'

It was almost easy for Diana to pretend she was only trusting Taylor with information to get more information out of her, and not because she genuinely wanted to hear what Taylor had to say.

'I saw… I don't know. It was right before Hollis and Orson had that argument. Fred had his back to the wall and Xander was in front of him. He pulled away from Fred, like he'd been caught.'

'If that's the case, this is the first I'm hearing of it. And if they were being that obvious, I'm surprised it took this long for anyone to see.'

Diana nodded, her mind already moving on to the possible motives either Fred or Xander could have for staging one death, let alone two. A secret relationship didn't feel like enough, unless there was significantly more to it. She scanned the list of names again.

'Who the fuck's Lyle?'

'The other security guard? I saw you talking to him earlier, you met him,' Taylor said.

'Yeah, but *who* is he?'

'He used to be on nights, he's taken over the day shift I think. I only met him once before.'

'What about Baker?' Diana said suddenly, who *shouldn't* be on the list jumping out at her.

'Who?'

'The DP who left, Donny Baker? Nobody seems to know where he went or knows anything about him apart from… photographing,' Diana said, making a mental note to look up a better way of describing the job. 'He hadn't been seen in thirty-six hours after you— *the body* was discovered, but why would he turn up to work and then leave?'

'Maybe he'd just had enough. Signed in and thought, *nah*, and left again. If I didn't want a permanent job if this thing gets picked up, I'd be right there with him. I don't think him leaving is a big deal, though.'

'Ask Alannah if anyone commented on it.'

'She says Orson told her he was gone. Again, I ask why?'

'Call it a hunch.'

Taylor smiled at her. 'You're the investigator, not me.'

SIXTEEN

Two days to the Spring Equinox ball

'You were up late,' Cornelia said, pulling her shoes on at the top of the basement stairs. Diana had been up for at least an hour, working on her Larkin Studios diorama and trying to make sense of why the killer would pose the figures, but also ransack the dollhouse. Why the killer would warn of more potential murders to come, or why the killer would murder 'Taylor' and 'Orson' in the first place. Why nobody on set seemed to be able to give her a straight answer on anything.

Mallory waited for Cornelia to move, fighting off a yawn. 'I tried doing a listening spell, but couldn't really hear. Did Taylor have anything interesting to say?'

Diana had driven Taylor back to the hotel she was staying in sometime after midnight. She had put music on loud in the car and left the windows open, trying anything she could to distract herself from how close they were in the car, Taylor's gentle floral perfume – that might not even be perfume, but just the way she smelled – threatening her sensibilities.

This was a murder investigation. Diana could not afford to make mistakes.

This time.

'I could hear fine before I went to bed,' Mallory said to Cornelia, yawning again. 'But you kept talking as they were talking, and I missed bits.'

Instead of fighting her, as she would've if it was Diana, Cornelia dipped her head as though to avoid Mallory seeing her smiling.

'Here's the situation: I got a list of people who were on set from Alannah, who is playing detective and that might be a future concern, but she established that security have lists of who's signed in on set at any time. If we put it with Mallory's call sheet from Sandi, we can see the overlaps are interesting.'

'This is what I've been trying to focus on,' Mallory said. 'The inconsistencies. Taylor is alive, Orson seems to be alive and well, but we've two bodies that tell a different story. I can't stop thinking about the Baker aspect: where is he? So much doesn't add up, and it doesn't help that everyone has a different version of events. Even taking into account the fact that Alannah is faerie and can't lie, she doesn't actually *know* what happened.'

Cornelia got to work writing the names from Alannah's list on the whiteboard while Mallory folded herself neatly into a chair. She looked tired, and when she caught Diana's gaze she smiled. 'I'm going for a nap right after this, don't worry.'

'Hey, who the fuck's Lyle?' Cornelia asked as she finished writing.

'I also had this question. He's security. His name rings a bell too, I can't put my finger on it.' Diana had played it out over and over, a sense of having heard his name before somewhere, and recently, on the tip of her tongue. 'He's Occult, that much I know – demon. I've only met him once, yesterday, when he was poorly managing the crowd at Oakpass Manor.'

'Then you need to meet him again and impress upon him the importance of telling you everything he knows,' Cornelia said. 'Easy.'

'There's a very good chance production will be shut down indefinitely while they try to process what happened,' Diana said. 'But I can try. Rachel said to plan to be there for call time tomorrow, when Hollis is due back. I can't see him letting them stop, especially as he was going to continue when Orson quit.'

'What if that's the killer's goal? To get production shut down? It would make sense if it was Baker with a grudge… but everyone else seems to want – or need – the work,' Mallory said. 'I'm still really struggling with *why* someone would do this. I can't see the link. If we hadn't seen the posts on his socials, we'd think Orson was dead. The fact that nobody else seems to realise he's alive is even weirder. Folk were meant to think Taylor was dead, except she wasn't gone long enough for that to be the case. What's the point of it all? Why are the murders so different?'

'Maybe it's something interpersonal, like you said – a grudge of some sort,' Cornelia said.

Diana clicked her fingers at her, an idea popping into her head. 'I saw Xander and Fred together, and I think they were kissing, or about to kiss. Taylor raised an interesting point – there were rumours Jenna had a thing with Xander years ago. Could jealousy be a big enough motive?'

'Coupled with the fact Jenna insists Sandi was with her and she wasn't anywhere near the scene, I'd say that's something to wonder about,' Mallory said. 'Except I don't understand how those two things relate to pretending Taylor was dead, and presumably pretending Orson is dead. What's the goal?'

'Ruining the show, or trying to find something in Larkin Studios or Oakpass Manor, are the only reasonable goals I can think of,' Cornelia said, yawning again.

'Ruining the show for a specific individual is possible – say if Jenna did want revenge on Xander, getting production shut down when he's got such a big part would be one way to go about it. It just seems... unlikely,' Mallory said. 'My gut, and the staging in the dollhouse, tells me that it's about Oakpass Manor.'

'So maybe that's what the killer was doing – looking in the dollhouse for Lady Larkin's long lost treasure?' Diana said. In her mind she saw herself shrinking an object and hiding it in a diorama, and blinked it away. That was something for another time.

'It's a dollhouse,' Mallory said. 'Who hides things in dollhouses?'

'That feels very you-coded,' Cornelia said, and Diana had a split-second of wondering if Cornelia knew, then brushed it aside. She was not Mallory. She could hide her secrets well, and sometimes the best way to do that was in plain sight.

'If I was going to hide something, it would certainly be in miniature.'

'Say someone was looking for... something,' Mallory cast around. 'Something small or worthwhile, and the goal was to get to the dollhouse so they could find its real-life counterpart in Oakpass Manor but... murder had to happen first? For some reason?'

It made even less sense than the Whistler case, and Diana hated it. She did not like feeling out of control. The best way to get through a case was to be a step ahead of the killer, but she had a lot of pieces and no order to place them in.

'This is starting to feel like Murder Case Madlibs,' Cornelia said. 'A game I do not really want to play.'

'It could be fun, though! The killer is in the entrance hall of the former vampire stronghold, with the... mysterious Occult object,' Mallory tried, then wrinkled her nose. 'Did we get anywhere with the symbol?'

'It's a Celtic knot,' Cornelia said.

'Wow,' Diana said. 'I expect you think I'm being sarcastic, but I'm genuinely impressed.'

'It's supposed to symbolise knotted roots of an oak tree.'

'Thematically appropriate. What's it mean?'

'That I'm still working out.' Cornelia grinned.

'We can come back to that,' Mallory said. 'Unidentified Occult Object in Larkin Studios or Oakpass Manor might be a thread to follow, though. Have there been any updates on Orson, actually?'

Cornelia pulled out her phone. 'No news stories anywhere, just old pieces about him maybe being connected to a potential *Undead Complex* TV show. He hasn't posted again, but— Aha! A fan-run *Undead Complex* account has tagged a sneaky photo of him from yesterday, and it looks like the same place he posted from on his own account.' She showed Diana, who agreed it did look like the same place.

'Unless it's a doppelgänger...' Mallory trailed off as the nauseating concept hit Diana full-force.

'That's... what if the bodies are the 'real' versions of the living folk, and the living folk are imposters? Like for real doppelgängers, or changelings?' Though Diana wanted to think she'd know if Taylor wasn't Taylor.

'This is going to sound strange, but I asked Observer Johnson about this the other day,' Mallory said. 'If he'd know if someone wasn't who they said they were. He said that, like all trolls, if he'd met the person at least once, he'd know them again to see, and he'd also know if they were not who they said they were.'

'And Orson is a troll,' Cornelia said. 'Who presumably possesses the same talent.'

They exchanged glances. 'Then the question is, did he see "Taylor's" body? Did he know it wasn't her?' Mallory bit her lip thoughtfully. 'Langdon hasn't come back to me yet on whether his uncles know Orson, but hopefully we'll get something there.'

'That's a lot of stuff pending,' Diana said, pushing down the idea that the Taylor she had been spending time with was not hers at all. Not that Taylor was hers to begin with. 'We're waiting on toxicology reports, an autopsy that may or may not be happening, the restarting of proceedings on set. Plenty of folk to talk to, but no real evidence of anything. What do we do now?'

'I think we call Felix,' Mallory said unexpectedly. 'They're a big fan of the comics, maybe there's something in them that would help us? You said Hollis cemented them in real lore, so it's as good a place to look as any.'

Diana texted Felix asking them if they could come now, just as there was a rustling at the back of the lab. The witchlights were out, and Diana was the first one on her feet, peering into the darkness.

'Theodore?' she called.

There was more rustling, and Diana took a step closer.

'Oh for the love of Blair.' Diana waved a hand. The witchlights flared on, revealing Kingston. He blinked at her, a conical flask and a Bunsen burner in his hands.

'What the fuck? Cornelia!'

'I was about to ask if you had any salicylic acid, I've a banging headache,' Kingston mumbled, holding an arm up against the lights.

'Oh hey, Kingston, I didn't know you were up,' Cornelia said, smiling as she saw him. Mallory stayed where she was, curled in a ball on the sofa. 'What are you rummaging around Mallory's lab for?'

'I was going to try make some aspirin,' he said vaguely. 'Headache, you know.'

'Go to a *shop*,' Diana said. 'Or *ask* someone.'

'Oh yeah,' Kingston said. 'Do you have any aspirin? Or painkillers of any sort?'

Mallory held up a packet of something and he waltzed into the research room, bowing as he took them from her. He swallowed two dry, waving away Mallory's horrified offering of a bottle of water.

'What's he still doing here?' Diana hissed. She would've thought he had broken in if Cornelia hadn't responded to him like he was an object she'd recently mislaid and recovered, all without realising it was missing in the first place.

'We've got room,' Cornelia hissed back. She looked up as Kingston came back to the lab. 'Are you hungry?'

'What's stopping Shit King from going home?' Diana knew she was being a little callous, but she didn't care. There was something suspicious about him; not the vampire part, not the boy part, but the timing of his arrival. Like he was wearing Beckett's face. The changeling hypothesis was making her skin itch uncomfortably.

'Stop it.'

'I'll hex you,' Diana muttered, the spell already on the tip of her tongue. 'You *and* Shit King.'

Cornelia rounded on her. 'He's staying, don't call him that, I'm ordering food now. For once, just shut up, Diana.'

Diana pursed her lips. Sometimes she wished she could forget that murders ever existed.

The food arrived with Felix. They bounced into the room and hugged Mallory first – something Diana noticed they'd made an effort to do every time they'd seen Mallory since the Whistler case. They were wearing a hot-pink boiler suit and a hat that bashed the side of Mallory's face, but she didn't seem to mind. Felix kissed Diana's cheek, no doubt leaving a shimmery red print behind, and pressed their face into Cornelia's hair, before turning to Kingston, who had settled on the floor of the research room and had not moved in the time it took Felix to do the rounds.

'Hey,' Felix said, looking at him properly for the first time. 'What the fuck?'

'We know,' Diana said wearily.

'This is Kingston, he's Beckett's cousin,' Mallory said.

'They are practically indistinguishable,' Diana said.

Felix's eyes narrowed. 'And…'

'And he's here because he misses Beckett. He was… indisposed, before now, so learned he'd died late,' Cornelia said, her tone unusually soothing.

'Oh.'

'I heard you lost someone too, in the same case. May he live forever in the Fair Kingdom,' Kingston said quietly.

Something on Felix's face softened, but only slightly. 'Thanks. Sorry about Beckett. Diana, Mallory, what are we doing?'

'I'm here too, you know,' Cornelia said.

'Yes, but you're rarely in the driving seat of these things,' Felix said, earning a sharp shove from Cornelia that almost knocked them off their cow-print creepers.

'We need you to tell us about *Undead Complex*,' Mallory said. 'We're working a case, and we're at the information-gathering stage of things. In particular' – she held up a hand before Felix could launch into anything – 'we want to know if there's anything in the comics about changelings, or doppelgängers.'

'Right.' Felix snuck another glance at Kingston. 'It doesn't really come up in the way you'd expect. Let me rewind a second, just make sure you know this – Apparents think that changelings are faeries swapping out an Apparent baby for an Occult baby, like a cuckoo situation, with the goal being to take the Apparent baby to the Fair Kingdom, allowing the Apparents to raise the faerie baby as their own. It makes for an excellent story, but doesn't quite work in reality. For one thing, faeries aren't that interested in Apparents, so I'm not sure of the purpose of the whole thing. Like, we'd definitely kill the Apparent child and leave the cuckoo in place, if there was something to gain from that.'

Diana tried not to look aghast, because what they were saying made sense. Even still, she was reminded of the ruthlessness all of Occulture was capable of, no matter how much it tried to insulate itself with rules and red tape.

'But in reality, it's about glamour magic. The real concept of changelings is probably folklore from the Vampire Wars – it's deeper, older magic, about trading souls to make something new. The comics draw on a lot of supposed Occult history – Ruthless Monroe, the necromancer queen, is basically meant to be Morrigan, as in the mother of Occulture, and anyone who worked under her were supposed to be daughters, like a pseudo-Ternion, I guess. Which tracks with Occulture teachings on the Vampire Wars and the rise of the Ternion in saving us all.'

Diana shivered; the Whistler case had made her never want to hear about the Ternion again.

'To be honest, I was always impressed that an Apparent got any details about Occulture even sort of correct. *Undead Complex* is mostly about the establishment of power of a world within a world, which is very meta when you think about Occulture and the Apparent world, but instead of witch goddesses, it's necromancers and zombies. My understanding of the glamour-magic aspect of the Vampire Wars is vague. In the comics it's about trading a reconstructed soul for a piece of the metaphorical chess board the necromancers are working across.'

'Told you there was chess involved. Keepers, or something?' Cornelia said triumphantly.

'Gatekeepers, yeah.'

'So changelings could never just have someone else's face?' Mallory confirmed.

'No, that would take something seriously fucked up.'

'Like Jacob's ring,' Cornelia said softly.

'It's Blair's ring, really,' Diana said airily.

'And they never found it,' Mallory said slowly.

They didn't, but Diana did.

She'd woken up with it on her bedside table in the hospital, a vague flash of it bouncing towards her as Jacob's body was torn asunder by the souls of his vengeful victims, and holding onto it for dear life, like it could keep her from dying where she lay. And she had meant to tell the others, but as the days passed and Jacob's body wasn't found and the tribunals and Theodore and everything that had gone on, Diana had never found a good time to mention it. It was safe in her diorama; she checked it every morning before she did anything else.

'The Undead Complex,' Kingston said. 'That's what vampires call it.'

Everyone's head whipped around to look at him. Diana's eyes narrowed; she did not like the idea of him sitting there and listening to them, and liked even less that he knew what Felix was on about.

'Did it not occur to you to mention this earlier, Shit King?' Diana asked.

Felix looked perplexed. Diana made fists until Kingston held his hands up. Felix's grin was back in an instant.

'We've mentioned this show in front of you repeatedly. What is the Undead Complex?'

'It has a few names,' Kingston said. 'The King Me Principle – that's nothing to do with me, I swear.' He held up a KING fist. 'It's also called the Undead Principle, but I've heard it called the Undead Complex more than a few times. In vampire folklore, it's a very old form of magic that can only be produced by... let's see...' He trailed off, deep in thought. Diana considered hexing him into moving faster. 'Occultures working in agreement. Maybe a demon involved too, or a faerie. I'm not sure. But there's more than just vampires. It was what made Oakpass Manor such a formidable stronghold.'

'How do you know it's formidable?' Felix had leaned back against a desk, giving Kingston their full attention.

'Because it's still standing,' Kingston said evenly.

'You still haven't explained what it is,' Diana said, impatience giving the words bite.

'It's an exchange of souls. A pure sacrifice, because the soul was claimed from death, with no other magic performed directly on the body before it was offered up. Changelings, in the sense that you are making an exchange, converting something from one form to another.'

'Ah, the law of thermodynamics, once again rearing its confusing head,' Cornelia said.

'Is it like ghosts?' Mallory frowned.

'Or necromancy?' Felix asked, clearly enjoying himself.

'How do I put this. Gotta be careful,' Kingston muttered, before returning to regular speaking volume. 'It's not ghosts. It's not even strictly bringing anyone back from the dead, but

I suppose it could be considered necromancy, yes. The story goes that whoever was leading the battle at Oakpass – if I'm not wrong, it was the Battle of Equinox, but don't quote me on that.'

As if Diana was going to quote him anywhere.

'Spring Equinox, like that half-moon you have there,' he said, nodding to the murder board. 'Or quarter-moon, if you'd rather be technical about it.'

'What, sorry?'

'The circle with half of it shaded in, under the Dara knot – that's what the squiggly rope drawing is, I think. But that quarter-moon is used to signify Spring Equinox, if I'm not mistaken. A quarter-moon with the opposite side filled in would be for autumn.'

'Saves me a job,' Cornelia said, a quick web search confirming he was right. 'And I've discovered that knot is all over the Oakpass Manor website. It's the official seal, instead of a Larkin family crest.'

It made sense, but Diana did not want to tell Kingston that.

'When's the next Equinox again?' Mallory asked.

'Saturday,' Diana said mechanically. 'The day of the ball.'

The ball at Oakpass Manor, when hundreds of Occult folk would be packed into the ballroom.

'That's… that's the deadline, isn't it?' Mallory said slowly. 'Equinox. Whatever the killer is doing, they're going to finish it at Equinox.'

Diana had the sense she was falling. Three more tiny bodies in the dollhouse. Five lines. An Equinox symbol. All suggestions they were up against a killer with a plan.

'Let's not jump ahead,' Diana said calmly. 'We can't make decisions based on what a dollhouse suggests to us. This could all still be something to do with *Undead Complex*.'

'Keep going,' Cornelia said to Kingston, unusually still. 'We can have a breakdown about our potential murder deadline in a few minutes.'

'There was a moment, in the story, where the leaders were losing, and they chose to initiate a back-up plan,' Kingston continued. 'Take a soul on the brink of death, and create a weapon from it. Like reclaiming a sacrificed player in a game—'

'King me,' Mallory said. 'In checkers. If you get a piece across the board, you get a lost piece back to stack on top.' At everyone's baffled look, she shrugged. 'Felix said something about chess boards a few minutes ago, it wasn't a big logical leap.'

'YES,' Kingston said, pointing at her. 'YES. Exactly. Like checkers. It's a soul of the fallen – someone on the brink of death – combined with a fallen soul – someone who has died already. I don't think sacrificing any of their own would've done it, this was a losing strategy. So this was a move, so to speak. The Undead Complex became a way to form the gatekeepers.'

'And what are they?' Diana prompted.

'Haven't a clue,' Kingston said cheerfully. 'The end of the story is that the gatekeepers were the downfall of the vampires in the Wars. I assume not telling us is a way of warding against any vampires trying to repeat history. Vampires live long, long lives, but the gatekeepers were supposed to signify living forever – we call it unlikely immortality, or *non versimilis immortalis*, if you want what I am sure is the terrible Latin translation. We're supposed to reject that idea, that living forever is something to want. It's a cautionary tale.'

'So this is really what they teach you?' Diana's own lack of knowledge on Occulture burned in her chest, like it wanted her to feel ashamed.

'How do we not know about this?' Cornelia demanded.

'Because they don't want you to.' Kingston clasped his hands. 'We say it's part of our secret teachings. But the truth is more that it isn't recorded in any written history, because someone – or several someones – ultimately wants to hide it. And I'm not about that. I think, for what it's worth, there is some truth to the idea of the vampire gatekeepers, or of some form of necromancy, and that it possibly really did happen at Oakpass Manor. I mean, why wouldn't there be? There's implausible magic everywhere else, why wouldn't this be real and true?'

He did not look triumphant, or anything Diana would expect from a relative of Beckett who had just made a really good point and was damn proud of it.

'You said something the other night,' Diana remembered, cutting through the haze of that evening. She really had not meant to drink as much as she had. 'Something about an apple cult?'

'Do you mean Appoccult?' Felix cut in, looking glad to have something useful to say.

'Yeah, the Appoccult Society,' Kingston said.

'That was the Larkins' secret society,' Felix said. 'Hollis used it as a sort of symbolism in the comics, it's why Oakpass is so important as the inspiration of the necromancer castle, and why apples are a recurring theme.'

'Oh! There's a certificate of membership to the Appoccult Society in the attic somewhere, Great-Grandad Broadwick was a member,' Cornelia said, slapping her leg. 'It was like a weird secret society! I found it years ago and thought it sounded pathetic.'

'But having yearly balls wasn't?' Diana asked.

Cornelia ignored her. 'Okay, so what does the Appoccult Society have to do with the price of sliced bread?'

'I bet you don't know the price of sliced bread,' Diana said, hoping nobody would ask her either. She looked to a frowning Mallory, where she could see cogs visibly turning. Diana felt reassured that at least one of them was making some sense of this information.

'Does anyone else think it's kind of strange that every time we have questions around the Vampire Wars, it's hard to ask them?' Mallory asked. 'Like last year when we were working on the Whistler case, we basically discovered we knew nothing about how they…' Diana had always thought Mallory trailing off was brain fog, but maybe not. 'But now, every time I want to ask about it, I…' Mallory trailed off again.

'That would explain *so* much about inter-Occulture relations.' Kingston nodded to himself, as though he was internally analysing unknowable data and enjoying the results.

'Is anyone going to make any sense, please?' Diana said, unable to take this. She wanted to ask questions but they were leaving her rapidly. She'd already forgotten most of what Kingston had told them, the words slipping away from her like a dream.

'I think there's something at play here. I've suspected it for a while, but this confirms it.'

'Confirms *what*?' Cornelia demanded. 'This is intellectual edging and I won't stand for it.'

Kingston shot her an amused look. 'It's really simple. Perfectly simple, really.'

Diana fought the urge to murder him. She had met two members of Kingston's family and had wished death upon both of them. She did not feel sorry for wanting Beckett to come back just so she could kill him again.

'Say it. Before I make you,' Felix said.

'It's magic.'

'Well no shit.' Diana scowled, thoroughly unimpressed by how much talking time they gave Kingston boys in this house.

'No, it's very specifically magic. Magic stopping you from asking questions.'

'Sorry,' Mallory said, pressing her hands to her face. 'Asking questions *about what*?'

Kingston pointed triumphantly at her. 'See? And I bet any time that happened you thought it was her memory, or her not paying attention.'

'Cornelia's the one most likely to not pay attention,' Diana said. 'But yes, there was an element of assuming that her working memory was affected.'

Even as she said this, her mind started churning up the words she was going to say next, a subconscious equivalent of walking through a doorway and forgetting why you were in the room in the first place.

'I'll have you know I have superior memory when it comes to bizarre and useless facts, genera and entomological care. It's the everyday things that get lost in the sauce,' Cornelia said.

Mallory looked helplessly at Diana, who couldn't move to reassure her, because she was also starting to get lost.

'You don't know anything about the Vampire Wars because you're not supposed to.' Kingston's voice sounded very far away.

'How do… how do you know?' Diana managed to struggle out, already not knowing what it was that Kingston knew that she didn't.

'That's also simple,' Kingston said. 'I've been micro-dosing blood for months.'

SEVENTEEN

'Sorry. I mean, I'm not sorry. But what?' Diana said, the first to recover among the four of them. Felix's face had twisted into a shape that Diana did not recognise, something beyond her comprehensions of rage or horror.

'I'm among friends, I think, so I don't mind explaining. I've been micro-dosing blood for about five months or so, give or take.'

'What exactly does micro-dosing mean?' Felix asked through gritted teeth. Even Cornelia had the sense to look mildly horrified.

'A precise number of drops of blood titrated into a solvent and consumed on an empty stomach every morning.'

'So you drop blood into a glass of water and drink it?' Mallory translated.

Kingston nodded, a smile crossing his lips. 'She gets it. Although sometimes I forgo the solvent.'

'But why?' Cornelia blurted. 'Beckett said no blood was hurting him – that it hurt all vampires in one way or another – and that you were researching it, but…'

She had not told him the full extent of the disaster of the last time she'd seen Beckett alive, then. Diana could not imagine how one would even make that conversation go.

'I micro-dose, I gain clarity.'

Diana raised an eyebrow. She'd been in enough clubs and dive bars around art students and musicians to have heard someone say that more times than she cared to remember.

'It's like having another eye open. I learn something new every time I take it. It feels like my vision becomes sharper, more focused, but it's my brain, my knowledge. Have you ever just… known something to be true?'

Diana, who relied on her sense of instinct an awful lot, did. She knew Cornelia as the monarch of hunches, however irrational they might seem. It was harder to convince Mallory of the power of instinct, even though hers had guided her well.

In short, they all knew what it was like, so they nodded in unison.

With the exception of Felix, who said, 'Not really. If you mean know something because I learned it, yes. If you mean know something because of something outside of myself, no.'

And because they were faerie, they spoke the truth.

'Right. Well. Imagine if you did know things. A constant dawning of realisations, the world unfolding before your eyes morning by morning. The movement of things, the meaning of things, the connections all piecing together in a kaleidoscope.'

Diana's eyebrows lifted higher. She'd heard this before too.

'I know, I know, you've heard this before. Believe me, so have I. You haven't comforted someone through a twelve-hour bad trip as they're telling you the secrets of the universe and come out not being slightly cynical about everything you've ever learned. But this is the real deal. This is magic. This is *vampire* magic. Because that knowledge doesn't fade as long as you keep micro-dosing.'

Mallory raised a hand suddenly, punching the air. 'Yes! That's something I've been trying to wonder for months now, if not years – what *is* vampire magic? What did vampires give up when they stopped drinking blood?'

'We gave up clarity. We gave up knowledge. Think about it – witches simply are magic, in the way someone is simply tall. Like you, Felix,' Kingston said, not looking at them. 'Faeries have glamour magic and they must speak the truth. Trolls never forget a face and have superior memories. Demons are great manipulators. What are vampires? What *were* vampires? You look at me and you see something dangerous, because someone told you that was so. I look at me now and I see potential. The potential to increase knowledge. To understand. To connect the dots, to keep our long history alive by knowing it, by learning it, by living it out loud, even if the rest of Occulture can't hear it. And the more blood I take, the more I understand – my ancestors didn't know what they were giving up when they signed the Covenant, but I can't understand why. Something unknowable happened at the end of the Vampire Wars.'

'And there must be a reason,' Mallory said, beating Diana to it. Diana was a little relieved they were on the same page, although she was simultaneously not convinced by his speech.

'So the answer is in the blood. A little bit at a time, giving me a full twenty-four hours each time to digest what I've learned. I do that every day for the rest of my life, I can explain anything to anyone. I can help anyone understand anything about themselves.

Incidentally, Cornelia, you might want to consider an ADHD assessment at some point? I think that's going to answer a lot of your questions you have about yourself.'

Diana bit back a grin as Cornelia's face fell – not in upset or disappointment, but with the dawning of clarity.

'All of you, really, might consider that you are not of a neurotypical persuasion.' He didn't wait for reactions, even as Diana paused to let that sink in, then put that notion away in a compartment for another time. 'But those kinds of things? I just know. Whether that's looking at patterns, or it's listening, I'm not sure, but the blood is absolutely facilitating it. You're detectives,' he said, waving a hand. 'You know about connecting dots. Imagine doing that on a grander scale.'

Diana had always privately thought that's what Mallory was doing every time she worked on a case, and was not sure there was a grander scale to reach in doing so.

'Three drops,' he said, tapping his forehead. 'No more, no less.'

'What kind of blood?' Felix asked.

'Apparent. Willingly parted with, before anyone raises any concerns. We get vials from a blood bank.'

'Blood that people need,' Diana started. The idea felt so wrong to her, life-saving blood being used in a way that was not intended.

'Are vampires not people?' He said it lightly.

That stopped her. She felt a vague, wholly unfamiliar flush of shame at her assumption. It wasn't like those who gave blood to a bank could expressly request that it not be used on someone who did not morally align with their values – part of it was the anonymity, and the hope that the blood you gave would save a life. Who owned that life was irrelevant to the proceedings, as was what constituted saving it.

'A single ten millilitre vial lasts me over a month, if I do it properly.'

Diana was saved from having to construct a diplomatic response by her phone ringing. Saved by the bell, if the bell was more of a quiet vibration.

'It's Dr Ray,' she said, answering. Mallory and Cornelia stood to gather themselves, anticipating the inevitable invitation to the autopsy.

'Get over here,' Dr Ray said abruptly. 'The three of you. You're not going to believe this. I'm not sure I do.'

Dr Ray met them at the door of the mortuary, which was the first red flag for Diana. Granted, the first red flag was probably the phone call, but this was certainly a concrete indicator that something was wrong. Dr Ray's face was inscrutable.

'Follow me,' she said, leading them down the corridor, moving past her usual autopsy room and into Room Three.

Diana knew what the metal containers on the wall held, but she didn't want to think about it, focusing instead on Cornelia's grim determination to not appear frightened, and Mallory's apparent determination to not look overly interested at being in a room where the walls were full of corpses.

Mallory's fascination with death confused and enchanted Diana, and she hoped her friend would never change.

She also hoped that she'd never need to set foot in this mortuary again.

'Is now an appropriate time to ask what's going on?' Cornelia said.

'Yes.' Dr Ray opened one of the cupboards and pulled out a tray. At least, Diana thought it was called a tray. She was not sure what else you'd call the metal slab that contained a body. The body of—

'That's the director of photography!' Diana stepped forward, his face fresh in her memory from his staff ID. 'Donny Baker, he's been missing since the day Taylor's body was found.'

And while they were right to question his whereabouts, he was, evidently, not the killer.

Baker was waxy and sunken, lividity spreading across his chest, lines from where an autopsy had already been completed and he had been sewn up evident, which annoyed Diana but not enough to actually say it to Dr Ray. There was a large stab wound in his chest that, to Diana's untrained eye, looked exactly the same as the one in fake-Taylor's. A faint scent of something turned Diana's stomach and she bit her cheek, forcing herself to take shallow breaths.

'It explains why you haven't been able to find him, I guess,' Cornelia said.

'Please don't create a correlation between his death and his missing-ness until we know more,' Mallory said. 'This is how we start barking up the wrong murder tree.'

'Unfortunately, Cornelia is correct,' Dr Ray said. 'Something I hoped to never have to concede. He's been missing for precisely as long as you've suggested, and I believe it's because he's been dead this whole time. Notice anything about the body?'

'Stab wound,' Mallory said. 'It's the same shape and size as the one on fake-Taylor's body, or as close an approximation as I could make without measurements.'

'Again, correct. That would be because this *is* fake-Taylor's body.'

A cold crawl descended on Diana, starting at her scalp and rocketing down her body.

'Oh, fuck,' Cornelia said, summing it up nicely.

'So it *is* a magical murder,' Diana said.

Mallory shot her an alarmed look. 'Dr Ray, can you tell us when you made this discovery? Namely, how do you know this is definitely the original body?'

'Because I watched it happen. There was an unusual smell – I can't place it, but trust me when I say I've smelled many things in my time here, and this was unusual.'

'How unusual?'

'It was pleasant.'

That would definitely fall under the remit of unusual.

'Can you describe it? Woody, floral or… one of the others?'

Dr Ray shot Cornelia a glare. 'If you think I have time to sit around and figure out scent notes when bodies are melting into other bodies, you have another thing coming. But I would definitely say it was somewhat floral, bordering on fruity, and warm.'

'Thanking you,' Cornelia said, typing into her notes app.

'And when I removed the body to see, Taylor… was in the process of fading away to be replaced with this man.'

'Is it possible to verify…?'

'We matched fingerprints, his were already in the system – travel related, not crime – and you doubly confirmed his identity when you walked in the door.' Dr Ray exhaled. 'In my professional opinion, there was magical interference. The print samples I kept are gone – or rather, denatured. Fake-Taylor's body had not begun the decomposition process at all, whereas this is more like it, for the time that has passed.'

'Then the question is, who'd kill Donny Baker, and then cover it up by pretending it was Taylor?' Mallory asked, though not of anyone in particular.

'And how does that relate to Equinox?' Cornelia asked.

Dr Ray looked between them. 'Either say nothing, or spell it out. I'm a pathologist, not a detective.'

Diana gave her the rundown on the dollhouse, the figurines, and the belief there were going to be more deaths, and soon.

Dr Ray closed her eyes. 'It would be needlessly selfish of me to express despair at the notion I could be back in here working on more autopsies before the week is out, so I will not. I can let Sully know the situation so she's at least prepared to go back to the UML.'

'Though maybe with production shut down for now, the killer won't manage to kill again?' Diana said hopefully.

'And then we all lived happily ever after, and I was never required to look at another corpse,' Dr Ray said dryly.

She had a point.

'Surely having reasonable belief that the killer is intending to kill again is enough evidence for the UML to decide this is an Occult issue? Especially given… whatever just happened with the body?'

'Mallory, your earnestness is lovely, but it has no place here. They do not care. If anything, the threat of more murders makes everything worse, because they will view it as Sully and I essentially permitting a killer to run rampant, besmirching the good standing of Occulture. And if I've learned anything in my five-month tenure as Night Mayor, it's that literally nothing under the sun is as pressing or important as the good standing of Occulture.'

Diana bit her lip, holding back the desire to simply scream as loudly as she could. If this was a fraction of the sort of nonsense Theodore had had to deal with every day since he'd died, he'd probably earned the right to go a little bit weird.

'Can I try the beetles again?' Cornelia asked, breaking the uncomfortable silence that had descended.

'Be my guest,' Dr Ray said. 'You can't make things worse, certainly.'

Cornelia let three beetles out onto Donny Baker's torso for good measure – 'Two of these are from Selene's colony, so they should react properly' – but they responded the same way they had before: a brief flash of green, then resolutely orange.

'Have you started on the autopsy of Orson Webb yet?' Cornelia asked, scooping them back into their boxes.

'I was not aware I was blessed with four arms and a number of heads. Goddess knows I've been assuming otherwise, given I have two full-time jobs with opposing hours of operation. But no, Cornelia. No I have not.'

Cornelia grinned. 'You'd be the first monstrous Night Mayor to not be an actual monster.'

'I need to go home, I need to eat some lunch, I need to sleep for three hours and four minutes precisely, then I need to get up and do the autopsy, then continue fighting with the UML.

I will have details on Orson Webb as soon as I can. Thank Blair nobody has been putting pressure on me to release these bodies to the families. I can't imagine how devastating it would be to believe your loved one was gone.'

'Ah. Slight problem with that,' Diana said. 'Not the releasing bodies part, but the Orson part – we're not entirely convinced that the body you have is Orson Webb, seeing as Orson Webb is alive and well and on a beach on the other side of the world.'

'You don't half find the strange ones, don't you? Any bright ideas who Orson Webb might be? Elisabella in a wig, this time?'

'No idea. Nobody else is missing, so your guess is as good as mine. Though I think my guess would've been a little more inventive,' Diana said.

'Thank you so much, Dr Ray,' Mallory said, cutting Dr Ray's undoubtedly biting response off. 'I appreciate you getting us out here to see this.'

Mallory opened the door and herded Diana and Cornelia out, pausing when they emerged into daylight. 'I'm too sore to walk home, I'm calling a taxi. And when we're home, we're not leaving until we get somewhere on this.'

Diana placed the last paper suspect into the Larkin Studios diorama, drumming her fingers on the table while Cornelia finished redrawing the murder boards. Mallory had come in and gone straight up to bed, promising to come back down within the hour. Diana hoped she'd take two.

Cornelia stepped back and dropped her marker emphatically. 'Ta da.'

Donny Baker took pride of place in the centre, a question over why the killer would disguise the DP as a propmaker. EQUINOX was written in huge letters to the right of that, and their scene photos were plastered around the board, along with the names of everyone who had access to set. BAKER and ALANNAH were so far the only names they'd managed to cross off the list.

'So we're set on the focus being Oakpass Manor, with a big question mark over Lady Larkin's treasure, but a small question mark over a potential Undead Complex like Kingston suggested, all with an Equinox deadline?' Cornelia said.

'Yes. I mean I hate it, but yes.' Diana pressed her head into her hands.

'How's the diorama going?'

'It's raised a question – what do we know about Nathan Tate? He's security, so he'd sign folk in, but would be able to come and go as he pleased. He'd know who was on set, and we haven't been able to get near him to ask. I'm running that reconstruction now, based on what limited information I gathered from the scene.'

She and Cornelia watched as paper Taylor, Xander, Fred, Sandi, Rachel, Lyle and Diana entered and exited the crime scene, a tiny paper Orson curled in a ball in the Oakpass Manor dollhouse she'd set at the scaled edge of the diorama. This was Diana's biggest diorama to date.

'This is not strictly relevant to proceedings,' Cornelia said. 'But the tiny dollhouse you made is both adorable and very meta. Like one of those dolls inside dolls.'

Diana flashed her a smile. 'The problem is, any one of them could've had the opportunity to do it once they got on set.

They were all there early, but nobody can account for who was where, because they were all doing their own thing. At least we know it's not me.'

'I sure fucking hope so,' Cornelia said. She ran her hands through her hair, the oversize sleeves of her jumper obscuring her face for a moment. 'Let's focus on what we do know for a second. It's not Baker, because he's dead. Why?'

'If this is about Shit King's Undead Complex or King Me Principle or whatever-you-call-it concept, it might not be personal,' Diana said. 'Wrong place, wrong time?'

'Could be. Though it has to be someone who knows him.' She tapped her fingers again, resetting the diorama. 'Does that make a difference?'

'Not necessarily. Say our killer got a job on the set because they wanted to be close to Oakpass Manor in order to carry out some killings. We know Oakpass is a former vampire stronghold.'

'But Kingston said that the Undead Complex wasn't just vampires, it was combining souls to make something new and it was about living forever,' Cornelia said.

'Is that what he said? He said so many things.'

'Be nice, he's not even here to hear you.' Cornelia picked up her marker again. Within ten minutes, their murder board was covered in questions.

'The Larkins,' Cornelia said. 'And the dollhouse.'

'What about them?'

'The dollhouse reappears after being missing for a hundred years,' Cornelia said, tapping the marker on the board so rapidly it set Diana's ear ringing. She whispered a spell and Cornelia dropped the marker.

'You could use your words, you know,' she grumbled.

'But then you'd stop saying useful things,' Diana said sweetly. 'The Larkin dollhouse reappeared after a hundred years.'

'And there were five Larkins,' Cornelia continued. 'And there seems to be five intended victims. What if… what the killer is looking for is not treasure, per se, but the Larkins themselves?'

'That is such a Mallory thing to say.'

'What is?' Mallory asked, padding down to the basement in her pyjamas. Theodore was close behind her, bringing warmth with him.

'Cornelia was making logic leaps without you present,' Diana said, and filled her in on what they'd figured out so far. Which wasn't much, and was admittedly making her very cranky.

'I think you're on to something there,' Mallory said, peering into the diorama. 'Though my main question is, even if that's the goal… why would you cover it up? Why not hide the body somewhere on the grounds?'

'A wonderful question, Mallory. Perhaps I can lend an extra pair of eyes. I've already got the extra ears covered,' Theodore said, stroking his cat ears.

'Please, be my guest. Maybe the deception is the point? But then, why hide in plain sight what was going to unravel in a few days? What's the goal of murdering one crew member, and then pretending that crew member was another?'

'Access,' Cornelia said, at the same time as Theodore said, 'SUBTERFUGE!' so loudly that Diana got goosebumps.

'Ah. Perhaps your idea is more concrete. Please, continue,' he said.

'What was that, Cornelia?'

'Access. You kill him to access part of Oakpass.'

'And then disguise him why?'

'More… access.'

'More access. That's what we're going with,' Diana said dryly.

'More access,' Mallory said firmly. 'I think she's right. I don't think this was personal at all – I did, when we thought it was someone maybe targeting Taylor, and could've, if it was just Donny Baker, but now we've got fake-Orson to contend with. What if killing Baker wasn't actually the goal, so they "killed" Taylor to shut down production for a while? All attention would be focused on the set where she was found, so everyone stayed there while her body was removed. What if that was strategic, and it let the killer look around areas they couldn't otherwise?'

'It's one possible explanation, but doesn't fully answer why there needed to be bodies at all,' Cornelia said.

'She's right,' Diana said. 'Baker was missing and nobody was particularly bothered; he could still be missing and nobody would know he was dead. It's not just about murdering. Why take the extra steps? Why *pose* the bodies?'

The others fell silent, thinking.

'I don't know,' Mallory said at last. 'I have absolutely no idea why someone would do that. Or even how. Dr Ray said it was like Taylor melted and was replaced with Baker. I can't even begin to fathom what sort of magic would do that. The closest we saw was Blair's ring, and that…'

That was upstairs in Diana's bedroom.

'Plants,' Cornelia said suddenly. 'Plants would do it. Plants would be magical but not, wouldn't they? That could explain so much. The beetles aren't broken, they were confused. But what plant, what plant…' She paced. 'I'll find a botanist. I've been talking to one about a suitable diet for Travis that I could safely grow here year-round, maybe they'll know.'

'With the greatest of respect I can bestow upon you, my dear friend. How does this help you solve the murder?'

'If we know the killer isn't using physical magic, we can stop looking for physical magic clues,' Cornelia said, already typing out an email. 'Frees up space in the old thinking brain.'

'I think our next most logical port of call is to talk to the security guards. Interrogate them, really, as we're running out of time here,' Mallory said firmly.

'Great plan, I'm ready,' Cornelia said, pocketing her phone.

'And how do we do that? It's not like there's a security guard café or whatever; they likely won't be back at Oakpass until it reopens,' Diana said fretfully.

'Their security company has a base about five minutes from Oakpass Manor, so either they're there, or we can get someone to tell us where Tate and Whitlock might be. And we see what they have to say.'

'That's it! Tate and Whitlock! Grey Quinn mentioned both of them approaching him, the night we were out. That's why I thought Lyle's name sounded familiar – it wasn't the Lyle bit I was remembering.' Diana slapped a hand to her forehead, relaying what she remembered of Hollis and Quinn whispering together in the bar. 'It suggests they know each other. I'm ready now, if you are?' Diana looked to Mallory, who stretched carefully, testing her body, then nodded.

'Right now.'

'I like this plan. It's a great plan,' Theodore said, but there was a look on his face Diana did not recognise. She glanced at Mallory, whose face had fallen. She'd seen it too.

'Thanks, Theo,' Mallory said shakily. 'Are you okay?'

'Oh yes,' he whispered. 'A pleasant pheasant plan, because the plan was probably very rich and I think rich folk love pheasant. At least they did when I was a boy. Long, long ago, a boy I was.'

The look was best summed up as a lack of presence, like he was there but not, saying words that might make sense to someone else, but Diana was not sure even he knew what he was saying, which, she knew, was definitely saying something. Mallory, who had paled significantly, mouthed a word to Diana: *Katherine*.

And all at once, Diana realised why she felt so uneasy: this was how Mallory had described her first interaction with Katherine. Word salad, looking like she wasn't really present, conversations circling.

Mallory touched Theodore's hand and he flinched.

'Sorry! Mallory, I'm so sorry.' He moved to hug her, the vacant expression gone. 'I was in a world of my own.'

She returned the hug, disappearing in a fog of static for a moment.

'Actually, Diana,' Mallory said, emerging from the hug. 'Probably doesn't make sense for me to come with you. I'll stay here, fire up the Magic Magical Machine, maybe do a bit of side project work, and see you when you get back.'

Diana caught the meaningful stare and nodded once. 'We'll do our best. Tate and Lyle, never a sweeter pair.'

'You've got this,' Mallory said, and Diana felt a shiver up her spine as she laced up her boots and tugged on a jumper. They had mere days left until Equinox, but she felt they were, finally, getting somewhere.

EIGHTEEN

Mallory had just relegated Theodore to his iron plate and fired up the Magic Magical Machine – hoping to re-test the samples they got from Donny Baker's body with plants, rather than magic, in mind – when she got a call she'd been nervously anticipating, in the way one does when they half-expect it'll never happen.

'I think I've found your Katherine,' a gravelly voice said as soon as she picked up the phone.

'Observer Johnson?'

'Are there others seeking Katherine for you?'

'No, I wasn't expecting to hear from you so soon. I appreciate you doing this, I'm sure Katherine would too.'

'The Ternion provide to all those who seek. I have some information here – Katherine Vane of Wrackton was of demon and witch heritage, and she was recorded missing some years ago.'

'How many years ago?'

'The dates are inconclusive, but we are perhaps talking around the end of the Vampire Wars.'

'Oh. So that's… that's quite old,' Mallory said.

'Quite. She had a sister named Rosemary, who we presume also died roughly around the same time. There is also an allusion here to there having been a child. Perhaps it was her own, but there is no complete record, and I am surmising the child died young.'

'Are the Vane family still in Wrackton?'

'No. The lineage died out with her, her sister and the child. A lot of lives were lost in the Vampire Wars, and not many records survived. Though I suspect blowing up the Mayoral Offices didn't help,' he added, almost as an aside.

'Thank you so much,' she said, skating over the barb. 'Do we know where her sister is buried?'

'No. She may have been a half-sister. The records are incomplete, as I say, but that could also be pure conjecture.'

Mallory thanked him a few more times before hanging up.

She looked at her phone for a moment then dialled another number. She'd normally have asked Diana to do this, but she felt confident enough that this particular request did not require that level of finessing.

'Night Mayor's office.'

'Dr Ray?'

'I do answer my own phone from time to time, yes.'

'Hi, it's Mallory,' Mallory said, trying to hide her surprise.

'If this is about the case, I already told Cornelia—'

'No! This is something else. I need… I need a favour. And I need you to not ask me what the favour is for.'

'I am not dignifying that with a response.'

'I need access to the Mayoral Offices.'

Dr Ray exhaled, the phone speaker fuzzing. 'It's incredibly dangerous,' she said. 'You could be risking your life.'

'It's important. I wouldn't ask if it wasn't.'

'Then give me at least an hour to get in touch with the Ghoul Council. The wards will be lifted for about three hours only. That'll be at a stretch, you understand me?'

'Thank you, Dr Ray.'

'And, Mallory?'

'Yes?'

'Take someone with you. If you get into distress, someone needs to be able to recover your body.'

'Oh it's fine,' Theodore said, hovering in the doorway of her bedroom as Mallory got ready. 'I don't need to know what you're doing, or where you're going, or why, or how. I don't need to know anything.'

'I'm—'

'Official Undetectables business, I'm sure. Party of one, Mallory Hawthorne.'

Her phone buzzed and she shooed Theodore away. He huffed loudly and vanished down the hall.

> *Langdon*
> good news and better news

She smiled when she saw the text. He'd been really happy to see her when she'd visited him to ask if he'd approach his uncles for information. There was no denying Langdon's uncles conducted all sorts of shady business, and Mallory normally preferred to mind her own. She scrolled up to the last message he'd sent, saying it had been so nice to see her and they should hang out properly soon. In so many ways, despite many things being worse, her life had improved drastically over the last five months. She had friends that weren't only Theodore, who wanted to see her.

> *Langdon*
> Good: i asked my uncles about Orson Webb for you,
> they know of him. Said he's unusually mild-mannered,
> even for a troll, and very strait-laced, so they don't have
> dealings with him, if you get me

Mallory frowned. This was deeply at odds with what she'd seen of Orson herself; she'd thought him a little greasy, Xander had suggested he was easy to piss off, and Hollis had seemed to dislike him. The argument with Hollis had made him seen anything but mild-mannered, as had other folks' dealings with him on set. Another text popped in.

> *Langdon*
> better: i have the afternoon free, what do you say to
> hanging out with me today?

She smiled. Although he'd said they should hang out, she hadn't thought he'd follow through.

> *Langdon*
> assuming it's a yes, we could watch a movie here, or go

> get a coffee and sit in the forest for a bit? I can bring
> a blanket or a cushion, if that would make it comfy
> for you :)

It was risky – involving anyone else in any of their cases was always risky, and this was a particularly suicidal mission she was about to undertake. In another world she'd bring Theodore along in a heartbeat, but she couldn't let him find out what she was up to.

Langdon, on the other hand, had grown up on the cusp of whatever shadowy underworld his uncles inhabited, and Mallory supposed that if Cornelia and Diana weren't available, Langdon would be the next best equipped – or at the very least, able to keep a secret.

> *Mallory*
> i have a better idea – meet me in the Mayoral Square
> in half an hour?

'Hey,' Langdon said, bouncing towards her with a huge smile on his face. He was wearing a coat with a furry hood and green tartan jeans that Mallory was certain belonged to Felix, rolled up to show off acid-pink combat boots that matched the bag slung over his shoulder. 'You look nice.'

Mallory smiled, looking down at her outfit. She had decided dressing up to talk to Katherine was a wise move, and had put on a skirt. 'So do you.'

'What day of fun have you got planned for us?'

'Well, it's less of a plan, and more of a daring rescue mission,' Mallory started.

Langdon laughed, his hands on his knees.

It had not, to Mallory's mind, been that funny.

'Oh,' he said after a moment. 'You're serious. Okay, cool. Who… or what are we rescuing?'

'Now you're asking the right questions,' Mallory said.

They stood at the ruined entrance to the Mayoral Offices and Mallory took an experimental step over the threshold. There was an uncomfortable sensation in her stomach, and it took a moment for her to recognise it as fear.

Fear, memory, her body primed to run.

She was going to need to lie down a lot when she left here.

If she left here.

There was no resistance from the wards. She stopped, shoving her hands in her coat pockets.

'Full disclosure: I've been given clearance to go in, but I was also told to bring someone in case I needed my body to be recovered.'

'So we're doing something dangerous, then?'

'If looking for a ghost counts as dangerous, then yes. And you don't have to come with me.' She gave him the short version, and Langdon ran a hand through his curls as he listened intently. 'As it's five months since Samhain and there was no recorded emergence – attempted or otherwise – of any creatures, and we haven't been hit with any further ghost… explosions, I guess, for want of a better way of describing it, it's probably safer than it seems.'

'Well. This is a very unusual situation.' Langdon grinned. To his credit, he looked little more than mildly surprised. 'But I suppose you're an unusual sort of girl.'

Mallory could not help a small frown pass over her face. She wished she'd called Diana back to do this with her instead. It had been a long time since she'd hung out properly one-on-one with anyone who wasn't a member of the Undetectables, not even Felix.

'Yes. I mean, not really. But… come on then.'

He took a step towards the wards and disappeared. Mallory yelped even as he reappeared outside the mortuary, already jogging towards her. He looked mildly baffled, but Mallory figured the wards had been lifted for her alone.

'Oops. We could go back to the movie idea?' he suggested.

'I really need to get this done today,' Mallory said apologetically, as though it were a piece of admin. 'I have an idea though.'

After several attempts, Mallory managed to get Langdon across the threshold by holding his hand.

The Mayoral Offices were significantly less charming than they had been pre-explosions. Lights flickered on as they crossed the threshold, Mallory stepping daintily over cracked tiles to avoid tripping as she blinked in the sudden neon light. There was a distinct hum coming from the ceiling, as though the building was straining to function at all.

One side of the Offices was obliterated – the side she and her friends had escaped the Whistler from, where the original Night Mayor's office had been.

'There.' She smiled triumphantly. 'Step one complete. Step two…' She tried to extricate her hand, but Langdon held on.

'Just in case,' he said, then winked at her. Mallory felt alarm bells go off in her mind – not big ones, not bad ones, but ones that told her they were perhaps not on the same page. She wondered if it was worth texting Diana for her objective assessment of the situation.

'I think if we go down here,' she said, and walked quickly down the corridor parallel to the Night Mayor's office, pulling her hand free. Langdon stuffed his hands in his pockets, his elbow gently brushing her arm. This close, he smelled like pine and amber, comforting and warm. She focused on this, trying not to think about the last time she'd been in the Offices. Her stomach was still telling her to run, that she was in danger, and that she didn't have time to be in danger, and this was starting to knot the muscles at the top of her shoulders. If a headache took hold, she'd have to leave. And she didn't want that. She might never have access to Katherine again.

'Isn't there a spell for this?' Langdon asked. 'Something to call her?'

'I know of one spell,' Mallory said. 'But I'm not sure it works properly.'

'What about a séance?'

Mallory shook her head. 'I don't know, given that she's walking around. I haven't found too much on Samhain ghosts and spectral magic, which I suppose isn't surprising, given how few of them there are. No, I want to try something else.'

She got to where she thought was parallel with the Night Mayor's office, and closed her eyes.

'This is going to deplete me very fast. As in, my energy.' Mallory paused. 'I'm not going to work very well after this.'

'Can I help in any way?'

'Stand back.'

She whispered under her breath a spell to find a doorway. The walls rumbled and Langdon jumped. Mallory stayed perfectly still until a Mallory-sized doorway had opened in front of her, clearing a path for them both that would take them to the passageway where she'd last seen Katherine. She felt herself flag instantly and carefully lowered herself to the floor. White tile dust and crumbled concrete clung to her hands and jeans as she lowered her head onto her legs.

'Do you need anything?'

'Give me a second,' Mallory said. If Diana had been here, she'd have come prepared with something ridiculous, like a slingshot to send Mallory home. This had been an awful idea.

'Sit for a bit. I brought snacks,' Langdon said, taking his messenger bag off his shoulder. 'Well. I brought lunch. Picked up a couple of sandwiches before I left the Larix. And some crisps.' He dug through the bag. 'And some home-made pink lemonade. I get to say that because I'm actually living above the Larix at the moment, and I made the lemonade.'

Mallory grinned.

They sat and ate and Mallory felt some of her strength return. She tried not to admonish herself for being underprepared. Every time she did something beyond her usual range of capabilities, she found herself unable to handle how hard she'd pushed herself.

Langdon chatted and told funny stories; stories from on tour; memories of Ben, their bandmate who'd been killed by the Whistler; the ridiculous things he and Felix had gotten up to.

Despite her exhaustion, she felt relaxed. Talking to Langdon felt natural, an ease she only really had around the rest of the Undetectables anymore.

'I didn't want to randomly bring it up, but the cut on your face has healed really nicely,' Langdon said. Mallory raised a hand to her cheek; she'd been injured after the Mayoral Office explosion, and there'd been a time she'd worried about it scarring. Now it was a vaguely red mark she could cover with makeup if she felt like it, but mostly didn't bother.

'The cream you gave me helped, thank you again.'

Langdon shrugged, rubbing a hand over his recently flattened chest. 'I bought extra after my surgery, it would've gone to waste. You wouldn't believe how good I look now; I'll be able to perform with no shirt on if I want next time we're out on the road and not have to worry about glamours fading.'

'What's happening with Crown and Hemlock, anyway?' Mallory asked, carefully picking her way through a packet of crisps.

'Felix wants to continue. So do I, so I'm not disagreeing with them. Cloud doesn't. They can't really picture doing this without Ben. I don't think we'd even be the same band without him, so I get what Cloud is saying, I really do. We just need to find the right individual. Someone who meshes with us, respects the vision, is good with going with the flow. Someone who can understand the hole Ben's left behind, in our lives and our art.'

'That makes total sense,' Mallory said.

'And speaking of.' He scooted closer to Mallory. She put her packet of crisps down and discreetly wiped her hand on her legs before he folded her fingers in his. 'Am I right in thinking we mesh well together?'

Mallory wished Diana was here to translate. She had an idea of what was happening, an idea of what was about to happen, but she was so desperately out of practice that there was a distinct possibility she'd never been in practice in the first place. Certainly not as an adult. Her heart rate picked up.

'By which I mean… we're friends. And as far as dangerous missions go, I'm having a really lovely time. I like spending time with you, I like talking to you.'

He smiled at her and lifted one hand to cup her chin, his fingers warm against her skin. He really did smell nice.

Langdon held her gaze, liquid amber flecked with grey, and Mallory felt a tingle run up her arms that was, for once, nothing to do with guilt, or pain, or pining.

'Would it be okay if I kissed you?'

'I just had crisps,' Mallory said. 'So yeah, but…' She trailed off at the amused expression on his face. 'Yes,' she said. 'Yes you can.'

Langdon pressed his lips to hers, his mouth soft and surprisingly sweet, despite the crisps. All the sounds faded away, and for a few moments it was just her and Langdon and their bodies barely touching, his hands ghosting down her arms, his mouth moving softly, tenderly, against hers. He pulled back, searching her face, and when she smiled, he carefully took her face in his hands and kissed her deeper.

Mallory waited for something to ignite within her. Some spark, something to tell her she wanted this, wanted *him*, beyond her immediate enjoyment. She felt a dull, creeping sense of guilt she couldn't put a name to, but nothing else. No spark.

Still, she didn't break the kiss. She wrapped her arms around his waist and pulled him closer, nudging his mouth open with hers, feeling his heart flutter. There had been other kisses, sure, when she was younger. Several boys at parties, and one girl that, had Mallory not already known she was bisexual, would've confirmed it. But the years since had been long and kissless, and a part of her had been longing for intimacy.

Langdon broke away first, mildly breathless, his face lightly flushed. He smiled sweetly at her, like she'd made his day. He really was pretty, Mallory reasoned. And kind, and considerate. She felt a piece of something crumble within her. A realisation that however nice that had been, it wouldn't ever happen again.

Not with Langdon.

'You're looking at me like you're really sad I'm not someone else,' Langdon said.

Mallory flinched. She didn't like it when people could read her that easily.

'Sorry, it's such a specific face, and it's also not the first time I've seen it.' He ran a hand through his hair, grinning ruefully. 'Am I that bad?'

'No! Goddess, no. That was... that was really nice,' Mallory said, reaching to touch his hand. 'I'm glad you did it. I'm glad we tried. I'm starting to realise that I'm not the best at picking up signals, even when it comes to folk signalling me directly.'

Langdon laughed. 'You didn't even know this was a date, did you?'

Mallory's eyes widened. 'Was I meant to?'

'I asked you to hang out. It's pretty universal date language.'

'Maybe you just wanted to hang out!'

'I did. And we did. And it was nice. It's okay, Mallory. I'm…
well I'm gutted.' He smiled ruefully. 'You're kind of amazing, right.
And you're beautiful, and smart, and brave. So yeah. I'm gutted.'
He gave her an assessing look. 'Whoever they are, I hope at the
absolute bare minimum, they think the same things about you.'

Mallory closed her eyes. 'Thanks, Langdon. Seriously.'

'If there's ever a time I'm off on my own adventure, and I
get into trouble, you'll be the first person I call.' He pressed his
fingers against the back of her hand. 'Let me clear these up,'
he said, gathering up the remnants of their picnic. 'And let's
continue with this adventure, shall we?'

It was less adventure than a straightforward walk through the
passageway Mallory had made. Her back had stiffened and her
arms ached, but she moved forward in the hope that Katherine
would be close by. And she was, standing against the wall at the
far end of the corridor, a burst of warmth greeting them even
before Mallory saw her.

In different light, she did not look at all like Cornelia. There
was a drawn element to her face, like she'd endured great stress
before she died.

'Katherine Vane of Wrackton,' Mallory said. 'We've met before.'

'WHO IS HE?' she shrieked. 'WHO IS THIS BOY?'

'I'm Langdon Ericsson of Wrackton. My uncles co-own the
Larix, and I'm here to support Mallory.'

'I remember you, witch.' Katherine reached for Mallory. She
stopped short of touching her and hissed close to Mallory's face,
'I remember your salt.'

'That was Diana,' Mallory said. 'And she is sorry. We were running from the bad man, the one who put my friend in the cage. The one who scared you.'

'Oh, the man,' Katherine said. 'The man, the man.'

'Does she mean Jacob?' Langdon whispered.

'The MAN,' Katherine shrieked.

'He's gone,' Mallory said. 'He died.'

'And you found his body? And you desecrated his grave? And you made sure he cannot rise again?'

'He— no,' Mallory said carefully. 'They're still looking for his remains, but I saw his tongue fall from his mouth, saw him set upon by other spirits. He did not survive that. He did not survive their wrath.'

Katherine looked pityingly at her, but swished to the other side of the corridor, pressing her hands back against the wall.

'Why are you here, witch?'

'You asked me to help you, when we thought Theodore was dead. I offered to help you, in exchange for helping us, in Theodore's absence. So I am here to try to help.'

To try to help both of you, Mallory wanted to say.

'Theooodooore,' she whispered. 'THEODORE. THEODORE. THEODORE!'

'This is the part where he appears, right?' Langdon whispered. Mallory ignored him.

'Yes. Theodore offered to help you, and I agreed to help you too. I found out who you are: Katherine Vane of Wrackton. You had a sister.'

'Theodore,' Katherine said again, not appearing to have heard, 'did a very bad thing.'

'What?'

'Theodore did a very bad thing and a very bad thing happened in turn. Once was cat, now is man. Theodore runs as fast as he can,' she said, twirling a piece of her hair around her hand. Mallory could see her coat sleeves were slashed, wounds deep in her arms. Defensive wounds. Something bad happened to Katherine, too.

A murder within a murder within a murder.

'What happened to Theodore, Katherine?' Mallory's heart hammered in her chest. Maybe, somehow, Katherine knew what had killed him. Or who.

'He died. But how he died, oh. *Bad*. And why he died… worse.' She cocked her head. 'Worse, worse.'

'Katherine, please. Tell me what happened to Theodore.'

'You said sister,' Katherine said suddenly. 'You said I had a sister. Where is my sister?'

'We don't know where Rosemary Vane is, only that she died too.'

'Rosemary. Rose. I'm so sorry, Rosemary.' Katherine howled, turning her head up to the ceiling. The walls vibrated. Mallory felt Langdon take a step back, but she held strong.

'That's all we know. We think you've both been dead a long time.' It did not feel like enough information. It didn't feel like enough at all. Katherine had presumably lived a long, complicated life and had met an untimely end, and Mallory's bare facts erased so many of those experiences. She was reduced to her relation to another Occult individual and not much else.

Katherine stopped howling. She sank to her knees, curling her body around her limbs. Static burst from her in waves that sent Mallory staggering back two steps.

'Dead? How long has… how long have I…?'

Mallory shivered, feeling the echoes of meeting a freshly dead Theodore and the younger, calmer, less-able-to-sense-danger version of herself speaking to him as though he was newly born.

'We think you died around what we call the Vampire Wars,' Mallory whispered. 'Which were several hundred years ago.'

'Who won?'

'What?'

'Who won the war?'

'The Ternion won it for everyone else. The vampires signed a covenant to ensure it stayed finished.'

'And they still live?'

'Yes. That was the agreement.'

She appeared to digest this information, chewing her lip and generating a spray of static.

'I'm getting a sense that the Vampire Wars has been coming up for you way more than you're necessarily comfortable with,' Langdon whispered.

'Tell me about it,' Mallory muttered.

'And so you allowed Morrigan and Hecate's daughters to live,' Katherine said finally.

'I thought you meant they let the vampires live, not the Ternion. They're long gone,' Mallory said. 'But they still watch over us.'

Katherine snorted, and paced the width of the corridor before coming to a stop in front of Mallory, so close that Mallory couldn't see anything else.

'You will find my sister,' Katherine said decisively. 'You will find her at the place where sunrise dies. That is where she will be. That is where she is.'

'Katherine, we don't really have time for…' Mallory didn't know how to tell her that there was a chance she'd be bricked up in here forever. That she might never see her again.

'I will tell you nothing for as long as I continue to exist if you do not bring me Rosemary. You will find her. I have waited, I will wait.'

'Is this…'

'Theodore promised. He promised to find her. You will find her instead.'

Mallory didn't know what to make of that; had he told her about it, Mallory could've helped him find her sister years ago. There was nothing else for it. 'I will. I take his promise as my own. Katherine, can you please tell me what happened to Theodore? I think he's in trouble.'

Langdon shot her a worried glance.

Katherine smiled then, like she had fully come back into herself. It was a wicked, gloating sort of smile that felt less human than Mallory thought possible.

'You find Rosemary, I will tell you everything. Find her. Bring her to me.'

'I don't know where—'

'NOW!' Katherine screamed, static waves pulsing in the air. Mallory was thrown back into Langdon, who managed to steady himself against the wall behind them.

Katherine disappeared, leaving the room cooling and Mallory very concerned about what was to come.

NINETEEN

Diana slammed the research room door open a few hours later, Cornelia hot on her heels. Mallory looked up in surprise, and Diana felt the full force of her own fury burst out of her.

'I cannot work in these conditions. We can't go out in the field together anymore, she is a *frustration*. A prize one. You'd get her out of a grabby machine and be like "look, I have won a fool" and be all delighted with yourself until you realised your fool was going to *ruin your life*.'

'YOU can't work in these conditions? YOU?' Cornelia shouted, but there was a look of delight on her face that made Diana even angrier. Her ear rang loudly, making her want to scream.

'What happened?' Mallory squinted, the sound of the Magic Magical Machine humming in the background. Theodore was behind an iron screen, absorbed in a stack of papers, and he didn't so much as look up as Diana stomped across the room in socked feet, her boots – mud-caked and potentially ruined – clutched in her hands.

'What happened, you ask? WHAT HAPPENED?'

'Diana,' Cornelia said in a reproachful tone that made fire flare in Diana's belly.

'Don't you "Diana" me. We had *one job* and that was somehow transmogrified into a fucking *hero's journey*, except it was led by the *anti*-hero, which is *you*.'

'So is this your way of telling me you didn't get to talk to the security guards, then?'

Diana frowned at Mallory. 'Of course we did. That is entirely beside the point!'

It was hard sometimes to explain to Mallory the intensity with which she and Cornelia could argue, how far they could push the limits of their friendship, and come to a grudging reconciliation some hours later. Whether that was particularly healthy, Diana didn't know, but there was safety in it too. She knew that Cornelia knew that no matter what they said, no matter how many hex wars they got into, they would always be friends, always be there for each other, and always have each other's backs.

Even when Diana was incandescent.

'We checked at Larkin Studios first, to see if there was anyone on the gate – figured it was worth a try,' Diana started. 'The gates were locked and I didn't notice any cars about. Cornelia suggested we *walk*, quote, "up the road" to where the security company is. It was raining, because of course it was, and there was no footpath, so I was half in a ditch, half tangled up in briars—'

'There was one briar, Diana. ONE. And you don't even know what a briar is; you guessed that's what it was and before that you said bramble.'

'This is not a helpful interjection, Cornelia. We walked very,

very far. I was wearing THESE,' Diana said, lifting her hand to show Mallory her boots. 'They are heavy and *not made for extensive walking*. They are *strictly* minor subterfuge boots. And she says, "just a bit further, just a bit further", oh what was it, Cornelia, one, two HUNDRED times?'

'Yes,' Cornelia said stiffly.

'And what did you say to me?'

'I believe I asked you to be quiet—'

'I believe the phrasing was "shut the fuck up, Diana, and let me be in charge for once, it's just a bit further".'

'Ah,' Mallory said. 'I feel like this is some kind of foreshadowing.'

'So I shut the fuck up—'

'If that's what you want to call complaining the ENTIRE time,' Cornelia cut in.

'Every day I trust Cornelia to make good decisions. I trust her even when she says things like, "Oh, a hedgehog!" and points to it, and I look at the exact moment she says, "No wait, don't look, it's been flattened," as if that wasn't the first thought most sane individuals would have when happening across roadkill.'

'Oh no,' Mallory said. She appeared to be very carefully keeping her face neutral, waiting for the punchline of the story, but Diana was admittedly enjoying herself.

'Get to the point,' Cornelia said.

'We do all this walking and find the security building and we're told, after much finagling and clever attempts to extort information—'

'If that's what you call "batting your eyelashes and asking politely",' Cornelia snorted.

'—that Nathan Tate no longer works for the company, and left two days ago. So his last night on the job would've had him leaving the grounds of Oakpass and Larkin Studios right around the time Fake-Orson was killed.'

'Oh good. No offence, but I was beginning to suspect you were never going to tell me what you got,' Mallory said.

'Imagine Diana going on and on and on about something,' Cornelia said.

Diana, with all her dignity, mustered up a rude gesture. Cornelia laughed delightedly.

'But it turns out that Lyle Whitlock is stationed back at the gates of Larkin Studios, so back we went. Mud on my shoes, leaves in my hair—'

'I thought it was briars?'

'And Cornelia had a funeral for a hedgehog.'

'What did Whitlock say? I assume you talked to him,' Mallory said. 'And I assume you got something good and you aren't wasting our precious time on this?'

'I took a video, because Diana was too busy cosplaying a hedgerow to think of it,' Cornelia said, handing her phone over to Mallory, who set the video to play on her laptop, turning it so they could all see. She turned to Diana. 'You've got something in your hair, by the way. I think it's an entire oak tree?'

The video started, shaky at first, but then Lyle Whitlock came into view. Diana tried to see him through Mallory's eyes: short, with dark blonde hair, pale features and an awkward yet polite manner.

Just so sad, Diana was saying on the video.

'Quite a travesty,' Whitlock said.

'I was new on set so I didn't really know any of them that well,' Diana said. 'But it was such a shock to me.'

'It was my first day as day guard. Unexpected turn of events,' he said. His mouth pressed into a sympathetic-seeming line.

'First day? Wow.'

'A friend pulled in a favour. It'll perhaps be my last, too, sadly. Though, of course, nothing is as sad for any of us as it is for the families, I expect.'

'Of course. Devastating. Never seen anything like it. Two murders on one set, horrifying.'

'Rightly so. I didn't know the first… victim, I suppose? But dreadful business altogether.'

'Horrible,' Diana agreed. 'Did you get a chance to get to know anyone on set? It was so tight-knit.'

'Ah well, I don't know if you'd have met him, but Xander Crane and I go way back,' he said, running a hand through his hair. 'He's a very normal guy. Very down-to-earth approach to life, which you wouldn't really expect. All these celebrities, they're normal people like us.' He smiled at Diana, adjusting the strap of his leather satchel. Embossed initials A.L.W. flashed silver in the weak sunlight. Diana had liked the bag and been momentarily distracted. 'I expect you understand it better than most, being Occult like myself – how extraordinary it is to be ordinary. Strange to step outside that bubble, sometimes. I often think about how our ancestors wouldn't be able to fathom the lives we lead now.' He shook his head solemnly.

'How was Xander after the news? I got the sense there was a bit of tension with Orson,' Diana said.

'Oh, Xander was as cut up as the others,' Whitlock said. 'Very down-to-earth, as I said. Not quite so sure about that American actress, but I try to take folk at face value. We all have our histories, our ways of being in the world. Our secrets, our hopes, our dreams. Sad to see anyone's cut short—'

The video stopped there. 'Fuck,' Cornelia said. 'Sorry.'

'Does he mention anyone else?' Mallory asked. She had been quietly studying the video, her expression inscrutable.

'We asked him about Tate next. He said he barely knew him, that he'd taken over his old job and was working all his scheduled shifts for the next while. When Quinn and Hollis were whispering about Tate and Whitlock, they made it sound like the two knew each other, but it could be as simple as Whitlock wanting a job, and Tate trying to fill the role without hassle. As a favour, maybe, but...'

'Do demons who presumably know Quinn's reputation simply ask him for favours, no matter how trivial-sounding?' Cornelia said.

'There's something we're not seeing,' Diana said. 'Something about the way Hollis was the one to bring it up. I just have this feeling...'

'Tate and Whitlock probably have equal opportunity, in terms of access,' Mallory said. 'If we take the fact they're both demons into account, they could potentially manipulate anyone they wanted to into not remembering they were around – that could account for why everyone seems to think different things?'

'Yes, but we'd have to consider all the demons – Jenna, and Quinn,' Cornelia said.

'And I suppose that doesn't explain any of the rest of it. Using plants, if that's what was done, for the disguising of a body to look like another body.'

'Can we see if we can rule Quinn in or out for certain? He wasn't recorded as being on the grounds, but he *owns* the grounds, so maybe is exempt from such mundanities.' Cornelia looked pointedly at Diana, who sighed. She knew where this was going.

'I'm on it.'

She scrolled through her phone contacts – most marked with a little tombstone icon, to remind her not to contact them again – until she came to the particular ex-girlfriend she needed. Lina picked up the phone after two rings.

'Hello, Diana,' she said coldly. 'I haven't heard from you in a while, which suggests one of two things: the Ternion have risen from their graves, or you want me to do something that constitutes spying on my employer.'

'I was just about to say, how *is* my favourite faerie receptionist at Hotel Indigo Blue?' Diana said brightly.

'I'm actually the general manager now,' Lina said. 'What's this worth to you?'

'Oh, name your price. I need you to do a tiny bit of digging...'

When Diana ended the call a few minutes later, she gave the others a thumbs up. 'Lina checked the cameras; he was actually on the premises on both the morning Baker's body was found, and overnight when fake-Orson was killed. Apparently a camera points right outside his office and sometimes he leaves the door open, so Lina has sped through several hours of her boss sleeping. Quinn wasn't at Oakpass.'

'Great,' Cornelia said, crossing him off their murder board. 'That's something.'

'Right—' Mallory started, but Cornelia interrupted her by shouting 'BOTANIST!' at an unreasonable volume, grabbing her phone. 'They emailed while we were out, probably around the time Diana was becoming one with nature. They said they'd only heard of one instance of a plant potentially capable of something akin to a glamour, and it's something called *Atropa miasma* – or Bellissima, colloquially. I think the name is a play on belladonna. Incidentally, did you know belladonna was used cosmetically—'

'Hollis Hadley mentioned Bellissima at drinks,' Diana said, cutting her off. 'I remember cause Shit King asked him if he was Italian.'

'It's a nightshade plant – which feels thematic to the show, given the pilot is called "Henbane" – but what's most interesting is that it only grows inside an oak tree in early spring. And they recommended a book. Hold on.' Cornelia disappeared off upstairs.

'Any thoughts, Theodore?' Mallory asked, rifling through the Magic Magical Machine charts that had samples from both fake-Orson and Donny Baker's bodies. 'It didn't occur to me that this could be a nightshade, but the signatures are actually very similar.'

He didn't look up, and it occurred to Diana that it was strange that he had not gotten involved in her dramatics, or protested being left out of the video viewing. Mallory walked around the iron screen and Diana followed. He was engrossed in something and didn't seem to hear them coming, but when he did he flickered twice, the book he was reading from disappearing.

Diana glanced at Mallory to check she'd noticed.

'We have some Machine charts for you to look at, if you're not busy,' Mallory said gently.

'Aha! Yes, wonderful. Goddess no, I'm not busy. Why would you think I was busy? Free as a bird, me. If a bird was confined to a single town and also dead. Free as a caged bird! That's not better. Nonetheless, I am available to assist you,' he said grandly.

Mallory passed over the charts and he looked at them for an impossibly long time.

'These are the same,' he said. 'Not sure why I didn't see that before.' He scratched a cat ear idly. 'There's a slight variation in signature, but that could vary plant by plant, I suppose, depending how they reproduce. Like cotton, Mallory.'

When Diana looked at her askance, Mallory waved a hand. 'All cotton plants are genetically identical, it's a whole thing in fibres.'

'Got it, got it,' Cornelia said, running back into the room what felt like an eternity later with the largest book Diana had ever seen clutched in her hands.

'Why do you have the book in question?' Diana asked, knowing it was futile. The Broadwicks had whatever the Broadwicks wanted.

'Agatha, or maybe Ethel, wanted rare plants painted onto her bedroom walls a few years ago and acquired obscure illustrated texts to show the poor painters. Took them hours and hours with both of them standing over the painters' shoulders, which is why I can't remember which twin wanted this done.'

'But none of the bedrooms have anything painted onto the walls,' Mallory said.

'Exactly,' Cornelia said, exhaling heavily. 'Exactly.'

'At least they've indirectly helped?' Mallory said. 'Point one to the Broadwick twins?'

'That should balance out their current score of minus nine hundred and sixty-three very nicely,' Theodore said primly.

'The botanist warned it was an old witch's tale, because the likelihood of one plant being able to perform all of these effects is slim, but I told them I had an affinity for old witches, given that I'd be one someday, and that made them slightly less sceptical, I think. Here it is, though. *Atropa miasma.* Aaaaaand...' She read quickly, pushing her glasses up her nose. 'Yes. Okay. One of the properties is "may produce mass hallucinogenic effects. Consumption was historically used in disguise. High concentrations can produce vomiting, paralytic effects and asphyxiation. N'Occ."'

'Knock?'

'No, at the end here, it says "N'Occ."'

'Noose Occlusion?' Theodore said. 'Norse Occipitals?'

'No Occult? Non-Occult?' Mallory said.

'That makes more sense. Then again, may I offer you Numb Occurrences?'

'No or Non-Occult what, though?' Cornelia said.

Mallory shook her head. Diana wasn't sure, and if Mallory couldn't figure it out, it was something to put aside. Cornelia held the book under her arm and wrote *N'OCC* on their murder whiteboard.

'I think confirming this was part of the method will stop me spinning my wheels on the *how* and get back to looking at the *why*,' Mallory said.

'Oh!' Cornelia ran off again, returning in moments with a cardboard box held aloft.

'What horror is inside that box, Cornelia? Do I want to know?' Diana demanded.

'Travis,' Cornelia said breathlessly.

'What the fuck does Horrible Travis have to do with this?'

'His main food source are nightshades,' she said, pulling on gloves and organising their samples. 'In the presence of which he unfurls his proboscis.'

'He *what*?'

'Sticks out his tongue,' Cornelia said impatiently. 'Look!'

Diana had the displeasure of watching a large, flapping moth unfolding a hideously long tongue, lapping the air over the samples. 'That'll do it. Nightshade. Likely *Atropa miasma*. Is that good enough for you, Mallory?'

'Yes.' Mallory wrote *BELLISSIMA: OAKPASS?* on the whiteboard, smiling. 'Thank you.'

'So that's a possible link between Tate and Whitlock, strange departure of Tate post-two murders. Three potentially still to go. Someone is using plants to make bodies wear other bodies for reasons we can't ascertain yet. But at least Quinn is probably definitely not actually involved.'

'We do need to try get a hold of Hollis Hadley soon,' Mallory said. 'And perhaps pay Sandi a visit; her reactions have been very interesting to me.'

'That's our next port of call,' Diana said. 'Something to pass the time until we find out who is wearing Orson Webb's face.'

That call came late that night, Diana's phone lighting up and waking her from a restless sleep. Her ear ringing, she held the phone awkwardly across her face.

'It's happened again,' Dr Ray said, her voice tense. 'Orson's body disappeared. The real victim is Hollis Hadley.'

TWENTY

One day before the Spring Equinox ball

'That was Rachel,' Diana said, throwing her phone down. They'd convened in the kitchen, where Diana's phone rang a surprising amount of times that night. 'Production is shut down indefinitely.'

'Shit,' Cornelia said. Mallory hadn't moved in a while, her hands cupped around a mug of tea. Diana had woken them in the night to tell them the news, pulling Mallory from a sleep she seemed to desperately need. She'd video-called Dr Ray first to get the details and confirm the person on the slab was Hollis Hadley, glad of the distance between her and the cold grey space of the mortuary.

'It was inevitable. They could do without Orson, but Hollis... Hollis is the brain behind *Undead Complex*.'

'What else did Dr Ray say?' Mallory said quietly.

'By the time she got to working on him, she could see the "overdose" was makeup. He died of something else, she thinks asphyxiation, but there are no outward indicators that it was manual.'

'Consistent with Bellissima,' Mallory said. 'That's what the book said, isn't it? Paralytic effects, vomiting, asphyxiation.'

'That would certainly explain the vomit they found, she said that was real.' Diana wrinkled her nose. She was not a fan of the unsexy parts of being a private investigator.

'What kind of makeup?' Cornelia asked.

'Someone spent time putting raised veins on him, circles under his eyes, track marks on his arms – Dr Ray said they lifted with isopropyl, and there was no evidence he had actually used any substance recently. She said she'd get a hair strand test done as part of the toxicology report, but she doesn't think any sort of recreational drug was the cause of death.'

'The sort of thing an MUA might be able to do?' Mallory said. 'Someone like Jenna? She insisted she wasn't close by when Baker's body was found, and makeup is certainly within her skillset.'

Diana nodded. 'It's all, what do you call it – circumstantial, but that's a lot of circumstance.'

'What about the bottle they found beside him?' Cornelia asked. 'I recall something about a bottle.'

'That was the aspirin bottle Sandi told me she gave him,' Diana said, replaying the moment in her mind. 'Though she could've told us about it to hide the fact she was involved. If we found out it was hers, she's already got her cover story.'

'Someone stages his death on set of *Undead Complex*, gets production shut down for a day or two. Ransacks the dollhouse, ostensibly to find something. Then a few days later, production gets shut down permanently? Is that what the killer wanted?'

'It doesn't make sense,' Mallory said. 'I've been trying to make it make sense, but it doesn't. We're missing something big. They killed Donny Baker but pretended it was Taylor. They killed Hollis Hadley but pretended it was Orson Webb. Why?'

'That's the question,' Diana said. The answer was on the tip of her tongue. Her head felt scrambled. 'And what does it have to do with Equinox? Or the Larkins?'

'It feels incredibly disorganised,' Cornelia said.

'Yes,' Mallory said. 'It does, and I'm starting to think that's on purpose.'

'We think of murderers as being meticulous,' Diana said, starting to see Mallory's point. 'And of everything they do having a reason. The ones who are bad at creating reasons get caught, and the ones who aren't end up taunting whoever is pursuing them.'

'Right. So what if this killer—'

'The Dollhouse Murderer,' Diana said decisively. She had named their last murderer, it wouldn't do for anyone to take that job away from her. 'They're arranging the victims like they're pieces in a dollhouse. And they ransacked the dollhouse. And also indicated further murders in the dollhouse. Hence the name.'

'The Dollhouse Murderer, what if they are going in messy, and cleaning up afterwards?' Mallory said.

Diana's gaze met hers.

'Two murderers,' they said together. 'Two!'

'What?' Cornelia looked between them. 'How did you come to that conclusion?'

'Followed a line of logic,' Diana said, at the same time as Mallory said, 'Occam's Razor.'

Mallory gestured for Diana to continue.

'We could assume it's one killer trying to hide things, which is something we shouldn't rule out fully, but it makes far more sense if it's one disorganised killer, and someone else is covering things up. It would explain the inconsistency in who was being chosen.'

'What does that mean, though?' Cornelia asked helplessly. 'Why would someone want to hide Hollis Hadley's death?'

'It makes sense if the goal was not to shut down production, and only stall it,' Diana pointed at her.

'Which would make sense if, say, you were the showrunner who wanted to get as far away as possible before Hollis's body was discovered,' Mallory said, her eyes bright despite how exhausted she looked. 'But would of course make less sense if, say, he continued to post online proving he was alive.'

'Has there been any update on Orson? The living one,' Diana asked, feeling as though they were, finally, on a roll.

Cornelia fished in her pocket for her phone. 'Yes, actually. I emailed him this morning – what? Sometimes I have ideas – and pretended to be a journalist, told him I'd had an anonymous source tell me he'd had a bad relationship with Hollis and that my paper was going to run a story on their feud now that Hollis is dead.'

'And you expected a response to that?' Diana asked, aghast.

'I got one,' Cornelia said, more smugly than Diana thought she strictly deserved. 'He said he regrets quitting, he wishes he could take it back, he wants nothing more than to continue with the project to honour Hollis's legacy. Blah blah something about regretting standing around smoking with colleagues and letting it cloud his judgement, he feels he was not in his right mind while he was there and that he has woken from a terrible nightmare that twisted his actions and true desires, he regrets ever fighting with Hollis and believes the Ternion will keep him safe forevermore.'

'A long shot, but – could he have planned to leave, killed Hollis accidentally, then ran away?' Diana asked.

'A valid question, bolstered very nicely by the follow-up email I got, which read, "Do not print that or you will be hearing from my lawyers, I was hacked."' Cornelia lifted her hands.

'He could've got someone else to help him cover it up while he was gone, so it wouldn't look suspicious,' Mallory said slowly. 'Someone like Jenna, which I'd more readily believe if she hadn't seemed as though she didn't like him. Though saying that, she had more of an issue with Hollis than Orson. I did see her chat to him privately while I was on set.'

'I saw Rachel and Orson do the same thing,' Diana added. 'But she seems to dislike his management style and his general personality quite a lot.'

Cornelia wrote up *ORSON + JENNA?* And *ORSON + RACHEL?* on the board, twirling the marker between her fingers. 'That would potentially be a theory if there was only one body, but we have two,' she said. 'Which means that they would've had to work together with Baker's body too. Him running away after a second kill doesn't fully track – if the dollhouse is to be believed, there'll be three more murders.'

'But what if shutting down production was the end goal and they want the place cleared before Equinox? Killing the Creative Director would do it,' Mallory mused.

'But only once everyone knew it was the Creative Director,' Diana said. 'Which doesn't fit that hypothesis, even if the end goal is a free run at Oakpass Manor.'

'Which isn't going to work, because Quinn's hosting a party this weekend. If anything it'll be harder to get into now that production's stopped,' Cornelia said.

'So say Baker and Hollis were in the way,' Mallory said. 'Think about it – Donny Baker arrives on set early one morning, surprises the Dollhouse Murderer—'

'Or Murderers,' Cornelia added.

'Or Murderers, as they're snooping around the grounds, and is killed. Maybe that's not planned – the wound suggests there was a rapid confrontation, as it was at the front and there are no signs of defensive wounds.'

Diana raised an eyebrow at her, prompting elaboration.

'If he was surprise attacked, he'd probably have been hit from behind, or on the head. This has the sense of happening upon someone and being attacked quickly. It wasn't a fight, it was a straight kill, and the killer – or killers – could've been surprised. Maybe that's not planned at all, maybe he was in the wrong place at the wrong time. And the killer saw an opportunity to buy even more time by staging it,' Mallory said, draining her mug.

'Or killers.' Cornelia reached over to pluck Mallory's mug from her hands and refilled it.

'Shut up, Cornelia. If anyone says killer, they mean killer or killers,' Diana said, lobbing a pen at her.

Cornelia grinned. 'So Hollis was killed, using *Atropa miasma*. But Baker was murdered with a sharp weapon and *also* asphyxiated, presumably with *Atropa miasma*. Why?'

'Baker could've been given Bellissima as he was dying? To make sure they could hide the body? Dr Ray wasn't clear on how quickly he bled out, it's possible it took a while for him to die –

284

there was quite a lot of blood at the scene, but not anywhere else – maybe the weapon stayed in the wound until the body was moved and posed. Hollis… it could've been easy to poison him. Maybe he was on the alert, after Baker, so the killer… s… had to be sneakier.'

'Nope, not working for me, sorry,' Diana said. She could feel it in her gut; they weren't there yet. 'We are on the right track, but we're missing something.'

'Is there any chance of getting back in there to see Hollis's place of death?' Mallory asked. 'Just to see if there's anything we've missed.'

'They're actively dismantling it as we speak,' Diana said. 'But I would like to snoop around properly. Oakpass was a museum.' She pointed to the impressive library in the dollhouse. 'The library has glass cases in it now, but a lot of the stuff is as it was left the day the Larkins absconded from society. 'We could have a look ourselves for… whatever it is the killer – *or* killers, don't you dare interrupt me, Cornelia – are seeking. See if there's anything to find.'

'I'll try Sully.' Cornelia moved to the corner to dial. She came back shaking her head.

'Oughteron PD have claimed Hollis as their own case, as it's hit international news – I mean, of course it has. Hollis was a beloved writer, and someone got wind that Orson was reportedly found dead, so there's now reporting of some sort of on-set epidemic. She said Orson turned himself in to a local police station in Barbados early this morning to give a witness statement, and they didn't have any reason to hold him so they let him go – and I guess he got a lawyer who told him to stop talking to the media in the meantime. Folk are reporting that they saw Hollis after he went on his forty-eight-hour silent retreat.'

'Dr Ray thinks he died around the time Orson got on the plane – not late enough to eliminate the possibility,' Diana said. 'There's something very strange going on that smells of magic. Lots of incorrect information from witnesses.' The whole thing was starting to feel like a tangled knot, and it was giving her a headache.

Mallory smiled slightly. 'Welcome to eyewitness testimony 101, where the truth is that eyewitnesses get things wrong *constantly*. It's to do with how we individually process information and assemble it, and also to do with how traumatic information is encoded in the brain. What?' she asked, as Diana and Cornelia both looked at her. 'Theodore has been doing some psychology reading lately. Out loud, so I guess it's been collaborative. Sometimes we don't get all the information and form conclusions, unaware of our subjectivity in the matter. It stands to reason that there would be conflicting information, it's just a matter of how we process it. I'm still working on it.'

'I don't know if voluntarily giving a statement necessarily clears him, but I keep thinking about how Langdon's uncles said Orson was mild-mannered and strait-laced, which flies in the face of the brief interactions we've had with him,' Mallory said, blushing for a reason Diana could not identify. She filed it away for later examination.

'Anyway, Sully said she can barely get herself in there, and unless we can figure out another way onto the set that isn't illegal – emphasis on *isn't*, by the way – we're shit out of luck.' Cornelia slumped down onto her chair. 'We didn't even manage to get around to talking to all our potential suspects.'

'There has to be a way to get them all back into a room together, or at least some of them,' Mallory said. 'I'll keep thinking about that. Even with two potential killers, I can't make sense of this. We've got questions over Sandi – she gave Orson what she says was aspirin, but could be poison, in the form of Bellissima. Orson's strange departure and remorse. Jenna's odd avoidance of saying where she was, and the special-effects makeup.'

'Xander and Fred, who haven't offered any alibi yet,' Diana said. 'Rachel too.'

'Taylor and Kingston,' Mallory said. 'Though increasingly less so, given our thoughts on access to the set.'

'And Tate and Whitlock,' Diana said.

'Great. Cool. So many suspects left,' Cornelia said.

Mallory pressed her mug to her face, deep in thought.

'Right. Well,' Diana said, standing. 'We know what we have to do then, don't we?'

Mallory frowned. 'No, I don't think so?'

Diana dialled a familiar number.

'Hey, gorgeous,' she said. 'It's me. Listen, I need a favour.'

'You know, I didn't at any point suspect you were up to anything untoward,' Grey Quinn said, looking hugely out of place standing in their research room. He took out a handkerchief and dusted down their battered sofa before perching on the seat, draping a hand over the back. His expression was steady, but Diana could see his eyes were red-rimmed, like he'd been crying.

'We're private investigators,' Diana said. 'I wouldn't call anything we do necessarily *toward*.'

She had unsubtly asked Cornelia to hang out in the kitchen, but kept Mallory for emotional support, knowing she could trust her to stay quiet.

'I don't know how I missed this,' he said, leaning forward. 'So that explosion at the Mayoral Offices, that was…?'

'Us, yes,' Diana said.

'Funny. I never put two and two together.'

'It was in the papers a lot,' Mallory said.

'I don't read those, waste of my time. Though I am reconsidering that… Anyway, what do you want?'

'Let me put it to you very simply – we need access to Oakpass Manor. We'd stay there, a day or two at most, look for evidence, which would mean full access to all the records, all the rooms. Anything in there, we need to be able to examine and consider. We won't touch anything you specifically ask us not to. But we need to get to the bottom of what the killer wants at Oakpass Manor, because it's something they deem worth killing for.'

'And if I say no?' There was a glint in his eye that Diana didn't like, one that said he knew they were over a barrel. He had not become as successful as he was by being kind.

This, Diana was prepared for.

'Well, you could. But you see, Apparent police are all over this.' She paused for effect. 'They want nothing to do with our Occult force, they're refusing to cooperate with the UML on this – so much red tape, these days. It's international news, and your property is at the centre of it. Which is fine, I suppose. Apparent folk like hauntings.' Diana looked at her nails. 'They're not a fan of new ghosts, though. For a while I suspect your clientele will be one of two sorts of people: thrill-seekers and daredevils. And they don't much care about preserving the historical nature of a space, do they? Nor do they care much about the luxury or experience of a Quinn Indigo hotel.'

Quinn didn't say anything. Diana felt a tug of persuasion on her scalp, asking her to stop talking, but it was half-hearted at best, less intense than the last time he'd tried it on her.

'And not only that, the Apparent force don't know half the things we already do. This could be tied up for months. Years, even. As you see, even when they walk away from the set, even when the trail has gone cold, this will be unsolved. This will probably hang over Oakpass Manor forever, even if the studio is never resurrected, and I'm not entirely sure they'll care.'

She knew what he was thinking, could see it written all over his face.

'I suppose old ghosts are interesting, but murder adds a certain… negative connotation that I would rather was not associated with the property,' he said slowly.

'We wouldn't want future guests to feel uneasy,' Diana said smoothly. 'Particularly if there's so few of them, after all of this. And I recall your plan was to have an Equinox party very soon? Hard to justify it, with a murder hanging over your head, and that's *if* the scene is cleared in time. Just ask the Broadwicks about the end of the Samhain balls,' Diana said, driving the knife in further.

There was a pointed cough, and a blast of warmth in the room. Diana and Mallory exchanged panicked glances.

'Oh, hello,' Theodore said bitterly. 'I didn't realise if I left home for a few hours, home would be filled with menaces and charlatans. And Mallory.'

Quinn looked at him, taking in the cat ears and the whiskers, something vaguely like dawning comprehension in his eyes.

'Oh hello,' he purred. 'I believe we've met before, haven't we?'

Diana felt a crackle in the air. Six and a half years since their last meeting, and it was going about as well as she'd expected.

It occurred to her for the first time that Quinn might not know the hand he played in Theodore's death. Or rather, the hand he'd played in Theodore's wardrobe.

'"Believe" we've "met"?' Theodore waved static air quotes. Quinn took a small but undoubtedly sensible step back, and Diana wondered if she should take Mallory and run.

'I feel I'm missing something here. You are the Broadwicks' ghost, I assume?'

'I belong to nothing and no one. Unless a library membership counts. Which I suppose it does, really, membership implies a sense of belonging. But I am not *anyone's*. I am my own ghost,' Theodore said. He was forcibly maintaining a steady tone.

'It's really rather unfortunate you died in your little costume.'

A fizz of electric tension filled the air, which was growing warmer by the second, like building storm pressure. Mallory was staring uncertainly at Theodore as he whipped the cat ears off his head, throwing them at Quinn. They glanced off his shoulder and reappeared on Theodore's quivering head.

'My opinion of you,' Theodore whispered, every syllable tight with venom, 'is *lower than Atlantis*.'

'I think you should go,' Diana said abruptly, moving between the ghost and the demon. 'You know what we want, it's in your best interest to help us out.'

The air cooled and Theodore moved into the lab, muttering angrily under his breath as he went, too quiet for Diana to catch. Mallory followed him, petting him on the arm as they went.

'You'll owe me,' Quinn said, his eyes still on Theodore. 'You might think you're doing me a favour, but I assure you it is the other way around.'

'What do you want?'

'I haven't decided yet.'

But Diana knew what to offer. 'New season preview and a full range of samples from the next Ivy Cheung collection.'

'And custom tailoring.'

'Done,' Diana said. She'd worry about convincing her mother this was a necessary swap at a later date.

Quinn leaned over and shook her hand.

'It's been… well. I won't say a pleasure. But it's always interesting. I'll get you a set of keys, and I'll make sure you have clearance. Once they're finished with the scene, they said I can access the property again, so. Give it a few hours.' He did not let go of her hand. 'In and out. Don't stay for any longer than you need to. And in the name of Elisabella, don't *break* anything.'

'One last thing,' Diana said, walking him to the door. 'Whitlock and Tate.'

'Rings a bell,' he said.

'Security, at Larkin Studios,' she said.

'Ah yes, my job sharers.' His eyes flicked through the research room partition, where a quick glance from Diana confirmed Mallory was in full calm-down mode for an utterly seething Theodore.

'Any stories to share?'

He levelled a gaze at her then, taking in her outfit. 'I'll tell you, but only because, despite all the deception, I quite like you. Tate and Whitlock... neither are particularly what I'd call high fliers.'

'By regular standards or demon standards?'

'Both,' he said crisply. 'It's very hard to find good security, so I shouldn't complain really. I have neither of them anymore. Whitlock had been moaning about traditional job roles for demons – some think we should all be lawyers, as if that wouldn't be dreadfully tedious – so I've no idea what he was doing in the job, but Tate...' He dragged his teeth over his bottom lip. 'A dangerous man, in a way, though no particular threat to me. That's all I have for you, there's no scandal. Fred will meet you at the studio and bring you around to Oakpass Manor – we'll be trying to avoid any obvious traffic. The vultures are circling. By which I mean the paparazzi. I'll see you at Equinox.'

He brushed the front of his jacket, smoothly closing the button as he turned to go.

'And, Diana?'

She waited.

'You are possibly too young to know the lingering pain of the light from a torch held by an old lover. One you'd do anything for even as the years pass and the light dims. To lose someone after you'd do anything for them, even buy a property that has brought you nothing but misfortune, all to see them realise a dream they've held for a lifetime.'

Diana suppressed a truthful response. 'But?'

He reached for his pocket watch, nimbly flipping it so Diana could see an engraving on the back: *love will always rise again*

'Avenge him,' he said simply, tucking it away.

The second he was gone, Diana allowed herself to jump up and down.

'Did you see that? I negotiated with a demon and *won*. I didn't even need to use subterfuge, that was a plain old negotiation and I won!' She stopped. 'Also, I did not pick up on the history between him and Hollis Hadley. He seems genuinely sad.'

'Oh BOO HOO. BOO BLOODY HOO,' Theodore shouted. 'Six and a half years I've waited to face him, to get a semblance of an apology, an *acknowledgement* of the state he left me in, and he… he…' Theodore shook a fist at the door. 'He *just talked to me.*'

Diana knew better than to antagonise him when he was this angry. Knew better, but chose not to take that particular tack.

'He did acknowledge it. He didn't say anything helpful, or soothing, or kind, but he did definitely acknowledge the cat costume.'

'FOUL MALEVOLENT UNFEELING BEAST,' Theodore shouted.

'I think you mean *unfeline.*'

'Diana!' Mallory shot an alarmed look at Theodore.

But Theodore had broken into a smile. 'That was quite good, Diana. I am rubbing off on you. Unfeline beast, what a solid insult *and* solid wordplay. Beautiful. I'm off for a walk,' he said, and disappeared through the wall.

Diana blinked after him.

'What was that about Hollis?'

Diana filled her in.

'Interesting. Quinn's also helping us, which… helps his case.'

'But let's focus on my brilliance,' Diana said, feeling a bubble of victory.

Mallory gave a tiny round of applause. 'Great job. Now we just need to get in there, and see if we can find anything that'll help us actually solve this case.'

It was as simple as it sounded, and yet it felt insurmountable.

PERIMORTEM III

The body put up more of a fight than the others. They felt like they were dissolving, a sensation of falling over and over, dolly-track framing pulling the set walls in and in and in around them.

They were being dragged. Their skull slapping the floor with every step, their hands clenched but refusing to comply with their demands to move. A muscle twitch told them they were still living, but only just.

No sound escaped them as they were dragged under a single spotlight, though it was not overhead. It beamed into their eyes from some unseen direction, blocking out the background, green shapes dancing in the body's eyes.

They didn't know where they were, but they were dropped unceremoniously onto a hardwood floor, then dropped again until they assumed a position whoever was dragging them seemed pleased with.

The figure split in two and for a moment the body recalled being asked to *breathe it in.* They tried to and couldn't, their lungs long past being able to gasp for air, and the memory vanished as quickly as it surfaced.

There was a face – one, now – the spotlight refused to let them focus on, a wavering beam that gave them moments of reprieve. Their vision furred at the edges, a sense the figure was growing larger and more distorted, an expansive shadow that felt anything but truly real.

They were facing death with despair.

The air was thick with it. Thicker than dust, than anger.

The figure's footsteps sounded hollow, like they were in a wide space.

It felt familiar.

And then there was another sound. One the body vaguely registered as not coming from them, or the figure, but somewhere else, off-screen, outside the realms of their awareness.

It was their last thought.

TWENTY-ONE

Despite all signs pointing to the contrary, the now-deserted Larkin Studios and the looming Oakpass Manor had a certain *l'eau du spectre* that Diana couldn't shake. A wind had picked up, howling across the stone exterior and drowning out their footsteps across the gravel.

'I still think it's weird Fred left us a key and no note,' Diana said. 'And even then, I'm not sure the keys being on the security-hut counter qualify as "leaving" them.'

'Maybe he told Quinn to fuck off over being asked to wait for us? I would too, if my boss was away and my other boss was dead and some rich dickhead tried to treat me as their PA,' Cornelia said.

'Yes, cause we don't know any rich dickheads,' Diana shot back, earning herself a shove.

'He could've left us a cart,' Mallory said, and Diana realised she was several paces behind. She slowed until she was in step with her, crossing over the bridge, Oakpass nearing with every step. For several minutes as they walked, Diana could only hear the three of them breathing, and a dull buzzing in the back of her head.

'We do need to find Fred, when we're done here, see if he has anything to say for himself,' Cornelia said.

'Finally, an interrogation! We're long overdue one.' Diana fit the key into the lock, mildly saddened that it was not comically large, and let them in to the entrance hall, uncertain. She held up a witchlight, casting the space in a fluorescent-green alien glow that bounced off the pillars in the centre of the hall.

There were ghosts of *Undead Complex* still present – set pieces, scattered folding chairs, a makeshift makeup table, even a dolly track that Diana carefully stepped over to reach the wood-panelled wild wall of the set that had yet to be disassembled at the entrance to the drawing room. Osseous candles Alannah had moulded were on every available surface around a bed piled high with furs, the empty eyes of a skull with a spine-shaped candle atop its head staring straight at her. Diana could imagine the set lit with an eerie orange glow, Xander's character lying in the grip of fever. Or whatever was meant to happen in the scene.

There was no blood marking the place Hollis Hadley had died. Just a small vomit stain and a dip in the blankets where his body had rested, an absence marred by mussed pillows that she imagined had been tossed to the ground when he was discovered. She lifted the witchlight, catching Mallory and Cornelia's faces in an eerie glow.

Mallory, with her hands in a pair of latex gloves, Cornelia, with a vaguely disquieted expression.

'Manor's haunted.' Cornelia grabbed a packet of salt and upended it into her pocket.

'What?' Mallory had produced a blue witchlight and was peering closely at the bed, presumably looking for physical evidence, though Diana could tell her heart wasn't fully in it; the scene had already been trampled on by police and there wasn't going to be much left to find. She held out a hand to accept a beetle from Cornelia, their fingers brushing for a fraction of a second. Diana pretended not to notice Mallory swallow her emotion.

'Manor's haunted,' Cornelia repeated.

'It isn't haunted, you're being an absolute baby,' Diana said, the witchlight wavering over Cornelia's face. 'Since when are you afraid of a little haunting, anyway? You've lived with a ghost in your house since you were fourteen.'

Predictably, the beetle reacted exactly as all the others had, and Mallory slotted it back into its little box, raising an eyebrow at Diana as she did.

'Goddess, I wish Theodore was here,' Cornelia said. 'Might cheer the place up a bit.'

Diana whispered a spell to make Cornelia's skin crawl, and smiled when Cornelia shrieked, wriggling frantically.

Mallory looked at them both reproachfully, tucking an evidence bag into her kit. 'We're here in an official agency capacity,' she reminded them. 'Please stop acting like children.'

'Us? Children? Never,' Cornelia said. 'Let's find some proper lights, and then find the library and some weapons. We need to find something to go on.'

She felt around the wall and screamed a tiny bit again.

'Wasn't me this time,' Diana said before Mallory could express her disapproval. 'She's freaked herself out.'

Overhead lights flooded on. Diana felt the space shrink before her as the shadows were banished and the manor felt less hostile.

'Yes, that's what we need. Twitchy investigators,' Mallory said crossly, her expression so fierce that Diana and Cornelia took one look at each other and burst out laughing.

'Sorry, sorry, Mallory, I'm trying to get it under control, sorry,' Diana gasped, not wanting to upset her so early into the mission. 'Do we remember the plan?'

'How could I forget the heist demonstration you did with the dollhouse?' Cornelia hit a second light switch, illuminating the upper floor.

Diana had already made a beeline for the stairs, pocketing her witchlight. 'Be glad I lovingly restored the dollhouse in time to give the demonstration in the first place.'

'Ah yes, all that work you did with Taylor,' Cornelia said. Diana fought the itch to push her down the stairs a little bit. 'How is she?'

'Had she anything useful to say?' Mallory asked, diplomatic as usual.

Diana wanted to give her a hug; she'd had so many opportunities to ask Diana outright what was going on with Taylor – not that there was anything to report – and she'd chosen not to.

'Like, the name of the murderer, or what in the name of the Ternion has been going on here?' Cornelia asked.

'Ha ha,' Diana said flatly, risking a glance back just as Cornelia's shoulder grazed a painting on the wall beside her. A hairy second passed as it swung side to side, before she steadied it with her hand. 'No, I haven't really heard from her.' She hadn't texted her at all since she'd brought her home. 'I'm capable of following agency rules, you know – you said you wanted to keep things professional, so I'll let you handle the progress reports when we have something worth sharing.'

Both Mallory and Cornelia blinked at that. 'Great,' Mallory said, recovering first, looking incredibly uncomfortable. 'I'm glad the things I say have some bearing on how we conduct ourselves.'

Diana would revisit whatever that was about when they were settled in. 'Next floor,' she said.

They climbed a second, shorter staircase covered in red carpet that led to one of the surprisingly vast Manor turrets – 'Not actually as decadent as you'd imagine when it houses approximately *nine thousand years*' worth of dust,' Cornelia grumbled between sneezes – and crossed a narrow hallway to a walnut-wood door, that admittedly *did* look somewhat familiar.

'This is it,' Diana said, and pushed. 'Aaand, of course it's locked.'

'Allow me,' Mallory said. She pulled out a set of lock picks and set upon the door handle, making short work of it.

'We should really all consider getting a set,' Cornelia said.

'I've got spares,' Mallory said, pushing the door open and feeling around the walls for a light. 'And hair clips. And honestly, worst case scenario, you could try kicking the door in. Oh wow,' she gasped, looking around.

Although Diana had worked on it in miniature, in person it was indeed an oh-wow-worthy room. Curved black bookcases stuffed full of volumes lined the walls, a tall polished ladder resting next to the door. Deer antlers took pride of place over a sloping hearth, with a deep burgundy period sofa set visible under the dust-laden white sheets covering it, glass cases that Diana remembered seeing when she was young clustered across the back.

Cornelia sneezed again, but Diana was certain it was for effect.

'What are we looking for?'

'Anything on the history of Oakpass Manor, Larkin Studios or the Appoccult Society. We need to figure out what the Dollhouse Murderers are looking for, and see if we can establish any written basis for choosing Equinox. Start here,' Diana said, moving to the glass cases. 'There're diaries, newspaper cuttings, stuff we can't find online or in archives.'

The Undetectables clustered around to peer at a photo of the Larkin family, accompanied by clinically written museum text on cream card. Diana leaned her head on Mallory's shoulder as she examined the text, who patted her hair in response. It was always good to check Mallory wasn't furious with her.

'I do wonder what actually happened to the Larkins,' Cornelia mused. 'It's hard not to imagine the five lines Mallory found in the dollhouse, five potential murder victims, and five Larkins has some sort of link. It's especially weird that nobody seems to know where they went. Only that they were gone in the dead of night.'

'Stands to reason they're dead now, and have been for a long time,' Mallory said. 'Not just because over a hundred years has passed since the Larkins last lived here, but because it is very, *very* strange for a wealthy Apparent family to up and leave all their possessions behind. *Any* family, really. Why did they leave

Oakpass? And why was the dollhouse found, but not their bodies?'

'The plot, she forever thickens,' Diana muttered.

'Diana, look!' Mallory beckoned her towards another placard set on top of another glass case. 'This is about the dollhouse. It's not a great photo, but look! "Family friend and dollhouse enthusiast, F. Leon".'

A blurry photo of a woman with her hands placed primly in front of her, standing next to what was unmistakably a diorama. Diana's heart skipped.

Francine Leon.

'She was here! When is that photo from?'

'Nineteen-twenty, couple of years before the Larkins left-slash-died,' Mallory said.

'She hadn't even started her most salient work yet, this was just a hobby,' Diana said. 'She'd met her wife around then, I think – though they were officially "gal pals", because, you know, Apparent history.'

'I do know Apparent history,' Mallory said grimly. 'And its habit of erasing folk. Anyway, thought you might like to see it. What was her wife's name?'

'Delfina Sackville, she was an actress.'

'This Delfina?' Mallory pointed to another sign. '"*Cast of C'est La Vie, Larkin Studios, 1919. Delfina S, Patrick G, Isaac OP, R.E. Lam.*"'

'That's her! I didn't know she had anything to do with the Larkins.' Diana gasped, a thought striking her. 'Mallory, the dollhouse, do you think… do you…'

The idea was almost too much to handle.

'It could be,' Mallory said. 'She could've built it.'

'That means I have a tiny piece of Francine Leon in my house. I've held her work in my hands. I've reached through history to hold her hand in mine,' Diana said, feeling her face split into a grin. 'But she's Apparent, what was—'

'Appoccult Society,' Cornelia interrupted.

'Wild guess,' Diana said.

Cornelia held up the scrapbook in her hand. 'This is a combined record of all the newspaper stories about Oakpass up until the Larkins' disappearance. Francine was listed as an Appoccult Society member, as was Delfina.'

'That's an adorable meet-cute.' Diana beamed at her, then held up a hand for silence. 'Is that noise in my head, or can you hear it too?' she whispered.

A slow, dragging sound, like someone taking a step and pulling something along behind them.

The other two stopped, Cornelia cocking her head like a dog, listening.

The hair on Diana's arms rose as Cornelia's eyes widened.

Diana pointed towards the door, miming to walk quietly, and rolled her eyes when Cornelia darted across and out the door.

'She's going to get us killed,' Diana whispered. Mallory shook her head, and they both followed, still listening. The noise hadn't stopped, and when they got to the hall, the lights off, Cornelia was crouched at the bannisters, her nose pressed through the wooden dowels, her hand cupped to her ear.

Listening spell, Diana realised. Her ear was still ringing, and she couldn't focus on any one sound in particular.

Cornelia beckoned them over. Mallory crouched before they got to the stairs, trying to fold her long limbs around themselves so she could press up close to Cornelia's hand. Diana, who could not and also would not make herself small, grabbed Cornelia's hand instead to use her listening spell, for all the good it did her.

Step. Drag. Step. Drag. Step. Step. Step.

'Shit,' Diana mouthed. 'What do we do?'

'We run,' Cornelia said.

TWENTY-TWO

Before anyone could react, Cornelia took to the stairs, shouting, 'OI!' in the deepest, most un-Cornelia-like voice Diana had ever heard her use.

A hooded figure crouched in the hallway, shining a torch at the stairs – a big, industrial torch that made it impossible to see the figure's face. Spots danced in Diana's eyes as she strained to take in the scene.

Next to them, another figure. Someone sprawled out on the floor, unmoving, arms splayed at a crooked angle.

A body.

Dead.

Diana felt something tug at her mind, urging her to look away as Cornelia stopped mid-run, arms raised as though she was going to jump on the intruder like some sort of flying squirrel. Diana took a step back, treading on Mallory's foot, who let out a hiss of pain and they both stumbled to a stop. The figure dodged and Cornelia tripped on the rug they were standing on.

The figure dropped the torch and ran, past the staircase and into the entrance hall. Diana shook herself and followed, Cornelia right behind her. The figure paused as Diana gained on them, whirling around, then moved left, away from the door and behind a pillar. Diana rounded the pillars as the figure slipped into the back hallway, dodging a stack of light stands propped against the wall.

'Back door!' Diana gasped, and Cornelia pivoted away from the front door, a look of confusion on her face Diana didn't have time to question. Mallory came up behind her just as the door in question slammed shut behind the figure.

Diana wrenched it open magically and they emerged at the side of the manor.

There was no sign of the figure.

'I knew they went out the front door.'

'No they didn't,' Diana said sharply. 'Mallory and I followed them out here.'

'Mallory was still at the front door when I ran this way,' Cornelia said. 'She's still inside. I could've sworn to Hexana… never mind, it was confusing in there. Fucker's probably in the flowerbeds. Hold on,' Cornelia said, pulling out her phone and flicking on the torch.

Diana clapped her hands and the courtyard lights flooded on.

'Even better. COME OUT, COME OUT,' Cornelia called. There was something alarmingly alive in her face.

'I'll take this side,' Diana said. 'Whoever it is can't have gone far.'

But though they searched high, and though they searched

low, two thirds of the Undetectables did not find the intruder, or any trace of their escape.

'Hexana,' Diana said, wiping her face. 'What was that about?'

'I've no idea, but I wish they'd let me tackle them.'

'You'd have squished them like a bug.'

'That's the most hurtful thing you've ever said to me.'

'Diana? Cornelia?' Mallory called from inside. Diana trotted back in, Cornelia standing and wiping her flowerbed-muddied feet on the entrance rug. Diana did not need to turn around to hear Cornelia realise it was not actually a floor mat.

The lights were back on, and Mallory was crouched in front of the figure sprawled on the ground next to her. It reminded Diana of something, of seeing Mallory in this position before, calm and assured.

'It's like you were born to find bodies,' Diana said, trying to elicit a smile, but none came.

'You might want to see this,' Mallory said calmly. 'But it's going to upset you.'

Diana's thoughts instantly went to Taylor and a sickening feeling pooled in her stomach, her mouth drying.

'How upsetting could we find a dead body at this stage in our career?' Cornelia asked, nudging Diana further into the room. Her tone betrayed the fear that had descended over them, the adrenaline of the chase wearing off rapidly and transforming into palpable tension.

Someone else had died. She hadn't heard from Taylor in a while.

'No,' Mallory said. 'Not you. I mean maybe you, I can't tell you how to feel your feelings, I guess. But Diana will be upset.

Come here.' She held her hand out to Diana, who took it slowly, the body still obscured behind Mallory.

Diana knew then what she was going to see, and that it wasn't going to be Taylor.

She wasn't sure how, but she *knew*. Mallory would probably handle that kind of reveal differently. This was going to be worse.

Her gaze fell on the body.

On her own face.

Her heart plummeted. She lifted her hands, waiting for static to appear, afraid that the worst had happened somehow, even though it was impossible; it wasn't Samhain, and her friends could still see her.

She was not dead. She could not be dead.

But even still, tears rose up the back of her throat and she choked them down angrily, willing the body on the floor to not be hers, looking for any kind of proof that she was alive.

The body's face – Diana's face – flickered in and out of existence, becoming fuzzy and undefinable. The body changing size and shape repeatedly, skin changing from light brown to translucent pale. Her face blurred, barely recognisable, though there was something about it that seized at her. One moment Diana, the next moment…

'Oh,' Diana breathed, as relieved as she was horrified. 'That's Fred.'

Fred, the third victim. Diana had hardly formed an opinion on him, but her stomach still dropped at the sight. He didn't deserve this. Nobody deserved this. And he certainly shouldn't have been wearing her face.

'I'm looking down at my body and it looks like a discarded rag doll,' Diana said. 'But it's not my body, it's his, it's… That's my face. That's me.'

It was a less devastating feeling than when Ben died, than when Theodore and even Beckett had died, but Diana still felt a horrifying chill sweep through her again and again. Cornelia was wrong: murder would never get easier. Finding the bodies of people she knew would never get easier.

'That's not all,' Mallory said gently. 'But we can let you take a minute.'

Diana didn't want a minute; she didn't want to be there at all.

'We should've worried when Fred didn't show,' Mallory said. She was staring at the body on the floor like she was trying to see something other than what was there. Diana kept looking at the face – her face – and willing Fred to emerge permanently so she didn't have to keep seeing it.

'At least we can categorically eliminate Orson now, as he's still in Barbados,' Cornelia said.

'The killer has slipped up if we can see Fred beneath the Diana glamour. Either they didn't have enough time to make Bellissima work, or they didn't dose him correctly. Or… I don't know,' Mallory said. 'Fred was meant to be here, why would they disguise him with your face? Why bring him in here?'

'To the stairs,' Diana said, pointing. 'Like the dollhouse, there was a victim meant to have fallen down the stairs. And as this is victim three, like the dollhouse suggested… I think we're right in assuming there are to be two more, and that they're happening on or before Equinox.'

'What's the significance of the locations?' Cornelia asked. 'Baker wasn't even found inside Oakpass.'

'But that set was meant to be in the study,' Diana said. 'They didn't want to clean up the actual room, I heard. So study, drawing room, main staircase… courtyard. Maybe what Shit King said is what they're doing – some sort of Undead Complex ritual, raising the gatekeepers… whatever that means.'

'This is the two motivations problem again,' Mallory said, still kneeling next to Diana-Fred. 'It's a case of two parts. It's not a clear escalation of murder – though it is serial,' she added mildly. 'It all links together – presumably the killers link together too – but it's like… a dance. One killer takes a step, the other follows, sowing confusion in their wake.'

'That's a really good point,' Cornelia said. 'So the first killer is about finding treasure, the Undead Complex, killing people, and they're leading the charge. The second killer is fucking with people, possibly for fun, or else this staging is an important part of the ritual. If we could figure out where the treasure fits into all this, we might be able to get somewhere.'

'What if…' Mallory said slowly, looking thoughtfully into space. 'What if "Lady Larkin's lost treasure" isn't treasure in the conventional sense, but is *the Larkins*?'

'Elaborate,' Diana said.

'Think about it. We didn't have much time for snooping, but most of the rest of the crew might have managed it. Jenna, Sandi, Xander, Whitlock, Tate and Rachel would've had time to hunt for treasure under the guise of doing literally anything else – the person who had the least amount of time to run around was Taylor. If the treasure was something small, like a necklace or a book or an object, they wouldn't need to have cleared space or shut down production. But if they were looking for *bodies*, you'd want privacy and to have nobody around asking questions.'

'Think of what Kingston said, about the gatekeepers and the chess board and… I really didn't fully listen to everything he said,' Cornelia said. 'But the gist was something to do with two…'

'Two souls,' Mallory said. 'The King Me Principle. The Undead Complex could be the process of combining two souls, somehow. And, say, if you had five Larkins, and five murder victims, you could raise five gatekeepers.'

'And maybe the killer can't carry out the Undead Complex without them. Doesn't come close to explaining *why* or *who* would do it, but it's a great start,' Cornelia said, and Mallory beamed.

'Makes a lot of sense for Dollhouse Murderer One. And if someone was, say, investigating the murders you and your partner-in-crime had committed, you'd maybe want to scare them off,' Diana said, unable to take her eyes off her own flickering dead face, reminding herself it wasn't actually her, even when Fred's face refused to form fully.

It's Fred, it's Fred, it's Fred.

'It doesn't quite explain the changing faces, though,' Mallory said.

'I think this one is a message. The Dollhouse Murderers didn't expect to get caught tonight, but I think they knew we'd find Fred as me. If Taylor could find out who we are – as in, what we do – anyone could.'

'And we haven't fully eliminated Taylor yet,' Cornelia added. 'We can't discount the people that bring us in on cases ever again.'

Diana nodded, but didn't trust herself to speak.

'I found something,' Mallory said. She reached beneath Fred-Diana's body and pulled out a bag with gloved hands, forever a stickler for rules in the moments it mattered most.

'This was with him.' She unfolded something that looked like a makeup brush roll, revealing long candles, a bulb of mercury, some sort of animal fur – Diana thought it was rabbit, but she couldn't be sure – a bottle of something that bore such an uncanny resemblance to blood it could not have been anything else, a little steel spatula, and a sprig of a plant that Cornelia raised to her nose to sniff even as Mallory and Diana looked on in alarm. 'This is henbane,' Cornelia said, her nose wrinkling. 'I saw it in that book. It's known as the necromancy plant. Smells like – and I cannot stress this enough – absolute shit.'

'And this,' Mallory said, clearly not finished. She pointed to a bag discarded in the corner. Quick examination revealed a bottle of liquid latex, some sponges, cotton balls and body paint.

'And this,' Mallory said again. 'This is the last one, I won't say "and this" again.'

A ragged page torn from a book with a running head of *Alternative Occult for the Magick-less*, with a list of vague, flowery instructions entitled *FINDERS KEEPERS*.

'Various plants, looks like instructions for some kind of spell. But nobody, bar the Witches of Bonemarrow Lake, does that kind of shit anymore. I'm not even sure it'd work without an actual witch,' Cornelia said, leaning over Fred with a beetle in her hands.

'I was waiting for you to come back to start collecting evidence,' Mallory said quietly, accepting the beetle, and Diana understood that she was speaking only to Cornelia. She contemplated teleporting herself away from their private exchange with a witchlight, but realised she'd left it up in the library.

Cornelia's face softened. 'We didn't find the killer outside. Just in case that wasn't clear to you.'

Mallory smiled. 'I figured.'

Diana cleared her throat and then got to work taking photos of Fred's body, and a video, her skin crawling. It was eerie, watching herself flickering in and out of inhabiting a blurry face. Like she was having an out-of-body experience, but for real.

Like how Theodore must've felt the day he died.

'We need to call this in,' Mallory said when they'd finished. 'But I'll try Sully first, I'd rather not deal with the Oughteron police. Then we run our samples back at the lab, and hope for the best.'

Sully mercifully picked up on the second ring, and Mallory relayed the details quickly and with a calmness that Diana tried to soak in, her hands still shaking.

Sully's response was brief but vehement. 'Get out of there now. I mean it: safely extricate yourselves. I will tell Oughteron we got an anonymous tip, but you can't be there. Are you sure it's this Fred?'

'That's true,' Cornelia said. 'Maybe the spell has gone wrong and it's a secret third person.'

'Somehow, I don't think so,' Diana said dryly, seizing the opportunity to demonstrate just how fine she was. 'Despite the fact some details are not consistent with the previous two murders, we can confidently ID this body as Fred's.'

'How's that?' Cornelia demanded.

'His phone.' Diana pulled it from his pocket. The melting smiley face sticker was still there. 'This is Fred's phone.'

Mallory had the Machine on and samples running while Cornelia busied herself making them all hot chocolates with oat milk, adding extra marshmallows and sprinkles for Diana without her even having to ask, which was almost scary. Cornelia being nice made her feel untethered, like there was something wrong with her.

She resisted the urge to snap at Cornelia, to try to rebalance things, and accepted her marshmallows as a prize for doing so, feeling rebellious for drinking it in the lab.

'Mallory,' she said, intently trying to manoeuvre a half-melted marshmallow into her mouth. 'Do you remember anything specific happening when we encountered the intruder?'

'We fell over,' she said sadly, her attention on the Machine in anticipation. 'That was a bit pathetic.'

Diana laughed. 'Not what I mean.'

'Well, I froze. I had been really brave up to that point, and then I completely froze and couldn't move any further.'

'Did you feel anything when that happened?'

'Other than annoyed?'

'Yes.'

'Frustrated, also, like something was… something was stopping me.'

'It was like demon magic,' Diana said. 'Like something was freezing me in place, scrambling my thoughts, trying to persuade me to stop advancing on them. I know we thought about the demons in the crew, but Jenna, Tate, Whitlock… I really think we were up against one of them tonight.'

'Oh,' Cornelia said. 'So I *didn't* run out of fight halfway to starting it.'

The Machine beeped and Mallory reacted as a glass vial filled on the side.

She lifted it up where Diana could see the sapphire-blue smoke curling around itself.

'Well,' Mallory said softly. 'There is a trace here. And it's demon magic.'

TWENTY-THREE

'Definitely?' Cornelia pushed her glasses up her nose, squinting at the vial.

'Well, no. *This* is definitely demon magic,' Mallory held it up again. I need to run more tests to be sure that the samples are consistent, and *then* I can say for certain we've got a demon magic trace.'

Diana fizzed with impatience as she did so, offering assistance until it got to the point that she was certain she was being more hindrance than help.

'Okay so, our original theory was correct,' Diana said.

'We *have reasonable belief* our original hypothesis was correct,' Mallory said.

'What you said. Jenna, Whitlock and Tate are looking mighty suspicious. Although, Tate quit, and we don't know where he is.'

'He could've kept his access passes, he could've manipulated someone to continue getting access…'

'Difficult, if the other security guard is also a demon,' Cornelia said.

'And vice versa,' Mallory said, sitting carefully on the stool behind her. 'The other security guard is a demon, so how would he get past Tate when he was stationed there?'

'And vice vice versa,' Cornelia added. 'For Jenna.'

'None of them would've known we were there today, and there was no one on the gate – in theory, any of them could've walked in and surprised Fred, or targeted him specifically, to ensure there was no one around to witness... whatever they were doing.' Diana ran a hand through her hair, thinking. 'The rules of the Undead Complex are unclear to me still, but let's assume Mallory's right and the Dollhouse Murderers intend to kill five times, culminating with the grand finale on Spring Equinox. And let's also assume the goal is to find the Larkins, as Mallory suggested, and I am starting to get massively on board with this hypothesis because you're right, why else would you clear out the film crew if not for something big, Occult-y, and otherwise illegal?'

'Or generally frowned upon,' Cornelia said. 'Not the murder part, but the digging up corpses part. Generally speaking, it's not cool.'

'Let's assume that's the case for the time being,' Mallory said. 'If we take Whitlock and Tate, one was working each day of the first murders. Jenna was an essential crew member, so was there both days. What if we're looking for two demons? Jenna helps with the staging, and one of the security guards guarantees access?'

'That could be the case, but we'd be hinging the assumption on Jenna's ability to do makeup, more than on her being a demon,' Diana said.

'Quinn said something about them not being high fliers, either of them. He said something about Whitlock being obsessed with traditional roles or some shit, but said he wouldn't trust Tate. If Tate was working the evening Hollis was killed, he could've let the killer in – or he could be the killer himself,' Cornelia said.

Diana felt overwhelmed by the possibilities. 'We could say the same about Whitlock, though, on the morning Baker was killed.'

'But if we think about Dollhouse Murderer Two as the one doing the clean-up, why would a demon bother using plant magic?' Mallory asked. 'Or disguising the bodies? If it's two demons working together, that piece doesn't fit. That spell we found at the scene, the one that was non-magical magic… That could be an Apparent, or someone who isn't a witch. Why bother if you had other abilities at your disposal?'

'Our buddy the Whistler had plenty at his disposal, and he still used Blair's ring. Hey, do you think *Atropa miasma* was in the ring, and that's what made it work?'

'I think we're getting off topic,' Diana said quickly.

'But why would you hide the bodies inside other bodies, and still stage the scenes? Why would you pretend a different crew member was the one dead, when surely someone would notice the actual missing colleague? When Bellissima wears off, and everyone finds out who the real body is anyway? I know we wondered if it was part of the ritual, but does it *really* make sense for that to be the case? WHAT IS THE POINT OF THIS?' Mallory shouted suddenly, then pressed her lips together. Diana shot her an amused glance; Mallory was saying what she was sure they were all thinking. 'Sorry, I'm running on empty here and I want something to fall into place. It's like every time we think we're onto something with the Larkins and Oakpass and Equinox, a new thing pops up to scramble our thoughts. I just want to know why— oh,' she said. There was a glimmer in her eye and Diana felt herself smiling, her glance sliding to Cornelia to see she had seen it too.

They waited for Mallory's mouth to catch up with her brain. 'That's it.'

'What's it?'

'A wise ghost once said to me, evidence of absence is not absence of evidence,' Mallory said breathlessly. 'Bellissima is, first and foremost, *a hallucinogen*. We haven't been able to make interpersonal links between the victims, or really make sense of why each of them was murdered, because none of the stories lined up. We got conflicting reports on people's character, and what's been going on. Earlier, Diana shouted the killer had gone to the back door, but I thought they were still around the pillars. Cornelia had gone to the *front* door. We all saw slightly different things. When I saw fake-Diana's body, I could only see Diana in flashes, like Fred's face was blurred. Then Diana said it was her, and I couldn't see Fred anymore at all, even when the face flickered. The more I thought of the body as being Diana's, no matter how hard I tried to see Fred's face, I couldn't.'

'To what end?' Cornelia said patiently.

'I… have no idea,' Mallory said. When she got like this, the words tumbled out of her mouth and she seemed almost frustrated with herself for not being able to communicate her point. 'But what if that's an unintended outcome of using Bellissima as part of the ritual? And Dollhouse Murderer Two used it to their advantage? There's a guaranteed tangle of confusion around why the murders happened in the first place – we've spent *days* chasing down reasons why someone would kill Taylor, only to find it's Baker, and we'd probably have assumed Orson died by suicide if not for the dollhouse. And our direct line to—'

Diana's phone rang, the screen lighting up with the words *DR RAY – MORTUARY*.

Mallory pointed excitedly as Diana answered.

'Hi, Dr Ray. We have an audience listening in, so whatever sweet nothings you were going to whisper to me are going to be assessed by the judging panel.'

Mallory shot her a look and Diana batted her eyelashes in response.

'You will be getting sweet nothing if you *ever* say that to me again.'

Diana grinned. It was always a good sign when Dr Ray was receptive to her being ridiculous. It meant nothing terrible had happened. 'Did you get through the autopsy on Fred Hill already?'

'I would love to know where you think I get the time to move as fast as your little imaginations would like me to.'

'If I answered honestly, I think you'd hang up on me, so…'

'I got the toxicology reports back,' she said, ignoring Diana. It was perhaps the best course of action, all things considered. There was the sound of paper crumpling in the background. 'From the Donald Baker case and from Hollis Hadley, surprisingly – I had not expected the lab to move that quickly.'

Cornelia looked away, and Diana knew that what had made the lab move faster was not, strictly speaking, the bodies piling up. She made a mental note to speak to Mallory later about designing some sort of anti-corruption policy for the agency. If they weren't careful, Cornelia's efforts to help them were going to get them into a fucktonne of trouble.

'Regardless, and don't think for a second I don't know what greased that particular axle, Cornelia Broadwick,' Dr Ray continued, 'I am choosing to believe they made a decision from the goodness of their hearts. Hollis Hadley had no trace of aspirin in his stomach – nothing suspicious found in stomach contents at all for either victim.'

They exchanged glances – that meant it probably wasn't Sandi, unless she was hoping the mention of aspirin would provide a good enough cover for administering Bellissima.

'Blood tox analysis was a little more promising. Based on these reports, and my findings from the medical examinations conducted, I can confirm that both victims died of poisoning.'

'Poisoning with what?' Mallory asked, her face already telling Diana that she was satisfied enough that they were on the right track with Bellissima.

'It says "unknown" here,' Dr Ray said. 'Which is not very helpful.'

'We think we know what it is,' Diana said. She ran Dr Ray through the extent of their discovery, leaving out the various illegal and underhanded means by which they obtained the information. The less the Night Mayor knew about their shenanigans, the better.

'Then the killer is administering the poison through a more indirect method. Good work,' she said.

'Dr Ray, when do you plan to release the bodies to the families?'

'Not for a while. Thank Elisabella we haven't had to before now, the disaster that could've been. I— Alyssa?'

There was the sound of Dr Ray's phone being put down and low talking that Diana strained to hear.

'We're right,' Mallory whispered. 'Bellissima is tying all this together.'

'But it still doesn't explain why Murderer Two is going to such great lengths to hide the bodies. If it's just going to wear off, surely it's more efficient—' Cornelia started.

'But what if that's *accidental*? What if Dollhouse Murderer Two isn't Occult, or doesn't understand how to use Bellissima properly, and it's wearing off prematurely?' Mallory cut in. 'Then the goal isn't to change the faces of the bodies – it's a *consequence* of using Bellissima!'

'This is just bonkers enough that it's starting to make sense to me,' Diana said. It was not, she'd readily admit, the simplest explanation by any means, as it didn't explain *why* the bodies were also staged, but it fit another tiny piece of the puzzle into place. 'Great work, detective.'

'For fuck*sake*.' Dr Ray shuffled the handset. 'Sully's just heard there's been another police callout to set – another body, they fear – but she can't get access currently. Or possibly at all.'

The Undetectables exchanged glances. The dollhouse suggested there were only meant to be two more bodies, and they'd been banking on those turning up at Equinox.

'Are you sure?'

'No, but I don't think we can be sure unless a friendly face goes to confirm.'

'So what you're saying is, "Help me, Diana et al"?'

'If you think I'm going to poorly misquote Apparent cinema at you, you are mistaken. I cannot and will not ask you to do anything untoward, but I will leave you with this: some things can only be done in specific, underhanded ways.'

Spoken like a true Night Mayor of Wrackton.

'I cannot believe you have talked me into doing this,' Diana said, knowing full well this was entirely her idea and she was somewhat excited. The Undetectables were standing around a witchlight, the other two members looking apprehensive. They were about to do something very ill-advised, definitely illegal, but also brilliant. It was underhanded but would get them the answers they wanted. This was their case.

Diana's to solve.

'I'm undertaking a dangerous mission.'

'Are you done yet?' Cornelia asked. 'Mallory looks worried.'

'I'm not worried,' Mallory said worriedly. 'I'm thinking that you've possibly spent too much time around Theodore, that was a very him-thing to say. But seriously, what do we do if you get caught?'

'I'm not going to get caught,' Diana said airily. She had a rule for herself: to act confident enough about things that the thing or things in question did not sense she was frightened, and therefore did not backfire horribly. It mostly worked, much of the time. 'I've been through a witchlight before. I left one in the library when we came out to accost the intruder, there is no way this won't work.'

'Assuming it's still there.' A crease appeared on Mallory's forehead. She worried far too much for Diana's liking.

'If it's not, what's the worst that could happen? That is rhetorical, do not answer that. I'll be fine. In and out, confirm if there's a body and see what I can get from it. If there is a body and it doesn't match the positions of the bodies in the dollhouse, then maybe we're on the wrong track. But we need to know what we're up against.'

'This is breaking and entering, though,' Mallory said.

'I don't have to officially break into anywhere – just enter, but does it even count if I use a magical portal? Don't answer that either, I don't want to know. I want you to know that I am a motherfucking genius, and this is yet another example of that.'

'Take photos,' Mallory said finally. 'Lots of photos. And get samples if you can get close enough. Do a listening spell, if you can. And—'

'I think she's got this, Mal,' Cornelia said.

Mallory smiled softly. 'Okay.'

Diana held the witchlight in her hand and pictured the one she was trying to find, forcing all the sounds of breathing and rustling and life out of her head. There was a soft, high-pitched whine in her ear, but aside from that she heard nothing. She took a deep breath and felt herself being pulled inside.

There was one thing about witchlight travel Diana had neglected to mention to her friends, and that was that it hurt.

Not hurt the way Mallory hurt, or hurt in a way she thought Cornelia would recognise. It hurt her heart, her brain, shaking emotions out of her that she didn't know she had and forcing her to think about things she wanted to bury.

She arrived in the darkened Oakpass Manor library, landing with a thump behind the sheet-covered sofa, and all she could think about was Taylor.

She stayed perfectly still, suddenly aware that she was lying on something small and hard that was digging into her hip, but waited to find out if the sound of her body hitting the floor would bring anyone running. When the faint noises from below did not come closer, she cast a listening spell. Talking and shuffling and moving mixed with her own heartbeat and incessant ringing that would not stop no matter how much she willed it.

She sat up and pulled the offending object from beneath her, recognising it immediately as a planchette. It hadn't been there the last time they were in the library; someone else was here. At a loss for where else to put it, she shoved it into her bra for safekeeping.

Casting a cloaking spell, she moved across the floor as lightly as she could. The spell would obscure most of her movements, but there was no guarantee that she was being quiet enough, or that she wasn't about to encounter someone with exceptional hearing.

She crept down the stairs and was half-surprised to see someone lying right where they'd discovered Fred's body.

Not someone – *Diana*.

Sprawled out like a discarded rag doll was a mannequin; smaller than Diana in reality, its face utterly blank and featureless, but wearing the same outfit Diana had been wearing her first day on set. It was impressive attention to detail, especially given how long Diana had spent stalking a resale site to get her hands on the trousers.

Her arms were reaching for something. Small furniture was arranged around her body.

It looked for all the world like a blown-up version of one of her dioramas.

Diana inhaled sharply, then clamped a hand over her mouth, breathing as quietly as she could. She felt as though she might be sick. There was no question of this one being a message. The Dollhouse Murderers knew who Diana was. And they'd lured her into an obvious trap.

There were police in the entrance hall, radios squalling as they talked, none doing anything productive.

This wasn't a crime scene to them.

Diana reached into her pocket and pulled out one of Cornelia's beetles.

'Don't look at me like that,' she whispered. The little orange and yellow beetle turned its back on her nonetheless. 'Cornelia wants you to help.'

She set it on the ground and used a tiny breeze spell to make it move forward – barely stronger than if she'd blown a breath on it, but it was enough to make it twitch its wings and trundle towards the mannequin, little legs working mechanically, until it reached its destination.

There was a low chirp, and it turned green.

Bingo.

The beetle, deciding there were other things to examine, turned away from the mannequin, and Diana had to magically pull it towards her, stuffing it into its little matchbox-sized holder as it tried to escape.

'This is because I hate your friends the steel silk spiders and Horrible Travis, isn't it?' Diana hissed, shoving it into her pocket. She took out a swab and a pair of latex gloves, glad for the cloaking spell as she snapped them on, her hands getting caught up in the fingers because they were sweating so much.

All of her felt shaky, like she was inches from being caught.

Which, in a way, she was. She was not hidden from view. At any moment anyone could turn around and find her here.

She crept closer still, keeping an eye on the police. She was taking risks now, needing to look closer at the body, to confirm it was soft and full of stuffing and wire, not flesh and blood and bone and some poor soul's forever-stilled heart.

'If this doesn't tell you you've gone too far,' Diana said, her voice raspy. 'I don't know what will.'

But it was not the real Diana speaking.

Its face, with no mouth, no eyes, no nose, no way to make a sound, had turned towards her, her voice emanating from somewhere inside it.

The real Diana jumped, freezing as the police moved towards her. She was rooted to the spot, her mind screaming at her to move, her body ignoring her.

'Who the fuck are you?' one of the officers asked, and as he came closer Diana wanted the ground to swallow her up. She cursed herself for not keeping the witchlight in her hand.

Nathan Tate, former security guard, wearing a police uniform.

Diana knew, like she knew how to do magic and like she knew she was gay as hell, that she had fucked up big time.

'Um,' Diana said intelligently. 'Crime scene clean-up.'

'How'd you get in here? Where's your clearance?'

Diana climbed slowly to her feet, just as her brain seized on a fact: he did not seem to remember her.

'Which character do you play?' Diana asked, widening her eyes.

'What?' a second police officer said, joining Nathan.

'On the show, which character do you play? Is there some sort of military operation this time? Ooh, have you met Sandi Clementine?' Diana clapped her hands together.

Her mind was whirring; she was not able to process why a demon was on an Apparent police force, particularly one that had been viciously unkind to the witch DI that had been on it previously. She had too many questions – if Sully knew about him, if he was the reason why they'd been buried under red tape, if he really didn't remember her, and why he had been security on a gate to a privately owned building but was now standing here, clearly in charge of the scene. Too many questions to have at the same time as trying to finesse her way out of a situation.

'Is this part of the show?' Diana cooed. 'I've never been on a real set before. Your costumes are so realistic.'

'What's your name?'

'It's Merr…edith,' Diana said, picking the first name that came into her head, even as her mouth tried to say her own.

'Well, Merrrrredith,' Tate drawled. 'I'll ask again. What brings you here?'

And then Diana knew it was magic freezing her in place, not panic. There was pressure building behind her eyes, her ears rushing, the need to tell the truth swimming over her but she fought back at it, like she'd fought to not tell him her name. Merriweather had almost slipped out, her brain skipping over her other names, but almost betraying her in a way she was not happy about.

'Oh my goddess. You're real police, aren't you?' Diana said, moving towards Tate while every instinct told her to run. She could feel the coldness of the planchette she'd picked up shifting against her skin, and she hoped to Elisabella it wasn't about to make a slow, shameful descent out the bottom of her t-shirt.

'You're familiar,' the other police officer said suddenly.

And then Diana realised her second mistake: she knew the second officer too. He had previously been on the Wrackton force; she could picture him guffawing in the Larix basement, standing over her dead friend, and she wanted to punch him.

'I've told you how many times, you can't say shit like that, Malcolm,' Tate said. 'And I'm a detective chief inspector,' he said to Diana. 'Not a "policeman".'

'Oh wow,' Diana said, batting her eyelashes, not sure she was going to get out of this one alive. It took every ounce of her willpower not to react to what he'd said, or how he'd jumped to the top of her list of suspects. Nobody went from security-for-hire to DCI in a matter of days unless there was something untoward going on.

'I was going to say something like "in my dreams",' Malcolm complained. 'Can't bloody say anything anymore. What are we doing here anyway? This whole thing is a joke.'

'I need the dream to answer some questions,' Tate said softly. 'You're a fan of the show, right?'

Diana forced a giggle, recognising his attempt at a bluff instantly. 'This is like one of those "name three songs if you're really a fan" things, right?' She leaned forward and touched his arm, the squawk of his radio forcing her to grit her teeth as her ear rang with renewed fervour.

Tate scrutinised her. 'You know it's an offence to enter a crime scene?'

'I had no idea this was a crime scene! I always thought crime scenes were… oh, I shouldn't say. Should I? Oh, fine, you pushed me,' she said, not letting Tate get a word in. 'I always thought there was a certain… sexiness to them. Abstractly. You know, blood, weird messages, the way it looks on TV.'

Tate's expression didn't change, and Diana wondered if she'd fucked it.

'Are you sure you're done with snooping around? Don't have anything else to look at? Want to tell us how to do our jobs?'

Malcolm chose to speak up then. 'You could help us figure out what that means,' he said, nodding at the wall behind her.

She turned and her mouth dropped open. Daubed on the wall behind her, written in what she hoped was paint, were three words, followed by an attempt to erase a fourth:

Blame it on

TWENTY-FOUR

Mallory checked the time on her phone and huffed out a breath. The Magic Magical Machine hummed behind her, a hollow sound that reminded her of liminal spaces. She had the items they'd taken from the Fred-Diana scene laid out in front of her, but was distracted with worry and not making much progress.

'She's only been gone ten minutes,' Cornelia said, looking up from one of the books she'd 'borrowed' from Oakpass Manor that she was now taking messy, borderline illegible notes from. 'And it's Diana. She's much less impulsive than I am.'

'I have a sense something is wrong,' Mallory said, her fists clenched. It was a gut feeling, and not a pleasant one. 'I should've overridden her request.'

'The day you pull agency rank will be a *very* interesting day. If it'll make you feel better, I'll go in after her,' Cornelia said, dropping a witchlight onto the table. 'I could talk my way out of anything easier than you would, and I'm not afraid to hex Diana if she's doing something ill-advised.'

'No!' Mallory put out a hand to stop her. Her fingers brushed the fabric of Cornelia's third-favourite jumper – black, distressed, incomprehensibly long in the sleeves – and she withdrew her hand. 'I could be wrong. She might be fine and we don't know where exactly her witchlight is. If you arrive and make a scene it could blow her cover.'

'*Make* a scene?' Cornelia raised an eyebrow. 'I'll have you know I *craft* all the scenes that unfold around me. It's an art form.'

Mallory smiled, despite herself.

'But yes, I suppose you're right. We trust in her motherfucking genius.' Something that looked like relief passed over her face. Mallory wanted to probe it, but stopped herself. She didn't even know what she wanted to ask, and she didn't know how it would be received.

'Okay. We give her…' Mallory checked her phone. 'Twenty minutes, and then we figure something out.'

'Perfect,' Cornelia said.

Silence stretched out between them. It had been, Mallory realised, over five months since they had properly spent time alone – there had been times where they'd been in the same room without Theodore or Diana, but they'd both been focused on doing something else.

The last time they'd been alone, they had been in a cage at the Whistler's behest.

'Mallory,' Cornelia said, her tone light and careful in a way it wasn't usually. 'Are we…'

Mallory felt a small fizz of something in her chest.

'Are we okay?' Cornelia gestured between them. 'You and me.

Like, right now we are worried about Diana, so I don't mean that. I guess I've felt…'

'What—'

'Oh, I don't know. Forget it, I don't think there was a coherent thought attached to that question. It's clearly nothing,' Cornelia waved a hand. 'How's the Katherine search going?'

Mallory felt a blush colour her cheeks as she recounted most of her encounter with Katherine, leaving out the picnic-and-kissing prelude. She hadn't even told Diana about Langdon for reasons she couldn't quite express, even to herself. She wished she was brave enough to steer Cornelia back to the conversation she'd tried to have.

She had no idea if they were okay.

'So that's the whole thing? Find her sister, and she'll tell you what she knows? Seems easy enough. How many Vanes could there be in Wrackton?'

'That's just it,' Mallory said. 'I don't know if she was definitely buried in Wrackton, or was buried at all. If her ghost is trapped inside the Mayoral Offices, she could have died there.'

'It does feel on-brand for the Offices to have a load of secret skeletons in its walls.' Cornelia spun the sleeve of her jumper as she thought. 'Have you checked all the tombstones? And if not, want help doing it? I assume it's a lot of walking, so…'

'I tried the witch cemeteries and there were no Katherines of interest at all there, nor in the demon mausoleums.' The double-jobbing was not doing her any favours physically; she was currently wearing the least-painful clothes she could handle touching her skin.

'When was that?'

'When I went to appeal to the trolls about Orson, I took a detour on the way home.' She showed Cornelia her camera roll. 'I found nothing useful.'

'Sorry I was such a hungover mess, or I'd have gone with you. If you ever want a helpful assistant who can run around, let me know.'

'Observer Johnson said the records were incomplete,' Mallory said, ignoring her offer mostly because she didn't know how to respond to it in a way that sounded both human and un-lovelorn. 'So we don't know if she's even really Occult – the only reason I'm sure it's her is because she responded to being called Vane of Wrackton. There were records in the Offices, but...'

'Who knew how important the Offices were to our continued functioning as a society?' Cornelia said. 'If we'd known before, we could've tried to explode them less.'

Mallory laughed, then sobered, thinking of Katherine stalling the Whistler as they made their escape. She hadn't saved them in the end, but she'd tried. Mallory needed to try harder.

'Do you think it's worth it? Finding her sister, I mean. Is this going to answer anything for you?' Cornelia asked softly.

Mallory looked away. 'I don't know, but I'd rather try than not. She had no reason to mention Theodore when I first met her, much less describe him pre-cat ears.'

'And Theodore...'

'Won't say shit,' Mallory smiled sadly. She ran her fingertips over the edge of her Theodore case notebook. 'I've tried. He's not right.'

She opened it to a summary of events over the past five months and let Cornelia scan the notes.

'Oh. That's… I hadn't noticed all that. Some of it, yeah, but he's always been a little eccentric so I ignored it. Did she give you any indication of where to find her sister? And is she aware she might be Cask of Amontillado'd very soon?'

'Yes to the first, no to the second – I didn't know how to break it to her, and she didn't really seem to be in the right headspace for listening. Before we— I left, she said, "You will find her at the place where sunrise dies. That is where she will be. That is where she is".'

'Bold, coming from the ghost who didn't know she was dead in the first place.'

'It made me think she knew at some point, and was remembering something,' Mallory said. 'Like she's scrambled now, but there are parts of her still in there.'

'Could it be some sort of horizon thing? Behind a hill, or over by the Redwoods or something where the sun "dies" in a visible way?'

'I have no idea,' Mallory confessed. 'I've no idea at all.'

'What I wouldn't give for the days when I could sit here and try to convince you that Van Doren killed Theodore and also offed Katherine. Especially as he'd be such a good villain in this situation.' She snapped her fingers. 'Hey, why don't I ask Kingston what he thinks? He's good at word puzzles and stuff, he might have some suggestions.'

Mallory turned away, suddenly very motivated to start testing her samples. 'Maybe,' she said, not caring that her tone sounded cold and disinterested, and busied herself with the Machine. She didn't speak for the next few minutes, testing and labelling items.

'The item we thought was mercury is definitely mercury,' she said, holding it up. 'The vial of blood has something in it – I think another plant-based poison, based on the blood coagulation, though I can't be sure.'

'Could be bittersweet?'

'I mean, I can't think what about murder is sweet, but—'

'I mean the plant,' Cornelia said. 'Bittersweet. It's something Kingston said recently, that the vampires have an old folkloric tale that goes something like, "I daren't speak, a witch's curse is bittersweet".'

Mallory did not know how to politely formulate a question to ask how, exactly, this helped them, but Cornelia held up the spell page they'd found in Oakpass.

'The spell instructions include bittersweet, I was unrelatedly informing you of a fun fact.'

Mallory smiled again, feeling it drop into a frown as her mind ran through possibilities. 'So if this is a finding spell, then surely they'd have… found whatever they were looking for?'

'Assuming they're looking for the Larkins, would it work on corpses? It's never occurred to me to look for a corpse with magic, largely because that is not a reasonable pastime, unless you're an anthropologist.'

'It's been twenty minutes,' Mallory said, looking at her phone again. She put the question about the spell aside, fear that something had gone wrong gripping her chest.

'Give her another five.'

'Cornelia—'

'Just five more minutes.'

'Fine.' Mallory could feel a dull ache starting in her back and she pulled out a stool to perch on.

'I think you were right earlier,' Cornelia said suddenly. 'That it's probably not two demons working together. I think we need to focus on Xander, Sandi and Rachel – if you think about it, there are nine possible combinations of demon-and-not-demon, and that excludes two demons working together.'

'We've only got Apparent potential suspects left,' Mallory mused. 'Do you think Taylor could be involved? Honestly.'

'No,' Cornelia said, sitting on the desk beside Mallory. 'But in the same way I know Kingston isn't involved – it's a hunch. I'd have to think about it more broadly, but I can't see her faking her own death and then trashing the dollhouse and getting Diana involved. I know we've been stung on that one before, but this is different – she's staying out of it.' She swung her legs, her arm lightly touching Mallory's shoulder. 'If Diana comes back with news of another victim, we've got one more shot to figure out who the Dollhouse Murderers are, before they do whatever they're doing.'

'The answer probably lies in that finding spell. Did the spell itself give you any clues?'

'Nothing. Can't find it anywhere, can't even identify where it might've come from.'

'I wish I could understand what they were doing.'

'If anyone can understand, it's you,' Cornelia said. She was close enough that Mallory could see every freckle on her face, so close Mallory could lean forward and brush her lips against the soft skin of her cheek.

Mallory inhaled, trying to clear her head.

'We need to talk to the three of them, figure out possible links. No stone unturned, no ignoring anyone. Three demons, three

Apparents… one day to Equinox. I'd be fretting about what to wear, but I'm sure Diana has that covered already.'

'Speak of the devil,' Cornelia said, holding up her phone so Mallory could see it.

Diana
There's been something of a predicament

TWENTY-FIVE

'I told you to be careful!' Mallory said, her eyes wide with what Diana was starting to realise was genuine fear. Her friends had looked mildly worried when she'd emerged from the witchlight, and Mallory's expression had grown more exaggerated as Diana had filled them in. 'I'm sorry, I'm not trying to be all "I told you so" but... Diana!'

Diana closed her eyes. She did not like to be wrong. Her ear was buzzing, her heart full of painful Taylor-shaped thoughts, and all she wanted was a quiet little sit-down. Maybe even a little snack.

'It could be worse.'

'Could be worse *how*? We're not allowed on the grounds of Oakpass anymore because they know what you look like now, and you were our main shoo-in! We aren't able to access the very place we need to solve these murders!'

'You flirted with the enemy!' Cornelia said.

'It's no big deal,' Diana lied. It was probably a big deal, but she did not have the capacity to grapple with it. 'This isn't what we need to be concerned about at the moment, or even for the rest of the day.'

'Tell us again what the message on the wall said, I was barely able to hear you over the sound of Mallory's emotional upset,' Cornelia said.

'Hey,' Mallory protested, earning a laugh from Cornelia. She smiled to herself and Diana resisted the urge to roll her eyes. If they could just get a kiss over with, she wouldn't have to worry about them getting hurt or heartbroken.

Her own heart hurt.

'The mannequin said, "If this doesn't tell you you've gone too far, I don't know what will", and the wall said "Blame it on" and a big smudge.' She showed them a photo.

'This might be the blurriest photo you've ever taken,' Cornelia said, squinting. 'Hey, do you think that says "Francine"?'

'You're right,' Mallory said, her head close to Cornelia's. 'It does kind of look like it originally said Francine.'

'We probably just think that because we've got Francine on the brain,' Diana said.

'Who's "we" in this scenario?' Cornelia snorted.

Diana ignored her, reaching into her pocket to feel for the planchette she'd rescued from her bra the second she was free of Tate. 'And I found this in the library, before I found me. I mean it. This was on the floor before I got to the scene.' Diana wrinkled her nose. She hated thinking of that mannequin as her, hated the idea someone had made her voice come out of it.

She held it up. It had some weight to it, not like the wooden ones Apparents usually messed around with. This felt heavy, crafted from stone, some details worn.

'We should show that to Theodore,' Cornelia said. 'He loves weird old shit like that.'

'If by "loves weird old shit" you mean "was practically a doctor of para-anthropology before he died", then yeah I guess he does,' Diana said wryly.

'Wait! This scene is familiar,' Cornelia said, riffling through a stack of *Undead Complex* comics. 'Here!'

She showed them a full-page panel of a character Diana didn't recognise lying on the ground at the bottom of a staircase, hand outstretched, bloody words daubed on the wall: *BLAME IT ON*, and the word next to it blurred.

'Actually,' Mallory said. 'I've had a thought. If the mannequin spoke in your voice, then the Dollhouse Murderer must've known you were there – would Tate draw attention to himself like that?'

'If the goal was to send Diana a message – which, clearly, it was, based on everything about that scene – I don't think that matters. Plus, the fact we're even doubting Tate suggests that Tate could've had that same thought, should he be the suspect. Which he might be.' Cornelia pointed to the board, which had three lists drawn out, showing their nine possible Dollhouse Murderer pairings.

'So one – or both – of the Dollhouse Murderers saw us when we confronted them, and they decided to go back and finish the scene they were staging with Fred's body, with a mannequin dressed like Diana, that only Diana would know for sure was meant to be her,' Mallory said.

'Possibly attempting to get me arrested in the process,' Diana added. 'By getting the mannequin to speak, and getting me caught. Given that, if we're right and this is a ritual, if the placement of the bodies matters, surely they'd kill someone else, rather than bother with a mannequin.'

'I hate to ask,' Mallory said, in a voice that said she really did hate to ask. 'But did you, at any point, and I fully acknowledge that you had a lot going on during this absolute disaster of an attempt to access a place that we shouldn't have had access to at all, but did you happen to— Manage to? Get… a sample I can test.'

'Oh, Mallory,' Diana said.

'It's okay,' Mallory started.

'Of course I did.'

Mallory beamed.

'Cornelia, your beetle was being a little dickhead by the way. It did not want to do its job at all, but we got there in the end.'

'He's a good Lawrence,' Cornelia said. 'Such a good Lawrence.'

'Your beetle names are getting stranger.' Diana handed over the beetle box.

'Ah but you see, with this colony, I call them all Lawrence.'

'Are these the ones I got from Kansas?' Mallory asked, as though it had been as simple as placing an order at the beetle shop, and not weeks of internet searches, emails and breeder vetting to find the 'correct' *Sonata lutumae* colony that would replace the ones she had accidentally killed. This was also where Horrible Travis had come from. Diana wished she could honestly say she'd never lived in a place where boxes of insects were delivered semi-regularly.

'Yes! They're all Lawrence, because they're not in Kansas anymore,' Cornelia said, as if it was the most obvious answer in the world. 'Don't even worry about it. They're not as magic-hungry as Selene's colony, but the introductions seem to be going well and there's been some colony convergence.'

'As much as I would love to hear more about beetle fornication—'

'Is the magic-hungry thing a problem? Should I call the folk I got them from? I can call them,' Mallory said. 'They said to, if I had any problems.'

'No, I like my wayward little sons,' Cornelia said.

'Anyway,' Diana said, keen to keep things moving in a direction she understood. 'I got a sample. So here.'

It wasn't long before Mallory and the Machine confirmed what Diana had expected – demon magic.

'And no Bellissima, which would change the MO if not for the fact you couldn't poison a mannequin,' Cornelia said.

'I couldn't steal an automobile,' Theodore boomed, appearing with a *crack* as a static burst took out every page in the room, dotting the space with a flurry of loose leaves. The Magic Magical Machine beeped in protest and Mallory shoved Theodore back towards the iron plate, trying to contain the discharge. Diana grabbed an iron screen and ushered Theodore into the research room.

'I'm sorry,' Theodore said in a small voice. 'I thought appearing would be more fun, I didn't think… is the Machine okay?' He looked forlornly at Mallory.

'Really, don't worry about it,' Cornelia said. 'If it breaks, we can fix it.'

Diana raised her eyebrow at Cornelia, but said nothing. This was a fight for another day, and it was not a new one. She did not want to imagine the state of their PI agency if there was ever a situation where they could not access Cornelia's money anymore.

'I'd rather not have to wait for that,' Mallory said carefully. 'It's not a problem, Theo. Really, don't worry. It might just need a reset.'

'What were you talking about? It sounded fun. You couldn't poison a mannequin, you couldn't steal an automobile… but I suppose it's just me that couldn't do that. You probably shouldn't. For reasons of morals, and such.'

Diana explained the situation as Mallory and Cornelia tried to get the Machine to stop beeping. Mallory had the operating manual in her hands and was frantically turning pages, while Cornelia unhelpfully pressed buttons, gathered up the scattered paper, and kept waving at Mallory to calm down.

'Oh, goddess. You really *couldn't* poison a mannequin,' Theodore said. His static charge had calmed down, and he looked a little more like himself. 'That's very bizarre. And did anyone point out that the mannequin having your voice was likely the killer trying to get you arrested?'

'Yes, we've already been horrified by this notion,' Diana said. She held up the planchette. 'I found this, too. Thought you might like to take a look, you like old things.'

'Is that an unkind dig at my age? I'll have you know that the ageing process halts at the point of death. From that day henceforth, I am forever going to be… the age that I was.'

'No, it's a kind, observant acknowledgement of the fact you're a para-anthropologist. I thought maybe you might also like weird physical objects too.'

'That's an entirely different discipline. Plus in life I had butterfingers; there were too many potential pitfalls to my handling objects. Although if we were to take a plus side from me potentially breaking precious artefacts, it's likely they wouldn't have killed me. Oh,' Theodore said, dropping the planchette on the ground. It hit the tile with a *crack,* but thankfully neither the floor nor the planchette had been damaged when Diana stooped to pick it up.

'What's wrong?'

'I don't know. I mean, I do know.'

'Which is it?'

'Both. Neither. Hmm.' Theodore rubbed his hair. 'For some reason I'm having trouble expressing myself adequately.'

'How very unusual for you,' Cornelia said.

'Hand it over again. I'll be careful this time. They call me Two Hands Wyatt, you know, because that's how many hands I have.' He held his hand out again for the planchette, but Diana placed it down carefully on Theodore's desk.

It seemed as good a time as any to share the next plan she'd cooked up that was bound to upset everyone in the room.

'I'm thinking maybe our next move is to try a ghost-summoning spell on the Larkins,' Diana said. Theodore looked up sharply, his hand inches from the planchette.

'No, I don't think we *do* try that, Diana. That should never be attempted. By anyone. You know the Ghoul Council rules, but you also know mine – ghosts are dangerous, and should never be summoned. They could possess you, and you could die. Or worse, be stuck with a ghost living in your head. But probably die as well.'

'But Mallory already—'

'Perhaps she shouldn't have done that.'

'Theodore.' Mallory appeared in the doorway, her face falling. Diana had known she felt guilty for bringing Theodore back, but did not know until precisely this moment how deep that guilt ran.

'You know I am immensely grateful that you wanted me back here. Among my friends. In my home, with my work.' He beamed at her. 'But the gratitude I feel would positively smother you should it come from *several* ghosts. Especially if they were malevolent and wanted to possess and kill you, which is something ghosts are wont to do. Plus, I belong here. What happens if the Larkins can't leave Wrackton should you summon them here? Preposterous! We would have a haunting on our hands.' He pulled his cardigan around himself. 'Now. I have an examination to complete.'

He bent to peer at the planchette as closely as he could manage, his nose sparking static as it brushed against the gilded edge.

There was a shift in the air, something that made Diana's vision feel like it flattened. Pages lifted around Theodore, a blue aura building around his body.

'No. No, no, no,' he muttered, backing away. 'I don't… I don't like it.' He recoiled, the blue aura staying where he'd been, then falling towards the planchette, as though it was trying to pull the aura inside it.

'Theodore?'

'I… I…' He shook his head rapidly, whiskers and eyes and hair and cat ears fading into fuzz. 'Get out.'

He was twitching, his head a blur, the aura fading and his body disappearing behind a wall of static.

'What's happening?' Mallory asked, as Theodore's mouth opened, his jaw slackening, his eyes widening.

'Evil… it's evil. It's evil. Make it go make it GO!'

'Theodore?' Cornelia reached towards him, but he had practically flickered out of existence, his body nothing more than floating neon fragments, like reflections hovering in mid-air.

Diana put out a hand to stop her, turning on the spot and throwing the planchette onto Theodore's iron chair.

'Take this back to where it came from,' Theodore hissed, flickering into view again. 'And never bring it back again. This *evil*.'

He shook his head once, twice, raising a hand to brush over his cheeks.

There was a *snap*, like static discharging, and Theodore blinked.

'What's going on? Mallory?'

Mallory pulled him into a hug, her hand spraying static as she stroked his hair, both of them fuzzing out of view.

'Theodore, you need to tell us what's going on. Now. No more bullshit,' Cornelia said. She looked frightened. 'I'm going to level with you – we're the only thing between you and the Ghoul Council stepping in and taking you away from here in a ghost light. No more hedging. You need to tell us what you've been doing in the Mayoral Offices, what you've been doing since you got back, and *why* you've been like this.'

It was not quite the interrogation Diana had been imagining, but it was something at least.

Theodore let out a wail that was closer to a miaow, and buried his face in his hands.

'I've been trying to get you to tell me *anything*, Theo,' Mallory said, holding him away from her so she could look him in the eye. He wriggled free and wrapped his arms around himself, the picture of woe.

'Are the Ghoul Council really that close to stepping in?' Diana asked quietly.

'I don't like to play the "my parents are in the Ghoul Council and some of the only rules I think are worth following are the ones that mean everyone gets to live here safely" card, but I will. Theodore knows the terms of staying here.'

'Cornelia…' He shook his head miserably.

'Couldn't you feel it? The tension in the room, like it was going to ignite?' she demanded. Cornelia, who was never really serious about anything – other than basic lab safety – was trembling, and Diana had to swallow the urge to cut the tension with a joke.

She wanted her friends to skip to the part where they addressed more than the potential dangers, and thought about *why* he'd reacted that way. She wanted her friends, her scientist friends, to sit down and contemplate what could possibly make their ghost friend behave the way he just had – if it was the planchette, or if this was a result of him being brought back to unlife.

She mostly wanted them to stop being so incredulous, because she didn't want to tell them that for several exciting seconds, where Theodore was fracturing and her vision had sharpened, she didn't think of film sets, or running to a different far corner of the planet, or Taylor. She thought of life, and of being on the edge of it, just like she had in the Mayoral Offices last October, and she'd wanted to be nowhere else. Her hands trembled from the adrenaline rush, a dull noise in her ear that might've been her own heartbeat.

'She's right,' Theodore said quietly. 'One of my promises to your parents, Cornelia, when you were small, or smaller – you were never actually small, I don't think. At least… never mind. Not just because those are the rules, but because the promise meant something – that I would never, ever harm anyone in Wrackton. I promised them, and I promised myself. I wouldn't forget what it meant to be alive. Back then, I couldn't even fathom a situation where I would feel less than myself. And yet, here I am.'

He rubbed his face. 'I don't know what's wrong with me,' he said finally. 'Mallory, you are not a very subtle investigator. Or maybe you are and I just know you very well. But even before Cornelia made her demands, I know what you've been doing, who you've been talking to. I even know why, I think. And I thank you. I think the world of you. Of all three of you. But I cannot be responsible for hurting you. I cannot guarantee I won't lose control again.'

'Theodore—' Mallory started, but he held up a hand, looking to the planchette nestled against the back of his chair.

He sniffed exaggeratedly. 'Stop looking into my case. I'm officially withdrawing permission from the Undetectables. You solved one of my murders, that's enough.'

'Theodore, I made you a promise too,' Mallory said firmly. 'I promised you I'd solve your first murder. If you can't go back on your promises—'

'Or experience significant distress from doing so,' Theodore added.

'Then I don't see how you could dare ask me to.'

Diana almost laughed at how fierce Mallory was being, though she held it in. Theodore was rarely this serious, and he was certainly never this calm.

'I need to go,' Theodore said. A frantic note was building in his voice. 'I need to leave. I have to go.'

'You don't, you can stay here,' Mallory said.

'No. I *have to go*. I can't be around any of you until I can find a way to be... to be Theodore. The proper one.'

'Don't,' Mallory pleaded, a note of desperation in her voice.

'Mallory's right, you don't have to go,' Cornelia said. Her tone had softened, her eyes concerned behind her glasses. 'There's no real reason to. So you've been a bit...'

'Erratic,' Mallory supplied.

'I would've gone for "enigmatic",' Theodore said. 'But have it your way. I will be back, when I can. I need you to trust me. Even if I don't deserve it. I need you to understand that I would never, ever hurt you. I could never forgive myself if I did.'

Mallory held out her hand to him. 'I trust you. We've all trusted you for years.'

Had Diana been forced at knifepoint to explain how she knew Mallory was lying, she wouldn't have been able to, but something in Mallory's voice told her the unspoken ending to that sentence was, *until now.*

'Then you shall have to trust I will return.'

He pulled his cardigan around himself, and ran at the basement door, passing through it in a whirl of static.

'Fuck,' Mallory said. 'Fuck fuckity fuck.'

'Couldn't have said it better myself,' Cornelia said, rounding on Diana. 'Next time we try to interrogate someone, could you refrain from questioning my bargaining chips? I was trying to make it clear to him that this was serious.'

'Oh come on—'

'We need to keep going. Summoning the Larkins is not it, by the way. We need to talk to Sandi, Jenna, Rachel and Xander, and we need to do it now.'

Diana reached over and picked up the planchette, an idea of who to talk to first forming. She swallowed down the urge to fight with Cornelia; there was plenty of time to do that when the case was solved.

'Maybe the planchette was, indirectly, a very direct clue? I've got some calls to make.'

TWENTY-SIX

'You know when you said, "What would happen if we just… called Sandi up?" I did not think we would actually be doing that and calling it legitimate investigation,' Cornelia said.

'Do I sense a tone of begrudging respect?' Diana asked. She set up a laptop on Cornelia's kitchen table as Cornelia plugged in Mallory's heat mat and draped it over the back of her chair.

'No,' Cornelia said. 'Because you're making me pretend I'm a historian writing about folk with familial links to the Appoccult Society and you know I am very, very bad at role play.'

'She's met me, and cried all over Diana,' Mallory said. 'While I'm inclined to believe her great-grandmother living at Oakpass was an exaggeration, perhaps she *did* spend time there, in the Appoccult Society. I just wish she'd given me enough information to figure out her name. We need something that looks like motive, Sandi's whereabouts, and her links to Jenna as well as her thoughts on the murders. Anything to get a picture of if she could be involved.'

'Fine, but I don't have to like it.' She joined the video link and

Diana and Mallory pulled their chairs away so they were out of frame but could still see the screen. Cornelia raked her fingers through her hair, pulling at the neck of the jumper Diana had foisted upon her in an effort to make her look the part.

'I'm working on talking to Xander and Rachel,' Diana said, tapping her phone. 'They're going to be harder to nail down, on account of not being ludicrous people. Ditto for Jenna, and Tate.'

'She's connecting, everyone be quiet!' Cornelia pushed her glasses up her nose.

'The necromancer is IN!' said Sandi Clementine as she appeared on screen, raising her arms so Diana could see she was dressed in a set of sweeping blue robes.

'Oh, goddess,' Cornelia said, and Diana was not sure if this was a tone of reverent awe, or condemnation.

After what felt like hours of vague pleasantries and Cornelia circling the drain of getting to the point, Diana was getting ready to urge her along with a well-timed hex when she seemed to snap out of it. 'So your family have some history with Oakpass Manor, I've heard? A little bird told me. Have always wondered where that phrase comes from but now I expect it's not the time. Something to do later with my historian…cy.'

'Oh, yes,' Sandi nodded vehemently. 'I once thought my great-grandmom lived in Oakpass, but upon further research, she was actually part of a society. The Apple Occultical Society, I believe.'

'It's—'

Diana kicked her.

'Yes. The Apple Occultical Society, I am very interested in the historical accuracies of this. I have… I believe I have a list of names of members going back through the years, what was her name?'

'She… well she was an actress, actually,' Sandi said, her eyes shining. 'It's in our blood, literally. Her name was Delfina Sackville.'

Cornelia paused with her pen over her notepad, as Diana's mind turned, trying to make the words make sense.

And then they did, just as Mallory turned to mouth something in her direction, her face a stormy mix of fury and elation. Diana was already diving for paper and a pen, scribbling and holding it up for Cornelia to see, tapping it insistently so the page was covered in ink dots.

DELFINA SACKVILLE = FRANCINE LEON'S WIFE

Cornelia squinted, then nodded once as Diana continued scribbling, holding up a second page.

'Oh, yes, the movie star. She was linked to Larkin Studios too, wasn't she? I know this from my historical… records.'

'It's where she got her big break,' Sandi said brightly. 'Sad the Larkins all disappeared, but she was heavily involved in the Society. She made all sorts of Occultical friends – witches, trolls, vampires, demons – even people from something called the "Ghoul Council", which sounds so haunting. Ha ha!'

She leaned forward to bark out a laugh and Diana, Cornelia and Mallory all involuntarily leaned back.

'It's so nice to continue on her work, in a way. You know, as an actor. Not in any other way,' Sandi said.

Diana looked to Mallory to confirm she'd heard that. Mallory bit her lip, scribbling in her notebook.

'Your great-grandmother, she had a…'

'Live-in best friend. Gal pal. Her and my great-grandpa lived apart when her career took off, and after he died, she never seemed to want to take a man. She did… something, the friend. I think she was into science, maybe? There's a lot of history, good and bad. Half the family didn't talk for a time. I'm following in her footsteps despite not really knowing her. You know, I bet I have a cousin out there somewhere who's doing the exact same thing as me, and I'd have no way of knowing. But I suppose if someone was a relative of hers, they'd make it known.'

Diana fought the urge to cut in and correct all of her Francine Leon misinformation.

'But you didn't?' Cornelia asked.

'I have talent,' Sandi said. 'Delfina was amazing, but I don't want to be known as her great-granddaughter. I want to make it on my own, with my own talent. But that's just me, someone else wouldn't have that kind of backbone.' She blinked earnestly.

'Speaking of Larkin Studios, you were working there?' Cornelia let the end of the sentence tick up as though it was a question.

'Oh yes, yes. Yes, yes, yes. A trying time. A beautiful time. A difficult time.' Sandi nodded.

'I heard there were some issues on set?'

'Oh, no not really.' Sandi blinked. 'It was a nice workspace.'

'I was referring to the, erm… the three murders that occurred on set.'

Sandi pressed a hand to her chest. 'Oh *those*. Harrowing. Devastating.'

'Do you have any idea how it could've happened?'

Sandi looked pensive for a moment, tapping her chin. She took a deep breath.

Cornelia leaned forward in her seat. Diana saw Mallory's hand snake out to hold Cornelia in position.

'None at all.' Sandi shook her head emphatically.

'No enemies? No fights on set? No… animosity?'

'Nothing of the sort,' Sandi said. 'We worked hard, the deaths were very sad but it happens sometimes. It closely related to my script, you know – there were so many things I saw in there that were like they had been peeled from Oakpass and put into my hands.'

'Like what?'

'Oh you know, things like— oh my, is that the DOOR?' Sandi stood, and for a moment the screen was filled with masses of billowing blue robes.

'I didn't hear anything—' Cornelia started, but then there was the sound of a door opening, and a quiet voice whispering.

'Jen-Jen, so happy to see you,' Sandi cooed in a stage whisper.

Cornelia turned up the laptop speaker as loud as it would go.

'I wish technology and magic mixed,' Diana grumbled, straining to hear over the rustling of Sandi's robes.

'—Can't stay long,' a voice that Diana immediately recognised as Jenna's was saying. She closed her eyes, hoping shutting out everything else would help her hear better.

'—Illegal in this country,' Jenna said. A crinkling, plasticky sound filled the speaker.

'What, would they arrest me?' Sandi exclaimed. 'They wouldn't, it would look so bad for them. Don't worry about getting caught, you're an upstanding citizen' – pronounced, *city-zine* – 'they'd hardly look twice at you, let you off with a slap on the wrist.'

'I don't want to… are you in an interview?' Jenna whispered.

'Yes, a historical society or historical… historian, I think, asking me about my grandmom's links to Larkin Studios and Oakpass Manor. Very nice young person. Looks exactly how you'd expect a historian to look.'

Jenna muttered something unintelligible and Diana pressed her ear to the speaker, catching '—digging into the murders, be careful.'

'Of course I'm careful, don't you worry, dollface,' Sandi said. 'If they ask about treasure, I'm *pffft!* Gone. Swift as a bird. See you later, Jen-Jen.' She blew an exaggeratedly loud and wet-sounding kiss. They waited for what felt like five minutes for Sandi to wander back into frame.

'Oh, you're still here. Where were we?'

'You were telling me how the script had things taken straight from Oakpass Manor,' Cornelia said.

'Oh, yes! Here's my favourite line from the script. Ahem. Ahem-hem,' she said, shuffling to the edge of her seat. She raised her arms again, and in an instant Diana could see the transformation from Sandi Clementine to her necromancer character, Ruthless Monroe. 'You pass through the oak, to avoid the elder,' she intoned.

She waited a moment, then lowered her hands. 'Like that.'

'Oh. Erm, well done,' Cornelia said, clapping a little. 'Thank you for that. What does… what does it mean?'

'I think it's about passing through something, to avoid something else. Metaphorically. In the context of the show, it was about avoiding something and taking a safe path to find what my character needed to find. Deeply profound. So sad that Hollis Hadley had to die; he was a talented man.'

'And you really don't know why anyone would do it?'

Sandi lowered her eyes, then looked up, embodying Ruthless Monroe once again. 'These were questions from the Historical Society, I see not how murder is relevant. Murder, you see, is one of life's greatest mysteries. I do not deal in murders; I deal in character. Substance. All we can do is bear witness.'

Cornelia blinked. Sandi's face relaxed, and Diana had no idea what to make of it.

'Apologies, it's a fascinating topic. We can get back to the Larkins; I'd love to get your thoughts on the return of the dollhouse—'

Sandi fanned her face. 'I'm feeling a little unwell all of a sudden, so I'll bid you *adieu*, as Delfina would say.'

It was not, to Diana's knowledge, something Delfina would particularly say.

'Thank you for your time,' Cornelia said. 'The Historical Society will be very pleased with this.'

'Thank *you*, whatever your name may be. And please, if you remember nothing else, avoid the elder.' She winked, and hung up.

'A lot to unpack there,' Cornelia said, breaking the bewildered silence that had elapsed.

'So Jenna turns up, they talk about not being arrested, specifically about not talking about treasure… and Sandi bolts,' Diana said.

'Plus all the other weird stuff she said,' Mallory added. 'What did she mean Hollis "had to" die? She phrases things oddly all the time, but that in particular struck me as strange.'

'Odd choice of words for sure. The Delfina Sackville link is most interesting to me – that was Francine Leon's wife. What she said about continuing on her work… I think that's what we need to do. Establish a historical link, someone who'd know a lot about Occulture, and the Larkins, and consequently the Undead Complex,' Diana said.

'But that would've been Hollis,' Mallory said. 'And anyone who'd paid any attention to the source material. It doesn't help us, sorry, Diana.'

She was right, even if Diana wished she wouldn't say it.

'I don't know how to view that conversation between her and Jenna as anything other than particularly damning,' Mallory continued. 'But we will suspend judgement until we've spoken to everyone. Any luck on getting hold of Xander or Rachel?'

'No answer from Rachel yet,' Diana said, 'but Xander said to give him a call. I got his number from Alannah.'

'Darlin', hello,' Xander said hoarsely. 'And to what do I owe this pleasure?'

'I'm trying to make sense of everything,' Diana said, somewhat truthfully. 'All the things that happened on set. And I wanted to see how you were doing. Is this a good time?'

'Right, right. Yeah, no, just Rachel here with me; she said sorry for not answering your text, but she's been busy babying me. Awful shit. Just fucking awful.'

'I guess I want to try and understand. I know we talked about Taylor, but… it turns out Donny Baker was the one killed, not Taylor, then Hollis Hadley, then Fred…'

Xander's breath caught and Diana waited for him to say something else.

'Fred was important to you, wasn't he?'

There were the sounds of Xander moving away, a voice quietly asking him what was going on, a door closing.

'How… how did you know?' Xander whispered. 'I'm… I didn't…'

'I've lost a lot of people recently,' Diana said. 'I know when I'm staring into the face of grief. Metaphorically or otherwise.'

'And the grief howls back.' He sniffled, and made aggressive face-wiping sounds. 'I haven't told anyone at all, not even…' He stopped.

'I'm so sorry. I really am. Xander, do you have any idea who could've done something like this? Anything you saw, or heard.' Diana didn't even care that she wasn't being subtle anymore.

'No. Honestly, no. I told the police what I could – DCI Tate, or whatever his name is. He was a security guard a few days prior, chap must've been undercover or some shit, but he pretended not to know me, the prick. I left feeling more confused than when I went in there, but that's it. Rachel brought me in. She's been so good. I haven't told her either – the way shit gets around in this industry, never mind a closed set. I'm not ashamed of myself or anything, but he wanted to keep things quiet.'

'Are you and Rachel friends?'

'Yeah, she's been a good sort, particularly the last little while, really looking out for me, making sure I didn't have to deal with anything else that happened on that set. Private, though. Has a partner she doesn't talk about, she could have about seven dogs and fifteen children and we wouldn't know. I put her forward for the job, knew her from another show we were on. She was a great choice, even if it's not actually what she wanted to be doing. She'd have had a much better time if Orson had…' He coughed. 'But she gets on with everyone. Better than some people.'

'Like who?'

He exhaled loudly. 'Some actors get too big for their boots, and it's all for show. You don't know what you're getting, but you know it's not authentic. Anything they say could be a lie. But, man, I could fight with anyone. Fought with that security guard cause I was smoking two feet away from where he'd designated the smoking area.'

'Did anyone else fight with him? This is Whitlock, right?'

'Yeah, no, I dunno. Fred stayed out of his way. Bit prim and proper, that lad – like he's looking down his nose at you. Not surprising, seeing as he got left in the lurch when everything kicked off and he became the only security guard, but…'

'Did he say anything about it?'

'Nah, never said a word, darlin'. I better go. Keep in touch.'

He hung up before Diana could ask to talk to Rachel.

Diana pressed her face into her hands, finally looking up at the other two.

'To the murder board,' she said finally.

'Right, so Jenna and Sandi are our frontrunners,' Cornelia said, sorting through the pile of scrapbooks she'd taken from Oakpass. It was an impressive amount, given the way they'd had to exit. 'Because that was bizarre.'

'Then DCI Nathan Tate, who is an enigma wrapped in a bow,' Diana said. 'I find it very hard to believe the same police department that despised Sully's witchliness would readily take on a demon as their boss. Plus, why was he working security if he was waiting for a promotion of that size? I don't think you can simply transfer in at that rank. Either he was moonlighting, or undercover, or there's something seriously dodgy going on there.'

'I didn't think transfers happened that quickly,' Cornelia said. 'It took Sully weeks to get a transfer rushed through when she moved to Wrackton. She was a DI, and I don't think they've managed to replace her.'

'But maybe he's been keeping Sully and Dr Ray out deliberately,' Diana said, sitting up. 'If he was involved in the killings, he wouldn't want other Occult folk muscling in. I haven't been able to find out anything about him – Sully doesn't know him personally, but if he's DCI, he's who has been refusing Wrackton's involvement.'

'One hypothesis,' Mallory said carefully. 'He's a demon. How easily could he convince someone to transfer him into the Oughteron force? Then again, why go to all that trouble?'

'It got out of hand,' Diana said. 'It should've stayed his own case, but someone called Dr Ray and we got Sully to start sticking her nose in. Maybe he wasn't aware of how fraught the Apparent-Occult relations were these days and had to take drastic measures?'

'Despite how complicated this case seems to be, it does seem like a needless extra complication. It has to have a simple answer,' Mallory said.

'Ugh.' Diana pulled her hair down out of its ponytail, running her fingers through the ends. 'I can ask someone, hold on.'

She sent a text to Quinn, who replied promptly.

> *Quinn*
> Was about to contact you – party is still on, we've recast it as a memorial service for Hollis and the police have promised to clear the scene

> *Quinn*
> When I said Tate was dangerous, but not to me, that's what I meant – I believe he was posted by the NCA undercover

'What's the NCA?' Cornelia asked, craning over Diana's shoulder.

'National Crime Agency,' Mallory said.

> *Quinn*
> So not dangerous, just annoying. Found nothing of interest and was pulled off the case when I contacted the NCA myself. We've reached an agreement on the use of my property…

> *Diana*
> And now he's a DCI??? How does that work

> *Quinn*
> He's enjoying a reward for being put in a compromising position.

And before Diana could type anything else,

> Quinn
> See you tomorrow

'Okay, well. That's potentially an explanation bordering on alibi, but...' Cornelia sighed. 'He's implying *something* dodgy went down. If Tate could manipulate his way into a position of power, he could also kill several people as part of a ritual.'

Mallory pursed her lips, but didn't add anything. It would be too easy to let it go and focus elsewhere.

'Go back to Jenna and Sandi for a moment. Jenna sounded actually scared about being arrested, which I for one think is pretty suggestive of her having done something worth being scared about. Say, murdering several colleagues.'

'But would you get off with a slap on the wrist like Sandi said if you were caught for murder?' Mallory said seriously. 'Jenna swore she wasn't there, that she was with Sandi, but folk saw her – Alannah said she saw Sandi. Even if Bellissima was affecting people's memories, I think Alannah remembering seeing her at *some* point during the discovery of Baker's body means she probably did.'

'Right. And Jenna didn't like Hollis.'

'She liked Fred, though,' Diana said, knowing even as she did that likability was a meaningless concept when it came to murders and rituals.

'But what if Fred knew what was going on, and she silenced him?'

'And if that's the case, would Sandi be competent enough to

help her commit three murders? There's no accounting for taste when it comes to partners in crime, but... I'd choose better, personally,' Diana said.

'Actually, that reminds me – we do need to talk about Taylor,' Cornelia said. She rested her hand on Mallory's shoulder. Mallory froze in place, but Cornelia seemed not to notice. 'I think it's exceedingly difficult to fake your own death, then fake a number of other deaths, and while I'm not certain she had the opportunity at any point, I am on a little bit of a wobbly fence when it comes to her.'

'Even when we figure out who the demon involved is, the second could literally be anyone,' Mallory said diplomatically, but Diana knew she was agreeing with Cornelia. And as much as she didn't like it, they were right not to close off that particular line of enquiry.

'Two killers, two motives, one Equinox, one goal, potentially. Two victims left – assuming that Equinox is the goal,' Mallory said, closing her eyes. 'How long do we have until Equinox?'

'Please stop saying Equinox, it's giving me a headache,' Diana said. 'It's tomorrow.'

'Great! Something terrible is going to happen tomorrow, and we don't really know what it is or who's doing it,' Cornelia said.

'But we can be legally at Oakpass Manor to see it,' Diana said triumphantly. 'Quinn's party is still going ahead. At the very least, if the world ends, we'll be there to see it happen.'

'A cheery concept,' Cornelia said brightly, clapping her hands once. 'Okay. Mallory this pile is for you, this is for Diana, and I'll take the middle pile.'

'I notice your pile is the smallest,' Diana said.

'I noticed that you were waiting for me to make tea. I can't do everything,' Cornelia said, sweeping a scrapbook from the top of the closest pile into Mallory's hands and busying herself with tea, a packet of biscuits clutched between her teeth.

'Oh, it's more cuttings from all the times Oakpass was mentioned in the papers!' Mallory exclaimed, turning the pages carefully.

'They used to invite novelists around,' Diana said, reading over Mallory's shoulder. 'Romance novelists, who'd write Oakpass in as a setting. "The Larkins invited me around for a tour and a fine dinner, answering questions I had about the grounds. All they asked in exchange was a copy of the book for their private collection." Some Apparent writer in 1920,' Diana read.

'It's a lot of wanking over an old building, isn't it?' Cornelia heaped four spoons of sugar into Mallory's tea and gave it a stir, completely missing the wince on Mallory's face.

'Bold, coming from someone who lives in a house that is referred to by name,' Diana said.

'Shut up. It is though, like that all suggests a family wouldn't just up and leave the house unless they had to,' Cornelia said. 'Everything I learn about the Larkins makes me wonder where they went.'

'Here's the Appoccult Society in 1921,' Diana said. 'But it's damaged.'

'That's not damage,' Mallory said, peering at it closely. 'Well, it is. Someone's face has been burnt out of it. Their name's been scratched out, too. I can make out the letters *u* and *i*, and an *f*. And an *l*, I think. Could be a *t*.'

'You sound like me during an eye test,' Cornelia said, reaching over to turn the pages. 'Appoccult Society, 1922.'

'That's Delfina!' Diana tapped the page excitedly, recognising her even in the blurred photo. 'Francine's wife. And allegedly Sandi's great-grandmother – the only thing she got right on that call was that she was married before and he died shortly before she met Francine. I didn't think she had children, but it's not *impossible*; she would've been twenty-five when she started acting.'

'Everyone else in this photo is in the other photo,' Mallory said. 'I can't see the person with the scratched-out name.'

They flicked back through the pages, trying to find society announcements in the paper clippings, until Cornelia slapped the page, her glasses slipping down her nose. 'Aurelius L. Waldorf Visits Oakpass Manor,' she read out. 'Prominent Ghoul Council member pays visit to the Larkin family.'

'That has all the letters I saw,' Mallory said. 'And his name isn't on any of the other photographs – not that there's many. That's the same year this photograph was from. I don't know how we're going to verify that, it's not like we can just *ask* the Ghoul Council for past membership.'

'Cornelia,' Diana started, but Cornelia had already figured out what Diana was going to say, hopping up with an excited gleam in her eyes.

'I'll be right back.'

She bounced up the stairs, returning with two frames balanced on her hip.

'Bit dusty, but here's the Society certificate Great-Grandfather had, and a photo from a Samhain ball where the whole Council was in attendance, in 1919.' She dropped it on the table. It was covered in a sticky film of dust, and Cornelia wiped it with her sleeve, ignoring Diana's look of disgust. 'There's Aurelius.'

Mallory picked up the frame gingerly between her fingers and looked at the back of the frame. 'He's here too, and his roles. "Aurelius L.W., preservation (GC)".'

'So he was actually very prominent,' Diana said, chewing over the information. 'What in the name of Hexana would you need to do to get excommunicated from a society obsessed with Occulture?'

'Did he come before or after Delfina? Maybe she knew him.'

'I think we're getting side-tracked here.'

'I know,' Diana said, grinning. 'But it felt good to solve something in one go. We're looking for *Undead Complex* stuff, anything that might indicate a link between that and the Larkins.'

'Hey,' Mallory said suddenly. 'Listen to this. "Missing – reward offered. Necklace on silver chain, precious family heirloom. Authentic green jewel, oval cut, base cut for ring." And look.' She flipped back a page. 'Look at Lady Larkin. Look what she's wearing.'

She turned the photograph so they could all see, and Diana's stomach dropped.

'That's the ring Jacob was using, isn't it?' Mallory said quietly. 'That's Blair's ring.'

There was a beat where Diana considered brushing past it again, but the look on Mallory's face – one of absolute worry, that the ring was behind all of this – made her mind up for her.

'I suppose while we're all on the cusp of veering off in the wrong direction, now is as good a time as any to admit that I have a secret,' Diana said brightly. 'I'll show you the secret. But no matter how upset or otherwise you feel, remember I was on the verge of dying when I took it, and hiding it was about keeping you both safe. Let that temper your rage. Got it?'

The others exchanged glances.

She waved her hand and a diorama floated down the basement stairs. She turned it as it landed on the desk so the others could see a small bedroom – one she'd made during their first case. She lifted the mattress with a flourish and pulled out the ring, returning it to its original dimensions.

'What the fuck is this?' Cornelia asked. 'I mean, I know what it is, but what is THIS?'

'I took it. The night we almost died. I was in and out of consciousness and at one point it was right beside my face, so I grabbed it. And I woke up with it sitting on my bedside table in the hospital, and hid it in the diorama.'

'Fuck yeah,' Cornelia said, fist-bumping Diana. 'Nice work.'

'I'm not trying to rain on your parade,' Mallory said hesitantly. 'But why didn't you tell us about this before? We could've put wards up, made sure it was hidden.'

'It was fine. It's not like anyone was going to look in there.'

'But a simple spell would've told them where it was, if anyone even thought we had it,' Mallory said. 'The fact people have been looking for this ring means they know it exists. Not to mention someone has been *searching Oakpass Manor* for something that might not be the Larkins. What if we're wrong, and this is what they've been after the whole time?'

'I wanted to keep it safe, and I figured the best way to achieve that would be if only I knew it was here.' Diana rarely got defensive with Mallory, but Mallory was normally able to see things better than this.

'I know, but—'

'We can argue about this when the case is done,' Diana said.

'I'll put it back where I had it. Mallory, if it makes you happier to figure out a ward or two, make sure it's extra safe, Cornelia can perform those spells, she's not half bad at it.'

'But—'

'We have hours before Equinox, and hours before there's about to be a lot of Occult folk in Oakpass Manor for a ball. Two people could die tomorrow, we're wasting time.' She pulled the scrapbook in front of her, the whine in her ear drowning out the softened protestations of her friends.

TWENTY-SEVEN

'I think we need to all take a nap for a bit,' Diana said. 'Come back refreshed.' They had drifted from the basement up into Mallory's bedroom, as it had become clear Mallory was hanging on by a thread.

'I'm so glad you're actually voicing your thoughts, Diana. It would be terrible if you'd kept things hidden from us for *months for no reason*,' Cornelia said, her eyes glued to her phone.

Diana ignored her. 'I RSVP'd for all of us for tomorrow night and asked Quinn to confirm if Xander, Jenna, Whitlock, Rachel and Sandi were coming. He said Xander declined, but Jenna, Rachel and Sandi all RSVP'd yes, and he doesn't expect to have to, quote, "fraternise with the help". Whitlock was not invited.'

'Goddess, he's the worst,' Cornelia said. 'And if this wasn't a murder case, I'd also be declining. Who wants to stand around wearing hideously restrictive clothes for a whole evening?'

'People who like fun,' Diana said.

'Anyway, I can't stop thinking about what Sandi said,' Cornelia continued, ignoring her. 'Not any of the suspicious shit, just the line she recited from *Undead Complex*. I felt like she was trying to tell us something.'

'That she's an amazing actor, obviously.'

'Your sarcasm is not welcome. I'm going to check in with our not-resident *Undead Complex* expert, in case she was hinting something at us that we have literally no context for.'

'Felix?' Diana was slightly annoyed at herself for not thinking of it sooner.

'No, Langdon. Obviously Felix!'

Mallory turned a very interesting shade of pink and Diana raised an eyebrow. Cornelia looked at her curiously, like she was about to say something, then thought better of it.

'I want snacks. I'll be right back.'

As soon as Cornelia was gone, Diana turned to Mallory. 'We have not had a chance to speak about certain things I've noticed but have been very kind to not mention or point out,' Diana said.

'What do you mean?' Mallory looked genuinely worried, and Diana wanted to smooth out the wrinkle that had appeared on her forehead. She always went straight for thinking she'd done something wrong.

'Langdon. Whenever he comes up you... do that.'

Mallory's face, still flushed, fell. 'Shit. Is it obvious?'

Diana felt her lips twitch. 'That something happened? Yes, I think even Cornelia has noticed.'

'Oh, goddess.' Mallory hid her face in her hands. 'It... I... I was really stupid. Like, really, really oblivious. I went to talk to him about the trolls, and he gave me a lift to do more work on my other case. It was nice, and he kept saying we should hang out, and I didn't think anything of it. I got access to the Mayoral

Offices while you two were off questioning suspects, so I asked him to come with me, but…'

'But it was a date.'

'It took me an *embarrassingly* long time to figure out. He was being really lovely to me.' Mallory buried her face in her hands again, a small scream of distress escaping her. She pulled the blanket up around her face.

Given that it was normally Diana squirming while trying to tell Mallory stories, she would have been lying if she said she wasn't enjoying the role reversal.

'And then what happened?'

Mallory mumbled something into the blanket.

'Sorry, didn't quite hear that.' Diana cocked her head. 'Did you have sex in the Mayoral Offices? You did, didn't you? You're the first person to do that since Van Doren! I am so proud.'

'No!' Mallory pulled the blanket away from her face. 'No I didn't. Also, ew, thanks for that Van Doren visual.' She twisted her mouth. 'We just kissed, that's all.'

Diana smiled at her. She hadn't really thought Mallory had it in her, though she was glad she'd found a way to distract herself from the Cornelia and Shit King stuff. 'That's really sweet. It's actually *adorable*.'

'Shut up,' Mallory said, smiling back. 'It was nice, but…'

'But?'

'That's all it was. Nice. I won't be doing it again. He knows that, I know that, everything's okay.'

Diana sighed. She knew why, even if Mallory had never been able to say it out loud.

'Did he know why?'

'Not specifically, but he guessed something like it.' Mallory picked at the blanket covering her legs. Her whole face sagged with exhaustion. 'It's fine, seriously. It proved to me that I am capable of at least kissing someone, and of being somewhat attracted to someone else. Maybe there's a chance someday I'll actually want to pursue something of my own volition, and you'll be able to stop trying to set me up with every single person you've ever met ever who you think I might even vaguely like.'

'But I'm so good at matchmaking!'

'I beg to differ,' Mallory said. 'We've all seen your various girlfriends to date.'

'I didn't say I was good at matchmaking *for myself*, Mallory.' Mallory grinned at her, and Diana laughed, a Taylor-shaped vice taking hold of her heart. 'Point taken. Are you okay, though?'

'I promise it's fine. I'm fine. Langdon is being nice, and he will continue being nice, and he won't make things awkward, and everything will be fine. I don't need any more matchmaking, thank you.'

Diana knew that Mallory would not say this if Diana was capable of matching her with the person she wanted to be with.

'Can someone clear a space for all this shit?' Cornelia shouted up the stairs, the sound of tea cups rattling on a tray. Diana pulled papers and books out of the way as Mallory settled back into her blanket, a faint blush still on her face, as Cornelia threw down her spoils from the kitchen.

'I multitasked while I was gone – Felix says that "The Oak Pass" is a whole arc in the early comics, and they've heard it's rooted in Occult history.'

'So probably vampire lore,' Diana said.

'Yes, actually. They said it's about Oakpass as a stronghold. But, you know, in zombie form. They're typing. They're typing. They're typing.'

'Could you stop please?' Mallory said, before Diana could lightly hex Cornelia. 'I can't take the tension.'

'They saaaay…' Cornelia drew the word out slowly. 'It was something to do with an elder tree, where two of the necromancers were embroiled in a battle of wits – that's literally what they've said – and were trying to poison each other as a metaphor for the poisonous nature of a desire for power. Felix said it was meant to be magical and it took them years to realise that elder berries contained cyanide, which is, apparently, less fun.'

'It's not really helping, is it?' Diana said, feeling a glut of frustration in her stomach, like it had been building for days. 'At this rate we're just going to have to go to the party, keep an eye out, and hope we catch a killer.'

'Or killers,' Cornelia said. Diana threw a crisp at her.

'It's always got to be something bigger than it seems, doesn't it?' Mallory rubbed her temples. 'And I can't think about that again until I've had a nap.'

'Maybe we should all just sleep on it,' Cornelia said at last. Diana noticed for the first time that Cornelia looked drawn, and helpfully didn't point out that she accepted the suggestion when Mallory made it.

Diana accepted her tea and tucked a packet of crisps under her arm, clenching two biscuits between her teeth for good measure. 'Sfee oo soon.'

There was a soft knock on the front door as Diana was carefully rubbing oil into the ends of her damp hair. She had thrown on a fresh big t-shirt and her gaudiest bed socks; anything to stave off the panic that they still had no real idea what the undead complex ritual was or who was going to be doing it at a ball surrounded by all the most important figures in Occulture and beyond.

'Cornelia, can you get that?' she called, but there was silence from her room. Diana didn't want to disturb Mallory.

'Fine, I will get the door myself. Hope whoever it is doesn't mind maybe seeing my knickers,' Diana muttered, stomping down three stairs before remembering again that Mallory was resting and hurrying lightly down the rest.

Taylor stood with her shoulders drawn up to her ears against the rain, strands of her hair plastered to her face. She was wearing a pink beanie and her eyeliner had smudged under her eyes.

'What are you doing here?'

'I wanted to come check in on you,' Taylor said. 'I figured, since you haven't updated me in a bit on the case, that you're stumped. Is this a bad time?' She shoved her hands into the pockets of her cardigan.

'No, I… I'm… clean,' Diana said, wishing whatever piece of her capable of assembling coherent sentences hadn't fucked off. 'And everyone's asleep.'

'So it is a bad time? A good time? On a scale of one to ten, where would you rate your current experience of time?' Taylor teased.

Diana laughed. 'Just get in here.'

She took Taylor's hand and guided her up the stairs to her room, turning back to put a finger to her lips as they passed Cornelia's room.

'Hold on.' Diana cast a cloaking spell as she closed the door behind them. 'Now we can talk at a normal volume,' she whispered.

'It's hard to do that when you're not talking at a normal volume,' Taylor whispered back.

She stood awkwardly in the middle of Diana's room, looking around at the stacks of model-making equipment, dioramas in various stages of completion, and rails upon rails of clothes that took up most of the space.

Or maybe she wasn't being awkward, and Diana was the one feeling off-kilter. She had left a pair of socks on the ground and she mumbled a spell so they disappeared to the best place she could think of – down the side of her bed. It was the only thing she could see that made her feel uncomfortable, other than her own state of undress.

And it wasn't like Taylor hadn't seen that before.

There was a quiet pause that Diana filled with a muffled laugh.

'Feels weird,' Diana said at normal volume.

'Your bedroom is *cute*,' Taylor said, throwing herself down on Diana's bed. 'I love the colour of this, it matches my hair.' She ran her hands over the bedspread, her nails pink, and Diana instantly fell into a memory of the two of them in the backseat of her car in Vancouver.

Diana was staring, and she shook the memory away, running her fingers through her still-damp hair.

'Can I get you anything? Hot chocolate?'

'With marshmallows,' Taylor said, her eyes on the ceiling. 'Goddess, this bed's like an actual cloud. This is Cornelia's *guest* bedroom?'

'One of many,' Diana said. 'I'll be right back.'

She padded down to the kitchen and assembled a plate of treats she knew Taylor liked, mentally cajoling herself for not being able to get it together. She also wasn't sure why she was hiding Taylor's presence from the others. She knew Mallory would get it. Cornelia wouldn't give a shit that she had a girl over. This – engaging non-professionally with someone involved with a case while the case was active – was not expressly against their agency rules, even though it probably should be.

But Diana was not in the business of cutting off her own nose to spite her face.

She brought the hot chocolate back upstairs.

'Hope you don't mind, I made myself at home.'

Taylor had removed her beanie and found one of Diana's jumpers, her wet clothes in a pile on the floor. She was reclining against Diana's pillows, her legs crossed.

It almost took Diana's breath away to see her there, looking like she belonged in her room. Like she belonged to Diana.

'I come bearing gifts.' Diana rested the tray on her bedside table and Taylor leaned forward to take a cup.

'Oh, a bourbon cream! My favourite,' Taylor said, dunking one into her hot chocolate. Diana hovered beside her, suddenly feeling at odds with herself. It took a moment for her to recognise the feeling: self-consciousness.

'It's your bed,' Taylor said. 'Sit.' She patted the space beside her, scooting over until she was beside the wall. Diana would not be able to avoid touching her, and it filled her with a strange terror. Diana did not usually go to pieces like this and yet here she was pulling an absolute Mallory.

There had been dozens of pretty girls. There had been dozens of situations like this.

But Taylor. *Taylor.*

Taylor was the first time Diana felt evenly matched. Like she understood Diana and operated on the same level as her. She was the missing piece in Diana's life – she occupied the space Mallory and Cornelia could not fill. She felt safe; she felt like home in a way Diana couldn't explain.

Plus, she was really hot.

Diana climbed up beside her and Taylor handed her a mug.

'How are you doing? And don't give me the bullshit answer, I want the real answer.'

'Ugh, fine.' Diana smiled. 'Bad. Really, really fucking bad. But it always works out for me in the end.'

'That's what you said in Vancouver, too.'

'Let's not talk about that,' Diana said lightly.

Taylor fixed her with a look over the rim of her cup. 'Like I said at the time, I didn't mean any offence. I wanted to tell you as I saw it, because there's no point in lying to you. And what I saw then is that your whole "everything works out" thing' – she wiggled her fingers – 'is bullshit. Diana, look. You're brilliant, you're talented, you're special… but you don't fully know who you are. And I can't be with someone who is always primed to find the ejector seat.'

'I'm working on it,' Diana said, anxious to move the conversation on. The moment had been set up too perfectly to let it be spoiled by something as mundane as reality. 'Let's talk about something else.'

'How's the case going?'

Diana fought the urge to scream.

'Anything else, at all.'

Taylor snorted. 'Right so, this sounds like a lovely dose of existential crisis. Do you want solutions, or do you want me to listen?'

'Listening,' Diana said, smiling softly.

Taylor licked marshmallow off her spoon. 'Go for it then.'

'Actually,' Diana said, feeling mildly out of control even as tension was rapidly leaving her body for the first time in days. Taylor's arm pressed against hers, their legs almost touching as they sat side by side. Diana had to crane her neck to look at her, conscious that there were mere inches between her lips and Taylor's neck. There was a fine layer of stubble against her jawline that Diana wanted to stroke her fingers across.

'Actually?'

'Sorry. What I want to talk about is ridiculous, cause it's fully not any of my business, even though it sort of is. But I don't have anyone else to talk to about it, so you're hearing it.'

'Careful, you'll kill me with anticipation,' Taylor said.

'Say I had a friend—'

'A tall friend or an impulsive friend?'

'Who was possibly in love with my other friend—'

'An impulsive friend or a tall friend?'

'And maybe *love* is taking it too far, but I think we're in love territory, even though the friend in question has not said,' Diana said. Taylor had dropped her spoon into her mug, her face turned to Diana. 'And say one of those friends has seemingly got someone new. Someone who looks exactly like her ex-boyfriend – who is dead, by the way. Five months ago. They'd just broken up… it's a long story. And the other friend seems crushed by it, but also pretending she's not crushed, and they are both pretending they don't have any feelings for the other. And say it's driving me up the wall to be the silent witness to it, because they could be together, and it would literally be fine. Hypothetically.'

'Hypothetically speaking, maybe they don't want to risk it,' Taylor said. 'Maybe they can't run back home from Vancouver just because they have to face down some genuine feelings.'

'I resent that remark,' Diana said.

'I'm sure you do.' Taylor winked. 'But, sure look, here's the deal– this is your home, right? This is their home too. If it's meant to be, it'll work out. If it's not, well… enjoy the sexual tension for the rest of your life.'

'I guess,' Diana said, though she did not guess at all. She wanted to be told meddling was the answer.

'You wanted me to tell you meddling was the answer,' Taylor said.

'How did you know that?'

'I might be a lowly Apparent, but I don't need to be a witch to know that's not what you wanted to hear.'

'Yeah, yeah,' Diana said. 'I guess my fear is that if I *don't* meddle, things are going to end in an implosion, sooner or later. I feel bad for even talking about it. It feels like I'm gossiping about them, when I've never gotten a proper answer out of either of them. I tried with one of them last year, but I don't think I can push it. It's at the point where if they thought anyone suspected they were interested in each other, they'd spontaneously combust.'

Taylor laughed, a rich, warm sound that shook the bed as Diana looked at her quizzically.

'I'm just remembering the last time someone said spontaneous combustion. It was before you got to set; one of the ways we'd entertain ourselves were several rousing rounds of Fuck Marry Kill among the crew members. It… you had to be there.' Taylor waved a hand. 'It was funny at the time, cause it was before any crew members had… well.'

'Yeah,' Diana said, at a loss for what else there was to say.

'Anyway,' Taylor said. 'Someone asked Rachel and her options were Xander, Jenna and one of the security guards.'

'Which one?'

'I've actually no idea. For some reason – tiredness, giddiness, I don't know – some eejit told Sandi that Rachel and Xander had been at it in the makeup trailer. I've no idea where this started, but your man the security guard overheard it and lost his shit, saying how unfair it was to insinuate something like this. As if Rachel even gave a shite. Xander's a bit of a ride, if you're into that sort of thing.'

Diana scrunched up her face. 'I mean, maybe.'

A persistent ring in her ears had started up, unignorably irritating. Taylor's voice sounded like it was coming from under water.

'Anyway, someone suggested he was about to spontaneously combust and Alannah offered to glamour him so it looked like he was burning, and Rachel started calling Xander her husband. Orson got wind of it and called a crew meeting to remind us of the appropriate way to behave on set, as if this wasn't the third day of shooting and we weren't pulling off an impossible task. Anyway, the security guard realised he'd got the wrong end of the stick and was really embarrassed, kept quoting philosophers. Something about life being simple but man makes it complicated, I don't know. I'm babbling now. It was the combustion part.'

'I'm so glad you've helped me solve my problem,' Diana said, trying to speak at a normal volume. Taylor's voice kept getting lost in the screaming ring of her own ear.

'Oh, yeah, no. If you think there's any chance they won't thank you for meddling, don't do it. And I know you asked for listening, but it would be irresponsible of me not to warn you of a potential mistake.' Taylor stopped, taking Diana's mug from her hands. 'Hey, are you okay?'

Diana scrunched up her face further. 'Can't hear. Ear ringing,' she mumbled, her voice sounding wrong in her ears.

'Hold on,' Taylor said, and shifted her body, pulling Diana towards her. Diana was forced to straddle her legs, barely catching herself from smacking her head against Taylor's.

'Hey,' Diana laughed. 'What are you doing?'

'Trust me,' Taylor said. She took Diana's face tenderly in her hands, covering her ears and pressing her fingers to the base of her skull. She tapped her fingers percussively, the sound beating inside Diana's head, and when she took her hands away, some of the ringing had stopped.

'What the fuck magic was that?' Diana lifted her head. She was inches from Taylor's lips, and forced herself to look at Taylor's eyes, which wasn't any better.

Taylor's mouth curved upwards. 'I keep telling you, I may be a lowly Apparent but it doesn't mean I'm not magic in some ways.'

'I don't think that's what you said before,' Diana said, lifting her hand to Taylor's face. She traced her thumb around Taylor's lower lip, worrying briefly that she might be hurting her legs, just as Taylor's hands came up to settle on her waist, shifting so Diana's body was tight against hers.

Diana was so close now that she could see Taylor's pupils had dilated, her eyelids heavy.

Diana stroked her thumb over her jawline, feeling the soft fuzz there as she rested her hand on her cheek. Taylor's breath tickled her face. She smelled of sugar, chocolate, and something gently floral and familiar. Diana breathed it in, afraid to move in case the moment ended, in case there was a repeat of Vancouver. In case she'd read every signal wrong.

'What was that you said about not being with me?' Diana's voice had dropped to a silky whisper.

'I think you said you were a work in progress, or something?' Taylor said, her eyelashes brushing her cheeks with every long, slow blink.

'I think I did say that.' Diana let her lower lip brush Taylor's, holding her face so she couldn't move any closer. Taylor exhaled shakily. 'As long as we both remember that, everything will be fine, I'm sure.'

'That,' Taylor said, pulling her closer so there wasn't a single millimetre of space between them, her hands on Diana's thighs beneath her t-shirt. 'Will not be a problem.'

TWENTY-EIGHT

Nine hours to the Spring Equinox ball

Diana slammed the front door shut and padded to the kitchen, post in hand to cover the fact she was sneaking Taylor out. She had half expected to be woken in the night by an angry Cornelia, but that hadn't happened, seemingly because nobody in the house had realised Taylor was there in the first place.

Unobservant heathens.

Until she realised that they were busy observing something else – Mallory was crouched at the doorway to the basement, her arms around her knees, shaking slightly with the effort. Cornelia's voice travelled into the room from below. Diana put a cushion down behind her and Mallory sank into it gratefully.

Taylor's perfume clung to Diana's clothes and raised in pleasant wafts, and she fully expected Mallory to notice. 'What are we doing?'

Mallory shook her head, pointing. Cornelia was sitting beside a recalcitrant Theodore, a growing blue static charge in the air in front of him. It crackled and glowed, pulsing as it gained more energy from the air. Worse than he had been with the planchette.

'Cornelia, get away. I've got the emotional equivalent of a chainsaw, I will raze this room. I am unsafe. Warning, warning, destructive ghost in the house.'

A strange howl escaped him and Cornelia backed off, moving until her ankles hit the stairs. Diana held her hand out automatically and Mallory struggled to her feet, descending until they stood next to Cornelia.

Theodore smiled up at their arrival, his whole body quivering with the effort.

'Oh good, Mallory, you're here just in time for me to say the exact same thing I said to Cornelia already. I am feeling dangerous today, and you must give me space.'

Theodore looked haunted, which, for a ghost, was pretty difficult to achieve.

'What's happening?' Diana muttered to Cornelia. 'Short version, please.'

'Short version is that he showed up here like this and has not made any sense, and then you came down here.' Cornelia sniffed, then sniffed again, moving her face around Diana's clothes. 'You smell nice. And different.'

'Fuck off,' Diana said pleasantly. 'Focus.'

'Theodore, I'm not going to come any closer, but we really do need you to tell us what's going on. I've been worried about you,' Mallory said, forcing their attention back to the matter at hand.

'You should all leave,' Theodore said.

'But I'm here now. Came all the way down the stairs for this. I really don't want the lab to explode – not least because it will make Mallory sad, but also because it would destroy my dioramas, and most of our research. Think of the murder board, Theodore.'

'It would also probably make my house fall down,' Cornelia added.

'That too.'

'We want to help, Theo. We always want to help.' Mallory reached towards him carefully. 'I'm going to pat you on the arm now.'

'That sounds really nice and reassuring,' Theodore sniffed, allowing Mallory to comfort him.

'Theodore, I don't want to alarm you,' she said. 'But you're… really hot.'

'Thank you, Mallory, but as you know, I don't swing that way. Besides, it would be most inappropriate for us to acknowledge each other in such a way, given that I see myself as a bit of a mentor and there would be an unequivocal power imbalance—'

'No, I literally mean you're not *warm*, you're physically hot to touch,' Mallory interrupted.

'Ah.'

'And that is unusual.'

'Ahh.'

'And a bit alarming.'

'Ahh.' He nodded sagely, flickering.

Diana crept up to stand next to Mallory. She handled him best out of all of them and always had, but Diana wanted to be close in case magic became necessary. She'd almost had her fill of incomprehensible ghost behaviour. She made sure there was nothing directly behind Mallory, should Theodore make good on his promise to raze the basement.

'I should inform you that I went away for a while, because things were not okay within me. The Rot House had spread, you see, and I became rotten. It was almost Shakespearean levels of rot, but not literal as of course I cannot be affected by something as mortal as mould. Though I do sometimes harbour regret that I was not wearing a mushroom-patterned cardigan the day of my demise. Imagine the joy I would've brought. "There he goes," they'd say. "That's a fun guy right there."'

'Are things improved now?' Mallory asked gently.

'Goddess no, if anything everything is much, much worse. But I returned because I have…' He took a deep, unnecessary breath. 'I have a message. For you. All three of you. From… well, we'll call them An Unnamed Source. Capitalised, you know, as though it is their name.'

'Who is this unnamed source?' Cornelia asked.

'An Unnamed Source does not wish to be named in the traditional sense, so you're just going to have to trust me. If you can trust me to leave when I am a danger, you can trust me to come back when me returning makes the most sense.'

Diana did not need to check if the others agreed: they were not sure what they were trusting anymore.

'Can you tell us where An Unnamed Source was?'

'It… hmm. The Mayoral Offices. I don't think that's illegal to tell you. Illegal, a-hahah.' He giggled wildly. 'I don't think any of this is illegal; you'd know best though, given that you're detectives and detectives know things. Although do private investigators know things too? I don't know. You know what your agency outfit is missing? A decent camera! Cornelia, I'd expect you to have done the thing of getting really expensive camera

389

equipment, then you could double as a paparazzo if your career ever took a turn for the worse—'

'Okay. What did they say?' Mallory interrupted.

Diana figured this was a better attempt at keeping him on track than what she wanted to do, which was to grab him by the head and force him to explain in simple words what the fuck was going on.

'An Unnamed Source told me something about Oakpass Manor that I thought was important enough you should hear it.'

'And that thing was?' Mallory prompted. She was so calm in the face of danger, so assured, that Diana did not know how Mallory could see her herself any other way.

'There's a ritual,' Theodore said. His face flickered as he spoke, his mouth moving out of time with his words, and it looked to be an act of enormous concentration. 'A ritual to be performed, and I quote, "sometime around Equinox". And as Equinox is tonight, I feel the warning is less than timely.'

'The Undead Complex? Theodore, what does it do?' Cornelia demanded.

'This next part doesn't mean anything to me, but maybe it means something to you. "The… elders… will gallantly return and restore the past… to the present,"' he choked out, every word a labour, cat ears quivering on his head. '"They will stop at nothing to do it."'

'Who told you this?' Diana asked.

His eyes rolled back as he turned, blinking slowly, only the whites showing.

'Iiii… can't… say…' Theodore managed.

'Theodore, please. Please, any clue you can give us.'

'Mayoral Offices,' he said slowly. 'Clue.'

Mallory looked at Diana, who understood. This could be Katherine.

Cornelia's phone rang, and she darted up the stairs, swearing under her breath.

'You know I trust you so much,' Mallory said. 'And you know I wouldn't ask you to tell me something you didn't want to tell me unless it was really important. I think this is really important. I need you to stop hiding things, Theodore, I need to— HEY!' She reeled backward. 'Stop that!'

'Sssss… sorry. Trying to bypass… wards.' He clenched his fists so hard the blue static in front of him grew bigger.

'What did he do?'

Mallory held up a hand and nodded at Theodore. Diana watched Mallory's jaw unhinge and her face slacken, her eyes rolling back as her entire body stiffened. Theodore fractured into a fog that filled the entire basement. Diana's eyes widened.

She'd never seen a possession happen before, but she knew one when it landed in her best friend.

'Theodore!' Diana said, grabbing Mallory's arm. 'Stop!'

Mallory's neck twitched, her head lifting jerkily as though she wasn't in control of it.

Which, by all accounts, she wasn't.

'I can't tell you,' Theodore-as-Mallory said. 'I can't tell you anything more, and I wish I could. There are powerful things happening, there is something wrong with me, and I am a danger to you. This is worse than last time, this is bigger than last time. This is bigger than us. I think you should leave. I think you should all get your things and leave Wrackton and maybe never come back.'

'Theodore, what are you talking about?' Diana grabbed Mallory's hand, gripping it so tightly it had to be hurting her.

'You have to leave Wrackton. I will miss you, but I would rather miss you and know you were living your lives than miss you and know you were gone. I have to be here forever, but I'd prefer if part of that forever meant you were out there somewhere.'

Tears fell from Mallory's eyes and Diana had no idea if they were Theodore's or Mallory's.

'I'm sorry, Mallory. I'm sorry, Mallory. I'm sorry, Mallory...' Mallory's lips continued to move soundlessly. A crackle of static swept across her clothes, the corner of her sleeve smoking as her skin paled, turning grey.

Cornelia screamed, something flying through the air over Diana's head. Only as it arced down over Mallory and a static burst erupted from Mallory's body did Diana realise it was salt.

'Get out of her. Get OUT OF HER!' Cornelia's eyes were wild as she raced into the basement, taking Mallory's other arm.

Mallory stumbled and Cornelia caught her, holding her until she had steadied herself.

'Forgiveeee... me,' Theodore said, reappearing before them. His hands shook and his face scrunched as though he was crying.

Something flickered in him again and he straightened, looking like himself.

'I'm so sorry. I cannot... I should never... I...'

'You wouldn't steal a vehicle, I know,' Mallory said softly.

'But you'd try to POSSESS one of your FRIENDS?' Cornelia

shouted. She had stepped beyond being reasonable and was now roaring unnecessarily. Diana put a hand on her arm.

'Samhain ghosts always go bad, after a fashion. I am so scared of hurting you. Please understand my intention was not to hurt you, Mallory. It never is. I wish I could turn back the clock, make all of this stop, but I can't. Just. Leave. Wrackton.'

He let his body fall to where he disappeared into a waiting witchlight. The static charge he left behind vanished, leaving Diana's clothes and hair crackling.

Mallory lowered herself to the floor, her hand over her smoking wrist, Cornelia kneeling beside her.

'Are you okay?'

Mallory nodded. 'Just took me by surprise. It was like he was hammering on the door to my mind. I could've said no, and he'd have stopped, but part of me... part of me was afraid of what would happen if he didn't say what he needed to say, and I thought... I could try one last time to ask him to tell me what he's been doing with Katherine.'

'That was possibly the most reckless thing you've done so far in your short tenure as Director of the Undetectables,' Diana said. 'Did it work?'

'I saw a flash of Katherine, but he had all his thoughts locked down. Maybe she really is bad news, maybe that's why he's kept her from us this whole time. He wanted to keep us safe.'

'At least we know for absolute certain that something dreadful is meant to happen tonight,' Diana said. 'So there's that.'

'Yeah, and all it took was Mallory almost spontaneously combusting,' Cornelia said. Only now could Diana see how rattled Cornelia really was.

'You saved her,' Diana said. 'So everything's okay, and now you're overreacting.'

'I think you are grossly *underreacting*. I don't want our safety to hinge on my remembering to carry salt around,' Cornelia said frostily.

'Did you… had you meant to carry it?' Mallory asked quietly.

'I love Theodore as much as you two, but he's not right,' Cornelia said finally. 'He hasn't been right for some time. I didn't want to have to use it – I was hoping carrying it would somehow ward against ever having to.'

They were quiet for a moment.

'Let's do breakfast. We can figure out what to do after breakfast,' Diana suggested.

'I'll get the kettle going, and get my notes,' Mallory said, in a voice that said she'd like to be alone.

Cornelia barely waited a beat after Mallory closed the basement door. 'I wanted to ask you something.'

'If this is about the ring, I don't want to hear it. If it's about why we've never dated, I want you to know you're the sibling I've never had or wanted, and the desire to cross that line does not exist. Plus you are very annoying,' Diana said, touching the Machine as if that could determine if it had been damaged in Theodore's static outburst. Cornelia was quiet for a moment too long.

'I sincerely hope your silence is because that was such a funny and irreverent joke that you were stunned by my wit, and not because anything I said was true.'

'No, fuck no. You're more a sibling to me than my actual sisters. It's… did something happen between Langdon and Mallory?'

There it was. Diana fought back a smile, the urge to meddle rising again. It was so easily fixed, a non-issue that would make her feel so much better about everything else going on in her life.

'Why'd you ask?' She had to tread carefully, lest she scare Cornelia off.

'I... just a vibe I got.' Her tone was casual; Diana read it as restrained. 'Nothing specific. I realised I've been distracted lately, and maybe I wasn't paying enough attention to something others were very aware of. It's not any of my business either way, but they're both my friends, so I'm... curious.'

'So curious that you've asked me and not Mallory.' It wasn't a question.

'Well.' Cornelia raked a hand through her hair. 'I didn't want to ask and it not be something, did I? We both know if I brought it up and nothing was going on, Mallory would be second-guessing everything she said around him for the rest of time. Plus there's the distinctly problematic cis-heteronormative thing of assuming a boy and a girl standing next to each other are in some way involved. I don't want to add to the current problems of society just because I'm nosy. And besides, I take from your avoidance of answering the question, something *did* happen.'

'If you'd taken a single breath of air from running around with Shit King, you'd have noticed a lot more's been going on,' Diana said, a tendril of anger curling in her stomach. She hadn't even said anything wrong and Diana wanted to hex her out of the room.

'I haven't seen him in days, I've been as focused on the case as you have.' Cornelia looked genuinely confused.

'Yeah well… you've been texting him, probably,' Diana said. Sometimes, fifty percent of being an arsehole was knowing you were being one and proceeding regardless. 'You've barely left the house this entire case. Mallory and I have been in the driving seat while you've been throwing piles of money at whoever'll take it from you.'

'And yet you brought us a pro bono case.' Cornelia pushed her glasses up, an expression Diana did not think she'd ever seen on her face before – something like hurt.

'I haven't been feeling great lately, that's all. I wanted to ask a question and get your honest answer. You know, the thing you sometimes value.'

Diana had not been expecting that response, so she changed tack. Maybe Taylor was right, and maybe she had to choose the right moment.

'If something had happened between Mallory and Langdon, what would you think?'

'Oh, you know.' Cornelia waved a hand airily. 'Good for them.'

'Shut the fuck up,' Diana said. 'Seriously. Shut the fuck up. Cornelia, when are you going to admit the truth?'

'What truth?'

'I can't even be bothered to be more subtle, I'm trying to sledgehammer finesse this out of you,' Diana said, exasperated. 'When are you going to admit how you feel about Mallory?'

Cornelia blinked. 'I have no idea what you're talking about.'

'You don't know what I'm talking about. So you don't have feelings for Mallory?'

'I really don't know what you're talking about, Diana.'

There was a creak at the basement door and Diana paused, listening, trying to hear around the ever-present whine in her ear.

'What?'

'I thought I heard something.' The house was silent once more, and Diana redirected her attention. 'You really have to stop parading Shit King in front of her. Especially this soon after Beckett. It's not right, on either point. That's his cousin, you are not in a Victorian novel.'

'You… you have literally no idea what's going on, do you?'

Diana threw her arms up, frustration pouring from her like wisps of magic. 'I don't. I have no idea what's going on.' The words were ready to explode out of her now. 'Everything has changed horribly since the Whistler. There's no going back. I can't hear very well and I feel like I'm constantly missing a step, fading in and out of conversations and losing hours to my ears ringing. I've been trying to find us cases worth taking. I got us this one and I – no understatement – *hugely* regret starting because it's once again so much bigger than just investigating something and coming to a conclusion. There's a reason the old Wrackton PD wouldn't touch magical murders with a bargepole, and it's because they suck donkey arse!'

A dam had broken somewhere within her and she couldn't stop the flow of words, angry that Cornelia was listening, that she wasn't reacting, that there were no hexes forthcoming.

'I don't want Mallory to not always be here, I don't want you to leave Wrackton, but I don't know if I want to stay here forever. I want to have the option to come back and for you to be crystallised in place, suspended in amber, and it's selfish and mean of me but I want to know I have options, that no matter where I go in life there is a home, and home is you and Mallory.' *And Taylor,* she added silently. 'If we don't solve this case, if more people die because we didn't figure it out in time, I don't know what I'm going to do.'

Her eyes had the courtesy to wait for her to finish before the first tear fell.

'Oh shit,' Cornelia said, wrapping her arms around her. She squeezed tightly, burying her face in Diana's hair and held her while she sobbed, waiting until Diana caught her breath before speaking again. 'I'm so sorry. I… I literally have no excuse for not checking in on you sooner. I assumed you were fine – you were looking after Mallory, and looking after me by not looking after me, in the way you do. I decided that you were fine and didn't need anyone to check in on you. I didn't even notice you were still struggling with your hearing.' She raised a hand. 'Like of course you are, I was there when the doctors told you. I assumed if it was bothering you this much, you'd say something. You're always complaining – that's not an insult, just a fact. You always complain when stuff is wrong, and then you go and fix it. I assumed you'd fixed this. Wrongly.'

Diana sniffed, not caring that her nose was running. Months' worth of tears had been fighting to get free; she had not cried at all since the Whistler case.

'I didn't know how. I didn't know how to bring it up, or admit that in my head I thought everything would resolve itself in a few weeks, and that we'd move on to the next case and the next and the next and suffer no single repercussion for doing so. It happens like that in the movies, right? Even

Mallory's procedural manuals assume that's the case. So why not here, in reality?'

'You should talk to Mallory,' Cornelia said. 'About this. She knows what it's like to have your life ripped out from underneath you. She'll get it. Nobody is going to look sideways at you for needing support. That's not what we do here.'

'As much as I hate to ever give you credit,' Diana said, glad Cornelia couldn't see her face. 'You're right.'

'I'm what, sorry?'

'YOU'RE RIGHT,' Diana said loudly. 'And that is *not* a funny or appropriate joke to make in this instance.'

'That's what I thought you said.'

Diana snapped her fingers and Cornelia yelped at the small hex that claimed several of her arm hairs.

'When this is over, I will talk to her properly. I guess I felt as though I would be claiming something that I didn't have a right to, which doesn't make sense now that I say it. And anyway, it's not like I don't have my own experiences outside of what you and Mallory can understand,' Diana gestured at herself.

Cornelia bobbed her head in agreement. 'But what's different here is that Mallory gets completely what you're going through.'

'What about you?' Diana asked, shrugging out of the hug and magically acquiring a tissue, blowing her nose loudly.

Cornelia wrinkled her face. 'Why?'

'We're being honest and having a conversation,' Diana said. 'I thought I'd be nice and reciprocate.'

'I'm fine,' Cornelia said. 'You've nothing to worry about here.'

But there was something in her voice that told Diana she was lying out her arse.

'So, Shit King,' she said. 'To circle back. I really didn't think you were inclined to answer *every* ad that told you hot young vampires want to meet in your area, but you're making me question both myself and how well marketing strategies work on you.'

Cornelia's eyes widened. 'Me and *Kingston*?'

'Your taste in men has always baffled me, but even I am capable of seeing that he bears a striking resemblance to an ex-boyfriend you were with only because of how he looked, don't even lie to me otherwise,' Diana said. 'Hence the hot young vampires joke. But the joke is that I don't get it.'

Cornelia laughed then, a wild, loud laugh that seemed to release some of the tension in the room.

'No! We really are just working through some grief together. Plus, he's kind of fun to have around. I've realised he's more like what I wanted Beckett to be. He's who *Beckett* wanted to be. He looked up to him so much. I think had Beck not died, we'd... we'd be friends now,' Cornelia said. 'And it would've been nice. So I'm grieving a friend, and he's grieving his closest family. That's literally it.'

'So...' Diana did not want to spell it out. 'If you've got nothing going on...'

'I have more time to be happy for my friends,' Cornelia said.

'But I didn't—'

'Forget I said anything,' Cornelia waved a hand. 'It is what it is.'

'It—'

'I think it's time for breakfast,' Cornelia said firmly. 'Oh, Hexana! I forgot – that phone call I took was a representative from the UML.'

'What did they say? Is the Whistler investigation closed?'

'Not quite.' Cornelia bared her teeth. 'We've been issued a verbal, binding cease-and-desist for investigating anything to do with Oakpass Manor on account of it not being "lawful or licensed behaviour", whatever that means.'

'Cornelia,' Diana said. 'Why didn't you lead— focus. "Whatever that means" sounds like it's actually important to understand. So what does it mean for us, exactly?'

'It means we are not permitted to enter Oakpass Manor grounds, without UML approval, which could take thirty-odd business days.'

'But the Equinox party—'

'Is, at my last estimation, less than thirty-odd business days away, given that it's tonight.'

'But the owner of the property invited us in,' Diana said incredulously. 'Surely they can't—'

'That's what I said!'

'What did they say?'

'They said that processes must be observed. They also said that we cannot seek contact with any organisations affiliated with, or enter into correspondence with anyone related to, the ongoing proceedings at Oakpass, and that to participate in future cases, we would need an ongoing licence, that will expire and require re-application every ninety days or at the completion of each case, whichever comes first.'

'Oh, for the love of ELISABELLA,' Diana shrieked. 'What are we going to do now?'

'I had an on-the-spot idea. I think our director would call it "taking initiative",' Cornelia said, her voice not nearly as soothing

as Diana imagined she thought it was. 'I've enlisted some outside
help in keeping an eye on all the goings-on at Oakpass for the
next few hours. Help for which I am assuming full responsibility,
especially if this goes wrong.'

Diana goggled at her. 'What the fuck have you done?'

'It's a two-part plan. The second part is me avoiding increasing
liability by letting you in on it before I have to, so I won't tell you
any more. Okay, see you in the kitchen!' Cornelia said, leaving
Diana in the near-quiet wondering what on earth they were
going to do.

TWENTY-NINE

Three hours to the Spring Equinox ball

Mallory had retreated to the comfort of her room for a nap, and woke hours later with a heavy heart – heavier than normal – her back and neck seized and the skin on her arms sunburn-tender, though she hadn't had any sun in a long time.

It took her a minute to figure out why, on this particular occasion, she felt so sad, and the memory of the words fell like a hammer on her head.

'So you don't have feelings for Mallory?'

'I really don't know what you're talking about, Diana.'

She hadn't meant to eavesdrop. She'd been coming down to tell them the bread had gone mouldy, and thought she'd heard Cornelia say her name. She hadn't had the energy to do a listening spell, so had stood behind the door, trying to hear over the panicked blood rushing in her head.

And then she wished she hadn't.

At least that was that. She was just going to have to get over it. Get over her, get over herself, lest she ruin their friendship with her stupid, pointless pining. She'd ruined it months ago with

403

what she'd done to Cornelia's beetle colony; even if Cornelia had forgiven her, it wasn't something you forgot about.

But Langdon had made her feel like she could be wanted.

And she could be. Just not by the person she wanted to be wanted by.

Cornelia was so opposite to Mallory – carefree, impulsive, brash, reckless, likeable. They would be too opposite, too much in the wrong direction from each other, that it did not surprise Mallory in the slightest that Cornelia was baffled by Diana's question.

Not surprised, but hurt nonetheless.

She pushed her fists against her eyes until bright colours burst behind her eyelids, then fumbled in her bedside drawer for her meds. She wished she could magically bring herself a cup of tea and didn't want to get out of bed to do it, anxious to save energy for the Equinox party.

She shoved all thoughts of what she'd overheard out of her head and went back to something that had been gnawing on her. A question the others had fairly ignored, given the circumstances, but that had bothered her since Diana had told her about it: the question of why someone had written 'Francine' on the wall, then tried to erase it.

It was the one piece among all their clues – the murders, Equinox, the Larkins, the Undead Complex, the demon trace, the non-Occult magic, Bellissima – that didn't make sense. There was no evidence Francine was particularly engaged in the Appoccult Society; Mallory had the impression from various tiny snippets they'd found that Francine only joined to keep Delfina happy. Francine had offered up the dollhouse as the trinket one had to produce in order to join the Society. If Diana's deep and personal biography of Francine Leon's life was to be believed, Francine did not enter the business of murders while she was around Oakpass Manor. That came much later – years, in fact, and was utterly unrelated to the disappearance of the Larkins.

As much as Mallory desperately wanted to believe Sandi and Jenna were the Dollhouse Murderers, she'd had a growing sense in her stomach that they weren't necessarily right, and her mind had hooked on Francine.

Hooked on the fact Sandi had not seemed to know much about her when asked. Hooked on the fact the dollhouse was at the centre of the murders – 'They're the Dollhouse Murderers, for the love of Blair,' Mallory muttered to herself – and feeling strongly that they were missing something. Something glaringly obvious, a sense she'd forgotten a small but important detail. It was as familiar to her as forgetting simple words these days; an answer on the tip of her tongue that she couldn't quite reach.

Mallory groaned into her hands, wishing she had the energy to go out into the Redwoods, lie on the ground, and scream until every bird in the vicinity screamed back as they flew away.

She wished Theodore was with her, then thought about the amount of time she spent wishing Theodore was around in the last few months. She was failing him again, and failing Katherine in the meantime. There was a weight in her stomach as she pushed thoughts of him possessing her out of her mind – she didn't know how she felt about it yet.

She took a deep breath. One thing at a time. She'd focus on Francine, pull that thread and see what was making her feel so unsettled. She pulled her laptop onto her lap, balancing it on a cushion and wincing at the pressure on her legs. It was going to be a terrible day.

She searched Francine Leon's name, noting that few results came up, and the ones that did were the same rehashed articles over and over about her contributions to science, and a few books that had been written about her. Diana knew much more about Francine than any of the scholars.

An obituary popped up, a blurred image of a newspaper article, written by her stepdaughter. Mallory skimmed over it until she got to a word that stopped her in her tracks.

'My darling stepmother Francine, or "Francie" as she was specially known in our house, will be dearly missed by Lockie, June and Brady, and her dear great-granddaughters, Tiff and Rachie. We hope she is safe with her dearly loved wife, Delfina.'

Rachie.

Rachel.

Mallory froze. Rachel, as in *Undead Complex* Rachel. She searched her memory for her name, feeling it on the tip of her tongue.

Rachel *Lyons.*

She had called Francine 'Francie' in front of Mallory and Diana, and Diana had corrected her. She was the only other person they encountered on set who seemed to even know who Francine was, and she was the only person there who could've known Diana's particular interest in her.

In a way, it was the opposite of clever, and Mallory was furious at herself for not realising before.

'CORNELIA!' Mallory shouted. 'COME HERE.'

Cornelia bounded in, wearing a particularly oversized blue jumper, a book in her hands raised as if she was planning on hitting someone. Mallory's heart ached again. *I really don't know what you're talking about, Diana.*

'What?'

'I think I know who one of our killers is.'

Diana was clearly pissed off at not figuring it out herself, but Mallory was determined that they saw it as a win nonetheless.

'Rachel. Rachel as our second killer. It makes sense,' Mallory kept saying, as they looked through their case notes to date for the fifth time since Mallory had run down the stairs, knowing she'd regret it later.

It was late afternoon, dusk falling rapidly outside as they sat in the basement, Mallory curled on a chair. The room felt cold and empty without Theodore.

'She was there for Taylor's murder, and she works in the prop department with Taylor. Jenna said she'd worked with her before. Jenna has only ever been a makeup artist, but Rachel does have access. She's been here, so she could conceivably have worked out who Diana really is. She would have everyone's trust on set, because—'

'She's been the one smoothing everything over,' Diana cut in. 'Life imitating art.'

'Rachel didn't ransack the house,' Mallory added. 'If she did, she wouldn't have asked Diana to fix it. Her role in the duo is to smooth things over, keep them both safe.'

'How do you know?' Cornelia asked.

'She asked Diana for help, and then potentially realised who Diana was when she got here. Maybe the big pink pentagram outside our HQ made her suspicious, maybe she searched for her online, maybe someone told her,' Mallory said. She could feel the answers starting to slot together. 'And then used Fred to try scare her off, and when that didn't work, tried again with the mannequin.'

'So what would the motive be here?' Cornelia asked.

'I've absolutely no idea, because I still can't get a grasp on why someone would want to perform the Undead Complex ritual or *what it even is*,' Mallory said, dangerously close to snapping. It wasn't Cornelia's fault she didn't have answers. 'We know it's likely to summon the gatekeepers, but we don't know what that functionally means beyond a ritual that'll be performed later tonight. If we had some sort of demonstration, or way of seeing what it might look like, I'd probably feel a lot more certain it was Rachel and Jenna working together, but as that's impossible, I—' She stopped, the answer hitting her. 'The spell.'

'What spell?' Diana asked.

'The finding spell,' Cornelia said, her gaze following where Mallory's had landed on objects they'd recovered from Fred's scene. 'We didn't try it ourselves.'

'Elisabella wept, WHY are we so bad at this?' Diana shrieked. 'Oh we'll start a PI agency! Can't possibly be a learning curve associated with INVESTIGATING MURDER.'

'Is this a regularly scheduled breakdown, or can we skip it? Not like we're on a deadline or anything,' Cornelia said, poring over the spell and arranging the items on the lab bench.

'Shut the fuck up,' Diana said eloquently, though Mallory did not miss Cornelia reaching over to squeeze her hand briefly.

'Focus. Focus,' Mallory urged again. 'We've been assuming the finding spell would lead us – and the killers – to the Larkins, but what if the dollhouse is more important than we thought? It's been bothering me, how it all fits together – I think the dollhouse is a set of instructions on how to carry out the Undead Complex ritual.'

'But why?' Diana asked.

Mallory scrunched up her face. 'I don't know. But think about it – the Larkins have been missing for years, and the dollhouse was missing just as long. If the Larkins were targeted by the original killer – because I think there was an original Dollhouse Murderer – they'd have had no idea what was coming down the line. The perfect murder, still unsolved, because nobody knew it *was* murder.'

She could feel it, that exciting, intoxicating sense of the pieces forming a clear picture in her head. 'The dollhouse surfaces a hundred years later, the murders start up shortly after. It stands to reason the dollhouse was an integral part of the Undead Complex for whoever was originally trying to carry it out a century ago. So if Rachel is Dollhouse Murderer Two, Dollhouse Murderer One got frustrated and couldn't figure out the instructions.'

'Sorry, back up a bit,' Cornelia said. 'You think Francine…'

'I think someone got Francine to make it.'

'She was hardly involved, though?'

'Maybe Delfina was, or someone else in the Appoccult Society,' Mallory said, her eyes finding her Machine sample jar, the curl of smoke inside. 'Maybe she was under instructions to do so, and didn't realise the repercussions. Or maybe the person who set the original trap for the Larkins was a demon, and Delfina and Francine had no choice but to carry it out.'

'And perhaps those symbols we found in the walls, the Oakpass knot in the courtyard, were meant to provide protection.' It was hard to miss the hopeful note in Diana's voice, how hard she was trying to not think of her hero as someone who was partially responsible for the Larkins disappearing. 'Apparents used to be weird about Occult stuff years ago, maybe she was told it was a way to stop the Larkins being burned at the stake or dunked or whatever happened to witches back then.'

'Depends where you were geographically and also what time period,' Mallory said absently. 'Although burning at the stake is the common Apparent aphorism, that really only happened in European countries, and not all of them. In Ireland, they just locked some witches up for a year and then let them go because they didn't know what else to do. I've always wondered if they were actually Occult—'

'Mallory,' Cornelia said. ''Tis your turn to focus. I'm ready to do the spell.'

'I'll do it if you read, Mallory.' Diana grabbed the page, and then realised there was a second page stuck behind it. 'Hexana, it doesn't half go on.'

'What am I meant to do?' Cornelia demanded.

'Shush. Shush. Mother's working,' Diana said. Mallory snorted and Cornelia kicked Diana's ankle.

She stumbled through the spell while Diana sprinkled the

ingredients over the house, so tired the words were coming out jumbled. She had to restart the spell twice.

Diana sat back, her eyes darting over the house expectantly.

'What do we think—' Cornelia started, but the lines within lit up one after another, a fine dust rising from the tiny floorboards. The circle beneath the pillar in the entrance hall glowed, and then the nightmare began.

'For the love of BLAIR,' Diana said, jumping back. Mallory shook with the effort of joining her, her skin crawling, her mind trying to focus on what was happening around her repulsion.

The pillars twisted, opening the floor beneath them, and five insects crawled out of the hole. Two had hundreds of scuttling legs, one some sort of spotted cockroach Mallory vaguely recognised from Cornelia's bug room, and the final two—

'Fucking steel silk spiders, CORNELIA,' Diana shrieked.

'Hexana, I'll get a jar, hold on.'

'Why did that happen? What was the point of finding… those?' Mallory squeaked, uncertain it wasn't her bad reading of the spell that had done it, somehow.

Cornelia returned with several jars specifically designed for bug catching. 'Hold on,' she said. Her glasses had slipped down her nose, her eyes bright with interest. 'Hand me a magnifying glass, Mal?'

She was silent, and Mallory realised the bugs had moved to the outside of the Manor and were not moving any further, the spiders utterly still.

'They're dead, and look like they have been for a long time,' Cornelia said. 'Curious.'

'I would really like for them to go away,' Mallory said. 'In the nicest way possible.'

'They are so cute,' Cornelia said, holding up the centipedes. 'When I get a chance, I'll pin and frame them. I bet these are a century old.'

'Stop that,' Diana said.

Mallory felt vaguely unsettled seeing how close Cornelia put her face to the bug corpses.

Diana peered into the dollhouse. 'Where's your borescope, Mallory?'

She tilted it, turning the screen so Mallory could see down into the space beneath the pillars.

'Stairs,' Mallory said. 'Like a secret passage?'

'It ends there, there's no button or catch, so hard to know if this is in the real Oakpass, or if it was just a hiding place for the bugs.'

Diana removed the borescope just as the dollhouse glowed again, and the floor twisted back into position.

'It wasn't backwards!' Diana said, pointing. 'When the floor was open, the doors in the entrance hall lined up on the right sides, but when it's closed they aren't! I noticed it when I was restoring it with Taylor, but thought it was a mistake. But of course, Francine would never. I should never have doubted her.'

Mallory half-smiled at that.

'What do bugs and murder have in common? And no, that's not the start of a terrible joke. Though I wish Theodore was here to make one,' Mallory continued, feeling a flutter of sadness that he wasn't there to help.

'Mallory was right! This is why the Dollhouse Murderers have been interested in Oakpass, why they've been using the dollhouse as their own personal diorama. It's not just a replica of the Manor, it's instructions!' Diana said, certainty gripping her. 'I bet this is part of the Undead Complex ritual – the mechanics of it, at least, the same way I make my scenes. But what sort of ritual makes bugs emerge from someone's house?'

'What you said, as much a fan as I am of them,' Cornelia said.

'One where there's five,' Mallory said softly. 'Five Larkins, five… creatures. I know what Theodore said about coincidences, and I think this is a glaring exception. Kingston said that the Undead Complex was about combining souls to make gatekeepers, and I think we've met a gatekeeper before.'

Diana rounded on her. 'In the Mayoral Offices. The creature – the mantis I killed?'

'Yes. I think the Dollhouse Murderers are making giant creatures, and I think tonight they're going to release five of them into Oakpass Manor.'

'But WHY?' Diana asked. 'Why would they do this, if that's vampire folklore? If it's Rachel and Jenna, or Rachel and Tate, or Rachel and Whitlock – what would the point be? An Apparent and a demon working together to do this. To what end?'

'What's the easiest way to find that out? Do we get Rachel here, try scaring her into giving up the answer?' Cornelia asked, flexing her hands.

Mallory checked her watch, her stomach plummeting. They were up against the wire.

'No. We need to get ready for the Equinox party, and figure out how we're going to confront her. We'll need to warn Quinn and get him to organise an evacuation plan. Maybe if we warn Dr Ray— what?' she asked, seeing the expression on Cornelia's face.

'One small problem with that.'

Cornelia explained.

'Oh, Hexana,' Mallory whispered. 'There has to be a way in. I can't believe I'm saying this, but there has to be someone Cornelia can put some pressure on to let us into Oakpass Manor, or some loophole we can work around. I'll contact everyone, maybe if we even try Tate…'

'That in itself begs a valid question,' Cornelia said. 'The UML has never moved swiftly on anything before – not without months of build-up. And yet suddenly, we're banned from getting involved in a case that's only been going on for a week.'

'Almost like someone ran interference,' Mallory said, catching on.

'And who would have the most power in doing something of that sort?' Cornelia asked. 'While it must be noted I have learned from my past mistakes in latching onto a suspect, I'm only eighty-seven percent certain that Nathan Tate could do something like that. If we're out of the way, we can't stop him. It doesn't have to be Jenna – it could still be… well, any of them. But I feel very strongly about Tate.'

Mallory was about to comment gently on Cornelia's impulsive attitudes to key suspects, when two things happened at once:

First Cornelia's phone rang at an ear-splitting volume.

And second, her words were drowned out by a wailing siren screaming into the night sky above Wrackton.

THIRTY

Fashionably late for the Spring Equinox ball

Cornelia answered the phone, alternating roaring down it and shaking it, like that was going to do anything.

'Yes, we're all here,' Cornelia shouted, plugging one of her ears with a finger. 'There's some kind of incident happening here. What's your status? HELLO?'

Diana grabbed a jacket and watched as Mallory pulled herself to her feet, allowing her ten precious seconds before she bent and performed the compression spell. Mallory shot her a grateful look and jammed her feet into her boots. Diana was already out the door, ignoring Cornelia's flailing attempts to be heard on the phone and to stop her going out without her.

Diana still had at least one "you once led us into a trap, don't I get to do insert-dangerous-thing-here" saved up. She ran to the front door, throwing it open. Her ear rang and the siren got louder as she took the stairs down to the street two at a time, looking in the direction of the blue searchlights roving the sky in the direction of the Mayoral Offices. Cornelia's neighbours stood in doorways and windows, peering out anxiously, as telescopic concrete bollards rose from the ground, preventing cars from going through. She'd only ever seen them deployed for crowd control when there was some sort of festival happening at Mayoral Square.

She could hear, dimly, the screeches and roars of cars peeling away a few streets over.

A barrier rose at the end of Cornelia's street, blocking any chance of Diana getting her car out.

'FuckSAKE,' Diana screamed, as Mallory joined her, still struggling to get her arms into her jacket. She pointed at the bollards, covering her ears, and Diana screwed up her face in acknowledgement.

Cornelia bolted out of the house, joining them as the sirens cut off abruptly. Mallory pointed at the bollards again. Cornelia frowned, holding up her phone. 'That was Kingston trying to call me.'

'Why?'

'That's my liability,' she said, dialling.

'What the fuck, Cornelia?' Diana snapped.

'I told you, this is my liability,' Cornelia said. 'So don't start. Kingston!'

'Am I on speakerphone? It's cool if I am, I just like to know,' Kingston's voice burst through the phone speaker. The siren had made Diana's ear go wild, a cacophonous symphony playing inside her own head.

Kingston's voice wasn't helping, and neither was the raucous background noise that suggested he was at a party.

'I am at the top secret location otherwise known as PASSOAK,' Kingston said. 'This is King Shit, reporting a sighting.'

'My liability,' Cornelia mumbled. 'Doesn't mean I have to like it.'

'Myself and GlitterFae are here and we have spotted your potential… uh… unsubs,' Kingston said slowly. 'Was that a siren in the background, or has Diana taken up singing?'

Diana was going to hex him so good the first chance she got.

'Give me that,' another voice snapped.

'Felix?' This was Mallory, who had paused mid-tying her boots.

'No, they're GLITTERFAE and they're wearing a very snazzy suit, which should give you a clue to their identity. Ouch—'

'Yes, it's Felix, no I did not consent to the nickname. Yes, my suit is snazzy. We've been here about an hour and have done several rounds. Folk are acting really… strangely. It's hard to explain; they're talking to each other, but nobody seems to be particularly in the moment. I've spotted Jenna White—'

'I would like to note that I saw her first, I just couldn't remember who I was looking for,' Kingston cut in.

'—and we both saw Sandi Clementine. Jenna doesn't look well, actually. Also, there's something strange happening – every time I want to go into the entrance hall, I can't. Folk are funnelling in through there, then can't go back.'

'Looks like warding,' Kingston said.

'And as a final observation, someone has lit three flares in the internal courtyard – I spotted it as I was coming inside,' Felix finished.

'What about Rachel?' Diana asked

'I thought I saw her when I first arrived, but I can't be certain,' Felix said.

They exchanged glances.

'Are Sully or Dr Ray there?' Mallory asked.

'Not that I've seen. Ditto on your other demons – Tate and Whitlock are nowhere to be found.'

'Did you leave it somewhere?' Cornelia asked, bafflingly vague. Diana frowned at her.

'I left both of them, rest assured,' Felix said. 'We— Kingston, can you—'

There was a scuffle, some swearing, and the line went dead.

'We need to get to Oakpass now,' Cornelia said. 'We're out of time. The killers – Rachel, whoever else – they're there now. We have to go.'

'How? The roads are closed.' Mallory pointed helplessly.

Diana already had her phone out, gritting her teeth against the noise inside her own head, and dialled Sully, glad to have someone to sweet-talk.

But the line rang out twice, as did Dr Ray's. She tried calling the police station and found the phones were off the hook. There was something alarming about this that made Diana's stomach clench.

'Well. We'll have to go find Sully and Dr Ray ourselves, get clearance to leave Wrackton, and solve the murder. Slash stop the giant bug ritual.'

'Hold on,' Cornelia said, uncharacteristically not jumping straight into action. If Diana didn't know better, she'd say she looked genuinely worried. 'The Dollhouse Murderers sent you a specific message to get you to stop looking into them – what if we're walking into a trap? I say this with nothing but respect for your terrible affliction of being noticed by a killer, but maybe your focus should be on getting in touch with Dr Ray and Quinn, and Mallory and I will look for Rachel and… whatever demon she's working with that may or may not be Tate.'

'I vote no,' Diana said, raising her hand. She was being petulant and she was pleased about it.

'I vote yes,' Cornelia said. 'To you trying not to piss off a murderer.'

They looked to Mallory, who glanced between them with trepidation.

'You're the director, you get the deciding vote,' Diana said, knowing even as she did that it was very unfair.

'Pros and cons,' Mallory said. 'The pros need to be better than the con, which is that you potentially walk straight into getting murdered at Oakpass Manor.'

'I am going to say this once,' Diana said in her calmest voice. 'We have been in a life-or-death situation once before. While admittedly Mallory did a lot of the practical locating and rescuing, I did most of the fighting. We have no idea what we're facing at Oakpass. Well, if you'd like to be technical about it, we've half an idea. But if you think I am letting you walk into a place where there are actual killers and weird bugs without my help, regardless of the possible consequences – bearing in mind that if the Dollhouse Murderers know who I am, you can bet your arse they know who you are – you are both the biggest fucking twats I have ever had the misfortune of knowing.'

'That's not an actual pro, though,' Mallory said hesitantly. 'It's a good point, but doesn't follow the pros-and-cons format.'

Diana had a trump card ready, and she played it happily.

'Pro: I'm the only one of the three of us that can drive.'

Cornelia closed her eyes as Mallory raised a hand. 'Fine. Let's get dressed for a party.'

They managed to walk to within two streets of the Mayoral Offices, surrounded by cars full of officials constantly arriving, and bollards everywhere. Some UML representatives and what Cornelia was eloquently referring to as 'Import Police' were stationed at the end of every street, trying to stop them travelling closer.

'My house is up here,' Diana said no fewer than five times, beaming at every single person-shaped obstacle standing in her way. Each of them eyed the ballgowns she and Mallory were wearing, and the sharp black tuxedo they'd coerced Cornelia into, but said nothing and let them continue.

It also wasn't a lie; the home Diana had grown up in *was* close to the Mayoral Offices, it just wasn't hers or her family's anymore.

Cornelia had cast a listening spell and relayed her attempts to make sense of the whispers from the UML representatives and radio chatter emanating from the jackets of various Import Police, but after the fifth mishearing she insisted was something about 'three chicken nuggets and a great glass elf', Mallory suggested she should redirect her efforts to trying to contact Sully and Dr Ray.

Standing outside Diana's old house now, ignoring the flood of light and twitching curtains coming from inside, Diana shoved her hands inside her pockets.

'What now?' Cornelia asked. A sheen of sweat covered her forehead, and Diana frowned.

'We need to get to the Offices,' she said. 'As presumably that's where Sully and Dr Ray are if they're not answering, and we need someone to let us drive out of here.'

Mallory checked the time on her phone. 'It's been too many minutes since we heard from Felix, and I don't like how that phone call ended. Do you have an actual plan, apart from finessing our way through obstacles? Either of you?'

Cornelia bit her lip.

'We keep trying to get to the Offices,' Diana said firmly. 'Stay here, but follow my lead.' She marched to the end of the next road, her dress billowing as she left Mallory and Cornelia staring after her.

A barrier in the form of a single UML representative stood in her way, next to yet another bollard. His body was lit by the pale blue glow of the searchlights, the entrance to Mayoral Square behind him, full of cars and trucks but eerily quiet.

'Hello,' Diana said, approaching him. He looked like a child in a suit much too small for him, which for a witch, Diana felt was unforgivable. 'I'm with the Homeowners' Tidy Town City Committee, I'm sure you've heard of us.'

'Erm… not really, no.'

Diana planted her hands on her hips and levelled a gaze at him. He seemed to shrink, glancing around as though he hoped someone would come save him.

'We're a collective of concerned neighbourhood citizens of Wrackton, and I want something to put in our bi-daily email for tonight. The homeowners are going to be very, very, *very* upset to not know the reason for the sirens. We have a very strict noise threshold we stick to around here. There'll be fines to the town for violating that, you know.'

'There… that's… privileged information,' he managed.

'What's your name?' Diana asked, softening her tone.

'Hugo,' he whispered.

'Okay, Hugo. Here's what we're going to do. Nobody will ever know this came from you. But if my *darling* husband Ber… Bertrand can't get his *beloved* baby Suki out of the driveway for his dawn drive and I don't have a reason for it, I'll have to deal with so much *sulking*.' She reached a hand out and touched his sleeve. 'This is an interesting suit, what's it made from?'

'Fabric, I think.'

'Let me help you out.' She cast a resizing spell so the sleeves fit him properly, and he recoiled. 'Nice fabric, it's very… polyester. So, Hugo. For the sake of Suki. And Bertrand. And my peace. And the Homeowners' Committee. What say you?'

'There… there was a disturbance at the Offices,' Hugo said in a whisper. 'Some sort of… of creature, they said. I'm stationed here until it's done with.'

Diana swallowed. 'What kind of creature?'

He shook his head violently. 'A big one, that's all I know. I only caught a glimpse.'

Diana straightened up. 'Thanks *so* much, Hugo. We'll be on our way. Come on, girls!' She waved to Mallory and Cornelia, the latter of whom glowered at her as she passed.

'I'm not sure…'

'We're just heading home to deliver the news,' Diana trilled, waving as she trotted down the road. 'I'll send Bertrand your love!'

Once they were out of earshot, Cornelia grabbed her. 'Who the fuck's Bertrand?'

'There's a creature,' Diana said, ignoring her. Cornelia never got the games Diana liked to play, nor the creative efforts she put into her networking. Diana could be anyone she wanted to be in any given moment. 'Another escape from the Mayoral Offices. Frankly, I am sick of creatures.'

'We've had them before and there was no alarm,' Cornelia said. 'What's different this time?'

'Van Doren probably went out of his way to avoid broadcasting that anything was wrong,' Mallory said. She was hunched with her hands deep in her pockets like they were somehow holding her upright. 'And it's possible this one *is* different.'

They rounded the corner and saw cars, more police, but no Sully or Dr Ray. Instead, DCI Tate stood outside the Mayoral Offices barking orders to someone, the entrance cordoned off. There was an ambulance and several paramedics standing around talking.

'I'll go,' Mallory said decisively.

'Go where?' Cornelia looked bewildered.

'Talk to Tate. She can't' – she lifted an elbow in Diana's direction – 'but if he didn't remember Diana – or at least pretended not to – he likely won't remember me.'

'Be careful,' Diana said. 'He's our main suspect, we need to tread carefully.'

'I'll go with you,' Cornelia said, and the two approached him. Diana tried calling Sully again while she waited, hiding behind a pillar, watching Tate's body language change from suspicious to downright hostile. They were back in less than ninety seconds.

'What a class-A prick,' Cornelia said. 'So rude.'

Mallory was smiling grimly. 'He said we can't be in the area and we need to leave. But he also accidentally confirmed that neither Sully nor Dr Ray were there – we asked if we could speak to them, and he said, "If she was here do you think—" before seemingly realising what he'd said and telling us to fuck off away from a crime scene.'

'Crime scene?' Diana squinted. 'Are we classifying creatures as a crime scene?'

'I think we should go check the station,' Cornelia said. The sheen of sweat was still on her forehead, despite the crisp spring wind. 'I'll go.'

'I'll come with you,' Mallory offered, but Cornelia shook her head. 'Stay here, save your energy. I won't be long.' She took off at a jog, her dress shoes thudding as they hit the pavement.

'Listening spell?' Mallory suggested. 'I'm also curious about it being designated a "crime scene" when a bug isn't exactly a crime. Also this feels like the sort of thing Theodore should be around for.'

Diana cast the spell, choosing not to comment. Theodore missing was a worrying thing, but it was not a worry she could afford to chew over.

'—find of the century, especially if she's not here to see it,' DCI Tate was saying to someone who was clearly a subordinate, based on the amount of animated nodding he was doing.

'If we keep things cordoned off, we can probably get confirmation it's his body before the news breaks, get someone out to do a proper statement. Frankly amazing that thing chose tonight to escape, but it blew apart rubble they hadn't cleared yet, and there he was.'

Diana and Mallory exchanged alarmed glances.

'You— I don't care what your name is, go write me a statement. I don't care if that's not your job,' Tate snarled. 'You'll do it.'

The subordinate nodded.

'You,' Tate said, clicking his fingers at a paramedic.

'He really is a prick,' Diana muttered.

'We need her to confirm this is his body. They'll want to wrap up the serial killer story as discreetly as possible, and we can use that. I don't want to farm this out to one of ours, they won't do it.'

Mallory inhaled sharply, and Diana felt her insides still.

His body.

Serial killer.

It could only be Jacob's body.

THIRTY-ONE

'We can't trust it's him,' Mallory said after thirty nail-biting seconds of trying to listen for a name, for any confirmation, before Tate and the paramedics disappeared inside. Diana did not always appreciate Mallory's eternal dedication to being sensible, this time included.

'Who else could it be?' Diana demanded. 'Do we know of any other serial killers who died inside the Mayoral Offices? It's not like a load of folk have recently died all at once. Don't tell me, I heard it as I was saying it. But who else could it be?'

'Diana, as much as I appreciate your commitment to the answer being obvious, we're working an active case where nobody is who they look like. Jacob being found here, now? That timing is suspicious as hell,' Mallory said, smoothing back her hair. 'And the timing is not just suspicious because of whatever is happening at Oakpass, but because I was in there earlier this week. There was no sign of his body, they've had *months* to look for it, and they've only found his body *now*, after a creature escape? Almost like they want to cover up the creature escape with a bit of feel-good good news,' Mallory said.

'There are logistical concerns, now I think about it,' Diana said. She felt deflated.

'I'm worried this is going to speed up Katherine getting bricked in, too. Case suddenly closed, so they have no reason to not do it now. What if I've run out of time?'

'Mallory, as always, we have to be sensible and not panic. So Katherine gets Cask of Amontillado'd into the Mayoral Offices – I'm sure one of us could have a go with a big mallet and knock down a bit of wall at some point.'

'I don't know what sort of bricking-in you're imagining, but this is properly sealing it,' Mallory said, looking on the verge of tears. She sniffed. 'Though I will admit, if it is Jacob, I will feel relieved he's been found. I was so worried about his body hanging around in there, potentially with Blair's ring, before you cleared up that mystery. It feels like we're finally getting away from that case a little. It guess it's been on my mind – when I saw Katherine, she asked if his body had been found, and it's been weighing on me since, the fact no one had. I knew he was dead, but… I worried.'

'What a strange and unusual thing to have happen.' Diana grinned, and Mallory's lips broke the barest of smiles.

Diana jiggled her leg, trying to call Felix again. Their voicemail – instructing the caller to send a text – kicked in instantly. 'Felix's phone is off, or broken.'

'I don't like this,' Mallory said. 'We need to get to Oakpass now, we can worry about Jacob later.'

'Agreed. Where the hell is Cornelia?'

She spotted her jogging back towards them from the opposite direction they'd seen her go, her unbuttoned jacket flapping in the wind. Cornelia stopped beside her and took a big gulp of water from a bottle she produced from her bag, panting.

'Ugh, that's too cold. Station's closed,' she said, her glasses fogging. She wiped them on the edge of her jacket. Diana fought to not comment on her treatment of the suit. 'Like fully closed up, door locked, no lights on.'

'Something very weird is going on there,' Mallory said.

'That's an understatement,' Cornelia said. 'I have a very bad feeling about all of it. It's not like Sully took the rest of the team out for ice cream.'

'Much too cold for that,' Diana said, earning herself a glare.

'But even if she did, Dr Ray wouldn't also be missing. The fact she's not here is giving me the heebie jeebies. I did get these though,' she held up a set of keys. 'Mortuary. I checked – no Donny Baker, no Hollis Hadley, no Fred Hill. Empty drawers. Also, Dr Ray doesn't label her drawers very well. I got a really unfortunately good look at Mrs Blackburn's husband, Elisabella rest his soul.' She grimaced. 'But that's my news, anything exciting happen while I was gone?'

'You're not going to like this,' Mallory warned, before filling Cornelia in while Cornelia got her breath back.

'So a creature escapes on a night where we are trying to stop two killers from producing five of them, and they *happen* to find Jacob's body?' she said once Mallory had finished. The fact she'd waited that long to speak was nothing short of a miracle.

'That's what I said,' Mallory said.

'He said the creature broke free, and unearthed Jacob's body from an area they hadn't fully cleared yet,' Diana said. 'Which I suppose is precisely what the Dollhouse Murderer *would* say, if this was about distracting the police and Dr Ray.'

'But if Tate's here dealing with it...' Mallory gestured. 'It means he's not at Oakpass.'

'He could've come back,' Diana said unconvincingly. It did seem unlikely. 'But also, he's in with the UML. He knows about witchlight travel. It's still possible he's our guy.'

But she knew he wasn't. It wasn't Tate.

'There's something else bothering me too, just sort of tangentially,' Mallory said. 'If creatures are escaping and it's only Equinox and not Samhain, and say it's not a deliberate stunt to distract, then... was Theodore's presence having a significant effect on the creatures? He leaves, things get immeasurably worse.'

Cornelia's phone buzzed, but before she could answer it the call dropped. A text came through and she peered at it before flipping the phone so the others could see.

Kingston
COMEE QUIKC

'We need to move.' Cornelia spun in a circle, as though hoping a car would appear. 'Somehow. Maybe we can magically remove the bollards ourselves, or maybe it's all the power of suggestion and you could drive a car over them, Diana?'

Mallory was mid-trying to convince Cornelia that those were not actually valid options, when Diana shushed them, catching something happening behind them. She held up a hand as Tate walked out behind the paramedics, wheeling a gurney with a zipped body bag on top. He was speaking into a radio. There were no rings on his hands, nothing to suggest that he was not who he was meant to be.

'He's very definitely not our demon,' Diana said. 'I will, on this occasion, admit to being wrong.'

'How very magnanimous of you,' Cornelia said. 'Now, let's go.'

'How!' Mallory said, her frustration palpable. 'I'm all for going now, but *how*? We got a cease and desist from the UML, Felix and Kingston said there were wards up, so it's not like we can just… walk in!'

'We use witchlights again,' Cornelia said.

'I'm pretty sure that's out, if they've got the place warded.'

'Not if you've had two spies leave two witchlights inside the building in strategic locations – one in the ballroom, and one near the back entrance. Even if they're right and there is some kind of ward keeping them out of the entrance hall, we'll bypass all of that and land ourselves in the middle of Oakpass.'

'Why would you do that?' Mallory said, at the same time as Diana said, 'Excellent work, detective.'

'In case we couldn't figure out another way in,' Cornelia said to Mallory, patting Diana on the shoulder. 'If we can work out out what kind of wards we're up against – if any, I'm not sure the UML is truly this organised – we can decide if witchlight travel is the safest way inside.'

'But,' Mallory said, her voice coming out as a squeak.

'I love it when you get all worked up,' Diana said, earning a begrudging smile from her.

'I can't think of how we're going to get there except you two walking, my brain won't…' Mallory clutched her head. Cornelia placed a hand on her arm gently, her gaze on Diana.

'No car, no ability to get out of the town. We could walk, but it would take over an hour, which isn't good for Mallory *or* for our attempts to stop whatever's happening, and we'd still have the same problem of not being able to saunter in.'

'Would it be so bad if we were caught by the UML?' Mallory asked. 'We can tell them it's another case, so even if it's not our solve in the end, *someone* is dealing with the problem. Although they are unlikely to believe us, so that's an issue in and of itself. Maybe you should walk without me, see if you can get a cab on the other side of the town border?'

'Absolutely not, Mal. We go together or not at all. Right, I'm going to see which one of these Import Police can be bribed into letting us out. Surely we can fake an emergency between us? Mallory, do you know where an appendix is located and how to pretend yours exploded?'

'That's not going to work and you know it; they'll bundle her into the ambulance directly,' Diana said.

Mallory looked up at the sky and Diana followed her gaze. There were still searchlights raking the clouds above them.

'What we need now is some kind of miracle.'

'I don't know about a miracle,' a familiar voice said, bringing warmth with it as a crack of static filled the air. 'But would you settle for a hero?'

THIRTY-TWO

Impolitely late for the Spring Equinox ball

Mallory had thrown herself at Theodore before Diana had time to react.

'You're back! You are back, aren't you…?'

'I never really left. Though it feels good to be missed, like a seasonal special drink. Enjoyed in small batches, would become boring if available year-round.' Theodore closed his eyes, settling his face on Mallory's shoulder like a contented cat.

'What does that mean?' Cornelia asked, wrapping her arms around Theodore too. 'The never-really-left bit. The simile part was painfully overdrawn, but comprehensible.'

'The mind does allow for open interpretation from time to time,' Theodore said sagely, belying the fact he wasn't making a lick of sense. Diana swore in Cantonese under her breath.

'Theodore, I have to tell you something,' Mallory said, taking a deep breath. 'They've just found Jacob's—'

'Goddess, Mallory, you look half frozen,' Theodore said. 'Like a frappé. That's a sort of iced coffee, it pairs nicely with my earlier hot-drink simile.'

'Theodore, please listen. There were sirens, and a creature escaped—'

'What *is* a creature really, when you think about it? Are we not all creatures, in a way? There was a song that went like that, wasn't there, Mallory? Something about the sun on a creature-man, I think. Though that doesn't seem right, when you really ponder it properly. Let's all ponder it now.'

Diana met Mallory's gaze. Even for Theodore, this really was a spectacular avoidance of the issue at hand.

'We'll talk later, we're on a bit of a time crunch at present. What was that about a hero?' Mallory smiled at him, though it didn't quite reach her eyes.

Diana had to admit that Mallory was handling this better than she would, as Diana would by now have threatened him with a ghost light. She supposed there was more than one reason Theodore loved Mallory best; her ability to deal with him at his most ridiculous without resorting to threats was admirable, even under stress.

'Ah, yes. Well. You see. I am a ghost. And while I maintain that I am not a ghost-for-hire, I do have a certain skillset. One I am happy to share. Diana, my smallest witch friend, do you have a phone handy? One that can play music?'

Diana held up hers, hoping his static wouldn't break it, as that would be the final nail in the Hexana-forsaken coffin.

'Ready and waiting. What do you need?' She was trying to mimic Mallory's casual tone, knowing it was coming through urgent and strained. They rarely had time for Theodore's theatrics, and now felt like the wrong time to indulge him.

Theodore wriggled out of the hug Cornelia and Mallory still

had him in and twirled on the spot, pulling his cardigan close around him. His cat ears fluttered in the breeze.

'It's not about what I need, you see. It's about what you need.'

'And what's that?'

'Well. As the saying goes, you wouldn't steal an automobile. But I rather think you should.'

His plan was simple, brilliant and terrifying, in that order. Cornelia figured out where the speakers were that played the sirens – they were magically modified alphorns built into the Mayoral Square. 'They're audible over six miles away,' she said, earning a smile from Mallory and an urging to hurry up from Diana, who just wanted to get the show on the road.

She felt uncomfortable without her phone in her pocket, but had left Cornelia to follow Theodore's directions on how to hook it up to the speakers – 'It's simple science, Cornelia, they even had radios back in my day, you know' – while she and Mallory picked the car they were going to temporarily borrow.

'It's still stealing,' Mallory said. 'We can euphemise it all we want, it is legally stealing no matter what we call it. This is car theft *and* joyriding.'

'I wouldn't call what we are about to do a joy, by any stretch of the imagination. Anyway, we'll be fine. Cornelia will negotiate us out of trouble,' Diana said airily, not voicing the part where they'd be lucky if they were still around to have that negotiation.

'Fine. Fine, but I don't like it. As director I'm going to put a future veto on any and all crimes. It's be gay, *solve* crimes—'

'—Not be gay, do them, yes I know. Though we should consider that we can do a little bit of both doing and solving, on occasion, as a matter of agency policy.' Diana blew her a kiss, then pointed. 'That one?'

There was a sleek-looking red sports car next to the bollards near the end of the Mayoral Square that Diana quite liked the look of. She turned to Theodore and pointed discreetly, earning a big nod of approval and a thumbs up. She and Mallory stood on either side of the car, Mallory looking at her phone, Diana pretending to admire some graffiti on the wall beside her, juggling her keys to Cornelia's house like she was just waiting for her car to be let out.

With Jacob's body in the back of the ambulance, the paramedics climbed in and the Undetectables waited, bodies tensed, as a police car trundled down the road, the ambulance falling in close behind. The cars approached the bollard at the end of the square, and it started to retract.

When it was seconds from being completely flush with the ground, Theodore clapped his hands twice, causing a static crackle to flutter in front of them. This was the signal for Cornelia.

A strange, ethereal howling poured from the speakers, impossibly loud, then thunderous violins filled the air. Diana half expected an orchestra to pop out of the ground beside her. The ambulance driver jumped in their seat, but kept moving forward. Diana used an unlocking spell and clambered into their chosen vehicle, losing valuable seconds as she fruitlessly tried to adjust the driver's seat back and down.

'Can you start it?' Mallory asked, pulling her seatbelt on just as the engine roared to life, a thunderous drum beat joining the violins.

'HAHA! I keep telling you I'm a motherfucking genius.' Diana adjusted the side mirrors to see what was happening behind them.

Theodore fractured like he had in the basement when he'd possessed Mallory, a crackling cloud of blue and purple, small triangles and flashes of his semi-corporeal form present as he floated down towards the Mayoral Offices. They heard shouts as several uniformed police officers and suit-wearing UML representatives raced towards the nebulous cloud formerly known as Theodore, unable to hear each other over the screaming music.

'Where's Cornelia?' Diana said, slamming the car into gear. She'd never borrowed an automobile before, and was unimpressed by how slowly the proceedings were unfolding.

The back door opened and Cornelia vaulted in, hitting her head on the opposite door handle. 'Fuck. Here we go, go go go!' she shouted. 'Follow that ambulance!'

'If you don't stop backseat driving, I am turning this car around,' Diana snarled as she wrenched the steering wheel and pulled out. The ambulance had slowed ahead and Diana broke past the barrier, uncomfortable in the seat. She could barely see over the steering wheel and the seatbelt cut into her neck.

She glanced into the rear-view mirror as the lights in Mayoral Square extinguished, a lone figure walking through the centre of the square.

Phase two of Theodore's plan was beginning. Diana's heart pounded as Theodore leapt forward, drifting on the air in a way she'd never seen him do before. He passed the car even as she picked up speed, turning towards the main road, Mallory and Cornelia both holding on for dear life as the engine roared obnoxiously. Diana cut a glance at his face as he turned back. He looked serenely peaceful, which was at odds with the absolutely ludicrous thing he was about to do.

A frenetic strain of violin started, and he raised his arms like a conductor, a wall of static building around him, his entire form hidden in a haze. There was a crack and the parked cars either side of him rocked sideways, rushing away from the Undetectables' car and piling up behind them, stopping a number of cars who were in pursuit. Alarms screamed over the orchestral din and Mallory covered her ears as Diana gunned the engine, following Theodore, who was running and smashing everything in his path with elegant hand movements, barely visible in the milliseconds where they got close enough to him. He was lost in the music as he twirled and glided, static exploding everything around him in bursts. The ambulance had picked up speed ahead of them, invisible in Theodore's fog. There were shouts behind Diana and more sirens as Import Police got out of their cars and took off after them on foot.

'Faster!' Cornelia urged, gripping the headrest to shout directly into Diana's ear.

'I'M GOING AS FAST AS I CAN!' Diana bellowed, switching gears as the car skidded around another corner. The road to Oakpass was close; they were almost out of the maze of Wrackton's side streets. 'THE OWNER OF THIS CAR IS TALLER THAN ME AND I'M NOT WEARING MY DRIVING PLATFORMS!'

'Go to the Redwoods, Theodore will follow our lead!' Mallory said suddenly. 'We'll cut through the forest and circle back to Oakpass that way before anyone can catch up to us!'

'Reason number three hundred and fourteen why you're the director,' Diana said. She swung the wheel in the direction of the Larix, glad Theodore had managed to stay ahead as he effortlessly smashed through more bollards – Diana assumed the ambulance had gone in a different direction – exploded pieces of concrete littering the road. He noticed the turn and surged ahead, continuing to clear a path until they made it to the entrance to the Redwoods. He briefly returned to his natural form and waved as their car passed him, Mallory whispering their tally of crimes beside her.

Diana peered into the rear-view mirror, watching a glow of light surround Theodore, obscuring his form again just as the sirens caught up to him, the violins still screaming into the night sky. He held his arms out and disappeared into a static cloud. The sirens stopped abruptly. Diana wrenched her eyes away and narrowly avoided ploughing into a tree as Mallory shrieked, strings serenading them as they found the path out of the Redwoods.

'Now for part three,' Diana said grimly, accelerating again, leaving Wrackton and the chaos behind.

THIRTY-THREE

They burst through the other side of the Redwoods onto a quiet Oughteron road. Now they could see the flares Kingston and Felix had spoken of – three red clouds floated in the distance.

'Is this a good time to point out the very, very obvious?' Diana asked. 'Such as, what if this is a trap that Shit King has lured us into, that we are careening towards at a possible top speed of… apparently one hundred and sixteen-ish of your finest miles per hour?' Diana peered at the dashboard, underwhelmed by how simple it was for a relatively flashy car she was starting to think was a poor choice to borrow.

'If that is the case, and that's a big if, it's a trap that Felix is involved in now, so it's a trap we have to walk into,' Mallory said. She was, Diana noted, still sitting with her hand clenched around the door handle. 'We can't leave them there. Though I cannot fathom what situation would involve Kingston and Felix hanging out together, even at your behest, Cornelia.'

Cornelia bit back a small smile, but not before Diana saw it in the mirror. A trickle of horror descending in her stomach told her what she feared: that they would never really be rid of Kingston. Shit Kings were for life, not just for Equinox.

She turned onto the wide road that would lead them to Oakpass Manor, trying to focus. Darkness had fallen with the abruptness that only occurs during some of the coldest months of the year, and she was straining to make out anything in front of her headlights. The red flares, once visible, were indistinguishable from the clouds forming in the night sky.

'Oh for the love of Blair, is this fucking fog? The last thing we need is the ghost of a beloved author to show up or to roll off the road into a magically placed moor.'

'Surely it's more likely to be haunted demon dogs terrifying the neighbours, and *then* we roll into a magically placed moor,' Cornelia said.

'I think we need to try contacting Sully and Dr Ray again,' Mallory said, ignoring both of them. Diana thought this was rather reasonable.

Cornelia did the honours. The call, predictably, rang out.

'Then all we can do is send a semi-detailed text and not worry about it for the moment,' Mallory said, now folding her hands in her lap, her fingers tangling in the fabric of her dress. 'Focus on getting inside Oakpass. Do we know how we're going to manage that, given the whole we're-barred-from-doing so, and that barring presumably involves physical wards?'

'Don't worry,' Cornelia said. 'I have a plan.'

It should come as no surprise that two thirds of the attending members of the Undetectables did not, in fact, like Cornelia's plan.

'This is the worst thing you've ever come up with,' Diana said, annoyed – both because it was not a plan, and because she had briefly felt proud of Cornelia for coming up with something.

'I thought you were meant to be the motherfucking genius, how come you didn't have a better plan?'

'Because standing next to the gates of a location to feel "the vibes" is *not a plan*, Cornelia.'

Cornelia tightened the straps of her bag, ignoring her. She had a small knife in her hands for the briefest moment before Mallory took one look at it and hissed, 'Put that away *now*.'

Which, Diana had to admit, was much kinder than how she'd have personally put it.

'I can't feel any wards,' Mallory said finally.

'Me neither,' Diana said. 'Not anything obvious, anyway.'

'How did you know to tell Felix and Kingston to put down witchlights?' Mallory asked.

'I had a vague notion that there'd be a ward on the outside of Oakpass's walls, so my plan was we witchlight into a witchlight. Us telling the UML about witchlight travel doesn't mean they have a full grasp of how it works. It's a deceptively intelligent plan: I forgive you for not seeing it right away.'

'Since when did we start using "witchlight" as a verb?' Diana snapped, making sure her own bag was full of whatever she thought she might need. Her shoes had knives inside them, and she had another strapped to her thigh underneath her dress – a concept she was not fully able to appreciate, given the circumstances.

'It saves time,' Cornelia said. 'Are we ready?'

Diana tipped the witchlight, illuminating the three witches

in a violet glow. An attendant at the gates of Oakpass looked up, and Diana shuffled them all further away, pretending she was looking for something around the car.

'I'll lead, you hold onto me,' Cornelia said, taking Mallory's hand and holding her other out for the witchlight.

Diana handed it over and took Mallory's other hand, squeezing gently.

Cornelia hesitated. 'If you could talk me through the logistics of stepping through a witchlight, that would be greatly appreciated.'

'For the love of *Blair*,' Diana said, glaring at her. 'You're going to get us all killed.'

'Diana.'

'Fine. First things first – it's going to hurt. A lot – emotionally,' Diana said, catching sight of Mallory's face. 'It's an emotionally taxing experience. I'm sure there's science to it. But the most important thing is that you visualise where you're going to be.'

It had worked for Diana before; there was no reason it wouldn't work again.

'Can we all fit through at once?' Mallory asked, her gaze on the witchlight. Admittedly, the crystal did not seem like it was going to readily accommodate an entire PI agency.

'It definitely works with two, because we saw it happen. I don't see why it wouldn't work with three,' Diana said. 'Plus, do we have much of a choice? I've already voted no to the idea of us splitting up. Allowing it now would be unreasonably hypocritical of me.'

'I never want us to split up,' Mallory said. 'That's my greatest fear. Oh, *Hexana*. I don't know what it is about confronting killers, but I feel very fearful and confessional.'

Cornelia barked out a laugh. 'I think the most genuine conversations we've had in recent years have been centred around life-or-death moments.'

'It's true, though,' Mallory said softly. 'I don't want us to split up. The last five months have been the best and worst of my life. I never thought we'd end up with all of us back together, I never thought we'd be happy or working together on anything. I never thought I'd have a job again, if I'm honest. I love you both.'

'Can I tell you the truth?' Diana asked, knowing as she said it that there was no question of if she could. Her friends would listen.

'Always.'

Mallory said nothing, instead giving her full attention.

'I'm scared.'

Mallory squeezed her hand.

'We are about to face down some murderers again, so being scared is the appropriate emotion to be feeling at this moment in time,' Cornelia said. 'If you weren't scared, I'd be worried.'

'No,' Diana said impatiently. 'I am *scared*. There was a time not that long ago where the world would bend to my will. Everything I wanted, I worked towards and got. There was never any question of if I'd get it, just when and how. If something went wrong, I landed back on my feet moments later. If I thought something was going to go bad, I'd dip out.'

She could hear now what Taylor had meant, when she'd said Diana had a tendency to run for home. She'd always thought home was somewhere she aimed for: a film set, a set of abilities, the places she could show off or be the most skilled. But really, home was where her friends were. It was where she could be a witch, where she could be herself. Even with her family's house gone, Wrackton was still home. The guest bedroom in Cornelia's house was *home*. Home was a feeling, not a place.

'Whether that was friendships, jobs, whatever… one gut feeling that something was off, and I'd be out, believing that the world was doing what I wanted it to. What I asked of it. That I was luck personified, and the world was at my feet. Lately, that hasn't been happening. I love you, I love being in the Undetectables, but I keep asking myself if this is all there is. Is this just… life, forever? I always want to be moving, I always want to be working towards something, but I've never felt… I've never felt at peace with having something good.'

'Which explains your relationships,' Cornelia said. She lifted the witchlight towards Diana, bathing her in amethyst.

'Piss off, Cornelia,' Diana said, but there was no venom in it. 'Most of those were fun but fleeting, and that's what I signed up for.' She felt tears spring to her eyes and fought against them, rising in her throat and threatening to choke her. 'With my hearing, and Taylor… Taylor… Taylor?'

'We have rightly established her name is Taylor, yes,' Cornelia said, but Mallory shook her hand free to turn Cornelia around. 'Taylor! What are you doing here?'

Taylor, wearing a sequinned gown with a corset top, green hair falling softly in waves, was picking her way over the grass ditch.

'I couldn't leave you to your own devices, could I? Plus this felt like an excellent opportunity to play "get the girl", where I play the part of the girl who gets the girl. I figured I'd be heroic and come to your aid. I'm under no illusions though, you'll probably be peeling me out of here later.'

'How did you know to come?' Cornelia asked suspiciously, but Diana knew the answer. Taylor knew her better than she'd ever given her credit for.

'Diana sent me a weird text that felt like a goodbye, and I'm not a total eejit. Also, Sandi asked me to be her plus-one; she's convinced I have special talk-to-the-beyond powers after my brush with death.' Taylor held up an invite. 'But now I'm ditching Sandi and coming with you, because I heard some of your speech. I wasn't eavesdropping, like, you've just some mouth on you.'

'I... I mean, welcome,' Mallory said. 'It's just, this is a rescue mission, and... goddess, I don't mean to be rude, it's so lovely to have you here, but...'

'But I'm a useless Apparent? Yeah, I know. But I'm a useless Apparent who brought a big knife to a magic fight, and if that doesn't say something, I don't know what does.'

'Where's this big knife you speak of?' Cornelia asked. Taylor spun around and Diana saw a scabbard with an as-advertised big sword inside it.

Diana pulled it free, a gasp of delight on her lips before she had the chance to plan her reaction.

'A sword! You know how to treat a girl.'

'I had a few weapons in my hotel room – I took some to make moulds one night and kept forgetting to bring them back. I assumed we'd all be in enough danger to necessitate me producing a sword out of nowhere. Although the weight of that thing requires you to swing it quite hard.'

'If I'm going to die tonight, I'm going out the way Elisabella would intend for me.'

'What way's that?' Taylor asked, adjusting the scabbard so it fit over Diana's chest.

'As a motherfucking genius *and* a hot sword lesbian,' Diana said, taking Mallory's hand again and holding her other one out for Taylor.

'*Now* can I keep my small knife, Mallory?' Cornelia asked.

'Shh. Get going. This will hurt,' Diana said to Taylor, and closed her eyes, trying to calm the wild beating of her heart at the feel of her hand in hers.

Diana tensed for pain, but none came. She cracked an eye open. 'What's taking so long?'

'I don't… oh fuck,' Cornelia said, dropping the witchlight. Purple smoke rose from it, and they all jumped back, the shrubbery behind them scraping Diana's arms.

The witchlight flared and a besuited witch stood uncertainly on the road, blinking in the foggy air and wearing a *UML Liaison* badge. It was not, Diana noted, a nice suit, and given that UML stood for Unified Magical Liaison, the badge contained at least one redundancy.

'Someone needs to talk to your bosses about suit fittings,' Diana said.

'Greetings,' she said.

When it became clear nobody was going to respond, she cleared her throat. 'It is of note to the Unified Magical Liaison that you are about to perform a manoeuvre that we deem to be in violation of the verbally delivered cease-and-desist ordered to you on behalf of the UML, co-signed by the Ghoul Council.'

Diana shrugged. 'Is that all?'

446

'Please… refrain from doing so.' She nodded once, then stepped into the witchlight, vanishing from sight, leaving a wholly unnecessary puff of smoke behind her.

'I wish to FUCK we hadn't told them it was possible TO DO THAT,' Cornelia shouted. She picked up the witchlight and let out a groan as it disintegrated in her hands.

'Okay. New plan,' Diana said. 'Taylor, you're going to need to use your invite.'

THIRTY-FOUR

'What could possibly need my attention *this—*' a familiar silky voice said, and Diana straightened as Grey Quinn ambled to the gate, urged along by Taylor tottering beside him. 'And what do my esteemed guests need from me with such urgency?'

'Real talk?' Diana ventured.

'Always.'

'Someone's going to perform some sort of ritual tonight that's going to unleash giant creatures on Oakpass Manor and its inhabitants that may or may not be connected to all the deaths on *Undead Complex*, and I need you to help me stop them against the wishes of the UML by utilising a technicality.'

'Pardon?' Quinn blinked. Diana realised he didn't look like he was fully present, his eyes sliding over her face, unfocused.

Diana took a deep breath. 'I said, someone's going to—'

'Keep your voice down,' he said. 'Stop this from happening. Is that a *sword*?'

'I will, I will. Yes. I just need you to do something, and everything will be okay.' She held out an arm. Mallory took her other, and Cornelia followed suit.

'Drag me onto the grounds.'

'What?'

'Drag me onto the grounds and up into the manor.'

Quinn coughed a laugh.

'I'm not going to—'

'The terms of the cease-and-desist are about *entering* the properties,' Diana said. 'We are not technically entering if we are bodily dragged onto the grounds and refused permission to leave until the party is over.'

Quinn swallowed, and Diana could see, though he was fighting hard to show it, that he was impressed.

'Are you sure you're not a demon?' he asked, then flexed his fingers, tensing like a snake.

A waft of heat and an apple scent hit Diana as soon as they crossed the threshold into the entrance hall, all slightly rumpled but otherwise still decent-looking, nervously tensed for the arrival of another UML representative that never came.

One of the best things about magic was how deliciously literal it was.

Quinn instantly melted into the mass of guests, and Diana had a sense of being swallowed up by the crowd. Normally she loved socialising – years of attending Broadwick balls and the occasional Fashion Week events her mother had dragged her to as a teen had shaped her ascension to Occulture society –

but tonight she felt anxious panic tugging at her stomach at the jumble of conversation and music overlapping. All she wanted to do was clear out the room, find Rachel, and end this.

Her ear fuzzed, dampening some of the sound in an uncomfortable manner, and she looked around at the others, mostly to check they were still there, though the urgency of this was slipping away from her. Mallory was frozen in place, her hands clenched tightly into fists. Taylor looked as though she might fall asleep. Cornelia wrapped her hands around her bag strap, eyes flickering across the guests that were drifting away from the entrance and into the rooms beyond.

'Don't leave the entrance hall,' Mallory said, then closed her eyes. 'Does anyone else feel...'

'Yes,' Cornelia and Taylor said in unison, as the ringing sounded louder in Diana's head. She shook her head to clear it and turned on the spot.

'Is that Rachel?' Diana pointed at a figure drifting across the doorway, but the figure split in two and moved in opposite directions, neither of them red-haired or particularly Rachel-shaped.

'What're we at?' Taylor asked sleepily. 'I don't remember...'

'Diana.' Quinn passed by, a tilting wine glass in his hands. 'What are you doing here?'

Diana wasn't sure she knew anymore.

Felix. Felix. Felix.

'The air,' Mallory said, reaching into her bag and pulling out a handkerchief. She pressed it over her nose and mouth. 'That's how they've been doing it, *the air*. Diana, how do you get to the courtyard?'

'What courtyard?' Diana demanded. Mallory wasn't making any sense. The air smelled of apples, of lemon and sugar and light floral gin. She inhaled deeply.

'Dr Ray!' Cornelia smiled lazily. 'Hello.'

'Hi,' Dr Ray said. Her face was relaxed. Diana wanted to tell her she was beautiful, but then Dr Ray disappeared.

'Was that Sully?' she asked, blinking at the spot where two witches had been mere moments before. She blinked again, unsure why she cared about staring at the floor, at the five pillars that were holding up the ceiling. Sometimes Diana felt as though she was holding up the world within her own soul.

'What a party! What a world!' Sandi said, holding Diana's face under the chin. She was waving what Diana could've sworn was a sparkler around, and then she blinked and Sandi was lost in the crowd.

'I'm sorry about this,' Mallory said, her voice muffled. She grabbed a wine glass from a passing waiter's tray and tossed the contents into Diana's face, pressing her handkerchief over her nose and mouth. '*The courtyard*, Diana. NOW.'

Cornelia hadn't moved, but her eyes were not focused. Taylor had drifted and Mallory reached a hand out to grab her before she left the lobby.

'Back… door. Beside kitchens, door. Then door,' Diana said.

She took a step in what was probably the right direction and Mallory hurried ahead. She was wearing trainers underneath her dress. Diana followed to tell her the dress was pretty on her.

Mallory fumbled with a pair of lock picks – Diana was about to ask her if they were on a case – when the door fell open and Cornelia shoved Diana and Taylor through from behind. Mallory slammed the door behind them all, panting as she leaned against it.

Diana's head immediately began to clear, her head ringing but her thoughts coherent, like waking from a dream. A column of red smoke poured upwards.

A floodlight crashed on – white light this time – illuminating the Undetectables and their extended party of one.

Mallory winced away from the light and Cornelia put a steadying hand on her arm. Diana took a brave step forward, the weight of the sword bouncing on her back. She could barely make out the outline of a figure by the base of the smoke pillar.

'Ah, stop the *lights*,' Taylor said, just as Diana said,

'Well, well, well. What do we have here?'

THIRTY-FIVE

'I'm so happy to see you,' Kingston said, stumbling towards them. A second figure was crouched behind him, red hair catching in the light.

Diana waved her hand, though it took three tries for the floodlight to dim enough that they could all see. Just as it was in the dollhouse, the courtyard was round, with immaculately manicured lavender bushes in the centre surrounding a great glass dome. A pillar of smoke rose from a copper plinth like an offering – the source of the flare.

'What are you doing here?' Diana squinted in the direction of the second figure, who had pressed their head against their knees, red curls obscuring their face. 'With her?'

'Where's Felix?' Mallory craned her neck, as if hoping they'd emerge from behind a manicured shrub.

Out in the air, Diana's mind was sharper, the fog lifting. Something strange had happened to them all.

'Tell us something only the real Kingston would know,' Cornelia said, stepping in front of Diana. Diana scanned his hands, looking for any indication he was wearing a glamour. She tried to look through his face, see if there was something lurking behind it, but all she saw was a scraped vampire in a rumpled suit with a beaming grin.

'I didn't do this' – Kingston pointed at the pillar of flare smoke – 'Bad for the environment, promsbly.' He lifted his head. 'I don't think promsbly's a word, Cornelia. And she's sick, I think.'

Diana stumbled forward, but her steps felt leaden, like running in a dream. The distance between her and the figure – *Rachel* – closed slowly, giving Diana time to remember why she had been looking for her in the first place.

Rachel, the Dollhouse Murderer. She put a hand on her shoulder, and Rachel looked up.

Only it wasn't Rachel – it was Jenna, her red hair falling around her face, her eyes unfocused.

'Jenna?' Mallory crouched beside her, a quiet hiss escaping her as she struggled into a comfortable position.

'I felt so sick in there,' Jenna mumbled. 'So sick, the air… too hot.'

Diana turned back on Kingston.

'Is it you? Has it been the two of you, this whole time?'

'The two of us what?' He squinted at her. 'I know you were watching for her so I was keeping an eye on her, and then she found me and dragged me out here. I think?'

'I need to go home,' Jenna whispered. 'I shouldn't have come.'

Diana looked to Mallory, who was frowning hard, the cogs turning behind her eyes.

'Kingston—' Mallory started, but Cornelia raised a hand in warning.

'Tell us only something the real Kingston would know, or

Diana is going to cut you down with a sword,' she said steadily. There was no doubt in Diana's mind that she'd be expected to follow through on that threat.

'How do I even know if I'm the real Kingston? In the grand scheme of things, there are thousands of vampires in the world who know what I know, if not millions. What is real, when you think about it? What delineates reality from dreams?'

'What we really needed was some stoner philosophy,' Diana snapped.

'Tell me your name,' Cornelia insisted.

'What good's that going to do?'

'Do you know it, Diana?'

'I—' It had not occurred to Diana that she did not know Shit King's given name.

'Oh, no.' Kingston shook his head. 'Please, Cornelia. My street cred.'

'You don't have any,' Cornelia said. 'Tell us your name.'

'Egbert Atticus Kingston,' he said slowly. 'The First. I prefer Kingston, for obvious reasons.'

'It's him,' Cornelia said, pulling him into a hug.

'*That's* why you kept offering him eggs,' Diana said, a wave of realisation washing over her.

'It's a nice name,' Mallory offered. 'Very unique.'

Taylor, to her credit, did not comment on it, focusing instead on their suspect. 'Jenna, how did you know to bring Kingston out here?'

'I felt sick and needed air,' Jenna repeated. 'It's like everyone in there… everyone in there was on something. Something stronger, anyway.'

Diana looked at her then, noticed her pupils were enlarged, her eyes a little bloodshot.

'Stronger than what?'

'Nothing,' Jenna said. 'I misspoke. Please don't tell anyone.'

Mallory looked from Kingston to Jenna, dawning comprehension on her face.

'Diana,' she said slowly. 'There's a reason the two most lucid individuals at this party are who they are. What's something less concerning than murder that would be a slap-on-the-wrist offence for someone if they were caught doing it the first time? Especially if that person was chronically ill and genuinely remorseful?'

'I don't know.'

'Gloves,' Mallory said triumphantly. The cogs were turning behind her eyes. 'Gloves. I can't believe I didn't think of it before. GLOVES. Jenna wears gloves like mine, because she has chronic pain. We heard her and Sandi talking and assumed it was something criminal, but actually it's just not legal here the way it is in other countries. Jenna, can I look in your bag?'

Jenna nodded stiffly, and Mallory pulled on a pair of latex gloves. 'What?' she said to Diana's amused glance. 'It's procedure. Aha!' She pulled out a small pretty tin that, when flipped open, had several pre-rolled cigarettes in it. She lifted one to her nose. 'Weed, as I thought. It's why the air didn't affect Kingston as badly either, and I'm on so many painkillers that I was able to think, too.'

'Mallory, please get to the point faster,' Diana said, utterly lost.

'That's what Sandi gave her during the video call. Isn't it? When you called over to her hotel, that's what you were doing.'

'Yes,' Jenna said stiffly.

'You've been struggling to do physical tasks for a while, haven't you? Like carrying the dollhouse.'

Jenna nodded.

'Is this why you were so cagey about telling anyone where you were when Donny Baker was murdered?'

'I didn't want to get fired,' Jenna whispered. 'It's been so hard on me, being in charge of the whole department, and Orson… he didn't listen when I said I needed help. Promised me an assistant. It was meant to be Rachel, she wanted to help me out, but he kept saying she was needed elsewhere. I ended up crying one night shoot with Sandi in the chair, and she… she offered me some. I'd use it throughout the day. I wanted the job – I wanted to stay on when the pilot got picked up, but I knew they'd never hire me back if they thought I couldn't do it.'

'Couldn't you use magic on him, if he'd noticed?' Diana asked.

Jenna shook her head. 'It takes energy I don't have to use any sort of persuasion on anyone.' She sniffled.

Mallory closed her eyes. 'I've been wondering how they got the victims to take Bellissima if it wasn't showing in the stomach contents at autopsy. I've been wondering why we've all been misremembering things – it's Bellissima. The killers are piping it into Oakpass Manor somehow, into Larkin Studios as well. It's why the tox report didn't find anything in any of the victim's stomachs, but there was still some sign of poisoning in the blood samples. It didn't make sense that Alannah, who *has* to tell the truth, *also* wasn't making sense, and now it does. Everyone had altered perceptions of events. Jenna lied about where she was, but nobody was able to reliably dispute that, because *their* perception of events was altered. Their perceptions of *each other* were altered – they'd see things happening slightly differently. Someone who might've liked Orson or Baker would think they were difficult, and someone who would normally clash with them was indifferent. You and I were remembering different things when we were on set together – and when we were in Oakpass last time, we went in different directions after the intruder. It's all been confusing, *because everyone was artificially confused*,' Mallory finished triumphantly.

It took a moment to sink in.

'Good work, Mallory, that actually makes sense. That's why I've been smelling apples everywhere,' Diana said, feeling silly for not realising it before. 'It's probably aerosolised Bellissima!'

'That apple smell is the air freshener,' Jenna said quietly. 'In the bathrooms.'

Mallory shot Diana a look of dawning comprehension. 'The *bathrooms*,' she said.

'I thought it was disgusting,' Jenna continued. 'You won't tell them about me, will you?'

'You know they won't care?' Diana said. 'About the drugs. Lots of people smoke, I see it all the time. I wouldn't be surprised if Sandi had been supplying most of the crew.'

'But those people could probably stop if they were caught. It's different for me. Lots of places want to say they employ disabled people, but the reality never matches. I needed help they're not giving me – sharing the workload, not even reduced hours or anything – so I did what I could,' Jenna finished, looking utterly miserable.

'We won't say anything,' Mallory said firmly.

Taylor wrapped her arm around her, and Jenna leaned on her, eyes closed with relief.

Kingston let out a big sniffle, and Diana turned her attention back to him.

'I think we were drugged,' he said, collapsing onto Cornelia's shoulder. 'Also, I have a secret.'

'What is it?'

'I'm sort of afraid of dying.' He pressed his cheek to Cornelia's arm, his voice coming out sideways and muffled. 'I didn't remember until Jenna got me out of there – they took… they took Felix.'

'Who's they?'

'I… dunno,' Kingston shrugged one shoulder. 'I didn't see, or if I did they were wearing hats. No, cloaks. Maybe scarves? Something distracting. I came back to myself here, and there was this really, really big centipede running around. So big, too many legs, it ran around and around the edges of the courtyard, spent ages trying to get into that big dome thing' – he pointed at the glass dome – 'and then leapt over the wall. Then you guys showed up.'

Diana and Mallory were already advancing across the courtyard, leaving Taylor to try and get Jenna standing.

'Where did the centipede go?' Cornelia asked. It was impossible to tell if she was concerned or excited at the prospect of a giant centipede on the loose.

'Dunno, it's just not here anymore.'

Diana climbed over one of the bushes, bunching her dress and trying not to roll her ankle as she crouched next to the ornamentation around the dome. A line of greenish water was caught in the dip between where the concrete ended and the glass emerged from the ground. It was moss-covered, and compared to the immaculately maintained greenery around it, it seemed strange that this was not cared for.

Mallory carefully peered into it. 'I can't see into what's below, it looks really deep.'

'We thought it was a well when I looked at the blueprints,' Diana said.

'It's like a tomb. I can see the bottom, but it's so dark.' She grabbed for her phone, her hand brushing off some of the moss. A gilt-edged pattern of leaves emerged. 'Light's not helping,' she said, squinting down. 'It's too deep.'

'We've got a leaf pattern we need him to identify,' Diana called back. Taylor sprang into action.

'Kingston, come here to me, chicken. I've got a little job for you,' she said, extracting him from Cornelia and marching him over. 'Tell us what that is, there.'

'They're elder leaves,' he sniffled. 'It's a repeating pattern of elder leaves. I really need a minute to collect myself,' he said, rubbing his face. 'I can't keep crying in front of all of you like this.'

Mallory met Diana's gaze, telling Diana they were on the same page.

'Pass through the oak to avoid the elder,' Mallory said.

Diana saw the dollhouse floating in her mind's eye, and she turned it, thinking about the five lines that had been scratched into the walls.

The lines they assumed were to signify the Larkins.

'Five lines, five pillars,' Diana muttered, turning on her heel and examining the courtyard door up close. There was an *I* scratched into the surface; Diana was willing to bet the others were also visible tonight. 'We have to go back in.'

'Are you for real?' Taylor stepped in front of the door. 'Diana, we can't go back in there. Mallory's right, they're drugging us.'

'The Dollhouse Murderers have Felix. We don't have either Dollhouse Murderer. They're taking two victims tonight to unleash gatekeepers on Oakpass and everyone here. We have to save Felix.'

'But I don't think you're hearing me when I say the *air* is *drugs*.'

'We'll have to be smart about it. Shit King, give me your pocket square. Cornelia, yours too. Mallory has a handkerchief and we'll cut that in half – yes, Cornelia, you can use your small knife for that. We'll douse them in water. Jenna, you stay here and try calling for help. Shit King will stay too.'

'I won't,' Kingston said. 'I'm not leaving you in there.'

There wasn't time to argue. 'Fine. Fine! I don't think this is going to be more complicated than touching the lines – if it is we'll need to go back to square one. I'll take the one here, on the back of the door. Shit King, you're going to go into the first bedroom at the top of the stairs, you can't miss it. Mallory—'

'I'll go into the drawing room, it's the second closest.'

'Cornelia—'

'The study, on the wall. I know it.'

'Taylor, do you think you can get to the one on the main staircase?'

'I'll try my best.' She looked baffled, but as she didn't voice questions, Diana kept going.

'It'll be on the wall right in the centre. Try not to breathe too deeply. If we're right, they're going to open the floor in the entrance hall.'

'What about the wards?' Mallory asked.

'It's suggestion – demon magic. If you're conscious of it I think you can push through and still end up back in the entrance hall, at least for long enough to get down the stairs,' Diana said, more confidently than she felt. She had no idea if it was true, but it was worth a try. If there was a secret passageway, they'd figure it out when they got there.

'Shit King, you get a thirty-second head start, then Cornelia goes, then Taylor, then Mallory, then me. When you get there, count to ten, then touch your palm to the wall. Leave it for three seconds, then come straight back to the entrance hall. If nothing happens, come back out here.'

'Is that it?'

'No,' Diana said, casting around. 'And I'm going to – reluctantly, I might add – thank Horrible Travis and his aversion to things that inhibit nightshades for this one.'

Cornelia's eyes brightened. 'We're going to need some lavender.'

Diana nodded. 'And a miracle.'

THIRTY-SIX

Every passing second as the others ran though the Manor with nothing but dampened fabric protecting them was agony. It feel like years, every single nerve in Diana's body alive. There was a chance they wouldn't make it. That they'd get confused. That the ritual would go ahead. That Felix…

She refused to complete that thought. Her timer finished its lethargic countdown and she took a final deep breath, rubbing a piece of lavender under her nose, and hit the line on the wall. 'Open,' she whispered, hoping the others had made it. She waited three seconds and ran back into Oakpass. There were guests everywhere, the strains of violin filling her ears along with a burst of warmth and activity.

'Diana, come join us,' Sully said, appearing at her elbow. Diana shrugged her off, and Sully stood facing where Diana had been, talking animatedly to the idea of her.

She ran to the entrance hall, ignoring the tug on her brain that suggested she should go anywhere else in the manor. She pressed a hand to the pillars, her lungs screaming at her for air. Taylor ran across and took her hand, her eyes wild.

The ground beneath them rumbled. The guests drifted further from the entrance hall, like something was pushing them back, though they seemed otherwise completely unharmed. It made her feel better about repeating anything the Dollhouse Murderers were doing.

Diana spotted a line cracking across the floor between two pillars, then another, then another, until a jagged pentagram had cut itself into the floor and it was opening, the pieces giving way to damp walls and a stone staircase.

She loved being right.

Shit King clattered down the stairs seconds before Cornelia forced her way through the crowd, Mallory close behind her. Diana was running out of air, the need to breathe in almost overtaking her. Cornelia took Mallory's hand and led her down the stairs, her hand on the wall, and Diana took after them, bunching up her dress and asking the goddesses to not let her slip, even as Taylor tightened her grasp on her hand, steadying her. The floor closed up above them and Diana took her first gulps of air, her chest heaving.

A witchlight embedded in the wall flared to life, and Diana could see her hand was on something that looked suspiciously like—

'That's a bloody handprint. You're touching blood evidence,' Mallory said, examining it closely. Diana lifted her hand hastily. 'And there's some blood smears here on the stairs, too.

'We can worry about that later. Why can't we go down further?' Cornelia asked, peering around Kingston.

'Dead end.' Kingston pressed his hands over it like it was some sort of marvel. 'It's a wall.'

'No,' Diana said, pulling the sword free from its holster. A flash of the destroyed dollhouse in her mind's eye told her what to do next: the pike in the centre of the entrance hall. There had to be a reason for it. 'Move.'

She felt around the centre of the wall, cringing at how slimy it was, more sure now than she'd ever been that she was on the right track. The intuition strong in her stomach, like Hexana had placed it there. She shoved the sword with force into one of the bricks, and it gave way, the wall sliding back as though it was a door.

'Hey presto,' Taylor said, which made all the Occult folk present, Diana included, look at her in confusion.

'Come on,' Diana said, holding up her sword.

They emerged into a high-ceilinged crypt, with the maws of two dark tunnels beckoning at the back.

The walls were polished stone, though damp had seeped in over the years. In the centre was a wide raised platform, and on it, withered with time and magic and, perhaps, preservation interventions, were the musty, decaying bodies of what Diana was sure were the Larkins.

'Heather,' Mallory said softly, indicating the tallest mummified corpse.

'How do you know?'

'In the photographs, she was a head taller than Howard.'

They took a minute to take in the bodies, the urgency of their rescue mission fading briefly as collectively the Undetectables realised a hundred-year-old mystery had been solved: the Larkins had never left. They'd been down here all this time, waiting to be discovered, or to become unwitting participants in a ghoulish ritual.

It was, as Sandi would say, sad.

Cornelia and Mallory busied themselves examining the bodies, producing gloves from goddess-knew-where, and Cornelia pulled a beetle out of one of her socks. Diana took her phone out to film the bodies, the crypt, the staircase behind them, trying not to need air too badly again, the smell of rot coating the back of her throat. Kingston and Taylor moved to the tunnels, Taylor using her phone torch to peer down into them. Diana caught how she pressed her handkerchief to her mouth and realised Taylor had never seen a body like this before, much less five in a state of decay.

'We're in the right place,' Kingston said.

'How do you know?' Taylor demanded.

'I have good night vision,' he said.

'How do you really know?'

He held up a dropper bottle. 'I missed a dose this morning. Also, someone dumped a pike here. And... oh.' He held it up, beckoning Taylor to swing her torch around.

'Dried blood,' Diana said. 'That's the Baker murder weapon. And you're *touching* it. Put that down.' He dropped it, and she pretended she wasn't a hypocrite. 'That proves I'm right on how they got into the chamber – what I did with the sword, they did with the pike. In the ransacked dollhouse, the pike was left over the chamber entrance.'

Kingston moved down the tunnel and came back with a tarp clutched gingerly between his thumb and forefinger. 'There are bloody clothes down there too,' he said grimly, finally getting Mallory's attention, who instructed him to drop the evidence and write down exactly what he'd touched and how.

'The entrance must be where Donny Baker happened upon the Dollhouse Murderers,' Mallory said, imitating the movement. 'Came up behind them, and got stabbed with the pike. He must've fallen back, maybe tried to reflexively pull the pike out, then tried to pull himself upright using the wall, which would account for the handprint.'

'And then they somehow got him from here all the way back to Larkin Studios?' Diana asked.

'Think about it – if they hadn't found their way into the tunnel yet, the staircase is narrow. The Dollhouse Murderers would've had to keep clambering over a decomposing body any time they came down here. Besides, if they hadn't moved the body, we'd have no idea there was even a case, so I suppose we should be somewhat thankful.'

'Always great to thank murderers,' Diana said.

'There's where the tarp would come in handy,' Mallory continued, ignoring her. 'Roll the body up, move it, change it into the clothes fake-Taylor was found in, wrap the pike and bloody clothes back up in the tarp, hide it somewhere, then later discard the evidence down the tunnel when they got it open where, ostensibly, it would never be found,' Mallory said. 'We can test it later. If Baker was stabbed pre-Bellissima, there'll be hairs, fibres, maybe some traces or prints from the Dollhouse Murderers.'

Taylor and Kingston were ignoring this incredible feat of forensics, something Diana could tell both because they were engaged in a quiet, urgent conversation facing away from the action, and because she heard Taylor say, '—so it's three drops per bloke per day, is it?'

'We should keep moving,' Cornelia said finally. 'The Larkins can wait a little while longer.'

Diana cast a location spell, whispering Felix's name under her breath. The tunnel to the right lit up.

Shit King was right: this was the place.

Hope rising, she beckoned the others over. Cornelia and Mallory had moved to a wall where an array of ornamental weapons were mounted.

'—want to use the ceremonial mace, especially if *some people* get swords. It's way better than my knife, I could take someone's head off with it if necessary.'

'That's really what we need here, beheadings,' Mallory said, exasperated.

'It's better if we're fully armed,' Cornelia protested, trying to pull it off the wall.

'I doubt it's even oiled!' Mallory said.

'She doubts it's even oiled,' Taylor said solemnly in Diana's ear. She suppressed a shiver. 'I love her, in case I've never said that before.'

'You haven't mentioned it, no.'

'Your agency is a great little operation. Even if I die today, I'll die in safe hands.'

Diana squinted at her. 'What?'

Taylor shrugged. 'Sometimes you just have to believe in something, or you'll completely lose your fucking mind. I believe in you, and by extension, the Undetectables.'

Diana smiled slightly, then shook her head to focus. 'Cornelia! Felix is down there, come *on*,' she said.

Cornelia cast a listening spell and Diana and Mallory crowded around. There was a faint whispering, a soft groan of someone in deep pain, and the sound of a match striking.

'Let's go.' Diana held up her sword, less concerned than she should be at her lack of skill with it. Taylor raised the torch, and Cornelia her small knife. The Undetectables and their extended party of two marched down the tunnel, their footfall barely audible over the shaking rumbles of the party continuing above, to confront the Dollhouse Murderers.

THIRTY-SEVEN

'What has three victims and four hands and looks exactly like the sort of thing that dwells in a dungeon?' Diana said, wishing her wit did not desert her in moments of peril. She was funnier than her own brain liked to give her credit for.

They emerged into flickering candlelight, three steps descending into a deep antechamber that, bizarrely, contained furniture – high-backed chairs and a wooden coffee table. It was like a sitting room, if sitting rooms were circular, and had steps down into what was probably once a shallow water feature, and a jutting shrouded ledge crowding the back wall. The osseous candles Alannah had moulded were on every square surface, skulls and spines and femurs melting slowly under a rich amber glow.

A quick glance up confirmed they were under the moss-covered dome, some symbols daubed on it that made Diana feel nauseous.

Wards.

She felt a tug of her power dimming, and closed her hands more securely around the sword.

Rachel Lyons and Lyle Whitlock looked up as they emerged into the space, both wearing cloaks and expressions of contempt. There was no mistaking it: the Dollhouse Murderers, live and in stereo. Mostly because they were crouched in the former water feature that contained the decaying bodies of Baker, Hollis and Fred, lavender burning in a brass pot beside them.

'We're rather in the middle of something,' Whitlock said, waving a pike in their direction. 'And I'd ask you to mind your tone. This is a sacred space.'

'So is a mortuary, but you didn't seem bothered about stealing corpses from it.' Cornelia moved to Diana's side, Mallory on her other. Kingston and Taylor stayed close behind. Diana could hear Taylor's panicked breathing and forced herself to focus on the killers.

'Are you not interested in how they got down here?' Rachel asked Lyle. He didn't make any move to suggest he was.

'Pass through the oak to avoid the elder,' Diana said, pointing upwards. The sword dipped and her wrist strained to keep it upright. 'A clever puzzle, really. Just not clever enough for us.'

'Oh, piss *off*.' Rachel wiped her face with her forearm. Her fingers were covered in blood from a bowl she clutched in her other hand.

'Now hold on,' Whitlock said, resting a hand on her shoulder. 'We don't want to get worked up yet. There's so much to be done, still.'

'Where's Felix?' Diana scanned the dim space, candles casting long shadows over the walls.

'Who?'

'Our faerie friend. Where are they?' Diana fought to keep her voice steady.

Rachel smiled at her, her lipstick perfect, and Diana felt a wave of revulsion hit her.

'Drop that,' Whitlock said, pointing at Diana's sword.

Her fingers released before she even registered it had been a magical command. The sword clattered to the tiles below.

'And the rest,' he continued. 'I'll even drop mine, to make it fair.' He set the pike down as Diana heard Cornelia's knife fall to the ground.

Diana bit her cheek, trying to orient herself. Bringing a knife to a demon fight was, in hindsight, not the smartest move.

'Rachel,' Whitlock said. 'Could you be a dear?'

'I always am,' she said, and kicked the weapons away. Diana felt frozen in place, like she couldn't move. Terror crept in.

Felix. Find Felix. Don't let anyone die don't let them die find Felix

'I am surprised you made it this far, Diana, but I would prefer if you didn't live to regret it, if that's all the same to you,' Rachel said.

'You might be surprised, but I'm not. Turns out you're not as clever as you think.' Diana forced the words out despite the terror clawing its way up her throat. She felt a quiver of something in her legs: the urge to run away.

'Oh, please. Don't pretend you figured anything out,' Rachel said. Whitlock was bending over the bodies again, and Diana tried to divide her attention between the two of them.

'She thinks we didn't figure it out,' Diana stage-whispered to Cornelia.

'Embarrassing behaviour,' Cornelia said, her voice wavering.

'We were stumped, for a time, I will admit that,' Diana said, the need to get the words out greater than any magic holding her in place. 'All the murders felt so disconnected, so *messy*, until we realised it wasn't really anything to do with *Undead Complex* at all, but with Oakpass Manor. Until we realised it wasn't one killer, it was two. And you, Rachel... you revealed yourself to me days ago. Maybe you didn't mean to, but you did.'

She ignored the small throat-clear Mallory made beside her; Mallory would let her have this one, for the purposes of denouement. 'That was your first mistake. As for Whitlock, well. He made a fatal mistake, didn't he?'

'I made several fatal mistakes,' he said affably. 'I'm lucky Rachie's so good at quick thinking.' A curl of persuasion laced through his crisp, pleasant speaking voice. Diana could feel magic tugging on her scalp, stronger than anything Quinn had ever tried, stronger than Tate trying to make her tell him her name, stronger than she was happy with.

It was not stronger than her. She would not let it be.

'A lot of mistakes, and every single one so very expensive.' Rachel touched his sleeve, leaving a red smear behind. 'Oops.'

'Going to be difficult to clean that out,' he muttered. 'Do we have any oxy-bleach left?'

Diana could feel Cornelia about to cut in with something biting, and inched her hand out to rest on Cornelia's, hoping that was enough to stop her doing something impulsive.

'Oh, it won't matter soon,' Rachel said, taking a step towards the Undetectables.

Diana felt another scalp prickle, one that told her to take a step back, though weaker this time. Whitlock was occupied in pouring blood over the victims. Diana held firm.

'We know you have Felix, you might as well tell us where they are.'

Rachel paused, then turned dramatically to the shroud at the back of the room, her cloak billowing behind her.

'That cloak's a fire hazard,' Cornelia said.

Diana squeezed her hand in warning.

Rachel ignored her and pulled down the gossamer cloth covering the ledge, revealing what Diana had feared most: a limp Felix. Green runic symbols were daubed on their arms, elder leaves – for Diana would never forget what these looked like as long as she lived – threaded through their hair. Their head lolled to one side, as though they were already dead.

And Diana had seen this image before, as though it was plucked straight out of the *Undead Complex* comics.

'Are they alive? Did you hurt them?' Kingston pushed forward, moving like he might topple at any moment.

'I thought you took care of that one,' Rachel hissed at Whitlock.

'I did. Should be out cold still. Chap could barely walk, not my fault he could withstand three times the recommended dose.'

Kingston's eyelashes fluttered. 'Tolerance, baby.'

Whitlock tilted his head, like he was contemplating a poorly mown lawn. 'Hmm. Ah well.'

Diana felt another tug on her mind, this one asking her to kneel.

'Rachie, look at me. Ignore them for a moment.' He took her

hands, gazing into her eyes with what could only be described as pure adoration. 'We're about to finish everything we started. Everything we dreamt of. Isn't that exciting, my little love bug?'

Rachel closed her eyes, a small smile playing on her lips.

'All this planning, and here we are. At the end of it all. Though it's just the beginning, really. A complex thing made simple. Now look. Look at me. We could ask them to leave us to it?'

Mallory whimpered, and Diana could only wonder what sort of panic she was feeling underneath her regular layers of pain and worry.

'We can't leave you to it,' Cornelia said. 'We've come too far to stop now, metaphorically speaking. Also I doubt we still have a form of transport.'

'And we want Felix back,' Mallory added.

The antechamber rumbled, and Diana realised it was a band starting up above, the bass-filled buzz of a party in full swing.

'And we can't let you perform the Undead Complex ritual, or continue doing... whatever it is you're doing to your victims,' Diana said.

'None of that is of interest to me, unfortunately,' Whitlock said. 'Many apologies, I just can't get behind it. In my family we had a saying, and it was "never let a doubter or a naysayer alter your path".'

'Snappy,' Cornelia said, before Diana could stop her.

'Besides, what makes you think you can *do* anything?' Rachel asked. 'This is nature. Do you stop a hawk from hunting prey? Do you stop a bear defending its young? This is the old way of things. Sometimes older is better. Sometimes innovation is the source of pain.'

'Look,' Taylor said suddenly. 'I have never had to listen to one of these speeches before, hopefully never will again, but I'd give my Granda's bollix for this to be a neat, concise evil villain speech. Or better yet, if you'd leave it out altogether. Especially if the evil villain is shiteing on about a group they're not actually part of, like it means something. You're as powerless as I am, Rachel. This is their world, their magic. We get to visit it sometimes, but it's never been ours.'

'Who… is she?' Whitlock asked in an undertone.

'You know Taylor, you fucking idiot,' Rachel snapped. 'She's… that's who Baker became.'

'The one who left you in the lurch?'

'Nice of you to pretend you listen to me.'

'Let's not go over old ground,' Whitlock said, raising his hands. 'I said I was sorry for how I reacted when Baker interrupted us, but in my defence, I did not realise how fragile the human ribcage is. You'd think we'd have devised a better method of protecting the heart in thousands of years of evolution.'

'Oh don't worry, I don't need an apology,' Rachel said. 'It's not like you actually care how I feel about anything.'

Cornelia mumbled something under her breath that Diana could swear sounded like, 'And this is why people make fun of heteronormative couples on the internet.'

'I told you at the time how much I valued your quick thinking. Where's this coming from?' Whitlock asked, his eyes wide.

'Like you don't know,' Rachel snapped.

'Is this the same quick thinking that made an utter balls of a situation that this lot wouldn't have known to investigate if you'd just done something normal with Baker's body, like hide it *anywhere else* in the Manor?' Taylor asked.

Rachel blinked, recovering fast. 'Taylor, love. Get out of here. You're not part of this. I didn't mean to borrow your face, but it made some beautiful art.' She said it almost tenderly, a shiver rising up Diana's spine.

She tried to take a step, tried to summon some magic – something to shut the Dollhouse Murderers up, to incapacitate them. She wanted nothing more than to get to Felix, but the distance between them might as well have been miles.

'Fuck this,' Diana said, anger spiking. She reached for Cornelia's and Mallory's hands, who took them automatically.

The familiar power she felt when she held her friends' hands pulsed through her.

Diana was a witch and she was not afraid to use it.

'END,' she shouted, visualising the flares outside stopping and the halting of whatever they had in motion.

Her hands shook and she felt Mallory hold on tighter.

Nothing happened.

'DESIST.'

Nothing.

'REVERSE.'

'Are you done shouting out the script for a skincare ad, or can we get back to work?'

'Why is nothing happening?' Diana shrieked.

Cornelia shouted spells too, even Mallory trying a binding spell, but nothing happened.

'Can't you feel it? Didn't you feel it out there in the crypt? Haven't you felt it all along?' Whitlock asked softly. 'We're under protection of the old ways. My great-grandfather tried to warn them all, you know. They wouldn't listen. Before I was even thought of, I was given this chance to bring things back to the way they should've been all along.' He held his hand out to Taylor, who dropped to her knees obediently, hard enough that she cried out as her bare leg hit flagstone.

'Diana, I'm sorry, he—'

Whitlock raised a hand again. Taylor gagged and fell silent.

'She's sorry, she's just not very... *resilient*, that's all. Don't worry, happens to the best of us,' Whitlock said, his voice smooth, soothing. There was a lullaby-quiet to it, and Diana felt a creeping sense of absolute terror take her over.

'Does it make you feel strong, to use magic on those who can't fight back?' Mallory asked quietly.

'You know, it does, actually,' Whitlock said. 'And this is the way it was always meant to be. Occulture was never meant to be in any way subservient to the Apparent world. We were meant to exist among it, but maintain an edge that set us apart from the rest. Apparents were supposed to know we were special. We were the subject of societies, gossip columns, adoration greater than a movie starlet's. That's faded over time. A pity, but not one too far gone to rectify.'

Diana's head spun. Rachel crossed the room to pick up Cornelia's tiny knife, holding it in her hands, twirling the blade.

'This is nice. Cornelia, is it? Good choice.'

'Put that down,' Cornelia snapped.

'Now, now,' Whitlock said. 'I'd like you to treat her with the respect she deserves.'

'How does that fit with your subservient bullshit?' Cornelia asked. 'She's Apparent, isn't she?'

Rachel laughed. 'But I get it. I *get* it. My family got it. They saw Lyle's vision as clearly then as I do now. They adored Occulture. Adored magic. Adored the possibility, the excitement of what could've been. And sacrifices must be made, for the sake of undoing poor progress.'

A long shadow flickered across the antechamber. Diana looked up to see something pass over the dome. Something with too many legs. She swallowed.

'Francine Leon and Delfina Sackville,' she said. 'And your great-grandfather. I see it now.'

She thought she did see, or at least saw a way to make them pause. Never before in her life had she wondered at how, in movies and books, folk made it look so simple to stop a villain in their tracks.

But there was only one thing worse than a villain.

Two villains.

'I fucking told you not to write Francine on that wall, Lyle,' Rachel said. 'I *told* you someone would be able to read it.'

Diana barely heard her. She saw a flash of standing and talking to Whitlock in Larkin Studios, the embossed initials *A.L.W.* on his bag flaring in the sunlight. The pieces staring her in the face, slotting together finally.

'Let me guess. Aurelius... Lyle... Waldorf. A maternal grandfather.'

Mallory squeezed her hand so tightly, she thought it was going to fall off.

'What about him?' Rachel's tone was dangerous.

'Banished from the Appoccult Society for talking too much, too enthusiastically, about restoring the old ways pre-Vampire Wars at a time when that would've alienated the Apparent members of the Society. He grew angry at the Larkins. Enter Delfina Sackville, Larkin Studios' shiniest starlet. Maybe old Aurelius found out about her partner, Francine, and Francine's quaint little hobby. Your great-grandmother, Rachel.'

'How—' Rachel opened her mouth.

'And Aurelius set up a plan, didn't he?' Diana continued. 'He was so angry at being cast out. Angry at not getting the attention he thought he deserved. The adoration he thought he deserved, because he was born with a little bit of magic. So he convinced Delfina to join the Society, and to get the Larkins to accept Francine's dollhouse. And then the Larkins disappeared, but nothing happened. No gatekeepers. The dollhouse disappeared too – maybe Delfina felt guilty?'

'Aurelius is a revered member of my family,' Whitlock said quietly. 'He anchors our family values, and I rather think he had things right. The world has not improved since his time in the Appoccult Society. We are sinking lower and lower into a forced underworld. Gated little communities, a glorified council overseeing every single little thing we do.'

'So why didn't he raise the gatekeepers? Why did he stop after the Larkins disappeared?'

'Because he was a coward,' Whitlock said simply. 'Weakened constitution. When the time came, it seems he didn't have the stomach for it.'

'And you do?'

'You don't know the half of it,' Rachel said, and Diana got

a flash of how Rachel was on set, running around and trying to organise everyone. How those skills must've bled over into cleaning up after Whitlock, directing scenes.

'Ignore her, my little love. She's stalling, and we don't want to be short on time. Do what you're meant to do to finish this. On your knees, new friends.' Whitlock raised his arms again.

Diana felt the full force of a push on her head, felt her strength leave her, and her knees buckle. He had not been seriously using his magic before, she could see that now, and the truth of it made her want to throw up.

Cornelia folded a moment later, then Kingston. Mallory was the last one standing, her face drawn and serious, but eventually she too knelt, slowly sinking to the ground.

The most resilient among them, always.

'Why did you borrow my face?' Taylor asked suddenly.

'You pissed me off,' Rachel said. 'I had a plan – my skills were better spent elsewhere. Xander was kind enough to get me in front of Orson and Hollis, but they thought I was more useful wrangling the rest of the crew. I had my own ideas, my own vision. This show could've been everything, but you can't sell something on a promise – the potential has to be there if anyone's going to throw money at it. Orson promised me if I hired someone else, I could work with Jenna on SFX. Help create the face of *Undead Complex* and shape the image of the show. Make it something iconic, instead of the shit they had us throwing together. Do we even *need* another zombie show? We had a chance to do something different.'

'Let me stop you there,' Taylor said. 'Because that doesn't actually answer my question.'

'Bellissima made the vic— the bodies blurry. Blank canvases. I was pissed off that you'd called in sick, because I was sure you weren't coming back. As I worked, your face emerged. Made it easier to create a scene – a scene done the right way. This is how Ruthless Monroe's first death should've been.'

'So then when Orson quit…' Mallory said softly. 'You were angry.'

'Too right I was angry. I was fucking fuming. Hollis wasn't going to replace him, and I'd never get a chance to make it right.'

'And then, let me guess, because I'm sensing a theme – I pissed you off,' Diana added.

Rachel shot her a look. 'It's not all as simple as that. What I produced from what I was given was a miracle.'

'But why lure me back with a mannequin?'

'You were getting on my tits by always lurking around. That sign outside your big fancy house should've tipped me off sooner, but I found out who you were and I walked you into a trap. I had to do *something* – your little friends would've come after us harder if I killed you for real, so I adapted. Demonstrated my vision for the show while I was at it.'

'Rachie's very good at adapting,' Whitlock said. 'We had a plan – tonight we would choose five from the pool of attendees. And then, I must confess, we expedited the plan somewhat.'

'You did what Aurelius couldn't,' Cornelia said. 'You could kill.'

Whitlock tipped his head at her, then Diana felt another push holding her in place. 'But enough about me.'

'I've figured it out,' Diana said suddenly. 'You can make me kneel, you can use your magic on me, you can take mine away, but you can't stop me knowing things.'

'And what do you know, little witch?' Whitlock asked, gesturing at Rachel to move. She went back to check on Felix, pressing her fingers to their throat.

Diana forced herself to look at Whitlock, at his watery blue eyes that were steady and focused. She could hear it in the way they talked to each other. The façade of unity held together by barbed wire and a common goal.

'I know why you only took Felix and not the vampire. I know why, despite hundreds of folk upstairs to choose from, you have four victims, but five Larkins to perform the Undead Complex ritual on.'

He swallowed, quirking his head.

'And what, Goddess allow, could that possibly mean?'

'It means you never planned to take a fifth.'

She cut her eyes to Rachel for a split second, then stared him down.

Whitlock licked his lips, and Diana felt a thrill of triumph.

'I have no idea what you're talking about, and clearly, neither do you. Should we tell them, my love?' Whitlock asked.

'If you hurry up about it,' Rachel said sourly.

'This,' he said. 'All of this. Is an act of necromancy.'

'Like in the comics?' Cornelia asked bluntly.

'*Like in the comics*,' Rachel mimicked. 'Grow up.'

'No. The comics paled in comparison, as did the pilot. I jumped at the chance to visit Oakpass Manor, of course, to see where my great-grandfather – Aurelius, you seem to be familiar with him – worked, but we would've worked the job as normal if the dollhouse hadn't been recovered. A stunning coincidence that changed everything. Such fortuitous timing.'

Whitlock took a candle and brought it closer, pacing slowly back and forth in front of Diana and her friends like he had all the time in the world. The back of Diana's knees ached where the material of her dress had gathered, her skin damp with sweat.

In a way, she was panicking.

'Twelve minutes,' Rachel said, checking her watch.

'Perfect,' Whitlock said. 'Enough time to impress upon you how important this particular act of necromancy is. You know what it is – though I prefer the King Me Principle as a name – but you don't know *what* it is, what it means to bring the gatekeepers back to Oakpass. The folk upstairs, gathered for a party… they don't understand the true meaning of Equinox. It's a drink-swilling, shoulder-rubbing engagement for them that is far removed from the true significance of our holidays. Tell me, which goddess is associated with Occult Equinox?'

Diana, to her horror, didn't know.

'Morrigan,' Mallory and Kingston said in unison.

'Very good,' Whitlock said. 'We've scholars in our midst. Morrigan, the goddess of Equinox. Forgotten, because we focus so much on the Ternion. But who were we before the Ternion? Ask any of the guests upstairs, and I doubt they'll know the answer. Occulture meant something before the Ternion, before the Wars. Feared, revered, separate to the Apparent world. Witches were regarded with terror, demons were lawmakers and business-folk. Trolls and faeries ruled an underworld – though I understand they still do, it's just… smaller than before. And vampires… well, we've no idea, have we? But we could stand to find out. The Undead Complex will be a harsh reminder of the importance of tradition. It will be the beginning of a return to the old ways. Where the Ghoul Council call the shots, and we have no Unified Magical Liaison dictating what we can and can't do with our own power. We've got so *much* of it!' Whitlock exclaimed. 'So no more exclusivity for those who would inhabit our world. Rachel,' Whitlock held his hand out. 'Tell me which one.'

Diana saw the decision solidify in his mind in real time.

'Changing your mind now doesn't take away from the fact you had your fifth victim here in this room,' Diana said firmly. 'You had no intention of killing one of us.'

'Do shut up, you insipid little bitch,' Rachel snarled.

'Rattled, are we?' Diana asked.

'Don't listen to her, my angel. Which one will it be? It's your choice. My gift to you. Everything one does for the mothers of magic, must be done selflessly. Without imposition. You will make the right choice.'

'Wait,' Diana said. 'Before you get to killing. Or not, as would be my preference. Rachel, how well do you really know Whitlock?'

'Well enough, seeing as he's my husband. He's mine.'

'No disrespect, but, ew.' Diana wrinkled her nose. 'Possessiveness is one of the greatest icks the world has to offer. Saying that, why did you hide it on set? Especially with that stupid game everyone was playing.'

The stupid game that made more pieces fit together when Diana saw Whitlock standing in the antechamber.

'You try walking up to any set and announcing you're a ready-made partnership,' Rachel sniffed. 'There'll be assumptions made about your loyalties before anything really goes wrong. Besides, we had more reason to hide it as time went on.'

'Don't talk to her about this, my love,' Whitlock said. 'She's stirring the pot.'

'So would you call yourselves newlyweds, or have you been together long? I only ask because something is glaringly obvious to me,' Diana said, hoping she was convincing. 'And I wonder if it is obvious to you, too, or if this is about to be a *lot* of fun.'

'What the fuck's she talking about?'

'She's stalling,' Whitlock said. 'And we're letting her.'

'No, I want to hear this,' Rachel said. 'What are you talking about?'

'Oh, it's nothing. Just... Baker was an accident, wasn't he? You intended to kill eventually, but he was in the wrong place at the wrong time. And then Hollis... I'm not sure what happened there.'

'He didn't recognise Taylor,' Mallory pointed out.

'Aha. Mistaken identity, then? You went to kill Orson for real. He saw you, or saw one of you.'

'Something like that.'

'And then your suddenly blood-thirsty – sorry, Shit King – husband killed Xander's romantic partner, simply to get back at him for daring to be an unwitting participant in a rumour about you,' Diana said airily. 'Isn't that right? Someone spread a rumour that you and Xander were close – too close – and Lyle got very, very upset about it.'

'No,' Rachel said. 'Fred was in the way, there wasn't meant to be anyone there that night. It doubled up as a nice message for you.'

'I'm sure,' Diana said, smirking at her. 'It seems like underneath it all, he's got a bit of a vindictive little streak in him. He's acting out an old family grudge, really, isn't he? Old Aurelius got kicked out of a club, and a century later his great-grandson is still wanging on about it.' Her heart thumped loudly in her chest, urging her on. She was good at this. This was interpersonal relations.

'But what does she mean, "it's obvious"? What's obvious?' Rachel asked Whitlock, *sotto voce*. Her smile had faltered.

'Clearly nonsense, petal,' Whitlock said soothingly. 'Now, pick one. Please pick one, I want you to be happy with our choice.'

Diana had had enough.

'He had no plans of having you by his side when this was done.' Diana spat. 'Rachel, babe, he was going to kill you and turn you into a giant bug.'

THIRTY-EIGHT

'No he wasn't,' Rachel said, though a flicker of what Diana hoped was doubt passed over her face. Then another flicker, and Diana realised there was something moving over the dome again.

'We'll be using the faerie, and one of you can volunteer, or I'm choosing,' Whitlock said firmly.

'I'll veto Diana. I'd much rather her watch and know her big mouth was the cause of her friend dying.' It was clear Rachel was rattled.

'That's wise. We can't truly make a sacrifice to mother Morrigan if it has been tainted by satisfying our own ego,' Whitlock agreed. 'Fred had to die, but to kill Diana now would be… impolite.'

'One of my pet peeves is wild inaccuracy, so I want it to be undeniably clear that the only ones who've caused any deaths are the ones standing over three corpses who are intending on making two more,' Cornelia said. 'Just in case there was any confusion.'

'He really was going to sacrifice you, Rachie,' Diana added.

'Old magic loves a grand gesture. What could be more romantic than taking two intertwined histories, and restoring the Occult world to a former glory, all for the high, high cost of losing your wife?'

'You don't know anything about my history.'

'No, but I know Francine's,' Diana said. 'She was Apparent, and she loved Delfina. If she was asked to make a dollhouse, she'd have done it exactly as she was told – doubly so if the "request" was actually a forceful suggestion. I could guess, fill in the gaps about how Aurelius got Delfina on side, but I don't need to, do I? He was a demon determined to do something bad, a demon who really believed in his magic.'

'She's lying,' Whitlock said simply. 'Make your choice.'

'You think you know Francine's history, because you stole it,' Rachel spat. 'Your dioramas, your little PI agency... I was sick to my stomach when I realised what you were doing with her legacy. I was going to make something from it, someday. Be known for my work with miniatures on screen, carry on the family name. It's not fair some jumped-up little witch got there before I had a chance to.' Rachel moved up and down the line, pressing the edge of the knife against her fingers. 'Especially when *somebody* got overzealous and ruined the dollhouse.'

'I have apologised thrice for that,' Lyle said. 'Not my fault the instructions were unclear and did not explain what to do with the wall at the bottom of the staircase. I thought the answer was in the dollhouse, and, as I have also explained thrice, *I was right*. Now please, make a decision.'

'I'm waiting for guidance, Lyle,' she said. 'You promised guidance.'

There was a low rumble and Rachel and Whitlock tilted their faces to the skylight. Symbols on their cloaks flared and a strange green flash made Rachel inhale.

'I see,' she said quietly. 'Okay.'

'Do you have enough to make your decision?'

'Yes. She has provided so much to me. Thank you, Mother Morrigan,' she whispered. 'I am an unworthy daughter.'

Diana scoffed. 'You aren't a daughter at all.'

'Lyle,' Rachel said, her voice almost a whine. 'Are you going to let her speak to me like this?'

'Of course not.' He reached out and slapped Diana across the face. She sprawled back, her legs bending unnaturally behind her, tangled in her dress. Her face burned and her ears rang hard, fury biting her stomach. 'You have no idea of things. None at all.'

'I mean, she absolutely knows things,' Kingston said. 'Lots of things. She's a very competent young witch.'

'Thanks, Shit King,' Diana said.

Whitlock closed his fist and Kingston grunted, pressing his lips together.

'The art of persuasion is oft lost,' Whitlock said. 'But it shouldn't be. We know best how to deal with those who would lead us away from the old ways.'

'Who knows best?' Diana said at the same time as Cornelia said, 'You and what army?'

Whitlock smiled then, his teeth straight and white and glinting. 'You have no idea.'

'Again, for the sake of accuracy, you've readily and gladly established we don't know anything,' Cornelia said. 'Perhaps you've got something else to say?'

'Quiet her, please. I've had enough,' Rachel said, still walking up and down, the knife twisting in her hands.

'*You* quiet her.' There was a suggestive tone that Diana did not like one bit.

'It isn't her,' Rachel said quietly. 'Not her at all. You speak an alternate truth, though, and I will do it. I promise.'

'Very well.' Whitlock clapped his hands once, settling on the chair in front of Felix's limp body. He placed his hands on his knees. 'I'm going to tell them the truth. If we go into these things with information, the outcomes are better.

'Here is the truth: there was always a way back to the past. The monsters we make will command attention. In moments, we'll see the restoration of what came before.'

'Is this going to take long? I would rather die than have to listen to this,' Cornelia said.

'It won't take long at all. History never does. The Ternion had a goal at the end of the Vampire Wars – they planned to restructure society. But you see, that was never *forever.* They did not intend on suppressing Occulture for all time. They certainly did not intend for us to live alongside Apparents and become grateful for their indifference to us. No. A lot changed in the Vampire Wars – things we can know, and things we simply cannot, but one piece of knowledge I have been granted is that the Ternion had a failsafe. A preservation society, if you will.'

'The Appoccult Society,' Diana said. 'Old news, buddy.'

'We, thankfully, are not buddies. But you fail to understand, by condemning me for avenging my great-grandfather, that Heather and Howard Larkin were not chosen by accident. They were the chairs, for a time. Apparents who knew value when they saw it. Except, of course, when they didn't. But for a time, and usefully, they saw the importance of Occulture. They treated Occulture with the respect it deserved, the reverence it deserved. History is important, you see. Properly recorded history, though. When it is not properly recorded, we lose things. We lose our way. They all too often make monsters of the mavericks.'

Mallory inhaled sharply. Diana wanted to ask her what was wrong, but her eyes were flicking between Whitlock and Rachel, unwilling to break contact. She was straining to hear anything properly, his voice coming to her like she'd doused her head in a river. It reminded her of swimming lessons, holding her breath while trying to stay on the bottom of the pool, voices and shouts fading to nothing above her.

'Rachel?' Whitlock gestured.

'And we have our real monsters,' Rachel said, coming to a stop in front of Kingston.

'I hope you don't mean me,' he said.

She lunged for him and he struggled to dodge, but Rachel hauled him out in front of the others. Diana fought to stand, a scream rising in her throat, but nothing came out.

Kingston never had a chance.

The knife pierced his stomach and Rachel drew back, blood spattering her face in a wide arc, stabbing again and again, hitting the same spot with terrifying precision, guts spilling out onto the flagstones before him. Nobody made a sound. Diana suspected they couldn't, as she herself was screaming internally.

Pure silence settled over the chamber, but for the gurgling sounds of Kingston dying, and a rumble of something coming ever closer.

'Thank you, love, that's enough.'

Rachel dropped the knife. She reached into the mess on the floor and picked up a handful of Kingston's shredded guts, bringing it to where Felix lay. The dim light from the dome faded, shadows descending as the entire antechamber was illuminated only by candlelight.

A circle of fog surrounded the plinth, and Diana felt the pressure on her head release.

She could move again. She was surprised to feel tears on her cheeks and she wiped them with the heel of her hand.

'There's no point,' Whitlock said as Cornelia and Mallory lunged for Kingston, his eyes open and lifeless, his hand raised, blood covering his knuckle tattoos. 'It was what was meant to happen. In a few minutes the chosen five will rise as the noble gatekeepers of Oakpass Manor, and they will strike down anyone who opposes them. You can't stop it, or halt it any longer.'

He started the finding spell, the same one they'd spoken over the dollhouse, reciting it slowly and primly as though it was an Observatory refrain.

Diana was in control of most things in her life. She had the power to stop many things, had the power to convince anyone of anything she wanted. In her short life she had been very successful.

Too short a life, all things considered.

Which is why she felt comfortable doing what she was about to do.

'Wait – Lady Larkin,' Diana said. 'She had a ring, did she not?'

'What?'

'Lady Larkin. Heather, I think you said her name was.'

'And what does that have to do with anything?'

'I was wondering if it's something essential to your ritual,' Diana said. 'Given that I have it.'

'You stole it from the set, didn't you?' Rachel was smearing Kingston's guts all over Felix's body, mixing them with the runes. 'Or the dollhouse, when I gave it to you. What a fucking mistake that turned out to be.'

Felix, Felix. Please still be alive.

'I'm much cleverer than you'd ever give me credit for,' Diana said. 'I have the ring, and you have my friend. Perhaps we can trade.'

'Don't think I don't know what you're trying to do,' Whitlock said. 'It won't work.'

'That's fine. I have one final request, though.' She paused, letting her voice crack when she said, 'Please.'

'What?'

'It's... silly. But when I saw the mannequin you set up in Oakpass, and it used my voice, I felt like... maybe you were onto something.'

'Onto what?'

'I don't know.' Diana pulled her shoulders in, tilting her head coyly. 'It felt like glamour magic, and it felt like you'd maybe cracked the way to make one form of magic look like something else.'

Whitlock licked his lips, the almost-flattery intriguing him.

'It wasn't glamour magic. It was a very simple voice-throwing spell, and it can be very persuasive.'

'A voice-throwing spell? Like from a kid's magic set?' Diana tried to keep the condescension from her voice.

'There was a little more to it,' Whitlock said, a tad defensively. 'But essentially, yes. Sometimes the simplest of magic is the oldest, and therefore best.'

Diana could fault his logic in several ways, but she saw shadows forming at the edge of the antechamber, long, or with too many legs, or long *and* with too many legs, and shuddered. She looked around at her friends, trying to communicate what she wanted them to know.

That she was sorry.

That she was clever.

That neither of those were good enough.

'I don't know if I've got enough magic to make that work,' Diana said.

'Lyle,' Rachel said. 'She's stalling. Get moving.'

'No, please! This is... you can do old magic, this is my life's dream,' Diana said. 'I never liked the vampire. I'm with you. You're right. You and me and Rachel, we should've been running that set together. I should be able to have any job I want, like you. I should be feared.'

'Lyle,' Rachel said again. 'No.'

'Lyle,' Diana said, imploring him to look at her. 'I'm sorry I didn't see it before. You were doing old magic, and none of this has really been for your gain, has it? It's been about your ancestors. It's been about all of us. I've always wanted to be a powerful witch. I've always wanted to be able to command whatever magic I set my mind to. I want to see you do it. It's my last wish, before we enter the new order. When everyone upstairs sees what you're doing... I won't get a look in. And it'll be my fault, for not believing in you from the outset. This is to help us.

This is about Morrigan, and Hecate, and things that came before the Ternion. I get it now.'

Diana felt some magic surge back into her arms, like Whitlock was backing off.

'Everything one does for the mothers of magic, must be done selflessly. Without imposition.'

'LYLE,' Rachel snapped.

'It's one little wish. To see it up close,' Diana said softly. 'Please?'

She could feel Mallory's gaze boring into the back of her head, knew she knew what she was doing.

Whitlock adjusted his cloak, picking at the stain at his arm. 'Wish granted.'

'Oh my goddess, thank you! So it's like… pushing your voice out from yourself?'

'Not quite. You're imagining your voice is a balloon,' he started.

'We don't have all day,' Rachel snapped.

'Darling, patience is a virtue we will need soon. It will take a while for everyone to see us as Diana has. Look, her friends don't seem convinced at all. They look stricken.'

Diana did not turn to check.

'Okay, it's a balloon…' She closed her eyes, feeling around for her magic. It was weaker than it had been. She gave a pathetic little push and a candle flickered.

She begged Hexana, Blair and Elisabella to help her, to make this work.

'No, no. It's a balloon lifting up and *out*,' Whitlock said.

'It's hard to make it work on someone living,' Diana said apologetically. 'Or else I'm just not talented enough.'

'No, no, don't worry. Here.' Whitlock smiled widely and pointed to Kingston, crumpled on the ground. A wheeze emitted from Kingston's body where he lay.

His mouth opened with a crack, his tongue lolling out and bringing with it a trickle of blood.

In Whitlock's crisp voice, Kingston said, 'Join us, Diana!'

'See? Very simple.'

Diana fought back a smile. In telling them about the Undead Complex, Kingston had told them exactly what she needed to know. She had been unfair to him; even death couldn't stop him from being a genius.

'Oh, like this?'

Kingston's mouth opened again, Whitlock's voice saying, 'We can't truly make a sacrifice to Mother Morrigan if it has been tainted by satisfying our own ego.'

Whitlock's smile didn't falter, but his eyes widened.

'Oh dear,' Diana said, as the shadows grew bigger and the candles in the room extinguished one by one. 'I *do* hope using him like that doesn't count as tainting a sacrifice to satisfy your own ego.'

There was a pause.

'I fucking *told* you she was stalling.'

THIRTY-NINE

Something crashed through the skylight and Diana grabbed Cornelia's arm, Mallory's blood-soaked hand in the other.

'MOTHER MORRIGAN,' Rachel yelled.

The pulse had barely flown through them when Diana and Cornelia shouted 'BIND!' together, Diana pleased she and Cornelia were on the same page.

Whitlock and Rachel tried to move, but they were rooted in place from the waist down, their cloaks tangled around their legs.

A scream howled through the antechamber, wind picking up as voices filled the space and the candles went out. Diana squeezed her eyes shut as something big and multi-legged and positively centipede-like flashed across her eyeline, her whole body quivering with terror, Mallory's hand shaking in hers, Cornelia's arm rigid.

Chekhov's escapee-centipede really chose its moment.

The scream faded, and the candles relit. Diana opened her eyes cautiously.

The creature crashed back up through the skylight, and pieces of glass rained down on them. Diana felt them cut her skin, and Rachel screamed as a particularly big piece came down on her head, unable to move as it shattered. Diana looked up in time to see Heather Larkin's mummified corpse lifted up and out through the glass dome in the horrible legs – or arms, she wasn't sure what they were called – of the centipede.

A delighted cackle escaped Diana as Lyle's and Rachel's faces told her they were done. Equinox was passing and they'd run out of time. There was a distinct feeling of Lyle's power lessening as Heather's body left the space, as though he'd been deriving power from the ritual itself.

'Now that's what I call ironic,' Diana said, giddy with relief.

'Diana,' Cornelia whispered. 'What's the UML penalty for using magic on an Apparent?'

'It's who gives a fuck, we solved the case.'

'Let us go,' Whitlock urged. 'Let us go, you have no right to hold us. False imprisonment. My uncle is a lawyer, you know. A barrister. There's all sorts of charges you'll face. Mark my words, you will regret this. But I am a reasonable man,' he said unreasonably. 'So I will consider lessening those charges, should you let us go right now.'

'This is a citizen's arrest,' Mallory said. 'You are bound in place, Lyle Whitlock and Rachel Lyons, because you've murdered four times, attempted a fifth, and also planned to release giant gatekeeping bugs on Occulture.'

'I bet you love playing coppers,' Rachel spat. 'Doing their dirty work. Does it make you feel big? Does it make you feel good, stealing from other people's legacies?'

'Legacy! And tradition!' Whitlock said. 'The most important thing you can imagine!'

'Go to Felix,' Diana said to the others, who staggered across the chamber, Mallory dragging herself up to the platform in a manner that was painful to watch. Diana kneeled back, panting, using more magic to silence Whitlock, who was still screaming about tradition. She didn't know if she was actually out of breath or if it was the beginning of a panic attack.

She crawled forward trying to avoid as much glass as possible, wet blood that was not hers soaking her hands.

Kingston's body lay unmoving in an impossible pool of blood, his insides a visible mangled mess. His eyes were open. Diana felt the sharp pain of sorrow settle into her chest, wishing he'd just sit up and say something annoying. He'd been okay in the end. He'd literally allowed himself to be sacrificed, instead of staying above ground. Even though he was afraid, he'd had their backs.

'Kingston,' she whispered, taking the hand that said KING. 'I'm so sorry. Thank you for being a hero. Thank you for helping us.'

A whine started in her ear that she realised was coming from outside – sirens, and lots of them. The sound of hydraulics hissing made her think it was a fire truck.

'DOWN HERE,' Diana shouted, before remembering she was a witch and amplified her voice, stumbling past Rachel, who took a swipe at her, to where her friends were cradling Felix's lifeless body, trying to wake them – Mallory gently, squeezing their arm and shaking them, Cornelia offering short, rapid slaps to the face.

'There's a pulse. They're alive,' Cornelia said shortly.

'WE'RE DOWN HERE,' Diana called up through the shattered

dome. Jenna's pale face appeared over the broken glass, followed by the faces of paramedics and Wrackton police, then, mercifully, Sully, who looked sharper than she had when Diana last saw her. 'WE'VE APPREHENDED THE MURDERERS.'

'HOW DO WE GET TO YOU?'

'IT'S PERFECTLY SIMPLE,' Diana said, and then explained four times how to open the tunnel.

'You're under arrest,' Sully said what felt like hours later, bursting in with the rest of the Wrackton force in tow. DCI Tate was with her, a few straggling Oughteron PD officers behind him. They surrounded Whitlock and Rachel, though nobody touched them, police swarming the centre of the antechamber where the bodies lay.

'I should get the honours, it's my jurisdiction,' Tate said. 'You're under arrest for the murders of Donald Baker, Hollis Hadley, Fred Hill and… whoever this person is.'

'I'm not sure it matters who does the honours,' Sully muttered. The Undetectables shuffled towards her, Mallory barely able to stand, Diana not feeling much better.

'My goddess, are you okay? Oh.' Sully stopped, seeing Kingston properly.

'I know we look pretty good for witches who've been in a secret dungeon and seen a lot of death today, so you don't need to tell us,' Diana said dully, the words too heavy in her mouth. 'We can do statements or whatever, but I think we need to be at home for a bit, if that's cool.'

'And maybe some medical attention; there was a lot of broken glass and I think we've all been drugged,' Cornelia said.

'Drugged?'

'Yes, it's in the vents in the manor. If you go out to Larkin Studios, I'm sure you'll find it blowing from the air fresheners in the bathrooms.'

Mallory said nothing, and Diana cast her a worried look. She sank to the ground silently, Kingston's blood drying on her.

'That… would certainly explain some things,' Sully said.

'You turned up just in time,' Diana said. She still didn't trust Whitlock not to try taking control of the crowd, even with Tate there.

'I thought I was going to vomit at one point and found my way outside. Cleared my head enough to realise something was wrong. I thought it was something I ate,' Sully said ruefully. 'Before I left, everyone was lying down in the ballroom, to, and I quote, "wait".'

'You could've all been killed.'

'So could you,' Sully said. 'You aren't meant to be here, anyway. I saw the orders.'

'We were brought in by the owner of the property, nothing we could do. Then we were held captive by the murderers,' Diana said breezily. 'We can give you the run-down, I just really want to take my makeup off and to get my friend medical attention. Not in that order.'

'Yes, well, this party was a mistake and I'm growing mighty tired of the owner getting away with everything his little heart desires. It should never have gone ahead given it was an active crime scene. But that's Wrackton, even outside of Wrackton. Two phone calls to the right people and anything's possible. I only came along to keep an eye on things,' Sully said, a hint of bitterness in her voice. 'But that's a battle for another day. You'll need to give statements – this will be tricky, but we need your cooperation.'

She paused, then added, 'You did great. Thank you.'

'At least you got here in time, give or take a life,' Diana said, surprised to feel a tear rolling down her cheek. 'Sh— Kingston was sacrificed in front of us.'

'How did you escape?'

Diana looked to Mallory, who was also crying, great big heaving sobs that had turned her nose pink. She shook her head.

'They never got to finish the spell,' she said simply. 'Lyle Whitlock and Rachel Lyons admitted to killing Baker, Hollis and Fred. And Kingston…'

'Egbert,' Cornelia said, then burst into tears. Mallory slipped an arm around her waist. 'Egbert Atticus Kingston.'

'Poor bastard,' Sully said, and it could've been as much about his name as it was about his murder.

'There was also the attempted murder of Felix Cole, who was to be their fifth victim. They were trying to conduct what's known as the Undead Complex ritual, or the King Me Principle, which basically involves combining the souls of two of the dead into a gatekeeper, or… a giant bug, I guess. Which reminds me, did anyone see a centipede before they came down here?'

'No, we've got a BOLO out.'

'You should maybe BOLO somewhere on the grounds; it left via the emergency exit with Heather Larkin in tow.' Diana pointed up to the shattered dome above them. Her gaze landed on Kingston, who lay so still. So much blood lost. He did not look peaceful; he looked empty. Taylor crouched next to him, her hand gripping his as tightly as she could. She looked haunted, and Diana knew nothing she ever said or did would take back what Taylor had witnessed.

'You may have seen we found the Larkins too,' Cornelia said. 'Hidden in a secret passageway all this time.'

'There's always a secret passageway,' Dr Ray said, striding in. 'That bloody wall. Sully, I'll want a word with your team about following basic instructions in future. Please tell me you three have come to a conclusion, because this case has been coming between me and my limited hours of rest.'

'They were—'

'Nice of you to grace us with your presence,' Tate said acidly. 'Even I made it here before you, and some fucker stole my car.' He jabbed a finger at Diana. 'Take this magic off him.'

Diana snapped her fingers and words immediately burst from Whitlock's mouth.

'—on private property, you can't make a legal arrest, I'll never admit anything, this is a waste of your time, let us go, my wife did nothing, she is innocent, they're lying. This was my sword! My plan. My glory. MY GATEKEEPERS. And what do you mean we didn't finish the spell? You didn't start chatting shit about Heather Larkin until I got to the end of the spell, surely you saw the resulting *centipede*?'

'Clearly he didn't know there was a second page to that spell,' Cornelia said. 'And has no appreciation for the concept of a coincidental centipede. It said to tell you "fuck off", by the way.'

Diana shot her a look. 'What do you mean it *said*?'

'Three clicks of annoyance equal "fuck off", any entomologist would know that.'

'I'm asking you to unhand me and properly tell me my

charges before you escort us off this property,' Whitlock went on, oblivious to everything Cornelia had just said. Both he and Rachel, who was sensibly remaining quiet, moved past them in handcuffs.

Two paramedics entered with a gurney, stopping to look at Kingston, but Sully waved them on. 'I've called ambulances, the first is taking Felix. One will come to take Kingston to the mortuary. They're also going to check you all out and make sure you're okay. You cannot leave with Felix until you've been checked over.'

'Just give us a minute,' Mallory said softly. 'I think we'd all like that.'

Sully looked like she wanted to say something else, but thought better of it. The paramedics swooped in.

'HELLO?' a voice shouted through the dome. They looked up to see Sandi peering down at them. 'I HEARD YOU WERE LOOKING FOR A NECROMANCER.'

'They've been found, thank you,' Diana called up.

'Yes, they have, for it is I, RUTHLESS MONROE!' Sandi shouted back. 'THE NECROMANCER IS IN, AND SHE WILL RAISE HOLLIS HADLEY FROM THE DEAD! Does anyone have any henbane handy? I'm a good catch.' She held up her hands expectantly.

'What do you mean, "raise Hollis Hadley"?'

'HE'S LYING HERE WAITING FOR ME,' Sandi shouted back, her head twisting to look behind her. 'HE'S A BIT DEADER THAN I'D LIKE, LOOKS LIKE HE'S BEEN DEAD A HUNDRED YEARS. MUMMIFIED, YOU KNOW. BUT I'M NOTHING IF NOT ADAPTABLE.'

'Will you either shut up or FUCK OFF,' Tate roared from

above them, appearing beside Sandi, who took one look at him and tried to run away, distantly shouting utterly ineffectual spells. Diana wished it was actually possible to raise the dead; it would make their lives much easier.

In the quiet that followed, they looked at each other, Taylor standing off to the side, a silver blanket wrapped around her shoulders. Her gaze wouldn't focus on anything, and Diana was worried she'd gone into shock.

'That's it, then,' Cornelia said. 'Another case closed by the Undetectables.'

'Sometimes…' Diana hesitated.

'Were you going to say that sometimes you wonder if we're the cause of bad things happening in Wrackton? Cause yeah, I've wondered that too,' Mallory said.

'That, and…'

'And we're going to have to work on the whole "feeling incredibly conflicted about the concept of working with the police and the complications of sending people to prison" thing, aren't we?' Cornelia said.

'You could do that,' Kingston said, sitting up slowly. 'Or you could help me.'

The Undetectables, after a frozen millisecond where they simply stared, launched into action.

'What the fuck? What the fuck, what the fuck?' Cornelia kept saying, her hands trying to hold his abdomen together.

'I think I just need some stitches or something, it'll be fine. Hurts, though.'

'There's an ambulance coming for him,' Taylor said, running to the stairs. 'I'll tell them to be quicker about it.'

'I thought you were dead,' Cornelia said. 'You looked dead. You were dead.'

'Strange,' Kingston said. 'I thought I was too. But, here we go.'

'And he's not a ghost?' Mallory said, staggering to the other side of his body. There was only one Kingston.

'No static, his blood is warm, he's got a pulse...' Cornelia pressed her fingers to his neck.

'Has anyone ever told you that you're very gentle, Cornelia? Because they shouldn't, ouch,' he said. 'Wait, where's Felix?'

'They're being treated,' Mallory said. 'They were badly injured.'

'I need to see them,' Kingston said, moving to stand. More of his intestines exited the gaping wound, and Diana thought she might be sick.

'Nope,' Cornelia said, holding him down. 'Stay where you are.'

'Cornelia, you have to let me see them,' Kingston said, struggling.

'I can't understand how you're still alive,' Diana said.

'*Non versimilis immortalis*. Unlikely immortality. I think it's the blood. I died, but not for long. That's what my mind is certain of. Oops,' he said, as some of his own blood ran down his chin. 'Could we get that ambulance quicker?'

The Undetectables shuffled out into the antechamber, to the tunnel that would bring them into the courtyard in front of Oakpass, green light hitting their skin. Diana wanted to sit down. She wanted to sleep for a hundred years. She kept telling the medics that she was fine.

'KINGSTON!' a voice shouted, and she saw Felix trying to escape a gurney.

'He's fine!' Diana said, even though there was no way he possibly could be, but Felix ignored her, instructing the medic to wheel them closer so they could see him. Kingston's hand shot out and took Felix's, stroking their blood- and paint-covered skin.

'I thought we were goners,' Kingston said. 'But it would've been okay, because the last thing I saw before I was knocked out was your face.'

Diana ducked her head to hide her smile, but not before she saw the look of dawning comprehension cross Mallory's face. She backed off, and Diana stood next to her, wrapping her arm around Mallory's, mostly because it was the closest part of her in reach.

'For anyone confused,' Kingston said. 'I, Egbert Atticus Kingston – and you can laugh, but you can't carry the weight of it with the same finesse I have my whole life – love them. I love them more than anything. More than anything I have ever loved in my life. It has been three days, but I know it to be true.'

'I'm unsure about the ferocity or timing of that particular declaration,' Felix said. 'But I can confirm that when he's recovered, he's going to join Crown and Hemlock. If he has the guts to, that is.'

Cornelia groaned. 'I've been sitting on a guts joke for the last five minutes,' she said.

'I was in a band called Pissaxe before, I can do it again,' Kingston said. 'But first...'

He passed out, his hand never letting go of Felix's.

FORTY

Two weeks after Equinox

In all ways, but especially the ones that mattered, Diana Cheung-Merriweather was alive. She had found a renewed joy in the small things – sending an email, drinking a cup of tea, letting the mid-spring sunlight hit her face as she cooked dinner beside the open kitchen window.

Diana exhaled as she pressed send on *yet another* email to Mrs Blackburn, but this one, at least, seemed to be closing out the case.

The non-stop week-long televised broadcasting of the horrors they'd faced at Oakpass Manor, with a strategic leaking of the Undetectables' name and business contact information, had meant offers of work were pouring in at a much faster rate than before, the media hungrier than they had been after the Whistler case. It also meant Mrs Blackburn took pity on them, given they had seen a friend stabbed to death before their very eyes.

The subject of Kingston's apparent immortality had not come up, and Diana was happier to allow others to assume he was dead, mostly because Whitlock and Rachel *had* killed him. They just hadn't reckoned on him being unkillable.

The research room was quiet. Theodore had checked on them twice; once to ensure they were okay, and a second time to ensure they were proud of him for evading police capture after his antics the night of Equinox, but to let them know he would be in hiding for the next while.

Diana was just glad he seemed himself.

It had worried Mallory excessively, though she was unwell after the showdown and had not emerged from bed very often in the last couple of weeks. Her vague protestations about needing to close out the Katherine case resulted in Diana and Cornelia promising to spend time on it, combing records and casting as wide a net as they could to find Rosemary Vane. Dr Ray had promised, in her usually caustic way, that if she got wind of the Offices being bricked up while they were still recovering, she'd alert them. So long as they didn't bother her with why.

There was a knock on the basement door – one Diana had been expecting. She twitched her fingers to neaten the plate of biscuits she'd assembled next to a steaming teapot, and opened the door to reveal Taylor in a floral dress and green floral lace-up boots that matched her hair but clashed with the rest of her. Diana took a deep, delighted breath.

'Hi.'

'Can I come in?'

Diana set her up with a cup of tea.

'How are you feeling?' She hated how formal a question it felt. How awkward she felt around her, after everything.

'Like I saw the worst thing I've ever seen in my life,' Taylor said. 'Like it replays whenever I close my eyes. Like I'm dying.

Like I'm wasting my life if every single day is not worth living, if I don't make something of it, if I don't try, because he shouldn't have come back but he was dead and I saw it happen and couldn't stop it. You?'

'Same,' Diana said, earning a laugh. 'I don't know. I know I said I was afraid of not knowing how it all ends, but…' She trailed off, not knowing how to end that sentence. Not knowing how to end any of it. 'We solved the case. Your case. We know what happened. It just didn't end the way I thought it would.'

'It ended, though. And endings mean there can be beginnings.' Diana smiled.

'There was a moment, when the two of them were shiteing on about making monsters out of… what was it, mavericks? That I thought…'

'We all thought it. You know, Mallory said—' Diana paused. Mallory had said Jacob had said the same thing to her; the coincidences had stacked up high as they'd worked through the Dollhouse Murderers case. Bringing it up now felt like rehashing old ground. With Taylor, she preferred to let herself forget. 'Mallory said something similar.'

They ate their biscuits, Taylor working around the edges of a bourbon cream.

'I got a job,' Taylor said after a while. 'Not far from here, a few towns over, and it's a big show, one I've wanted to wrangle my way onto for a while. I'm renting a place, as I think I'm in it for the long haul. There's a job there for you too, if you want it. I got in touch with Orson. He's managed to convince a lot of industry people that he wasn't in his right mind, and he's working his way back in. References are ours, if we need them.

'I've been thinking about what I'd like to be remembered for. I like my work. I like taking risks and the wild hours and the pride in finishing what I set out to do. And maybe' – she stirred her tea, not making eye contact – 'maybe, if you came with me, I'd be remembered as a part of you. Prop maker, girlfriend of a brilliant PI…'

Diana closed her eyes, picturing what it would be like, illogically imagining them hand in hand carrying ice creams down a national road – she wasn't sure what the town in question looked like, but wasn't going to let that get in the way of a good bout of wishful thinking. She saw them curled up on the sofa shouting at crappy films under thick woollen blankets, watching the sunrise over good coffee, car rides with the windows down, endless nights of being able to turn over and pull her warm, sleeping body closer, kiss her face in the dark.

'Living with someone who won't try to store insects in my bedroom does sound nice,' Diana said lightly.

Taylor didn't look up, still stirring. Diana liked that she knew that was not an agreement.

She thought of Mallory, and of Cornelia, and of Theodore, and Felix, and even Kingston. She thought of Wrackton, her home, and all the times she'd wanted to run away from it all, and how many times she'd found herself drawn back to it. How she orbited her hometown and always would. How she'd set up a life for herself here.

And she found herself shaking her head.

'I would love to,' Diana said. 'And trust me, I would *love* to. But I can't.'

Taylor nodded. 'No, yeah. I get it. Last week I called Mam crying and she's been angling for me to go home ever since. I had this image of her crying over me every day, having to pick out my plot, tell Tommo I didn't leave anything for him to open on his birthdays and shite like that and… sorry. That's home. They're my family. You have yours. The ones who live here. And maybe you'll change your mind someday. I think I'm just realising that all dreams end eventually, but that doesn't mean you should fear the ending before it's even really started.'

Diana closed her eyes. 'I'm open to trying long distance,' she said. 'Really. I'll come visit whenever.'

Taylor put her cup down and gestured for Diana to do the same. She took her face gently, bringing her blue eyes and all those eyelashes so close Diana could see three eyes, which kind of ruined the moment, but Taylor kissed her and she forgot she'd ever found it funny, breathing in her floral scent and trying to take a snapshot in her mind.

'I'll be twenty minutes away, so if that's long distance to you I don't know what to tell you,' Taylor whispered, holding her face until Diana laughed, the first freeing noise she'd made in two long, difficult weeks.

'Then it's a date,' Diana said.

'It'd want to be, seeing as you're my girlfriend.'

Diana kissed her again.

'I'll see you when I see you,' Taylor said, standing.

'Saturday,' Diana said. 'There's something I have to make sure I finish first. Then I'm all yours.'

'I'll hold you to that.'

FORTY-ONE

Two and a half weeks after Equinox

In hindsight, it was obvious. Mallory Hawthorne just couldn't see it at the time.

'Kingston was really certain about this, which helps, but in the event he's right, I'm going to feel really stupid,' Mallory said, unbuckling her seatbelt.

'He likes to do that,' Cornelia said, already standing and stretching in the warmer spring air. 'Hey, isn't it nice to have the gang all together for something that isn't going to condemn us to death?'

'In fairness, Vampire Cemetery is the last place I'd have looked for Katherine's dead sister, given that the clue is in the title.' Diana climbed out of the car. Mallory was slower, taking Cornelia's arm to steady herself. More than two weeks in bed had not helped her much. Life had taken on an unreality since Oakpass, her body complaining and fatiguing faster and earlier than she was used to. It frustrated her and also felt not at all worth getting frustrated about at the same time.

'Why didn't the records have her in here? Observer Johnson's, I mean. Or any publicly available records,' Diana said, voicing a thought Mallory had had ten times over.

'I don't think she's in one of the mausoleums, she's likely in the main burial ground. Kingston said that's what the "sunrise dies" bit meant; it's where they'd traditionally burn their dead at sunrise. There's a number of empty graves in the Dawning Beds, where victims of the Wars were memorialised. You'd think we'd have figured that out ourselves,' Mallory grumbled. She hated how much time she'd wasted on it, how stressed she'd been when the answer was right in front of her face.

Within a half-hour, searching across rotting stones studded in a wall of a tumbledown mausoleum, they found the grave.

'It's not fully marked, but that says Rosemary Vane, doesn't it?' Mallory said, squinting. She was wearing compression shorts and socks under her clothes in an effort to keep standing, Cornelia's spell on top of it.

Cornelia stood with her arms wrapped around herself, staring at nothing in particular. Mallory and Diana had almost left her at home when the suggestion of going out had made her eyes widen and a sheen of sweat appear on her forehead. It worried Mallory, gnawed at her in a way she would've previously ignored, but there was something about her wild panic that made Mallory fear that the mere existence of the Undetectables was doing something irreparable to all of them.

'Okay.' She pulled out a Vampire Cemetery map and marked on it where Rosemary Vane was buried. 'Should we take anything with us?'

'How about a picture?' Cornelia said, her teeth gritted.

'We can't show her a pict— Printers are a thing,' Diana said, and Mallory smiled at her. 'A picture, then.'

Mallory took several, and Diana found the address of a pharmacy close by that would print one for them. 'Let's get to the Offices before they close.'

The Offices in question had reopened, though not fully, indecision over what to do about the unseasonal creature and the discovery of Jacob's body halting any progress on that end. It was still in disrepair on the outside, though inside the main chambers looked more secure.

Newly installed – but just as finicky – witchlights clicked on slowly overhead, as though they were daring Mallory and Diana to turn back. Cornelia had already paused twice, until Mallory had taken her hand, trying not to think about how soft and delicate Cornelia's was in her own.

A tile fell from the ceiling and the witchlight behind it flickered on moments later. The Offices were very clearly expressing their discontent at the Undetectables' involvement in its temporary demise, and Mallory did not have the energy to add 'angry building' to her growing list of problems.

'Katherine Vane of Wrackton, I call you into being,' she said. Diana took her other hand, and Mallory was glad her friends were there with her.

'Back so soon, witch child?' Katherine asked, appearing inches from Mallory's face. She shifted her weight, feeling the somewhat-comforting edge of a salt packet digging into her thigh. She did not think it necessary to point out that it had been weeks since she'd seen Katherine last.

'We have the information you seek,' Mallory said instead. 'And in exchange, I want the truth. I want to know what you know about Theodore.'

'Sister first, then answers. It is only fair. It is only right.'

'Rosemary Vane is in Vampire Cemetery, at the farthest corner of the Dawning Beds. She died not long after you did, but her soul is remembered there.' She was very careful not to insinuate any of Rosemary's remains were there.

'I do not believe you, witch child.'

Mallory nudged Diana to let go of her hand and produced the photograph.

'You can keep that. I know you don't really have… pockets, for that sort of thing. But that's yours. We found her resting place for you. She's at rest, and she will be remembered.'

'By us,' Diana added unnecessarily.

'By us,' Mallory confirmed.

Katherine stared at the photograph, static building around her. Mallory tensed for impact, afraid of the pain.

But Katherine instead let out a low, unnecessary breath.

'Rosemary is dead. She has been dead for some time. This is her grave. She's okay,' she said, almost like a mantra, like she was trying to make herself believe it.

'You can visit her, if you can get out of the Offices,' Mallory said. 'It's within the confines of Wrackton, so you should be okay.'

'I'm not like your cat man,' Katherine said, her face centimetres from Mallory's. Mallory tried not to blink. 'I cannot leave. But I thank you.'

She moved to go, static building around her.

'A deal is a deal,' Mallory said firmly. 'You promised me something in exchange, remember?'

'Cat man,' Katherine said.

'Cat— Theodore, yes.'

Katherine paused at this. Mallory willed the others to stay quiet while the ghost made her decision.

'I can tell you something I heard. Something I saw. No, better. Better, better. I can show you.'

Mallory surreptitiously dropped a salt packet, and let Katherine touch her hand to her forehead. It was, she reasoned, impractical to fear death when she kept surviving against the odds.

'Show Diana and Cornelia too.'

'Take her hand,' Katherine said. Diana placed her foot on the salt packet Mallory had dropped and took her hand at the same time. Cornelia, uncharacteristically silent, squeezed hers tighter.

Then Mallory was not Mallory.

A haze, then an office.

An office Mallory knew, purple ceilings and floors and grey everything else.

Two figures, facing the desk. Van Doren's face vignetted by the shadows curling in at the sides of the image.

He looked younger.

He looked alive.

One of the figures was talking. A voice Mallory recognised.

'He's dead, but we can watch him,' the voice said.

She couldn't place it, but it made her feel younger, unheard, small.

'He's distinctive, so we won't lose him,' the second voice chimed in. A woman's, also a voice she knew.

Murmuring from Van Doren.

'—goes bad, when he turns and does their bidding, we'll put him away. But for now, we can watch him. Study him.'

'—Of course we didn't mean for him to die on such an obvious night. What do you take us for, Vincent?'

'I especially am regretful, but it could work in our favour—'

'—There's been one in my sock drawer since we began this whole farce, of course we're equipped.'

More murmurings.

A name Mallory recognised.

'They're children. It doesn't matter. They'll never figure it out, who cares if they're pretending to look into it? They'll never be believed.'

'Of course it was an accident! I didn't mean to kill him.'

'He didn't mean to kill him,' the second voice echoed. 'Certainly not tonight.'

'Even still, this Theodore… he is your responsibility.'

Murmuring. Angry voices. Indignant voices.

'Ezra. Imogen,' Van Doren said, his voice placating. 'The Broadwicks have always been a stronghold. Keep it that way.'

They turned and Mallory saw their faces for a split second before Katherine wrenched her back into the hallway, blinking in the neon light.

Cornelia sank to her knees. Diana's eyes met Mallory's.

'That was my parents,' Cornelia said, every syllable dripping with dread. 'They killed Theodore.'

ACKNOWLEDGEMENTS

It's very strange to think that I started writing this book when *The Undetectables* was still a Word document, especially as I blinked and am somehow writing the acknowledgements. The years really do keep coming – and so do the thank yous!

First thanks goes to my tremendous editor George Sandison, for guiding me through the land of giant centipedes and out the other side. (I still think 'Making the Undead (less) Complex' is a very good bit, 10/10.) Thanks also to Elora Hartway, for your incredible murder board insight and for requesting more Sandi, which was absolutely the right call. Elsewhere in Titan: many thanks to Kabriya and Charlotte, for their kindness and support – we'll always have the haunted lift! To Julia Lloyd, for the sensational cover (Horrible Travis is everything to me), and to Hayley and Kevin, who worked hard to make the insides grammatically correct – thank you. To the Titan sales teams and everyone behind the scenes at Titan Books who's had a hand in getting *The Undead Complex* out into the world – thank you a million times over.

To my agent Zoë Plant who is utterly brilliant (and Theodore's official co-parent) – thank you for confirming I could, in fact, write a coherent sequel at such a critical point in the drafting process! And to *in loco agentis* Martha Perotto-Wills: thank you for taking such good care of me, you have my eternal gratitude.

A further, effusive thanks to the folks at Gill Hess – Jacq, Declan and Helen – for putting my book in the hands of Irish readers. You are magic.

A HUGE thank you to the booksellers, bookshops, bloggers, TikTokers and reviewers that got so firmly behind *The Undetectables* – I cannot express how happy the support makes me, or how much it means. Word of mouth is everything. If I've had an opportunity to thank you to your face, please know I mean every bit of it.

To the readers: thank you for your messages, your posts, your emails. I love hearing from you. I love knowing you've connected with Mallory, Diana, Cornelia and Theodore (it makes me cry every single time I get a message from someone who found Mallory's story resonated with them). All of you make this real on a daily basis.

I am sprinkling liberal amounts of thank-yous on Amy Clarkin, Deirdre Sullivan, Fran Quinn, Jacq Murphy, Meg Grehan and Nik Scully for their support, feedback, and generally being brilliant friends. Endless thanks to Michael, for being you and for reminding me that every time I experience a book-related wobble, I have experienced it before and it's always okay in the end.

Music plays a huge role in getting me to sit down to write and there are countless artists who help me achieve that, but thanks especially to IDKHow for constantly creating the perfect soundtrack – your weird-guy murder music speaks to my weird-guy murder writing – and to Mallory Knox, who returned at exactly the right time.

And last but not least: to you, holding this in your hands now. Thanks for coming back to Wrackton.

ABOUT THE AUTHOR

Courtney Smyth is a caffeine fiend, one web search away from their newest fixation, and, most relevantly, a writer of stories. Their work has also appeared in anthologies *Into Chaos* and *The Last Five Minutes of a Storm*, and in Paper Lanterns Literary Journal. They have been writing about ghosts, demons and murders since they were ten and have no plans to stop. They are from Dublin, currently living and writing in the West of Ireland with their partner and their pet corn snake, Steve.

@cswritesbooks
courtneysmythwrites.com

For more fantastic fiction, author events,
exclusive excerpts, competitions, limited editions and more

VISIT OUR WEBSITE
titanbooks.com

LIKE US ON FACEBOOK
facebook.com/titanbooks

FOLLOW US ON TWITTER AND INSTAGRAM
@TitanBooks

EMAIL US
readerfeedback@titanemail.com